SHADOWS OF FEAR

Daphne Du Maurier
Robert A. Heinlein
H. P. Lovecraft
Madeline Yale Wynne
Jean Ray
Robert Silverberg
Harriet Prescott Spofford
Peter Straub
Arthur Machen

Tor Anthologies edited by David G. Hartwell

The Ascent of Wonder (with Kathryn Cramer)
The Dark Descent
Foundations of Fear
Christmas Stars
Christmas Forever

SHADOWS OF FEAR

FOUNDATIONS OF FEAR VOLUME I

EDITED BY

DAVID G. HARTWELL

TOR
HORROR

A TOM DOHERTY ASSOCIATES BOOK
NEW YORK

SHADOWS OF FEAR: FOUNDATIONS OF FEAR, VOLUME #1

Cover art by Tom Canty

A Tor Book
Published by Tom Doherty Associates, Inc.
175 Fifth Avenue
New York, N.Y. 10010

Tor® is a registered trademark of Tom Doherty Associates, Inc.

ISBN: 0-812-51896-9

First Tor edition: June 1994

Printed in the United States of America

0 9 8 7 6 5 4 3 2 1

To the editors and anthologists who first gave the genre a canon in the 1920s–1940s;

To the publishers who stuck with it and gave the genre an identity for better or worse;

To the writers who often ignored them all and just wrote powerfully and well;

And finally, to my children, Alison and Geoffrey, without whom I couldn't have completed the book during difficult times.

Acknowledgments

This book continues the revaluation of horror literature I began in *The Dark Descent,* and so to the same people and books given credit there I continue my indebtedness. Discussions with Alfred Bendixen (and of course his books) have proven helpful, and with Robert Hadji, whose wide reading in and out of the genre and considered critical judgement have influenced several of my choices for inclusion herein. The support of those who were enthusiastic enough about *The Dark Descent* to demand that I continue working in this area—particularly Joanna Russ—carried me through a number of rough spots. Certainly the most important acknowledgement is to Kathryn Cramer, not only for discussion, critical commentary, and moral support, but for sharing with me her unfinished writings and researches on horror publishing and the distinctions between category and genre, and on Henry James, as well as her published work surveying influences among horror writers today. At every point her creative insights have been provocative and useful. The critical reconsideration of the evolution of horror in literature begun by Kathryn Cramer, Peter D. Pautz, and myself five years ago has borne a variety of fruits, including all our various anthologies. This is only the most recent.

No acknowledgement would be complete without proper recognition of the support of my publisher, Tor Books, who took a chance. To Tom Doherty, publisher, and Melissa Singer, editor, for patient enthusiasm, my sincere gratitude.

Contents

INTRODUCTION

I High and Low

There is no delight the equal of dread.

　　—Clive Barker, "Dread"

. . . if not the highest, certainly the most exacting
form of literary art.

　　—L. P. Hartley on the ghost story

Taken as a whole, the output . . . stands in need of
critical study, not to erect theories upon subterranean surmises, but by using direct observation
and following educated taste . . . to enlarge for all
readers the repertory of the well-wrought and the
enjoyable.

　　—Jacques Barzun, Introduction to
　　　*The Penguin Encyclopedia of
　　　Horror and the Supernatural*

We dislike to predict the future of the horror
story. We believe its powers are not yet exhausted.
The advance of science proves this. It will lead us
into unexplored labyrinths of terror and the human desire to experience new emotions will always be with us. . . . Some of the stories now
being published in *Weird Tales* will live forever.

　　—editorial, *Weird Tales* (vol. 4, no. 2; 1924)

This anthology of horror literature is a companion volume to *The Dark Descent,* continuing a panorama of examples and an examination of the evolution of horror as a mode of literary expression from its roots in stories in the early Romantic period to the rich varieties of contemporary fiction. In *The Dark Descent,* it was observed that the short story has, until the 1970s, been the dominant literary genre of horror throughout its evolution (horror was in at the origination of the short story and has evolved with and through it); and that it is now evident that the horror novel is in a period of rapid development and proliferation, for the first time achieving dominance over the shorter forms. So it is a particularly appropriate historical moment for us to look back over the growth and spread of horror stories.

Furthermore, a general consideration of literary examples yields several conclusions about the nature of horror. First, that horror is not in the end either a marketing category or a genre, but a literary mode that has been used in every genre and category, the creation of an atmosphere and emotional environment that sparks a transaction between the reader and the text which yields the horrific response. Horrific poems and plays and novels predate the inception of the short story. There can and have been western horror stories, war horror stories, ghost stories, adventure stories, mystery stories, romances—the potential exists in every category.

But by the early twentieth century, horror began to spread and separate in two directions, in literary fiction and in popular literature, mirroring the Modernist distinction between high art and low, a distinction that is rapidly disintegrating today in the post–Modern period, but remains the foundation of marketing all literature in the twentieth century. For most of the century, horror has been considered narrowly as a marketing category or a popular genre, and dismissed by most serious readers and critics. In many ways, horror is associated with ghosts and the supernatural, which in a way stand for superstition and religion—and one of the great intellectual, cultural and spiritual battles of the past 150 years has been on the part of intellectuals, to rid western civilization of the burdens of Medieval religion and superstition, especially in the wake of the great battles over Darwin and Evolution. The Modernist era, which began in the late nineteenth century, is an era of science.

The death of horror was widely announced by Modernist critics (particularly Edmund Wilson, who devoted two essays to demolishing it), the specialists such as Lovecraft and Blackwood denounced, and the psychological investigations of Henry James, Franz Kafka, Joseph Conrad and D. H. Lawrence enshrined as the next stage in literary evolution, replacing superstition and the supernatural as the electric light had replaced the flame.

Yet it was precisely at that moment, in the 1920s and 1930s, that the first magazines devoted to horror began to appear, that the first major collections and anthologies of horror fiction from the previous hundred years were done, and the horror film came into prominence. Significantly, Lovecraft, in his classic study, *Supernatural Horror in Literature* (1936, revised), in examining the whole history of western literature concluded that over centuries and in a large preponderance of texts, the true sensations of horror occur rarely, and momentarily—in parts of works, not usually whole works. He wrote this during the generation when horror was actually becoming a genre, with an audience and a body of classic texts. A threshold had been reached after a century of literary evolution, in which a parallel evolution of the ghost story and the horror story had created a rich and varied body of tropes, conventions, texts, and passed, and the horror genre was established as a vigorous variety of popular literature, in rich interaction with the main body of the literature of this century ever since. One can speculate that, since the religious and superstitious beliefs had passed from overt currency in the reading public, their transformation into the subtext of horror fiction fulfilled certain desires, if not needs, in the audience and writers. As was noted in *The Dark Descent,* the most popular current of horror fiction for decades has been moral allegories of the power of evil.

The giant of the magazines of horror was *Weird Tales,* founded in 1923 and published until the 1950s (and recently revived). It was there that H. P. Lovecraft, Frank Belknap Long, Robert E. Howard, Clark Ashton Smith, and many others flourished. Davis Grubb, Tennessee Williams, Ray Bradbury, and many other literary writers also published early work in *Weird Tales,* which was hospitable to all forms of the weird and horrific and supernatural in literature. "Up to the day the first issue of *Weird Tales* was placed on the stands, stories of the sort you read between these covers each month were taboo in the publishing world. . . . Edgar Allan Poe . . . would have searched in vain for a publisher before the advent of this magazine," said the editorial of the first anniversary issue in 1924.

One of the conditions that favors genrification is an accessible category market, and *Weird Tales* provided this, along with a letter column in which the names and addresses of correspondents were published. This allowed readers and writers to get in touch with each other, and they did. The Lovecraft circle was composed of writers, poets and readers, and generated thousands of letters among them over several decades, forming connections that lasted years after Lovecraft's death in 1937, some at least until the death of August Derleth in the 1960s. Some of the early correspondents were involved, as Lovecraft was, in the amateur journalism movement of the teens and twenties, and they generated amateur magazines and small press publications, which flourished from the 1930s to the 1960s—their descendents exist today. The World Fantasy Awards has a separate category award for excellence in fan publishing each year, and there are many nominees. So *Weird Tales* was seminal not only in creating a genre, but also in creating a field, a subculture of devotees.

In the 1940s and 1950s, the development of the popular form continued and, through a series of historical accidents, came under the protective umbrella of the science fiction field, as did the preponderance of fantasy literature. H. P. Lovecraft and many of his circle published in the science fiction magazines of the 1930s. And the letter-writing subcultures generated by the science fiction magazines interpenetrated with the horror field, creating one body, so that by the late 1930s the active fans commonly identified themselves as fans of the fantasy fiction field.

In 1939, the great science fiction editor, John W. Campbell, Jr., whose magazine, *Astounding Stories,* dominated science fiction, founded a companion magazine, *Unknown,* devoted to fantasy and horror, and to modernizing the style and atmosphere of the fiction. Campbell, who had written an influential science fiction horror story in 1938, encouraged his major science fiction writers to work for his new magazine, and in the five years of its existence, *Unknown* confirmed a bond between horror and science fiction that has not been broken, a bonding that yielded the flowering of SF horror movies in the fifties and encouraged a majority of the important horror writers for the next fifty years. Shirley Jackson once told me in conversation that she had a complete run of *Unknown.* "It's the best," she said. Several of Jackson's stories first appeared in the 1950s in *The Magazine of Fantasy and Science Fiction* (as did, for instance, one of the earliest translations of Jorge Luis Borges). Since the 1930s, a majority of the horror stories in the English language have first appeared in genre magazines.

> In times when censorship or conventions operated to deter authors from dealing specifically with certain human situations, the occult provided a reservoir of images which could be used to convey symbolically what could not be presented literally.
>
> Glen St John Barclay, *Anatomy of Horror*

Meanwhile, from the 1890s onward, to a large extent under the influence of Henry James, writers such as Walter de la Mare, Edith Wharton, and others devoted significant portions of their careers to the literary ghost story. "In a certain sense, all of his stories are ghost stories—evocations of a tenuous past; and his most distinguished minor work is quite baldly cast in this rather vulgar, popular form. 'The "ghost story,"' he wrote in one of his prefaces, 'as we for convenience call it, has ever been for me the most possible form of the fairy tale.' But at a deeper level than he consciously sought in doing his intended stories of terror (he called, we remember, even 'The Turn of the Screw' a 'potboiler'), James was forever closing in on the real subject that haunted him always: the necrophilia that has always so oddly been an essential part of American romance," says critic Leslie Fiedler.

At the time of his death, Henry James was writing *The Sense of the Past*, a supernatural novel in which a character named Ralph becomes obsessed with a portrait and is translated into the past as a ghost from the future. The supernatural and ghosts were major strains in the work of this great and influential writer throughout his career and, under the pressure of his Modernist admirers, have often been ignored or banished from consideration by being considered only as psychological metaphors during most of the twentieth century. Virginia Woolf, for example, in defending the ghost stories, says the ghosts "have their origin within us. They are present whenever the significant overflows our powers of expressing it; whenever the ordinary appears ringed by the strange. . . . Can it be that we are afraid? . . . We are afraid of something unnamed, of something, perhaps, in ourselves." True, of course, but a defense of the metaphorical level of the text at the expense of the literal surface—which is often intentionally difficult to figure out.

Since the Modernists considered the supernatural a regressive and outmoded element in fiction, the contemporaries and followers of James who were strongly influenced by the literal level of his supernaturalism have been to a large extent banished from the literary canon. Most of them are women writers. A few, such as Edith Wharton, still have critical support, but not on the whole for their supernatural works. Those whose best work was largely in the supernatural, such as Violet Hunt and Gertrude Atherton, Harriet Prescott Spofford and Mary Wilkins Freeman, have been consigned to literary history and biographical criticism, marginalized. In the recent volume, *Horror: 100 Best Books* (1988—covering literature from Shakespeare to Ramsey Campbell), five women writers were chosen for the list, omitting novelists such as Ann Radcliffe, Emily Brontë, and Anne Rice, and every short story collection by a woman—except Marjorie Bowen's and Lisa Tuttle's.

Horror, often cast as ghost story, was an especially useful mode for many woman writers, allowing them a freedom to explore the concerns of feminism symbolically and nonrhetorically with powerful effect. Alfred Bendixen, in the introduction to his scholarly anthology, *Haunted Women* (1985), says: "Supernatural fiction opened doors for American women writers, allowing them to move into otherwise forbidden regions. It permitted them to acknowledge the needs and fears of women, enabling them to examine such 'unladylike' subjects as sexuality, bad marriages, and repression." He goes on to identify stories rescued from virtual oblivion and observe that "most of the stories . . . come from the 1890s and early 1900s—a period when the feminist ghostly tale attracted the talents of the finest women writers in America and resulted in some of their most powerful and intriguing work." Alan Ryan, in his excellent anthology, *Haunting Women* (1988), adds the work of Ellen Glasgow, May Sinclair, Jean Rhys, and Isak Dinesen, extending the list into the present with works by Hortense Calisher, Muriel Spark, Ruth Rendell and others. "One recurring theme," says Ryan, ". . . is a female character's fear of a domineering man, who may be father, husband, or lover."

Richard Dalby, in the preface to his *Victorian Ghost Stories by Eminent Women Writers* (1988—from Charlotte Brontë to Willa Cather), claims that "over the past 150 years Britain has led the world in the art of the classic ghost story, and it is no exaggeration to state that at least fifty percent of quality examples in the genre were by women writers." And in the introduction to that same volume, Jennifer Uglow observes, "although—perhaps because—they were written as unpretentious entertainments, ghost stories seemed to give their writers a license to experiment, to push the boundaries of fiction a little further. . . . Again and again we find that the machinery of this most conventional genre frees, rather than restricts, the women who use it."

An investigation of the horror fiction of the nineteenth and early twentieth centuries reveals that a preponderance of the supernatural fiction was written by women and that, buried in the works of a number of women writers whose fiction has been ignored or excluded from the literary canon, there exist significant landmarks in the evolution of horror. Harriet Prescott Spofford, for instance, is emerging as one of the major links between Poe and the later body of American women writers. Gertrude Atherton's "The Bell in the Fog" is both an homage to and critique of Henry James—and perhaps an influence on *The Sense of the Past*. It is provocative to wonder, since women were marginalized in English and American society, and since popular women writers were the most common producers of supernatural fiction, ghostly or horrific, whether supernatural fiction was not in part made marginal because of its association with women and feminine concerns. Just as James (except for "The Turn of the Screw") was forgotten as a writer of supernatural fiction for most of the Modernist era (although it was an important strain throughout his career), so were most of the women who wrote in that mode in the age of electricity. But the flame still burns, can illuminate, can heat the emotions.

In the contemporary period, much of the most popular horror is read by women (more than sixty percent of the adult audience is women in their thirties and forties, according to the most recent Gallup Poll surveys of reading). Best-selling horror most often addresses the traditional concerns of women (children, houses, the supernatural), as well as portraying vividly the place of women and their treatment in society.

Intriguingly, the same Gallup Poll indicates that in

the teenage readership, an insignificant percentage ("0%") of girls read horror. The teenage audience is almost exclusively male. Perhaps this is because a very large amount of genre horror fiction (that is published in much smaller numbers of copies than best-selling horrific fiction) is extremely graphic and characteristically features extensive violence, often sexual abuse, torture, or mutilation of women alive, who then return for supernatural vengeance and hurt men. One wonders if this is characteristic of boys' concerns.

L. P. Hartley, in the introduction to Cynthia Asquith's anthology, *The Third Ghost Book* (1955), remarked, "Even the most impassioned devotee of the ghost story would admit that the taste for it is slightly abnormal, a survival, perhaps, from adolescence, a disease of deficiency suffered by those whose lives and imaginations do not react satisfactorily to normal experience and require an extra thrill." And a more recent comment: "Our fiction is not merely in flight from the physical data of the actual world . . . it is, bewilderingly and embarrassingly, a gothic fiction, nonrealistic and negative, sadist and melodramatic—a literature of darkness and the grotesque in a land of light and affirmation. . . . our classic [American] literature is a literature of horror for boys." So says Leslie Fiedler in his classic study, *Love and Death in the American Novel.* Still, one suspects that the subject of who reads horror, and why, and at what age, has been muddied by the establishment of genre and category marketing, and is more complex than has been illuminated by market research and interpretation to date.

II The Sublime Transaction

The sublime provided a theory of terror in literature and the other arts.

> —Carl Woodring, *The Penguin Encyclopedia of Horror and the Supernatural*

. . . confident skepticism is required by the genre that exploits the supernatural. To feel the unease aimed at in the ghost story, one must start by being certain that there is no such thing as a ghost.

> —Jacques Barzun, Introduction to *The Penguin Encyclopedia of Horror and the Supernatural*

Supernatural horror, in all its bizarre constructions, enables a reader to taste a selection of treats at odds with his well-being. Admittedly, this is not an indulgence likely to find universal favor. True macabrists are as rare as poets and form a secret society unto themselves, if only because their memberships elsewhere were cancelled, some of them from the moment of birth. But those who have sampled these joys marginal to stable existence, once they have gotten a good whiff of other worlds, will not be able to stay away for long. They will loiter in moonlight, eyeing the entranceways to cemetaries, waiting for some terribly propitious moment to crash the gates.

> —Thomas Ligotti, "Professor Nobody's Little Lectures on Supernatural Horror"

The transaction between reader and text that creates the horrific is complex and to a certain extent subjective. Although the horrifying event may be quite overt, a death, a ghost, a monster, it is not the event itself but the style and atmosphere surrounding it that create horror, an atmosphere that suggests a greater awe and fear, wider and deeper than the event itself. "Because these ideas find proper expression in heightened language, the practiced reader of tales in our genre comes to feel not merely the shiver of fear, but the shiver of aesthetic seizure. In a superior story, there is a sentence, a word, a thing described, which is the high point of the preparation of the resolution. Here disquiet and vision unite to strike a powerful blow," said Jacques Barzun. M. R. James said that the core of the ghost story is "those things that can hardly be put into words and that sound rather foolish if they are not properly expressed." It is useful to examine literary history and criticism to illuminate some of the sources of horror's power.

We do know, from our study of history, that there was a time in our culture when the sublime was the goal of art, the Romantic era. Poetry, drama, prose fiction, painting strove to embody it. Horror was one of its components. Carl Woodring, summarizing the subject in *The Penguin Encyclopedia of Horror and the Supernatural,* says: "As did the scholars of tragedy, [Edmund] Burke and others who analyzed the sublime asked why such awesomeness gave pleasure when it might be expected to evoke only fear or abhorrence. Immanuel Kant, in his *Critique of Judgment* (1790), explained: "Whereas the beautiful is limited, the sublime is limitless, so that the mind in the presence of the sublime, attempting to imagine what it cannot, has pain in the failure but pleasure in contemplating the immensity of the attempt." Kant noted that the sublime could be mathematical—"whereby the mind imagines a magnitude by comparison with which everything in experience is small—or it could be dynamic—whereby power or might, as in hurricanes or volcanoes, can be pleasurable rather than frightening if we are safe from the threat of destruction."

One response to this aesthetic was the rise of Gothic fiction in England and America, and in Germany, "the fantastic." Jacques Barzun gives an eloquent summary of this period in his essay, "Romanticism," in the aforementioned Penguin *Encyclopedia*. "What is not in doubt is the influence of this literature. It established a taste for the uncanny that has survived all the temporary realisms and naturalisms and is once again in high favor, not simply in the form of tales of horror and fantasy, but also as an ingredient of the 'straight' novel." He goes on to discuss at length the fantastic, the Symbolist aspect of Romanticism, tracing its crucial import in the works of major literary figures in England, France and America. Here, if anywhere, is the genesis of horror fiction.

If the short story of the supernatural is often considered as an "inferior" literary genre, this is to a great extent due to the works of those authors to whom preternatural was synonymous with horror of the worst kind. To many writers the supernatural was merely a pretext for describing such things as they would never have dared to mention in terms of reality. To others the short story of the supernatural was but an outlet for unpleasant neurotic tendencies, and they chose unconsciously the most hideous symbols. . . . It is indeed a difficult task to rehabilitate the pure tale of horror and even harder, perhaps, for a lover of weird fiction, for pure horror has done much to discredit it.

—Peter Penzoldt,
The Supernatural in Fiction

Now that we have an historical and aesthetic background for the origins of horror literature, let us return to the nature of its power. Horror comes from material on the edge of repression, according to the French critic, Julia Kristeva, material we cannot confront directly because it is so threatening to our minds and emotional balances, material to which we can gain access only through literary indirection, through metaphor and symbol. Horror conjoins the cosmic or transcendental and the deeply personal. Individual reactions to horror fiction vary widely, since in some readers' minds the material is entirely repressed and therefore the emotional response entirely inaccessible.

But as Freud remarked in his essay on the uncanny, horror shares with humor the aspect of recognition— even if an individual does not respond with the intended emotional response, he or she recognizes that that material is supposed to be humorous or horrific. Indeed, one common response to horror that does not horrify is laughter. Note again the M. R. James comment above.

The experience of seeing an audience of teenage boys at the movies laugh uproariously at a brutal and grotesque horror film is not uncommon. I have taught horror literature to young students who confess some emotional disturbance late in the course as the authentic reaction of fear and awe begins to replace the dark humor that was previously their reaction to most horror.

Boris Karloff remarked, in discussing his preferred term for the genre, "horror carries with it a connotation

of revulsion which has nothing to do with clean terror."
Material on the edge of repression is often dismissed as
dirty, pornographic. It is not unusual to see condemna-
tions of genre horror on cultural or moral grounds. One
need only look at the recent fuss over Bret Easton Ellis'
novel, *American Psycho* (1990), to see these issues in
the foreground in the mainstream. Certain horror
material is banned in Britain.

And I have spoken to writers, such as David Morrell,
who confess to laughing aloud during the process of
composition when writing a particularly horrific scene
—which I interpret as an essential psychological dis-
tancing device for individuals aware of confronting
dangerous material. L. P. Hartley, in the introduction
to his first collection, *Night Fears* (1924) said: "To put
these down on paper gives relief. . . . It is a kind of
insurance against the future. When we have imagined
the worst that can happen, and embodied it in a story,
we feel we have stolen a march on fate, inoculated
ourselves, as it were, against disaster." Peter Penzoldt,
in his book, *The Supernatural in Fiction,* concurs:
". . . the weird tale is primarily a means of overcoming
certain fears in the most agreeable fashion. These fears
are represented by the skillful author as pure fantasy,
though in fact they are only too firmly founded in some
repression. . . . Thus a healthy-minded even if very
imaginative person will benefit more from the reading
of weird fiction than a neurotic, to whom it will only be
able to give a momentary relief."

There is a fine border between the horrific and the
absurdly fantastic that generates much fruitful tension
in the literature, and indeed deflates the effect when
handled indelicately. Those who never read horror for
pleasure, but feel the need to condemn those who do,
like to point to the worst examples as representative of
the genre. Others laugh. But the stories that have gained

reputations for quality in the literature have for most readers generated that aesthetic seizure which is the hallmark of sublime horror.

III   Category, Genre, Mode

The modern imagination has indeed been well trained by psychiatry and avant-garde novels to accept the weird and horrible. Often, these works are themselves beyond rational comprehension. But stories of the supernatural—even the subtlest —are accessible to the common reader; they make fewer demands on the intellect than on the sensibility.

—Jacques Barzun, Introduction to
    The Penguin Encyclopedia of Horror and the Supernatural

Genres are essentially literary institutions, or social contracts between a writer and a specific public, whose function is to specify the proper use of a particular cultural artifact.

—Frederic Jameson, *Magical Narratives*

A category is a contract between a publisher and a distribution system.

—Kathryn Cramer,
    unpublished dissertation

. . . one thing we know is real: horror. It is so real, in fact, that we cannot quite be sure that it couldn't exist without us. Yes, it needs our imaginations and our awareness, but it does not ask or require our consent to use them. Indeed, both at the individual and collective levels, horror operates with an eerie autonomy.

—Thomas Ligotti,
"Professor Nobody's Little Lectures on Supernatural Horror"

Sir Walter Scott, to whom some attribute the creation of the first supernatural story in English, said, "The supernatural . . . is peculiarly subject to be exhausted by coarse handling and repeated pressure. It is also of a character which is extremely difficult to sustain and of which a very small proportion may be said to be better than the whole." This observation, while true, has certainly created an enduring environment in which critics can, if they choose, judge the literature by its worst examples. The most recent announcement of the death of horror literature occurs in Walter Kendrick's *The Thrill of Fear* (1991), which demise Kendrick attributes to the genrification of the literature as exemplified by the founding of *Weird Tales:* "*Weird Tales* helped to create the notion of an entertainment cult by publishing stories that only a few readers would like, hoping they would like them fiercely. There was nothing new to cultism, but it came fresh to horror. Now initiates learned to adore a sensation, not a person or a creed, and the ephemeral embarked on its strange journey from worthlessness to great price. . . . By about 1930, scary entertainment had amassed its full inventory of effects. It had recognized its history, begun to establish a canon, and even started rebelling against the stultification canons bring. Horrid stories would continue to flourish; they would spawn a score of sub-types, including science-fiction and fantasy tales. . . ." But three lines later he ends his discussion of literature, and his chapter, by declaring that by 1940, films had taken over from literature the job of scary entertainment. Thus evolution marches on and literature is no longer the fittest. It seems to me very like saying that lyric poetry is alive and well in pop music.

That an intelligent critic could find nothing worthwhile to say about horror in literature beyond the creation of the genre is astonishing in one sense (it betrays a certain ignorance), but in other ways not surprising. Once horror became a genre (as, under the influence of Dickens in the mid-nineteenth century, had the ghost story told at Christmas), it became in the hands of many writers a commercial exercise first and foremost. One might, upon superficial examination, not perceive the serious aesthetic debates raging among many of the better writers, from those of the Lovecraft circle, to Campbell's new vision in *Unknown,* to today's discussions among Stephen King, Peter Straub, Ramsey Campbell, David Morrell, Karl Edward Wagner, and others on such topics as violence, formal innovation, appropriate style (regardless of current literary fashion), and many others. That money and popularity was a serious consideration for Poe and Dickens, as well as King and Straub, does not devalue them aesthetically. Never mind that Henry James was distraught that he was not more popular and commercial, and expressed outrage at "those damned scribbling women" who outsold him—even his so-called "potboilers."

The curious lie concealed in James' last phrase (which he used to describe "The Turn of the Screw"), and in the public protestations of many writers before and since, up to Stephen King, today, is illuminated by Julia Briggs. In her *Night Visitors,* she states her opinion, based upon wide reading and study, that the supernatural horror story "appealed to serious writers largely because it invited a concern with the profoundest issues: the relationship between life and death, the body and the soul, man and his universe and the philosophical conditions of that universe, the nature of evil. . . . it could be made to embody symbolically hopes and fears too deep and too important to be expressed more directly." She then goes on to say, "The fact that authors often disclaimed any serious intention . . . may paradoxically support this view. The revealing nature of fantastic and imaginative writing has encouraged its exponents to cover their tracks, either by self-deprecation or other forms of retraction. The assertion of the author's detachment from his work may reasonably arouse the suspicion that he is less detached than he supposes."

To further complicate the matter, the marketing of literature in the twentieth century has become a matter of categories established by publishers upon analogy with the genre magazines. Whereas a piece of genre horror implies a contract between the writer and the audience, the marketing category of horror implies that the publisher will provide to the distribution system a certain quantity of product to fill certain display slots. Such material may or may not fulfill the genre contract. If it does not, it will be packaged to invoke its similarity to genre material and will be indistinguishable to the distribution system from material that does. As we discussed above, horror itself may exist in any genre as a literary mode, and, as a mode, is in the end an enemy of categorization and genrification. It is in part the purpose of this anthology to bring together works of fiction from within the horror genre together with works ordinarily labelled otherwise in contemporary publishing, from science fiction to thriller to "literature" (which is itself today a marketing category).

I have previously discussed, in the introduction to *The Dark Descent*, my observations that horror literature occurs in three main currents: the moral allegory, which deals with manifest evil; the investigation of abnormal psychology through metaphor and symbol; the fantastic, which creates a world of radical doubt and dread. Whether one or another of those currents is dominant in an individual work does not exclude the presence or intermingling of the others. Rather than taking the myopic stance that horror means what the marketing system says it does today, I have applied my perceptions of horror to the literature of the past two centuries to find accomplished and significant works that manifest the delights of horror and which mark signposts in the development of horror. Horror literature operates with an "eerie autonomy" not only without regard to the reader, but without regard to the marketing system. Critic Gary Wolfe's observation that "horror is the only genre named for its effect on the reader" should suggest that the normal usage of genre is somewhat suspect here.

IV Short Forms

Why an ever-widening circle of connoisseurs and innocents seek out and read with delight stories about ghosts and other horrors has been accounted for on divers grounds, most of them presupposing complex motives in our hidden selves. That is what one might expect in a age of reckless psychologizing. It is surely simpler and sounder to adduce historical facts and literary traditions. . . .

—Jacques Barzun, Introduction to
*The Penguin Encyclopedia of Horror
and the Supernatural*

It is all the more astonishing to find English weird fiction the property of the drama in Elizabethan days, and later see it confined to the Gothic novel. On first reflection this development seems strange because the supernatural appears to flow more easily into the short tale in verse or prose. The human mind cannot leave the solid basis of reality for long, and he who contemplates occult phenomena must sooner or later return to logical thinking in terms of reality lest his reason be endangered. . . .

—Peter Penzoldt,
The Supernatural in Fiction

A horror that is effective for thirty pages can seldom be sustained for three hundred, and there is no danger of confusing the bare scaffolding of the ghost story with the rambling mansion of the Gothic novel.

—Julia Briggs, *Night Visitors*

Commentators on horror agree that the short story has always been the form of the horror story: "Thus if it is to be successful the tale of the supernatural must be short, and it matters little whether we accept it as an account of facts or as a fascinating work of art," says Peter Penzoldt. At the same time, most of them have observed that some of the very best fiction in the history of horror writing occurs at the novella length. Julia Briggs, for instance, after having given the usual set of observations on the dominance of the short form, states: "There are, however, a number of full-length ghost stories of great importance. Most of these, written in the last century, are short in comparison to the standard Victorian three-volume novel, though their length would be quite appropriate for a modern novel.

More accurately described as long–short stories, or novellas, they include Robert Louis Stevenson, Vernon Lee, Oscar Wilde, Arthur Machen, Henry James. They are quite distinct from the broad-canvas full-length novel of the period not only in being shorter, but also in using what is essentially a short-story structure, introducing only a few main characters within a strictly limited series of events. The greater length and complexity is often the result of a sophistocated narrative device or viewpoint. In each of these the angle or angles from which the story is told is of crucial importance to the total effect, while the action itself remains comparatively simple."

Only in a collection of this size could one gather a significant selection of novellas, and I have included a number of them to emphasize the importance of that length. I have excluded familiar masterpieces such as Robert Louis Stevenson's "Dr. Jekyll and Mr. Hyde," Henry James' "The Turn of the Screw," and Conrad's "The Heart of Darkness" in favor of significant works such as Daphne Du Maurier's "Don't Look Now" and H. P. Lovecraft's sequel to Poe's *Narrative of Arthur Gordon Pym,* "At the Mountains of Madness," John W. Campbell, Jr.'s "Who Goes There?" (from which the classic horror film, *The Thing,* was made), Gerald Durrell's "The Entrance," and others.

I have included several examples of horror from the science fiction movement by writers such as Robert A. Heinlein, Frederik Pohl and Philip K. Dick, Octavia Butler and George R. R. Martin, wherein horror is the dominant emotional force for the fiction, and a sampling of horror stories by women often excluded from notice in the history and development of horror, such as Gertrude Atherton, Violet Hunt, Harriet Prescott Spofford, and Mary Wilkins Freeman. Contemporary masters and classic names in horror are the backbone

of the book, Peter Straub and Arthur Machen, Clive Barker and E. T. A. Hoffmann, and many others, but for most readers there will be a few literary surprises. Horror literature is a literature of fear and wonder. Here, then, the *Foundations of Fear*.

This is the first of three volumes, published in paperback by Tor Books, that together comprise the entire contents of the large hardcover book, *Foundations of Fear*. The whole work, subtitled "An Exploration of Horror," is a sequel to *The Dark Descent*, the anthology that defines the nature of horror literature for contemporary times. Readers whose interests are piqued by the general introduction and the story notes in this book would do well to go back to *The Dark Descent*, in which similar concerns are addressed.

All of that having been said, the primary purpose of this book is to entertain. The devotee of the weird, horrific, and bizarre will find a feast herein, including much unfamiliar material. The general reader will also find a number of surprises and perhaps some unexpected illumination about literary types and literary politics. This work challenges the notion that the supernatural in fiction has in modern times been supplanted by the psychological, the idea that horror is dead.

Horror is one of the dominant literary modes of our time, a vigorous and living body of literature that continues to evolve and thrill us with the mystery and wonder of the unknown. This book explores where it has been and represents some of its finest accomplishments to date. Vampires, ghosts, and witches still plague us, along with many less nameable monsters—including, at times, ourselves.

Read on, in fear and wonder.

David G. Hartwell

Daphne Du Maurier (1907–1989)

DON'T LOOK NOW

Daphne Du Maurier was the granddaughter of George Du
Maurier, who invented the infamous Svengali in his
popular Victorian novel, *Trilby*. One of the most popular
novelists of the last fifty years, she almost single-handedly
kept alive the Gothic romance tradition in the mid-
twentieth century, in such novels of mystery and sus-
pense as *Rebecca* (1938) and *My Cousin Rachel* (1952).
Her stories are collected in the volumes *The Apple Tree*
(1952), *The Breaking Point* (1959) and *Echoes from the
Macabre* (1976); *Classics of the Macabre* (1987) re-
prints the best stories from the others. Her story "The
Birds" was the basis of the famous Alfred Hitchcock
movie. Nicholas Roeg filmed "Don't Look Now" superb-
ly. "I have always enjoyed," she says, "the challenge and
discipline of constructing a short story generally based on
some personal experience . . . I saw two old women, the
twins, who in the story are like a sinister Greek chorus,
sitting at a table in St. Mark's Square. On the way back to
my hotel after dark, a child, as I thought, was jumping
from a cellar into a narrow boat. These two quite different
incidents and the atmosphere of Venice, especially the
eeriness of the back streets at night, set me thinking, and
ideas began to develop into a story." And the result is one
of the finest supernatural horror novellas of the century,
slick, colloquial, yet attaining high intensity and tragic
force. It makes an interesting comparison to Gertrude
Atherton's "The Bell in the Fog." Rarely do stories of the
occult generate such conviction (usually they have the

same defect as religious fiction—requiring an a priori belief—in order to attain convincing horripilation). "Don't Look Now" also mixes a good bit of humor into the early scenes, only to emphasize the darkness underneath later. This novella is a triumph.

D on't look now," John said to his wife, "but there are a couple of old girls two tables away who are trying to hypnotise me."

Laura, quick on cue, made an elaborate pretence of yawning, then tilted her head as though searching the skies for a non-existent aeroplane.

"Right behind you," he added. "That's why you can't turn round at once—it would be much too obvious."

Laura played the oldest trick in the world and dropped her napkin, then bent to scrabble for it under her feet, sending a shooting glance over her left shoulder as she straightened once again. She sucked in her cheeks, the first telltale sign of suppressed hysteria, and lowered her head.

"They're not old girls at all," she said. "They're male twins in drag."

Her voice broke ominously, the prelude to uncontrolled laughter, and John quickly poured some more chianti into her glass.

"Pretend to choke," he said, "then they won't notice. You know what it is—they're criminals doing the sights of Europe, changing sex at each stop. Twin sisters here on Torcello. Twin brothers tomorrow in Venice, or even tonight, parading arm-in-arm across the Piazza San Marco. Just a matter of switching clothes and wigs."

"Jewel thieves or murderers?" asked Laura.

"Oh, murderers, definitely. But why, I ask myself, have they picked on me?"

The waiter made a diversion by bringing coffee and bearing away the fruit, which gave Laura time to banish hysteria and regain control.

"I can't think," she said, "why we didn't notice them when we arrived. They stand out to high heaven. One couldn't fail."

"That gang of Americans masked them," said John, "and the bearded man with a monocle who looked like a spy. It wasn't until they all went just now that I saw the twins. Oh God, the one with the shock of white hair has got her eye on me again."

Laura took the powder compact from her bag and held it in front of her face, the mirror acting as a reflector.

"I think it's me they're looking at, not you," she said. "Thank heaven I left my pearls with the manager at the hotel." She paused, dabbing the sides of her nose with powder. "The thing is," she said after a moment, "we've got them wrong. They're neither murderers nor thieves. They're a couple of pathetic old retired school-mistresses on holiday, who've saved up all their lives to visit Venice. They come from some place with a name like Walabanga in Australia. And they're called Tilly and Tiny."

Her voice, for the first time since they had come away, took on the old bubbling quality he loved, and the worried frown between her brows had vanished. At last, he thought, at last she's beginning to get over it. If I can keep this going, if we can pick up the familiar routine of jokes shared on holiday and at home, the ridiculous fantasies about people at other tables, or staying in the hotel, or wandering in art galleries and churches, then everything will fall into place, life will become as it was before, the wound will heal, she will forget.

"You know," said Laura, "that really was a very good lunch. I did enjoy it."

Thank God, he thought, thank God. . . . Then he leant forward, speaking low in a conspirator's whisper. "One of them is going to the loo," he said. "Do you suppose he, or she, is going to change her wig?"

"Don't say anything," Laura murmured. "I'll follow her and find out. She may have a suitcase tucked away there, and she's going to switch clothes."

She began to hum under her breath, the signal, to her husband, of content. The ghost was temporarily laid, and all because of the familiar holiday game, abandoned too long, and now, through mere chance, blissfully recaptured.

"Is she on her way?" asked Laura.

"About to pass our table now," he told her.

Seen on her own, the woman was not so remarkable. Tall, angular, aquiline features, with the close-cropped hair which was fashionably called an Eton crop, he seemed to remember, in his mother's day, and about her person the stamp of that particular generation. She would be in her middle sixties, he supposed, the masculine shirt with collar and tie, sports jacket, grey tweed skirt coming to mid-calf. Grey stockings and laced black shoes. He had seen the type on golf-courses and at dog shows—invariably showing not sporting breeds but pugs—and if you came across them at a party in somebody's house they were quicker on the draw with a cigarette-lighter than he was himself, a mere male, with pocket-matches. The general belief that they kept house with a more feminine, fluffy companion was not always true. Frequently they boasted, and adored, a golfing husband. No, the striking point about this particular individual was that there were two of them. Identical twins cast in the same mould. The only difference was that the other one had whiter hair.

"Supposing," murmured Laura, "when I find myself in the *toilette* beside her she starts to strip?"

"Depends on what is revealed," John answered. "If she's hermaphrodite, make a bolt for it. She might have a hypodermic syringe concealed and want to knock you out before you reached the door."

Laura sucked in her cheeks once more and began to shake. Then, squaring her shoulders, she rose to her feet. "I simply must not laugh," she said, "and whatever you do, don't look at me when I come back, especially if we come out together." She picked up her bag and strolled self-consciously away from the table in pursuit of her prey.

John poured the dregs of the chianti into his glass and lit a cigarette. The sun blazed down upon the little garden of the restaurant. The Americans had left, and the monocled man, and the family party at the far end. All was peace. The identical twin was sitting back in her chair with her eyes closed. Thank heaven, he thought, for this moment at any rate, when relaxation was possible, and Laura had been launched upon her foolish, harmless game. The holiday could yet turn into the cure she needed, blotting out, if only temporarily, the numb despair that had seized her since the child died.

"She'll get over it," the doctor said. "They all get over it, in time. And you have the boy."

"I know," John had said, "but the girl meant everything. She always did, right from the start, I don't know why. I suppose it was the difference in age. A boy of school age, and a tough one at that, is someone in his own right. Not a baby of five. Laura literally adored her. Johnnie and I were nowhere."

"Give her time," repeated the doctor, "give her time. And anyway, you're both young still. There'll be others. Another daughter."

So easy to talk. . . . How replace the life of a loved lost child with a dream? He knew Laura too well.

Another child, another girl, would have her own qualities, a separate identity, she might even induce hostility because of this very fact. A usurper in the cradle, in the cot, that had been Christine's. A chubby, flaxen replica of Johnnie, not the little waxen dark-haired sprite that had gone.

He looked up, over his glass of wine, and the woman was staring at him again. It was not the casual, idle glance of someone at a nearby table, waiting for her companion to return, but something deeper, more intent, the prominent, light blue eyes oddly penetrating, giving him a sudden feeling of discomfort. Damn the woman! All right, bloody stare, if you must. Two can play at that game. He blew a cloud of cigarette smoke into the air and smiled at her, he hoped offensively. She did not register. The blue eyes continued to hold his, so that he was obliged to look away himself, extinguish his cigarette, glance over his shoulder for the waiter and call for the bill. Settling for this, and fumbling with the change, with a few casual remarks about the excellence of the meal, brought composure, but a prickly feeling on his scalp remained, and an odd sensation of unease. Then it went, as abruptly as it had started, and stealing a furtive glance at the other table he saw that her eyes were closed again, and she was sleeping, or dozing, as she had done before. The waiter disappeared. All was still.

Laura, he thought, glancing at his watch, is being a hell of a time. Ten minutes at least. Something to tease her about, anyway. He began to plan the form the joke would take. How the old dolly had stripped to her smalls, suggesting that Laura should do likewise. And then the manager had burst in upon them both, exclaiming in horror, the reputation of the restaurant damaged, the hint that unpleasant consequences might follow unless . . . The whole exercise turning out to be

a plant, an exercise in blackmail. He and Laura and the twins taken in a police launch back to Venice for questioning. Quarter of an hour. . . . Oh, come on, come on. . . .

There was a crunch of feet on the gravel. Laura's twin walked slowly past, alone. She crossed over to her table and stood there a moment, her tall, angular figure interposing itself between John and her sister. She was saying something, but he couldn't catch the words. What was the accent, though—Scottish? Then she bent, offering an arm to the seated twin, and they moved away together across the garden to the break in the little hedge beyond, the twin who had stared at John leaning on her sister's arm. Here was the difference again. She was not quite so tall, and she stooped more—perhaps she was arthritic. They disappeared out of sight, and John, becoming impatient, got up and was about to walk back into the hotel when Laura emerged.

"Well, I must say, you took your time," he began, and then stopped, because of the expression on her face.

"What's the matter, what's happened?" he asked.

He could tell at once there was something wrong. Almost as if she were in a state of shock. She blundered towards the table he had just vacated and sat down. He drew up a chair beside her, taking her hand.

"Darling, what is it? Tell me—are you ill?"

She shook her head, and then turned and looked at him. The dazed expression he had noticed at first had given way to one of dawning confidence, almost of exaltation.

"It's quite wonderful," she said slowly, "the most wonderful thing that could possibly be. You see, she isn't dead, she's still with us. That's why they kept staring at us, those two sisters. They could see Christine."

Oh God, he thought. It's what I've been dreading. She's going off her head. What do I do? How do I cope?

"Laura, sweet," he began, forcing a smile, "look, shall we go? I've paid the bill, we can go and look at the cathedral and stroll around, and then it will be time to take off in that launch again for Venice."

She wasn't listening, or at any rate the words didn't penetrate.

"John, love," she said, "I've got to tell you what happened. I followed her, as we planned, into the *toilette* place. She was combing her hair and I went into the loo, and then came out and washed my hands in the basin. She was washing hers in the next basin. Suddenly she turned and said to me, in a strong Scots accent, 'Don't be unhappy any more. My sister has seen your little girl. She was sitting between you and your husband, laughing.' Darling, I thought I was going to faint. I nearly did. Luckily, there was a chair, and I sat down, and the woman bent over me and patted my head. I'm not sure of her exact words, but she said something about the moment of truth and joy being as sharp as a sword, but not to be afraid, all was well, but the sister's vision had been so strong they knew I had to be told, and that Christine wanted it. Oh John, don't look like that. I swear I'm not making it up, this is what she told me, it's all true."

The desperate urgency in her voice made his heart sicken. He had to play along with her, agree, soothe, do anything to bring back some sense of calm.

"Laura, darling, of course I believe you," he said, "only it's a sort of shock, and I'm upset because you're upset. . . ."

"But I'm not upset," she interrupted. "I'm happy, so happy that I can't put the feeling into words. You know what it's been like all these weeks, at home and everywhere we've been on holiday, though I tried to

hide it from you. Now it's lifted, because I know, I just
know, that the woman was right. Oh Lord, how awful of
me, but I've forgotten their name—she did tell me. You
see, the thing is that she's a retired doctor, they come
from Edinburgh, and the one who saw Christine went
blind a few years ago. Although she's studied the occult
all her life and been very psychic, it's only since going
blind that she has really seen things, like a medium.
They've had the most wonderful experiences. But to
describe Christine as the blind one did to her sister,
even down to the little blue-and-white dress with the
puff sleeves that she wore at her birthday party, and to
say she was smiling happily. . . . Oh darling, it's made
me so happy I think I'm going to cry."

No hysteria. Nothing wild. She took a tissue from her
bag and blew her nose, smiling at him. "I'm all right,
you see, you don't have to worry. Neither of us need
worry about anything any more. Give me a cigarette."

He took one from his packet and lighted it for her.
She sounded normal, herself again. She wasn't trembling. And if this sudden belief was going to keep her
happy he couldn't possibly begrudge it. But . . . but
. . . he wished, all the same, it hadn't happened.
There was something uncanny about thought-
reading, about telepathy. Scientists couldn't account
for it, nobody could, and this is what must have
happened just now between Laura and the sisters. So
the one who had been staring at him was blind. That
accounted for the fixed gaze. Which somehow was
unpleasant in itself, creepy. Oh hell, he thought, I wish
we hadn't come here for lunch. Just chance, a flick of a
coin between this, Torcello, and driving to Padua, and
we had to choose Torcello.

"You didn't arrange to meet them again or anything,
did you?" he asked, trying to sound casual.

"No, darling, why should I?" Laura answered. "I

mean, there was nothing more they could tell me. The sister had had her wonderful vision, and that was that. Anyway, they're moving on. Funnily enough, it's rather like our original game. They *are* going round the world before returning to Scotland. Only I said Australia, didn't I? The old dears. . . . Anything less like murderers and jewel thieves."

She had quite recovered. She stood up and looked about her. "Come on," she said. "Having come to Torcello we must see the cathedral."

They made their way from the restaurant across the open piazza, where the stalls had been set up with scarves and trinkets and postcards, and so along the path to the cathedral. One of the ferryboats had just decanted a crowd of sightseers, many of whom had already found their way into Santa Maria Assunta. Laura, undaunted, asked her husband for the guidebook, and, as had always been her custom in happier days, started to walk slowly through the cathedral, studying mosaics, columns, panels from left to right, while John, less interested, because of his concern at what had just happened, followed close behind, keeping a weather eye alert for the twin sisters. There was no sign of them. Perhaps they had gone into the church of Santa Fosca close by. A sudden encounter would be embarrassing, quite apart from the effect it might have upon Laura. But the anonymous, shuffling tourists, intent upon culture, could not harm her, although from his own point of view they made artistic appreciation impossible. He could not concentrate, the cold clear beauty of what he saw left him untouched, and when Laura touched his sleeve, pointing to the mosaic of the Virgin and Child standing above the frieze of the Apostles, he nodded in sympathy yet saw nothing, the long, sad face of the Virgin infinitely remote, and turning on sudden impulse stared back over the heads

of the tourists towards the door, where frescoes of the blessed and the damned gave themselves to judgement.

The twins were standing there, the blind one still holding on to her sister's arm, her sightless eyes fixed firmly upon him. He felt himself held, unable to move, and an impending sense of doom, of tragedy, came upon him. His whole being sagged, as it were, in apathy, and he thought, "This is the end, there is no escape, no future." Then both sisters turned and went out of the cathedral and the sensation vanished, leaving indignation in its wake, and rising anger. How dare those two old fools practise their mediumistic tricks on him? It was fraudulent, unhealthy; this was probably the way they lived, touring the world making everyone they met uncomfortable. Give them half a chance and they would have got money out of Laura—anything.

He felt her tugging at his sleeve again. "Isn't she beautiful? So happy, so serene."

"Who? What?" he asked.

"The Madonna," she answered. "She has a magic quality. It goes right through to one. Don't you feel it too?"

"I suppose so. I don't know. There are too many people around."

She looked up at him, astonished. "What's that got to do with it? How funny you are. Well, all right, let's get away from them. I want to buy some postcards anyway."

Disappointed, she sensed his lack of interest, and began to thread her way through the crowd of tourists to the door.

"Come on," he said abruptly, once they were outside, "there's plenty of time for postcards, let's explore a bit," and he struck off from the path, which would have taken them back to the centre where the little houses were, and the stalls, and the drifting crowd of people, to

a narrow way amongst uncultivated ground, beyond which he could see a sort of cutting, or canal. The sight of water, limpid, pale, was a soothing contrast to the fierce sun above their heads.

"I don't think this leads anywhere much," said Laura. "It's a bit muddy, too, one can't sit. Besides, there are more things the guidebook says we ought to see."

"Oh, forget the book," he said impatiently, and, pulling her down beside him on the bank above the cutting, put his arms round her.

"It's the wrong time of day for sightseeing. Look, there's a rat swimming there the other side."

He picked up a stone and threw it in the water, and the animal sank, or somehow disappeared, and nothing was left but bubbles.

"Don't," said Laura. "It's cruel, poor thing," and then suddenly, putting her hand on his knee, "Do you think Christine is sitting here beside us?"

He did not answer at once. What was there to say? Would it be like this forever?

"I expect so," he said slowly, "if you feel she is."

The point was, remembering Christine before the onset of the fatal meningitis, she would have been running along the bank excitedly, throwing off her shoes, wanting to paddle, giving Laura a fit of apprehension. "Sweetheart, take care, come back . . ."

"The woman said she was looking so happy, sitting beside us, smiling," said Laura. She got up, brushing her dress, her mood changed to restlessness. "Come on, let's go back," she said.

He followed her with a sinking heart. He knew she did not really want to buy postcards or see what remained to be seen; she wanted to go in search of the women again, not necessarily to talk, just to be near them. When they came to the open place by the stalls he

noticed that the crowd of tourists had thinned, there were only a few stragglers left, and the sisters were not amongst them. They must have joined the main body who had come to Torcello by the ferry service. A wave of relief seized him.

"Look, there's a mass of postcards at the second stall," he said quickly, "and some eye-catching head scarves. Let me buy you a head scarf."

"Darling, I've so many!" she protested. "Don't waste your lire."

"It isn't a waste. I'm in a buying mood. What about a basket? You know we never have enough baskets. Or some lace. How about lace?"

She allowed herself, laughing, to be dragged to the stall. While he rumpled through the goods spread out before them, and chatted up the smiling woman who was selling her wares, his ferociously bad Italian making her smile the more, he knew it would give the body of tourists more time to walk to the landing stage and catch the ferry service, and the twin sisters would be out of sight and out of their life.

"Never," said Laura, some twenty minutes later, "has so much junk been piled into so small a basket," her bubbling laugh reassuring him that all was well, he needn't worry any more, the evil hour had passed. The launch from the Cipriani that had brought them from Venice was waiting by the landing stage. The passengers who had arrived with them, the Americans, the man with the monocle, were already assembled. Earlier, before setting out, he had thought the price for lunch and transport, there and back, decidedly steep. Now he grudged none of it, except that the outing to Torcello itself had been one of the major errors of this particular holiday in Venice. They stepped down into the launch, finding a place in the open, and the boat chugged away down the canal and into the lagoon. The ordinary ferry

had gone before, steaming towards Murano, while their own craft headed past San Francesco del Deserto and so back direct to Venice.

He put his arm around her once more, holding her close, and this time she responded, smiling up at him, her head on his shoulder.

"It's been a lovely day," she said. "I shall never forget it, never. You know, darling, now at last I can begin to enjoy our holiday."

He wanted to shout with relief. It's going to be all right, he decided, let her believe what she likes, it doesn't matter, it makes her happy. The beauty of Venice rose before them, sharply outlined against the glowing sky, and there was still so much to see, wandering there together, that might now be perfect because of her change of mood, the shadow having lifted, and aloud he began to discuss the evening to come, where they would dine—not the restaurant they usually went to, near the Fenice theatre, but somewhere different, somewhere new.

"Yes, but it must be cheap," she said, falling in with his mood, "because we've already spent so much today."

Their hotel by the Grand Canal had a welcoming, comforting air. The clerk smiled as he handed over their key. The bedroom was familiar, like home, with Laura's things arranged neatly on the dressing-table, but with it the little festive atmosphere of strangeness, of excitement, that only a holiday bedroom brings. This is ours for the moment, but no more. While we are in it we bring it life. When we have gone it no longer exists, it fades into anonymity. He turned on both taps in the bathroom, the water gushing into the bath, the steam rising. "Now," he thought afterwards, "now at last is the moment to make love," and he went back into the bedroom, and she understood, and opened her arms

and smiled. Such blessed relief after all those weeks of restraint.

"The thing is," she said later, fixing her ear-rings before the looking-glass, "I'm not really terribly hungry. Shall we just be dull and eat in the dining-room here?"

"God, no!" he exclaimed. "With all those rather dreary couples at the other tables? I'm ravenous. I'm also gay. I want to get rather sloshed."

"Not bright lights and music, surely?"

"No, no . . . some small, dark, intimate cave, rather sinister, full of lovers with other people's wives."

"H'm," sniffed Laura, "we all know what *that* means. You'll spot some Italian lovely of sixteen and smirk at her through dinner, while I'm stuck high and dry with a beastly man's broad back."

They went out laughing into the warm soft night, and the magic was about them everywhere. "Let's walk," he said, "let's walk and work up an appetite for our gigantic meal," and inevitably they found themselves by the Molo and the lapping gondolas dancing upon the water, the lights everywhere blending with the darkness. There were other couples strolling for the same sake of aimless enjoyment, backwards, forwards, purposeless, and the inevitable sailors in groups, noisy, gesticulating, and dark-eyed girls whispering, clicking on high heels.

"The trouble is," said Laura, "walking in Venice becomes compulsive once you start. Just over the next bridge, you say, and then the next one beckons. I'm sure there are no restaurants down here, we're almost at those public gardens where they hold the Biennale. Let's turn back. I know there's a restaurant somewhere near the church of San Zaccaria, there's a little alleyway leading to it."

"Tell you what," said John, "if we go down here by

the Arsenal, and cross that bridge at the end and head left, we'll come upon San Zaccaria from the other side. We did it the other morning."

"Yes, but it was daylight then. We may lose our way, it's not very well lit."

"Don't fuss. I have an instinct for these things."

They turned down the Fondamenta dell'Arsenale and crossed the little bridge short of the Arsenal itself, and so on past the church of San Martino. There were two canals ahead, one bearing right, the other left, with narrow streets beside them. John hesitated. Which one was it they had walked beside the day before?

"You see," protested Laura, "we shall be lost, just as I said."

"Nonsense," replied John firmly. "It's the left-hand one, I remember the little bridge."

The canal was narrow, the houses on either side seemed to close in upon it, and in the daytime, with the sun's reflection on the water and the windows of the houses open, bedding upon the balconies, a canary singing in a cage, there had been an impression of warmth, of secluded shelter. Now, ill-lit, almost in darkness, the windows of the houses shuttered, the water dank, the scene appeared altogether different, neglected, poor, and the long narrow boats moored to the slippery steps of cellar entrances looked like coffins.

"I swear I don't remember this bridge," said Laura, pausing, and holding on to the rail, "and I don't like the look of that alleyway beyond."

"There's a lamp halfway up," John told her. "I know exactly where we are, not far from the Greek quarter."

They crossed the bridge, and were about to plunge into the alleyway when they heard the cry. It came, surely, from one of the houses on the opposite side, but which one it was impossible to say. With the shutters closed each one of them seemed dead. They turned,

and stared in the direction from which the sound had come.

"What was it?" whispered Laura.

"Some drunk or other," said John briefly. "Come on."

Less like a drunk than someone being strangled, and the choking cry suppressed as the grip held firm.

"We ought to call the police," said Laura.

"Oh, for heaven's sake," said John. Where did she think she was—Piccadilly?

"Well, I'm off, it's sinister," she replied, and began to hurry away up the twisting alleyway. John hesitated, his eye caught by a small figure which suddenly crept from a cellar entrance below one of the opposite houses, and then jumped into a narrow boat below. It was a child, a little girl—she couldn't have been more than five or six—wearing a short coat over her minute skirt, a pixie hood covering her head. There were four boats moored, line upon line, and she proceeded to jump from one to the other with surprising agility, intent, it would seem, upon escape. Once her foot slipped and he caught his breath, for she was within a few feet of the water, losing balance; then she recovered, and hopped on to the furthest boat. Bending, she tugged at the rope, which had the effect of swinging the boat's after-end across the canal, almost touching the opposite side and another cellar entrance, about thirty feet from the spot where John stood watching her. Then the child jumped again, landing upon the cellar steps, and vanished into the house, the boat swinging back into midcanal behind her. The whole episode could not have taken more than four minutes. Then he heard the quick patter of feet. Laura had returned. She had seen none of it, for which he felt unspeakably thankful. The sight of a child, a little girl, in what must have been near danger, her fear that the scene he had just witnessed was in some way a

sequel to the alarming cry, might have had a disastrous effect on her overwrought nerves.

"What are you doing?" she called. "I daren't go on without you. The wretched alley branches in two directions."

"Sorry," he told her. "I'm coming."

He took her arm and they walked briskly along the alley, John with an apparent confidence he did not possess.

"There were no more cries, were there?" she asked.

"No," he said, "no, nothing. I tell you, it was some drunk."

The alley led to a deserted *campo* behind a church, not a church he knew, and he led the way across, along another street and over a further bridge.

"Wait a minute," he said. "I think we take this right-hand turning. It will lead us into the Greek quarter—the church of San Georgio is somewhere over there."

She did not answer. She was beginning to lose faith. The place was like a maze. They might circle round and round forever, and then find themselves back again, near the bridge where they had heard the cry. Doggedly he led her on, and then surprisingly, with relief, he saw people walking in the lighted street ahead, there was a spire of a church, the surroundings became familiar.

"There, I told you," he said. "That's San Zaccaria, we've found it all right. Your restaurant can't be far away."

And anyway, there would be other restaurants, somewhere to eat, at least here was the cheering glitter of lights, of movement, canals beside which people walked, the atmosphere of tourism. The letters "Ristorante," in blue lights, shone like a beacon down a left-hand alley.

"Is this your place?" he asked.

"God knows," she said. "Who cares? Let's feed there anyway."

And so into the sudden blast of heated air and hum of voices, the smell of pasta, wine, waiters, jostling customers, laughter. "For two? This way, please." Why, he thought, was one's British nationality always so obvious? A cramped little table and an enormous menu scribbled in an indecipherable mauve biro, with the waiter hovering, expecting the order forthwith.

"Two very large camparis, with soda," John said. *"Then* we'll study the menu."

He was not going to be rushed. He handed the bill of fare to Laura and looked about him. Mostly Italians—that meant the food would be good. Then he saw them. At the opposite side of the room. The twin sisters. They must have come into the restaurant hard upon Laura's and his own arrival, for they were only now sitting down, shedding their coats, the waiter hovering beside the table. John was seized with the irrational thought that this was no coincidence. The sisters had noticed them both, in the street outside, and had followed them in. Why, in the name of hell, should they have picked on this particular spot, in the whole of Venice, unless . . . unless Laura herself, at Torcello, had suggested a further encounter, or the sister had suggested it to her? A small restaurant near the church of San Zaccaria, we go there sometimes for dinner. It was Laura, before the walk, who had mentioned San Zaccaria. . . .

She was still intent upon the menu, she had not seen the sisters, but any moment now she would have chosen what she wanted to eat, and then she would raise her head and look across the room. If only the drinks would come. If only the waiter would bring the drinks, it would give Laura something to do.

"You know, I was thinking," he said quickly, "we

really ought to go to the garage tomorrow and get the car, and do that drive to Padua. We could lunch in Padua, see the cathedral and touch St. Antony's tomb and look at the Giotto frescoes, and come back by way of those various villas along the Brenta that the guide-book cracks up."

It was no use, though. She was looking up, across the restaurant, and she gave a little gasp of surprise. It was genuine. He could swear it was genuine.

"Look," she said, "how extraordinary! How really amazing!"

"What?" he said sharply.

"Why, there they are. My wonderful old twins. They've seen us, what's more. They're staring this way." She waved her hand, radiant, delighted. The sister she had spoken to at Torcello bowed and smiled. False old bitch, he thought. I know they followed us.

"Oh, darling, I must go and speak to them," she said impulsively, "just to tell them how happy I've been all day, thanks to them."

"Oh, for heaven's sake!" he said. "Look, here are the drinks. And we haven't ordered yet. Surely you can wait until later, until we've eaten?"

"I won't be a moment," she said, "and anyway I want scampi, nothing first. I told you I wasn't hungry."

She got up, and, brushing past the waiter with the drinks, crossed the room. She might have been greeting the loved friends of years. He watched her bend over the table and shake them both by the hand, and because there was a vacant chair at their table she drew it up and sat down, talking, smiling. Nor did the sisters seem surprised, at least not the one she knew, who nodded and talked back, while the blind sister remained impassive.

"All right," thought John savagely, "then I *will* get sloshed," and he proceeded to down his campari and soda and order another, while he pointed out some-

thing quite unintelligible on the menu as his own choice, but remembered scampi for Laura. "And a bottle of Soave," he added, "with ice."

The evening was ruined anyway. What was to have been an intimate, happy celebration would now be heavy-laden with spiritualistic visions, poor little dead Christine sharing the table with them, which was so damned stupid when in earthly life she would have been tucked up hours ago in bed. The bitter taste of the campari suited his mood of sudden self-pity, and all the while he watched the group at the table in the opposite corner, Laura apparently listening while the more active sister held forth and the blind one sat silent, her formidable sightless eyes turned in his direction.

"She's phoney," he thought, "she's not blind at all. They're both of them frauds, and they could be males in drag after all, just as we pretended at Torcello, and they're after Laura."

He began on his second campari and soda. The two drinks, taken on an empty stomach, had an instant effect. Vision became blurred. And still Laura went on sitting at the other table, putting in a question now and again, while the active sister talked. The waiter appeared with the scampi, and a companion beside him to serve John's own order, which was totally unrecognisable, heaped with a livid sauce.

"The signora does not come?" enquired the first waiter, and John shook his head grimly, pointing an unsteady finger across the room.

"Tell the signora," he said carefully, "her scampi will get cold."

He stared down at the offering placed before him, and prodded it delicately with a fork. The pallid sauce dissolved, revealing two enormous slices, rounds, of what appeared to be boiled pork, bedecked with garlic. He forked a portion to his mouth and chewed, and yes, it was pork, steamy, rich, the spicy sauce having turned

it curiously sweet. He laid down his fork, pushing the plate away, and became aware of Laura, returning across the room and sitting beside him. She did not say anything, which was just as well, he thought, because he was too near nausea to answer. It wasn't just the drink, but reaction from the whole nightmare day. She began to eat her scampi, still not uttering. She did not seem to notice he was not eating. The waiter, hovering at his elbow, anxious, seemed aware that John's choice was somehow an error, and discreetly removed the plate. "Bring me a green salad," murmured John, and even then Laura did not register surprise, or, as she might have done in more normal circumstances, accuse him of having had too much to drink. Finally, when she had finished her scampi and was sipping her wine, which John had waved away, to nibble at his salad in small mouthfuls like a sick rabbit, she began to speak.

"Darling," she said, "I know you won't believe it, and it's rather frightening in a way, but after they left the restaurant in Torcello the sisters went to the cathedral, as we did, although we didn't see them in that crowd, and the blind one had another vision. She said Christine was trying to tell her something about us, that we should be in danger if we stayed in Venice. Christine wanted us to go away as soon as possible."

So that's it, he thought. They think they can run our lives for us. This is to be our problem from henceforth. Do we eat? Do we get up? Do we go to bed? We must get in touch with the twin sisters. They will direct us.

"Well?" she said. "Why don't you say something?"

"Because," he answered, "you are perfectly right, I don't believe it. Quite frankly, I judge your old sisters as being a couple of freaks, if nothing else. They're obviously unbalanced, and I'm sorry if this hurts you, but the fact is they've found a sucker in you."

"You're being unfair," said Laura. "They are genu-

ine, I know it. I just know it. They were completely sincere in what they said."

"All right. Granted. They're sincere. But that doesn't make them well-balanced. Honestly, darling, you meet that old girl for ten minutes in a loo, she tells you she sees Christine sitting beside us—well, anyone with a gift for telepathy could read your unconscious mind in an instant—and then, pleased with her success, as any old psychic expert would be, she flings a further mood of ecstasy and wants to boot us out of Venice. Well, I'm sorry, but to hell with it."

The room was no longer reeling. Anger had sobered him. If it would not put Laura to shame he would get up and cross to their table, and tell the old fools where they got off.

"I knew you would take it like this," said Laura unhappily. "I told them you would. They said not to worry. As long as we left Venice tomorrow everything would come all right."

"Oh, for God's sake," said John. He changed his mind, and poured himself a glass of wine.

"After all," Laura went on, "we have really seen the cream of Venice. I don't mind going on somewhere else. And if we stayed—I know it sounds silly, but I should have a nasty nagging sort of feeling inside me, and I should keep thinking of darling Christine being unhappy and trying to tell us to go."

"Right," said John with ominous calm, "that settles it. Go we will. I suggest we clear off to the hotel straight away and warn the reception we're leaving in the morning. Have you had enough to eat?"

"Oh, dear," sighed Laura, "don't take it like that. Look, why not come over and meet them, and then they can explain about the vision to you? Perhaps you would take it seriously then. Especially as you are the one it most concerns. Christine is more worried over you than

me. And the extraordinary thing is that the blind sister says you're psychic and don't know it. You are somehow *en rapport* with the unknown, and I'm not."

"Well, that's final," said John. "I'm psychic, am I? Fine. My psychic intuition tells me to get out of this restaurant now, at once, and we can decide what we do about leaving Venice when we are back at the hotel."

He signalled to the waiter for the bill and they waited for it, not speaking to each other, Laura unhappy, fiddling with her bag, while John, glancing furtively at the twins' table, noticed that they were tucking into plates piled high with spaghetti, in very un-psychic fashion. The bill disposed of, John pushed back his chair.

"Right. Are you ready?" he asked.

"I'm going to say goodbye to them first," said Laura, her mouth set sulkily, reminding him instantly, with a pang, of their poor lost child.

"Just as you like," he replied, and walked ahead of her out of the restaurant, without a backward glance.

The soft humidity of the evening, so pleasant to walk about in earlier, had turned to rain. The strolling tourists had melted away. One or two people hurried by under umbrellas. This is what the inhabitants who live here see, he thought. This is the true life. Empty streets by night, and the dank stillness of a stagnant canal beneath shuttered houses. The rest is a bright façade put on for show, glittering by sunlight.

Laura joined him and they walked away together in silence, and emerging presently behind the ducal palace came out into the Piazza San Marco. The rain was heavy now, and they sought shelter with the few remaining stragglers under the colonnades. The orchestras had packed up for the evening. The tables were bare. Chairs had been turned upside down.

The experts are right, he thought. Venice is sinking. The whole city is slowly dying. One day the tourists will

travel here by boat to peer down into the waters, and they will see pillars and columns and marble far, far beneath them, slime and mud uncovering for brief moments a lost underworld of stone. Their heels made a ringing sound on the pavement and the rain splashed from the gutterings above. A fine ending to an evening that had started with brave hope, with innocence.

When they came to their hotel Laura made straight for the lift, and John turned to the desk to ask the night porter for the key. The man handed him a telegram at the same time. John stared at it a moment. Laura was already in the lift. Then he opened the envelope and read the message. It was from the headmaster of Johnnie's preparatory school.

> Johnnie under observation suspected appendicitis in city hospital here.
> No cause for alarm but surgeon thought wise advise you.
>
> Charles Hill

He read the message twice, then walked slowly towards the lift where Laura was waiting for him. He gave her the telegram. "This came when we were out," he said. "Not awfully good news." He pressed the lift button as she read the telegram. The lift stopped at the second floor, and they got out.

"Well, this decides it, doesn't it?" she said. "Here is the proof. We have to leave Venice because we're going home. It's Johnnie who's in danger, not us. This is what Christine was trying to tell the twins."

The first thing John did the following morning was to put a call through to the headmaster at the preparatory school. Then he gave notice of their departure to the reception manager, and they packed while they waited for the call. Neither of them referred to the events of

the preceding day, it was not necessary. John knew the arrival of the telegram and the foreboding of danger from the sisters was coincidence, nothing more, but it was pointless to start an argument about it. Laura was convinced otherwise, but intuitively she knew it was best to keep her feelings to herself. During breakfast they discussed ways and means of getting home. It should be possible to get themselves, and the car, on to the special car train that ran from Milan through to Calais, since it was early in the season. In any event, the headmaster had said there was no urgency.

The call from England came while John was in the bathroom. Laura answered it. He came into the bedroom a few minutes later. She was still speaking, but he could tell from the expression in her eyes that she was anxious.

"It's Mrs. Hill," she said. "Mr. Hill is in class. She says they reported from the hospital that Johnnie had a restless night and the surgeon may have to operate, but he doesn't want to unless it's absolutely necessary. They've taken X rays and the appendix is in a tricky position, it's not awfully straightforward."

"Here, give it to me," he said.

The soothing but slightly guarded voice of the headmaster's wife came down the receiver. "I'm so sorry this may spoil your plans," she said, "but both Charles and I felt you ought to be told, and that you might feel rather easier if you were on the spot. Johnnie is very plucky, but of course he has some fever. That isn't unusual, the surgeon says, in the circumstances. Sometimes an appendix can get displaced, it appears, and this makes it more complicated. He's going to decide about operating this evening."

"Yes, of course, we quite understand," said John.

"Please do tell your wife not to worry too much," she went on. "The hospital is excellent, a very nice staff, and we have every confidence in the surgeon."

"Yes," said John, "yes," and then broke off because Laura was making gestures beside him.

"If we can't get the car on the train, I can fly," she said. "They're sure to be able to find me a seat on a 'plane. Then at least one of us would be there this evening."

He nodded agreement. "Thank you so much, Mrs. Hill," he said, "we'll manage to get back all right. Yes, I'm sure Johnnie is in good hands. Thank your husband for us. Goodbye."

He replaced the receiver and looked round him at the tumbled beds, suitcases on the floor, tissue paper strewn. Baskets, maps, books, coats, everything they had brought with them in the car. "Oh God," he said, "what a bloody mess. All this junk." The telephone rang again. It was the hall porter to say he had succeeded in booking a sleeper for them both, and a place for the car, on the following night.

"Look," said Laura, who had seized the telephone, "could you book one seat on the midday 'plane from Venice to London today, for me? It's imperative one of us gets home this evening. My husband could follow with the car tomorrow."

"Here, hang on," interrupted John. "No need for panic stations. Surely twenty-four hours wouldn't make all that difference?"

Anxiety had drained the colour from her face. She turned to him, distraught.

"It mightn't to you, but it does to me," she said. "I've lost one child, I'm not going to lose another."

"All right, darling, all right . . ." He put his hand out to her but she brushed it off, impatiently, and continued giving directions to the porter. He turned back to his packing. No use saying anything. Better for it to be as she wished. They could, of course, both go by air, and then when all was well, and Johnnie better, he could come back and fetch the car, driving home

through France as they had come. Rather a sweat, though, and the hell of an expense. Bad enough Laura going by air and himself with the car on the train from Milan.

"We could, if you like, both fly," he began tentatively, explaining the sudden idea, but she would have none of it. "That really *would* be absurd," she said impatiently. "As long as I'm there this evening, and you follow by train, it's all that matters. Besides, we shall need the car, going backwards and forwards to the hospital. And our luggage. We couldn't go off and just leave all this here."

No, he saw her point. A silly idea. It was only—well, he was as worried about Johnnie as she was, though he wasn't going to say so.

"I'm going downstairs to stand over the porter," said Laura. "They always make more effort if one is actually on the spot. Everything I want tonight is packed. I shall only need my overnight case. You can bring everything else in the car." She hadn't been out of the bedroom five minutes before the telephone rang. It was Laura. "Darling," she said, "it couldn't have worked out better. The porter has got me on a charter flight that leaves Venice in less than an hour. A special motor launch takes the party direct from San Marco in about ten minutes. Some passenger on the charter flight cancelled. I shall be at Gatwick in less than four hours."

"I'll be down right away," he told her.

He joined her by the reception desk. She no longer looked anxious and drawn, but full of purpose. She was on her way. He kept wishing they were going together. He couldn't bear to stay on in Venice after she had gone, but the thought of driving to Milan, spending a dreary night in a hotel there alone, the endless dragging day which would follow, and the long hours in the train the next night, filled him with intolerable depression, quite apart from the anxiety about Johnnie. They

walked along to the San Marco landing stage, the Molo bright and glittering after the rain, a little breeze blowing, the postcards and scarves and tourist souvenirs fluttering on the stalls, the tourists themselves out in force, strolling, contented, the happy day before them.

"I'll ring you tonight from Milan," he told her. "The Hills will give you a bed, I suppose. And if you're at the hospital they'll let me have the latest news. That must be your charter party. You're welcome to them!"

The passengers descending from the landing stage down into the waiting launch were carrying hand-luggage with Union Jack tags upon them. They were mostly middle-aged, with what appeared to be two Methodist ministers in charge. One of them advanced towards Laura, holding out his hand, showing a gleaming row of dentures when he smiled. "You must be the lady joining us for the homeward flight," he said. "Welcome aboard, and to the Union of Fellowship. We are all delighted to make your acquaintance. Sorry we hadn't a seat for hubby too."

Laura turned swiftly and kissed John, a tremor at the corner of her mouth betraying inward laughter. "Do you think they'll break into hymns?" she whispered. "Take care of yourself, hubby. Call me tonight."

The pilot sounded a curious little toot upon his horn, and in a moment Laura had climbed down the steps into the launch and was standing amongst the crowd of passengers, waving her hand, her scarlet coat a gay patch of colour amongst the more sober suiting of her companions. The launch tooted again and moved away from the landing stage, and he stood there watching it, a sense of immense loss filling his heart. Then he turned and walked away, back to the hotel, the bright day all about him desolate, unseen.

There was nothing, he thought, as he looked about him presently in the hotel bedroom, so melancholy as a

vacated room, especially when the recent signs of occupation were still visible about him. Laura's suitcases on the bed, a second coat she had left behind. Traces of powder on the dressing table. A tissue, with a lipstick smear, thrown in the wastepaper basket. Even an old toothpaste tube squeezed dry, lying on the glass shelf above the washbasin. Sounds of the heedless traffic on the Grand Canal came as always from the open window, but Laura wasn't there any more to listen to it, or to watch from the small balcony. The pleasure had gone. Feeling had gone.

John finished packing, and leaving all the baggage ready to be collected he went downstairs to pay the bill. The reception clerk was welcoming new arrivals. People were sitting on the terrace overlooking the Grand Canal reading newspapers, the pleasant day waiting to be planned.

John decided to have an early lunch, here on the hotel terrace, on familiar ground, and then have the porter carry the baggage to one of the ferries that steamed direct between San Marco and the Porta Roma, where the car was garaged. The fiasco meal of the night before had left him empty, and he was ready for the trolley of hors d'œuvres when they brought it to him, around midday. Even here, though, there was change. The headwaiter, their especial friend, was off-duty, and the table where they usually sat was occupied by new arrivals, a honeymoon couple, he told himself sourly, observing the gaiety, the smiles, while he had been shown to a small single table behind a tub of flowers.

"She's airborne now," John thought, "she's on her way," and he tried to picture Laura seated between the Methodist ministers, telling them, no doubt, about Johnnie ill in hospital, and heaven knows what else besides. Well, the twin sisters anyway could rest in psychic peace. Their wishes would have been fulfilled.

Lunch over, there was no point in lingering with a cup of coffee on the terrace. His desire was to get away as soon as possible, fetch the car, and be en route for Milan. He made his farewells at the reception desk, and, escorted by a porter who had piled his baggage on to a wheeled trolley, made his way once more to the landing stage of San Marco. As he stepped on to the steam ferry, his luggage heaped beside him, a crowd of jostling people all about him, he had one momentary pang to be leaving Venice. When, if ever, he wondered, would they come again? Next year . . . in three years. . . . Glimpsed first on honeymoon, nearly ten years ago, and then a second visit, *en passant,* before a cruise, and now this last abortive ten days that had ended so abruptly.

The water glittered in the sunshine, buildings shone, tourists in dark glasses paraded up and down the rapidly receding Molo, already the terrace of their hotel was out of sight as the ferry churned its way up the Grand Canal. So many impressions to seize and hold, familiar loved façades, balconies, windows, water lapping the cellar steps of decaying palaces, the little red house where d'Annunzio lived, with its garden—our house, Laura called it, pretending it was theirs—and too soon the ferry would be turning left on the direct route to the Piazzale Roma, so missing the best of the Canal, the Rialto, the further palaces.

Another ferry was heading downstream to pass them, filled with passengers, and for a brief foolish moment he wished he could change places, be amongst the happy tourists bound for Venice and all he had left behind him. Then he saw her. Laura, in her scarlet coat, the twin sisters by her side, the active sister with her hand on Laura's arm, talking earnestly, and Laura herself, her hair blowing in the wind, gesticulating, on her face a look of distress. He stared, astounded, too astonished to shout, to wave, and anyway they would

never have heard or seen him, for his own ferry had already passed and was heading in the opposite direction.

What the hell had happened? There must have been a hold-up with the charter flight and it had never taken off, but in that case why had Laura not telephoned him at the hotel? And what were those damned sisters doing? Had she run into them at the airport? Was it coincidence? And why did she look so anxious? He could think of no explanation. Perhaps the flight had been cancelled. Laura, of course, would go straight to the hotel, expecting to find him there, intending, doubtless, to drive with him after all to Milan and take the train the following night. What a blasted mix-up. The only thing to do was to telephone the hotel immediately his ferry reached the Piazzale Roma and tell her to wait—he would return and fetch her. As for the damned interfering sisters, they could get stuffed.

The usual stampede ensued when the ferry arrived at the landing stage. He had to find a porter to collect his baggage, and then wait while he discovered a telephone. The fiddling with change, the hunt for the number, delayed him still more. He succeeded at last in getting through, and luckily the reception clerk he knew was still at the desk.

"Look, there's been some frightful muddle," he began, and explained how Laura was even now on her way back to the hotel—he had seen her with two friends on one of the ferry services. Would the reception clerk explain and tell her to wait? He would be back by the next available service to collect her. "In any event, detain her," he said. "I'll be as quick as I can." The reception clerk understood perfectly, and John rang off.

Thank heaven Laura hadn't turned up before he had put through his call, or they would have told her he was

on his way to Milan. The porter was still waiting with the baggage, and it seemed simplest to walk with him to the garage, hand everything over to the chap in charge of the office there and ask him to keep it for an hour, when he would be returning with his wife to pick up the car. Then he went back to the landing station to await the next ferry to Venice. The minutes dragged, and he kept wondering all the time what had gone wrong at the airport and why in heaven's name Laura hadn't telephoned. No use conjecturing. She would tell him the whole story at the hotel. One thing was certain: he would not allow Laura and himself to be saddled with the sisters and become involved with their affairs. He could imagine Laura saying that they also had missed a flight, and could they have a lift to Milan?

Finally the ferry chugged alongside the landing stage and he stepped aboard. What an anticlimax, thrashing back past the familiar sights to which he had bidden a nostalgic farewell such a short while ago! He didn't even look about him this time, he was so intent on reaching his destination. In San Marco there were more people than ever, the afternoon crowds walking shoulder to shoulder, every one of them on pleasure bent.

He came to the hotel and pushed his way through the swing door, expecting to see Laura, and possibly the sisters, waiting in the lounge to the left of the entrance. She was not there. He went to the desk. The reception clerk he had spoken to on the telephone was standing there, talking to the manager.

"Has my wife arrived?" John asked.

"No, sir, not yet."

"What an extraordinary thing. Are you sure?"

"Absolutely certain, sir. I have been here ever since you telephoned me at a quarter to two. I have not left the desk."

"I just don't understand it. She was on one of the

vaporettos passing by the Accademia. She would have landed at San Marco about five minutes later and come on here."

The clerk seemed nonplussed. "I don't know what to say. The signora was with friends, did you say?"

"Yes. Well, acquaintances. Two ladies we had met at Torcello yesterday. I was astonished to see her with them on the vaporetto, and of course I assumed that the flight had been cancelled, and she had somehow met up with them at the airport and decided to return here with them, to catch me before I left."

Oh hell, what was Laura doing? It was after three. A matter of moments from San Marco landing stage to the hotel.

"Perhaps the signora went with her friends to their hotel instead. Do you know where they are staying?"

"No," said John, "I haven't the slightest idea. What's more, I don't even know the names of the two ladies. They were sisters, twins, in fact—looked exactly alike. But anyway, why go to their hotel and not here?"

The swing-door opened but it wasn't Laura. Two people staying in the hotel.

The manager broke into the conversation. "I tell you what I will do," he said. "I will telephone the airport and check about the flight. Then at least we will get somewhere." He smiled apologetically. It was not usual for arrangements to go wrong.

"Yes, do that," said John. "We may as well know what happened there."

He lit a cigarette and began to pace up and down the entrance hall. What a bloody mix-up. And how unlike Laura, who knew he would be setting off for Milan directly after lunch—indeed, for all she knew he might have gone before. But surely, in that case, she would have telephoned at once, on arrival at the airport, had the flight been cancelled? The manager was ages telephoning, he had to be put through on some other line,

and his Italian was too rapid for John to follow the conversation. Finally he replaced the receiver.

"It is more mysterious than ever, sir," he said. "The charter flight was not delayed, it took off on schedule with a full complement of passengers. As far as they could tell me, there was no hitch. The signora must simply have changed her mind." His smile was more apologetic than ever.

"Changed her mind," John repeated. "But why on earth should she do that? She was so anxious to be home tonight."

The manager shrugged. "You know how ladies can be, sir," he said. "Your wife may have thought that after all she would prefer to take the train to Milan with you. I do assure you, though, that the charter party was most respectable, and it was a Caravelle aircraft, perfectly safe."

"Yes, yes," said John impatiently, "I don't blame your arrangements in the slightest. I just can't understand what induced her to change her mind, unless it was meeting with these two ladies."

The manager was silent. He could not think of anything to say. The reception clerk was equally concerned. "Is it possible," he ventured, "that you made a mistake, and it was not the signora that you saw on the vaporetto?"

"Oh no," replied John, "it was my wife, I assure you. She was wearing her red coat, she was hatless, just as she left here. I saw her as plainly as I can see you. I would swear to it in a court of law."

"It is unfortunate," said the manager, "that we do not know the name of the two ladies, or the hotel where they were staying. You say you met these ladies at Torcello yesterday?"

"Yes . . . but only briefly. They weren't staying there. At least, I am certain they were not. We saw them at dinner in Venice later, as it happens."

"Excuse me. . . ." Guests were arriving with luggage to check in, the clerk was obliged to attend to them. John turned in desperation to the manager. "Do you think it would be any good telephoning the hotel in Torcello in case the people there knew the name of the ladies, or where they were staying in Venice?"

"We can try," replied the manager. "It is a small hope, but we can try."

John resumed his anxious pacing, all the while watching the swing-door, hoping, praying, that he would catch sight of the red coat and Laura would enter. Once again there followed what seemed an interminable telephone conversation between the manager and someone at the hotel in Torcello.

"Tell them two sisters," said John, "two elderly ladies dressed in grey, both exactly alike. One lady was blind," he added. The manager nodded. He was obviously giving a detailed description. Yet when he hung up he shook his head. "The manager at Torcello says he remembers the two ladies well," he told John, "but they were only there for lunch. He never learnt their names."

"Well, that's that. There's nothing to do now but wait."

John lit his third cigarette and went out on to the terrace, to resume his pacing there. He stared out across the canal, searching the heads of the people on passing steamers, motorboats, even drifting gondolas. The minutes ticked by on his watch, and there was no sign of Laura. A terrible foreboding nagged at him that somehow this was prearranged, that Laura had never intended to catch the aircraft, that last night in the restaurant she had made an assignation with the sisters. Oh God, he thought, that's impossible, I'm going paranoiac. . . . Yet why, why? No, more likely the encounter at the airport was fortuitous, and for some incredible reason they had persuaded Laura not to

board the aircraft, even prevented her from doing so, trotting out one of their psychic visions, that the aircraft would crash, that she must return with them to Venice. And Laura, in her sensitive state, felt they must be right, swallowed it all without question.

But granted all these possibilities, why had she not come to the hotel? What was she doing? Four o'clock, half-past four, the sun no longer dappling the water. He went back to the reception desk.

"I just can't hang around," he said. "Even if she does turn up, we shall never make Milan this evening. I might see her walking with these ladies, in the Piazza San Marco, anywhere. If she arrives while I'm out, will you explain?"

The clerk was full of concern. "Indeed, yes," he said. "It is very worrying for you, sir. Would it perhaps be prudent if we booked you in here tonight?"

John gestured, helplessly. "Perhaps, yes, I don't know. Maybe . . ."

He went out of the swing-door and began to walk towards the Piazza San Marco. He looked into every shop up and down the colonnades, crossed the piazza a dozen times, threaded his way between the tables in front of Florian's, in front of Quadri's, knowing that Laura's red coat and the distinctive appearance of the twin sisters could easily be spotted, even amongst this milling crowd, but there was no sign of them. He joined the crowd of shoppers in the Merceria, shoulder to shoulder with idlers, thrusters, window-gazers, knowing instinctively that it was useless, they wouldn't be here. Why should Laura have deliberately missed her flight to return to Venice for such a purpose? And even if she had done so, for some reason beyond his imagining, she would surely have come first to the hotel to find him.

The only thing left to him was to try to track down the sisters. Their hotel could be anywhere amongst the

hundreds of hotels and pensions scattered through Venice, or even across the other side at the Zattere, or further again on the Giudecca. These last possibilities seemed remote. More likely they were staying in a small hotel or pension somewhere near San Zaccaria handy to the restaurant where they had dined last night. The blind one would surely not go far afield in the evening. He had been a fool not to have thought of this before, and he turned back and walked quickly away from the brightly lighted shopping district towards the narrower, more cramped quarter where they had dined last evening. He found the restaurant without difficulty, but they were not yet open for dinner, and the waiter preparing tables was not the one who had served them. John asked to see the *padrone,* and the waiter disappeared to the back regions, returning after a moment or two with the somewhat dishevelled-looking proprietor in shirtsleeves, caught in a slack moment, not in full tenue.

"I had dinner here last night," John explained. "There were two ladies sitting at that table there in the corner." He pointed to it.

"You wish to book that table for this evening?" asked the proprietor.

"No," said John. "No, there were two ladies there last night, two sisters, due sorelle, twins, gemelle"— what was the right word for twins?—"Do you remember? Two ladies, sorelle vecchie . . ."

"Ah," said the man, "si, si, signore, la povera signorina." He put his hands to his eyes to feign blindness. "Yes, I remember."

"Do you know their names?" asked John. "Where they were staying? I am very anxious to trace them."

The proprietor spread out his hands in a gesture of regret. "I am ver' sorry, signore, I do not know the names of the signorine, they have been here once, twice, perhaps for dinner, they do not say where they

were staying. Perhaps if you come again tonight they might be here? Would you like to book a table?"

He pointed around him, suggesting a whole choice of tables that might appeal to a prospective diner, but John shook his head.

"Thank you, no. I may be dining elsewhere. I am sorry to have troubled you. If the signorine should come . . ." he paused, "possibly I may return later," he added. "I am not sure."

The proprietor bowed, and walked with him to the entrance. "In Venice the whole world meets," he said smiling. "It is possible the signore will find his friends tonight. Arrivederci, signore."

Friends? John walked out into the street. More likely kidnappers. . . . Anxiety had turned to fear, to panic. Something had gone terribly wrong. Those women had got hold of Laura, played upon her suggestibility, induced her to go with them, either to their hotel or elsewhere. Should he find the Consulate? Where was it? What would he say when he got there? He began walking without purpose, finding himself, as they had done the night before, in streets he did not know, and suddenly came upon a tall building with the word "Questura" above it. This is it, he thought. I don't care, something has happened, I'm going inside. There were a number of police in uniform coming and going, the place at any rate was active, and, addressing himself to one of them behind a glass partition, he asked if there was anyone who spoke English. The man pointed to a flight of stairs and John went up, entering a door on the right where he saw that another couple were sitting, waiting, and with relief he recognised them as fellow-countrymen, tourists, obviously a man and his wife, in some sort of predicament.

"Come and sit down," said the man. "We've waited half an hour but they can't be much longer. What a country! They wouldn't leave us like this at home."

John took the proffered cigarette and found a chair beside them.

"What's your trouble?" he asked.

"My wife had her handbag pinched in one of those shops in the Merceria," said the man. "She simply put it down one moment to look at something, and you'd hardly credit it, the next moment it had gone. I say it was a sneak thief, she insists it was the girl behind the counter. But who's to say? These Ities are all alike. Anyway, I'm certain we shan't get it back. What have you lost?"

"Suitcase stolen," John lied rapidly. "Had some important papers in it."

How could he say he had lost his wife? He couldn't even begin . . .

The man nodded in sympathy. "As I said, these Ities are all alike. Old Musso knew how to deal with them. Too many Communists around these days. The trouble is, they're not going to bother with our troubles much, not with this murderer at large. They're all out looking for him."

"Murderer? What murderer?" asked John.

"Don't tell me you've not heard about it?" The man stared at him in surprise. "Venice has talked of nothing else. It's been in all the papers, on the radio, and even in the English papers. A grizzly business. One woman found with her throat slit last week—a tourist too— and some old chap discovered with the same sort of knife wound this morning. They seem to think it must be a maniac, because there doesn't seem to be any motive. Nasty thing to happen in Venice in the tourist season."

"My wife and I never bother with the newspapers when we're on holiday," said John. "And we're neither of us much given to gossip in the hotel."

"Very wise of you," laughed the man. "It might have spoilt your holiday, especially if your wife is nervous.

Oh well, we're off tomorrow anyway. Can't say we mind, do we, dear?" He turned to his wife. "Venice has gone downhill since we were here last. And now this loss of the handbag really is the limit."

The door of the inner room opened, and a senior police officer asked John's companion and his wife to pass through.

"I bet we don't get any satisfaction," murmured the tourist, winking at John, and he and his wife went into the inner room. The door closed behind them. John stubbed out his cigarette and lighted another. A strange feeling of unreality possessed him. He asked himself what he was doing here, what was the use of it? Laura was no longer in Venice but had disappeared, perhaps forever, with those diabolical sisters. She would never be traced. And just as the two of them had made up a fantastic story about the twins, when they first spotted them in Torcello, so, with nightmare logic, the fiction would have basis in fact; the women were in reality disguised crooks, men with criminal intent who lured unsuspecting persons to some appalling fate. They might even be the murderers for whom the police sought. Who would ever suspect two elderly women of respectable appearance, living quietly in some second-rate pension or hotel? He stubbed out his cigarette, unfinished.

"This," he thought, "is really the start of paranoia. This is the way people go off their heads." He glanced at his watch. It was half-past six. Better pack this in, this futile quest here in police headquarters, and keep to the single link of sanity remaining. Return to the hotel, put a call through to the prep school in England, and ask about the latest news of Johnnie. He had not thought about poor Johnnie since sighting Laura on the vaporetto.

Too late, though. The inner door opened, the couple were ushered out.

"Usual claptrap," said the husband sotto voce to John. "They'll do what they can. Not much hope. So many foreigners in Venice, all of 'em thieves! The locals all above reproach. Wouldn't pay 'em to steal from customers. Well, I wish you better luck."

He nodded, his wife smiled and bowed, and they had gone. John followed the police officer into the inner room.

Formalities began. Name, address, passport. Length of stay in Venice, etc., etc. Then the questions, and John, the sweat beginning to appear on his forehead, launched into his interminable story. The first encounter with the sisters, the meeting at the restaurant, Laura's state of suggestibility because of the death of their child, the telegram about Johnnie, the decision to take the chartered flight, her departure, and her sudden inexplicable return. When he had finished he felt as exhausted as if he had driven three hundred miles nonstop after a severe bout of 'flu. His interrogator spoke excellent English with a strong Italian accent.

"You say," he began, "that your wife was suffering the after-effects of shock. This had been noticeable during your stay here in Venice?"

"Well, yes," John replied, "she had really been quite ill. The holiday didn't seem to be doing her much good. It was only when she met these two women at Torcello yesterday that her mood changed. The strain seemed to have gone. She was ready, I suppose, to snatch at every straw, and this belief that our little girl was watching over her had somehow restored her to what appeared normality."

"It would be natural," said the police officer, "in the circumstances. But no doubt the telegram last night was a further shock to you both?"

"Indeed, yes. That was the reason we decided to return home."

"No argument between you? No difference of opinion?"

"None. We were in complete agreement. My one regret was that I could not go with my wife on this charter flight."

The police officer nodded. "It could well be that your wife had a sudden attack of amnesia, and meeting the two ladies served as a link, she clung to them for support. You have described them with great accuracy, and I think they should not be too difficult to trace. Meanwhile, I suggest you should return to your hotel, and we will get in touch with you as soon as we have news."

At least, John thought, they believed his story. They did not consider him a crank who had made the whole thing up and was merely wasting their time.

"You appreciate," he said, "I am extremely anxious. These women may have some criminal design upon my wife. One has heard of such things. . . ."

The police officer smiled for the first time. "Please don't concern yourself," he said. "I am sure there will be some satisfactory explanation."

All very well, thought John, but in heaven's name, what?

"I'm sorry," he said, "to have taken up so much of your time. Especially as I gather the police have their hands full hunting down a murderer who is still at large."

He spoke deliberately. No harm in letting the fellow know that for all any of them could tell there might be some connection between Laura's disappearance and this other hideous affair.

"Ah, that," said the police officer, rising to his feet. "We hope to have the murderer under lock and key very soon."

His tone of confidence was reassuring. Murderers,

missing wives, lost handbags were all under control. They shook hands, and John was ushered out of the door and so downstairs. Perhaps, he thought, as he walked slowly back to the hotel, the fellow was right. Laura had suffered a sudden attack of amnesia, and the sisters happened to be at the airport and had brought her back to Venice, to their own hotel, because Laura couldn't remember where she and John had been staying. Perhaps they were even now trying to track down his hotel. Anyway, he could do nothing more. The police had everything in hand, and, please God, would come up with the solution. All he wanted to do right now was to collapse upon a bed with a stiff whisky, and then put through a call to Johnnie's school.

The page took him up in the lift to a modest room on the fourth floor at the rear of the hotel. Bare, impersonal, the shutters closed, with a smell of cooking wafting up from a courtyard down below.

"Ask them to send me up a double whisky, will you?" he said to the boy. "And a ginger ale," and when he was alone he plunged his face under the cold tap in the wash-basin, relieved to find that the minute portion of visitor's soap afforded some measure of comfort. He flung off his shoes, hung his coat over the back of a chair and threw himself down on the bed. Somebody's radio was blasting forth an old popular song, now several seasons out-of-date, that had been one of Laura's favourites a couple of years ago. "I love you, Baby . . ." He reached for the telephone, and asked the exchange to put through the call to England. Then he closed his eyes, and all the while the insistent voice persisted, "I love you, Baby . . . I can't get you out of my mind."

Presently there was a tap at the door. It was the waiter with his drink. Too little ice, such meagre comfort, but what desperate need. He gulped it down without the ginger ale, and in a few moments the ever-nagging pain was eased, numbed, bringing, if only

momentarily, a sense of calm. The telephone rang, and now, he thought, bracing himself for ultimate disaster, the final shock, Johnnie probably dying, or already dead. In which case nothing remained. Let Venice be engulfed. . . .

The exchange told him that the connection had been made, and in a moment he heard the voice of Mrs. Hill at the other end of the line. They must have warned her that the call came from Venice, for she knew instantly who was speaking.

"Hullo?" she said. "Oh, I am so glad you rang. All is well. Johnnie has had his operation, the surgeon decided to do it at midday rather than wait, and it was completely successful. Johnnie is going to be all right. So you don't have to worry any more, and will have a peaceful night."

"Thank God," he answered.

"I know," she said, "we are all so relieved. Now I'll get off the line and you can speak to your wife."

John sat up on the bed, stunned. What the hell did she mean? Then he heard Laura's voice, cool and clear.

"Darling? Darling, are you there?"

He could not answer. He felt the hand holding the receiver go clammy cold with sweat. "I'm here," he whispered.

"It's not a very good line," she said, "but never mind. As Mrs. Hill told you, all is well. Such a nice surgeon, and a very sweet Sister on Johnnie's floor, and I really am happy about the way it's turned out. I came straight down here after landing at Gatwick—the flight OK, by the way, but such a funny crowd, it'll make you hysterical when I tell you about them—and I went to the hospital, and Johnnie was coming round. Very dopey, of course, but so pleased to see me. And the Hills are being wonderful, I've got their spare room, and it's only a short taxi-drive into the town and the hospital. I shall go to bed as soon as we've had dinner,

because I'm a bit fagged, what with the flight and the anxiety. How was the drive to Milan? And where are you staying?"

John did not recognise the voice that answered as his own. It was the automatic response of some computer.

"I'm not in Milan," he said. "I'm still in Venice."

"Still in Venice? What on earth for? Wouldn't the car start?"

"I can't explain," he said. "There was a stupid sort of mix-up . . ."

He felt suddenly so exhausted that he nearly dropped the receiver, and, shame upon shame, he could feel tears pricking behind his eyes.

"What sort of mix-up?" Her voice was suspicious, almost hostile. "You weren't in a crash?"

"No . . . no . . . nothing like that."

A moment's silence, and then she said, "Your voice sounds very slurred. Don't tell me you went and got pissed."

Oh Christ . . . If she only knew! He was probably going to pass out any moment, but not from the whisky.

"I thought," he said slowly, "I thought I saw you, in a vaporetto, with those two sisters."

What was the point of going on? It was hopeless trying to explain.

"How could you have seen me with the sisters?" she said. "You knew I'd gone to the airport. Really, darling, you are an idiot. You seem to have got those two poor old dears on the brain. I hope you didn't say anything to Mrs. Hill just now."

"No."

"Well, what are you going to do? You'll catch the train at Milan tomorrow, won't you?"

"Yes, of course," he told her.

"I still don't understand what kept you in Venice," she said. "It all sounds a bit odd to me. However

. . . thank God Johnnie is going to be all right and I'm here."

"Yes," he said, "yes."

He could hear the distant boom-boom sound of a gong from the headmaster's hall.

"You had better go," he said. "My regards to the Hills, and my love to Johnnie."

"Well, take care of yourself, darling, and for goodness' sake don't miss the train tomorrow, and drive carefully."

The telephone clicked and she had gone. He poured the remaining drop of whisky into his empty glass, and sousing it with gingerale drank it down at a gulp. He got up, and crossing the room threw open the shutters and leant out of the window. He felt light-headed. His sense of relief, enormous, overwhelming, was somehow tempered with a curious feeling of unreality, almost as though the voice speaking from England had not been Laura's after all but a fake, and she was still in Venice, hidden in some furtive pension with the two sisters.

The point was, he *had* seen all three of them on the vaporetto. It was not another woman in a red coat. The women *had* been there, with Laura. So what was the explanation? That he was going off his head? Or something more sinister? The sisters, possessing psychic powers of formidable strength, had seen him as their two ferries had passed, and in some inexplicable fashion had made him believe Laura was with them. But why, and to what end? No, it didn't make sense. The only explanation was that he had been mistaken, the whole episode an hallucination. In which case he needed psychoanalysis, just as Johnnie had needed a surgeon.

And what did he do now? Go downstairs and tell the management he had been at fault and had just spoken to his wife, who had arrived in England safe and sound

from her charter flight? He put on his shoes and ran his fingers through his hair. He glanced at his watch. It was ten minutes to eight. If he nipped into the bar and had a quick drink it would be easier to face the manager and admit what had happened. Then, perhaps, they would get in touch with the police. Profuse apologies all round for putting everyone to enormous trouble.

He made his way to the ground floor and went straight to the bar, feeling self-conscious, a marked man, half-imagining everyone would look at him, thinking, "There's the fellow with the missing wife." Luckily the bar was full and there wasn't a face he knew. Even the chap behind the bar was an underling who hadn't served him before. He downed his whisky and glanced over his shoulder to the reception hall. The desk was momentarily empty. He could see the manager's back framed in the doorway of an inner room, talking to someone within. On impulse, cowardlike, he crossed the hall and passed through the swing-door to the street outside.

"I'll have some dinner," he decided, "and then go back and face them. I'll feel more like it once I've some food inside me."

He went to the restaurant nearby where he and Laura had dined once or twice. Nothing mattered any more, because she was safe. The nightmare lay behind him. He could enjoy his dinner, despite her absence, and think of her sitting down with the Hills to a dull, quiet evening, early to bed, and on the following morning going to the hospital to sit with Johnnie. Johnnie was safe, too. No more worries, only the awkward explanations and apologies to the manager at the hotel.

There was a pleasant anonymity sitting down at a corner table alone in the little restaurant, ordering vitello alla Marsala and half a bottle of Merlot. He took his time, enjoying his food but eating in a kind of haze, a sense of unreality still with him, while the conversa-

tion of his nearest neighbours had the same soothing effect as background music.

When they rose and left, he saw by the clock on the wall that it was nearly half-past nine. No use delaying matters any further. He drank his coffee, lighted a cigarette and paid his bill. After all, he thought, as he walked back to the hotel, the manager would be greatly relieved to know that all was well.

When he pushed through the swing-door, the first thing he noticed was a man in police uniform, standing talking to the manager at the desk. The reception clerk was there too. They turned as John approached, and the manager's face lighted up with relief.

"Eccolo!" he exclaimed. "I was certain the signore would not be far away. Things are moving, signore. The two ladies have been traced, and they very kindly agreed to accompany the police to the Questura. If you will go there at once, this agente di polizia will escort you."

John flushed. "I have given everyone a lot of trouble," he said. "I meant to tell you before going out to dinner, but you were not at the desk. The fact is that I have contacted my wife. She did make the flight to London after all, and I spoke to her on the telephone. It was all a great mistake."

The manager looked bewildered. "The signora is in London?" he repeated. He broke off, and exchanged a rapid conversation in Italian with the policeman. "It seems that the ladies maintain they did not go out for the day, except for a little shopping in the morning," he said, turning back to John. "Then who was it the signore saw on the vaporetto?"

John shook his head. "A very extraordinary mistake on my part which I still don't understand," he said. "Obviously, I did not see either my wife or the two ladies. I really am extremely sorry."

More rapid conversation in Italian. John noticed the

clerk watching him with a curious expression in his eyes. The manager was obviously apologizing on John's behalf to the policeman, who looked annoyed and gave tongue to this effect, his voice increasing in volume, to the manager's concern. The whole business had undoubtedly given enormous trouble to a great many people, not least the two unfortunate sisters.

"Look," said John, interrupting the flow, "will you tell the agente I will go with him to headquarters and apologise in person both to the police officer and to the ladies?"

The manager looked relieved. "If the signore would take the trouble," he said. "Naturally, the ladies were much distressed when a policeman interrogated them at their hotel, and they offered to accompany him to the Questura only because they were so distressed about the signora."

John felt more and more uncomfortable. Laura must never learn any of this. She would be outraged. He wondered if there were some penalty for giving the police misleading information involving a third party. His error began, in retrospect, to take on criminal proportions.

He crossed the Piazza San Marco, now thronged with after-dinner strollers and spectators at the cafés, all three orchestras going full blast in harmonious rivalry, while his companion kept a discreet two paces to his left and never uttered a word.

They arrived at the police station and mounted the stairs to the same inner room where he had been before. He saw immediately that it was not the officer he knew but another who sat behind the desk, a sallow-faced individual with a sour expression, while the two sisters, obviously upset—the active one in particular—were seated on chairs nearby, some underling in uniform standing behind them. John's escort went at once to the

police officer, speaking in rapid Italian, while John himself, after a moment's hesitation, advanced towards the sisters.

"There has been a terrible mistake," he said. "I don't know how to apologise to you both. It's all my fault, mine entirely, the police are not to blame."

The active sister made as though to rise, her mouth twitching nervously, but he restrained her.

"We don't understand," she said, the Scots inflection strong. "We said goodnight to your wife last night at dinner, and we have not seen her since. The police came to our pension more than an hour ago and told us your wife was missing and you had filed a complaint against us. My sister is not very strong. She was considerably disturbed."

"A mistake. A frightful mistake," he repeated.

He turned towards the desk. The police officer was addressing him, his English very inferior to that of the previous interrogator. He had John's earlier statement on the desk in front of him, and tapped it with a pencil.

"So?" he queried. "This document all lies? You not speaka the truth?"

"I believed it to be true at the time," said John. "I could have sworn in a court of law that I saw my wife with these two ladies on a vaporetto in the Grand Canal this afternoon. Now I realise I was mistaken."

"We have not been near the Grand Canal all day," protested the sister, "not even on foot. We made a few purchases in the Merceria this morning, and remained indoors all afternoon. My sister was a little unwell. I have told the police officer this a dozen times, and the people at the pension would corroborate our story. He refused to listen."

"And the signora?" rapped the police officer angrily. "What happen to the signora?"

"The signora, my wife, is safe in England," explained

John patiently. "I talked to her on the telephone just after seven. She did join the charter flight from the airport, and is now staying with friends."

"Then who you see on the vaporetto in the red coat?" asked the furious police officer. "And if not these signorine here, then what signorine?"

"My eyes deceived me," said John, aware that his English was likewise becoming strained. "I think I see my wife and these ladies but no, it was not so. My wife in aircraft, these ladies in pension all the time."

It was like talking stage Chinese. In a moment he would be bowing and putting his hands in his sleeves.

The police officer raised his eyes to heaven and thumped the table. "So all this work for nothing," he said. "Hotels and pensiones searched for the signorine and a missing signora inglese, when here we have plenty, plenty other things to do. You maka a mistake. You have perhaps too much vino at mezzo giorno and you see hundred signore in red coats in hundred vaporetti." He stood up, rumpling the papers on his desk. "And you, signorine," he said, "you wish to make complaint against this person?" He was addressing the active sister.

"Oh no," she said, "no, indeed. I quite see it was all a mistake. Our only wish is to return at once to our pension."

The police officer grunted. Then he pointed at John. "You very lucky man," he said. "These signorine could file complaint against you—very serious matter."

"I'm sure," began John, "I'll do anything in my power . . ."

"Please don't think of it," exclaimed the sister, horrified. "We would not hear of such a thing." It was her turn to apologise to the police officer. "I hope we need not take up any more of your valuable time," she said.

He waved a hand of dismissal and spoke in Italian to

the underling. "This man walk with you to the pension," he said. "Buona sera, signorine," and, ignoring John, he sat down again at his desk.

"I'll come with you," said John. "I want to explain exactly what happened."

They trooped down the stairs and out of the building, the blind sister leaning on her twin's arm, and once outside she turned her sightless eyes to John.

"You saw us," she said, "and your wife too. But not today. You saw us in the future."

Her voice was softer than her sister's, slower, she seemed to have some slight impediment in her speech.

"I don't follow," replied John, bewildered.

He turned to the active sister and she shook her head at him, frowning, and put her finger on her lips.

"Come along, dear," she said to her twin. "You know you're very tired, and I want to get you home." Then, sotto voce to John, "She's psychic. Your wife told you, I believe, but I don't want her to go into trance here in the street."

God forbid, thought John, and the little procession began to move slowly along the street, away from police headquarters, a canal to the left of them. Progress was slow, because of the blind sister, and there were two bridges. John was completely lost after the first turning, but it couldn't have mattered less. Their police escort was with them, and anyway, the sisters knew where they were going.

"I must explain," said John softly. "My wife would never forgive me if I didn't," and as they walked he went over the whole inexplicable story once again, beginning with the telegram received the night before and the conversation with Mrs. Hill, the decision to return to England the following day, Laura by air, and John himself by car and train. It no longer sounded as dramatic as it had done when he had made his statement to the police officer, when, possibly because of his

conviction of something uncanny, the description of the two vaporettos passing one another in the middle of the Grand Canal had held a sinister quality, suggesting abduction on the part of the sisters, the pair of them holding a bewildered Laura captive. Now that neither of the women had any further menace for him he spoke more naturally, yet with great sincerity, feeling for the first time that they were somehow both in sympathy with him and would understand.

"You see," he explained, in a final endeavour to make amends for having gone to the police in the first place, "I truly believed I had seen you with Laura, and I thought . . ." he hesitated, because this had been the police officer's suggestion and not his, "I thought that perhaps Laura had some sudden loss of memory, had met you at the airport, and you had brought her back to Venice to wherever you were staying."

They had crossed a large square and were approaching a house at one end of it, with a sign PENSIONE above the door. Their escort paused at the entrance.

"Is this it?" asked John.

"Yes," said the sister. "I know it is nothing much from the outside, but it is clean and comfortable, and was recommended by friends." She turned to the escort. "Grazie," she said to him, "grazie tanto."

The man nodded briefly, wished them "Buona notte," and disappeared across the campo.

"Will you come in?" asked the sister. "I am sure we can find you some coffee, or perhaps you prefer tea?"

"No, really," John thanked her, "I must get back to the hotel. I'm making an early start in the morning. I just want to make quite sure you do understand what happened, and that you forgive me."

"There is nothing to forgive," she replied. "It is one of the many examples of second sight that my sister and I have experienced time and time again, and I should

very much like to record it for our files, if you will permit it."

"Well, as to that, of course," he told her, "but I myself find it hard to understand. It has never happened to me before."

"Not consciously, perhaps," she said, "but so many things happen to us of which we are not aware. My sister felt you had psychic understanding. She told your wife. She also told your wife, last night in the restaurant, that you were to experience trouble, danger, that you should leave Venice. Well, don't you believe now that the telegram was proof of this? Your son was ill, possibly dangerously ill, and so it was necessary for you to return home immediately. Heaven be praised your wife flew home to be by his side."

"Yes, indeed," said John, "but why should I see her on the vaporetto with you and your sister when she was actually on her way to England?"

"Thought transference, perhaps," she answered. "Your wife may have been thinking about us. We gave her our address, should you wish to get in touch with us. We shall be here another ten days. And she knows that we would pass on any message that my sister might have from your little one in the spirit world."

"Yes," said John awkwardly, "yes, I see. It's very good of you." He had a sudden rather unkind picture of the two sisters putting on headphones in their bedroom, listening for a coded message from poor Christine. "Look, this is our address in London," he said. "I know Laura will be pleased to hear from you."

He scribbled their address on a sheet torn from his pocket-diary, even, as a bonus thrown in, the telephone number, and handed it to her. He could imagine the outcome. Laura springing it on him one evening that the "old dears" were passing through London on their way to Scotland, and the least they could do was to offer

them hospitality, even the spare room for the night. Then a seance in the living room, tambourines appearing out of thin air.

"Well, I must be off," he said. "Goodnight, and apologies, once again, for all that has happened this evening." He shook hands with the first sister, then turned to her blind twin. "I hope," he said, "that you are not too tired."

The sightless eyes were disconcerting. She held his hand fast and would not let it go. "The child," she said, speaking in an odd staccato voice, "the child . . . I can see the child . . ." and then, to his dismay, a bead of froth appeared at the corner of her mouth, her head jerked back, and she half-collapsed in her sister's arms.

"We must get her inside," said the sister hurriedly. "It's all right, she's not ill, it's the beginning of a trance state."

Between them they helped the twin, who had gone rigid, into the house, and sat her down on the nearest chair, the sister supporting her. A woman came running from some inner room. There was a strong smell of spaghetti from the back regions. "Don't worry," said the sister, "the signorina and I can manage. I think you had better go. Sometimes she is sick after these turns."

"I'm most frightfully sorry . . ." John began, but the sister had already turned her back, and with the signorina was bending over her twin, from whom peculiar choking sounds were proceeding. He was obviously in the way, and after a final gesture of courtesy, "Is there anything I can do?", which received no reply, he turned on his heel and began walking across the square. He looked back once, and saw they had closed the door.

What a finale to the evening! And all his fault. Poor old girls, first dragged to police headquarters and put through an interrogation, and then a psychic fit on top of it all. More likely epilepsy. Not much of a life for the other sister, but she seemed to take it in her stride. An

additional hazard, though, if it happened in a restaurant or in the street. And not particularly welcome under his and Laura's roof should the sisters ever find themselves beneath it, which he prayed would never happen.

Meanwhile, where the devil was he? The square, with the inevitable church at one end, was quite deserted. He could not remember which way they had come from police headquarters, there had seemed to be so many turnings.

Wait a minute, the church itself had a familiar appearance. He drew nearer to it, looking for the name which was sometimes on notices at the entrance. San Giovanni in Bragora, that rang a bell. He and Laura had gone inside one morning to look at a painting by Cima da Conegliano. Surely it was only a stone's throw from the Riva degli Schiavoni and the open wide waters of the San Marco lagoon, with all the bright lights of civilisation and the strolling tourists? He remembered taking a small turning from the Schiavoni and they had arrived at the church. Wasn't that the alleyway ahead? He plunged along it, but halfway down he hesitated. It didn't seem right, although it was familiar for some unknown reason.

Then he realised that it was not the alley they had taken the morning they visited the church, but the one they had walked along the previous evening, only he was approaching it from the opposite direction. Yes, that was it, in which case it would be quicker to go on and cross the little bridge over the narrow canal, and he would find the Arsenal on his left and the street leading down to the Riva degli Schiavoni to his right. Simpler than retracing his steps and getting lost once more in the maze of back streets.

He had almost reached the end of the alley, and the bridge was in sight, when he saw the child. It was the same little girl with the pixie hood who had leapt

between the tethered boats the preceding night and vanished up the cellar steps of one of the houses. This time she was running from the direction of the church the other side, making for the bridge. She was running as if her life depended on it, and in a moment he saw why. A man was in pursuit, who, when she glanced backwards for a moment, still running, flattened himself against a wall, believing himself unobserved. The child came on, scampering across the bridge, and John, fearful of alarming her further, backed into an open doorway that led into a small court.

He remembered the drunken yell of the night before which had come from one of the houses near where the man was hiding now. This is it, he thought, the fellow's after her again, and with a flash of intuition he connected the two events, the child's terror then and now, and the murders reported in the newspapers, supposedly the work of some madman. It could be coincidence, a child running from a drunken relative, and yet, and yet . . . His heart began thumping in his chest, instinct warning him to run himself, now, at once, back along the alley the way he had come—but what about the child? What was going to happen to the child?

Then he heard her running steps. She hurtled through the open doorway into the court in which he stood, not seeing him, making for the rear of the house that flanked it, where steps led presumably to a back entrance. She was sobbing as she ran, not the ordinary cry of a frightened child, but the panic-stricken intake of breath of a helpless being in despair. Were there parents in the house who would protect her, whom he could warn? He hesitated a moment, then followed her down the steps and through the door at the bottom, which had burst open at the touch of her hands as she hurled herself against it.

"It's all right," he called. "I won't let him hurt you, it's all right," cursing his lack of Italian, but possibly an

English voice might reassure her. But it was no use—she ran sobbing up another flight of stairs, which were spiral, twisting, leading to the floor above, and already it was too late for him to retreat. He could hear sounds of the pursuer in the courtyard behind, someone shouting in Italian, a dog barking. This is it, he thought, we're in it together, the child and I. Unless we can bolt some inner door above he'll get us both.

He ran up the stairs after the child, who had darted into a room leading off a small landing, and followed her inside and slammed the door, and, merciful heaven, there was a bolt which he rammed into its socket. The child was crouching by the open window. If he shouted for help someone would surely hear, someone would surely come before the man in pursuit threw himself against the door and it gave, because there was no one but themselves, no parents, the room was bare except for a mattress on an old bed, and a heap of rags in one corner.

"It's all right," he panted, "it's all right," and held out his hand, trying to smile.

The child struggled to her feet and stood before him, the pixie hood falling from her head on to the floor. He stared at her, incredulity turning to horror, to fear. It was not a child at all but a little thickset woman dwarf, about three feet high, with a great square adult head too big for her body, grey locks hanging shoulder-length, and she wasn't sobbing anymore, she was grinning at him, nodding her head up and down.

Then he heard the footsteps on the landing outside and the hammering on the door, and a barking dog, and not one voice but several voices, shouting, "Open up! Police!" The creature fumbled in her sleeve, drawing a knife, and as she threw it at him with hideous strength, piercing his throat, he stumbled and fell, the sticky mess covering his protecting hands.

And he saw the vaporetto with Laura and the two

sisters steaming down the Grand Canal, not today, not tomorrow, but the day after that, and he knew why they were together and for what sad purpose they had come. The creature was gibbering in its corner. The hammering and the voices and the barking dog grew fainter, and, "Oh, God," he thought, "what a bloody silly way to die . . ."

Robert A. Heinlein (1907–1988)

THEY

Robert A. Heinlein was the greatest science fiction writer of the mid-twentieth century, author of the classic *Stranger in a Strange Land* and many other novels. A certain small but significant and influential portion of his work was done in fantasy and horror, particularly for John W. Campbell's *Unknown*. The single story that had the most impact, however, is "They," first published in *Unknown* in 1941. Along with L. Ron Hubbard's "Fear," Fritz Leiber's "Smoke Ghost," and Heinlein's own "The Unpleasant Profession of Jonathan Hoag," it became for many writers one of the paradigms of the "new style" of horror and supernatural fiction in the 1940s and 1950s, which rejected the traditional supernatural trappings of good and evil, and the traditional settings (old houses, antiquarian discoveries), along with the florid styles of earlier writers, especially the Lovecraftians, in favor of unornamented prose, contemporary urban settings, and an almost Existential approach to the psychology of horror, through which the nature of reality was brought into question, Existential doubts raised with horrifying potential. Fritz Leiber said, if you are looking for significant stories that underpin contemporary horror, look to Fitz-James O'Brien's "What Was It?" and Robert A. Heinlein's "They."

They would not let him alone.

They would never let him alone. He realized that that was part of the plot against him—never to leave him in peace, never to give him a chance to mull over the lies they had told him, time enough to pick out the flaws, and to figure out the truth for himself.

That damned attendant this morning! He had come busting in with his breakfast tray, waking him, and causing him to forget his dream. If only he could remember that dream—

Someone was unlocking the door. He ignored it.

"Howdy, old boy. They tell me you refused your breakfast?" Dr. Hayward's professionally kindly mask hung over his bed.

"I wasn't hungry."

"But we can't have that. You'll get weak, and then I won't be able to get you well completely. Now get up and get your clothes on and I'll order an eggnog for you. Come on, that's a good fellow!"

Unwilling, but still less willing at that moment to enter into any conflict of wills, he got out of bed and slipped on his bathrobe. "That's better," Hayward approved. "Have a cigarette?"

"No, thank you."

The doctor shook his head in a puzzled fashion. "Darned if I can figure you out. Loss of interest in physical pleasures does not fit your type of case."

"What is my type of case?" he inquired in flat tones.

"Tut! Tut!" Hayward tried to appear roguish. "If medicos told their professional secrets, they might have to work for a living."

"What is my type of case?"

"Well—the label doesn't matter, does it? Suppose you tell me. I really know nothing about your case as yet. Don't you think it is about time you talked?"

"I'll play chess with you."

"All right, all right." Hayward made a gesture of

impatient concession. "We've played chess every day for a week. If you will talk, I'll play chess."

What could it matter? If he was right, they already understood perfectly that he had discovered their plot; there was nothing to be gained by concealing the obvious. Let them try to argue him out of it. Let the tail go with the hide! To hell with it!

He got out the chessmen and commenced setting them up. "What do you know of my case so far?"

"Very little. Physical examination, negative. Past history, negative. High intelligence, as shown by your record in school and your success in your profession. Occasional fits of moodiness, but nothing exceptional. The only positive information was the incident that caused you to come here for treatment."

"To be brought here, you mean. Why should it cause comment?"

"Well, good gracious, man—if you barricade yourself in your room and insist that your wife is plotting against you, don't you expect people to notice?"

"But she was plotting against me—and so are you. White, or black?"

"Black—it's your turn to attack. Why do you think we are plotting against you?"

"It's an involved story, and goes way back into my early childhood. There was an immediate incident, however—" He opened by advancing the white king's knight to KB3. Hayward's eyebrows raised.

"You make a piano attack?"

"Why not? You know that it is not safe for me to risk a gambit with you."

The doctor shrugged his shoulders and answered the opening. "Suppose we start with your early childhood. It may shed more light than more recent incidents. Did you feel that you were being persecuted as a child?"

"No!" He half rose from his chair. "When I was a child I was sure of myself. I knew then, I tell you; I

knew! Life was worthwhile, and I knew it. I was at peace with myself and my surroundings. Life was good and I assumed that the creatures around me were like myself."

"And weren't they?"

"Not at all! Particularly the children. I didn't know what viciousness was until I was turned loose with other children. The little devils! And I was expected to be like them and play with them."

The doctor nodded. "I know. The herd compulsion. Children can be pretty savage at times."

"You've missed the point. This wasn't any healthy roughness; these creatures were different—not like myself at all. They looked like me, but they were not like me. If I tried to say anything to one of them about anything that mattered to me, all I could get was a stare and a scornful laugh. Then they would find some way to punish me for having said it."

Hayward nodded. "I see what you mean. How about grown-ups?"

"That is somewhat different. Adults don't matter to children at first—or, rather they did not matter to me. They were too big, and they did not bother me, and they were busy with things that did not enter into my considerations. It was only when I noticed that my presence affected them that I began to wonder about them."

"How do you mean?"

"Well, they never did the things when I was around that they did when I was not around."

Hayward looked at him carefully. "Won't that statement take quite a lot of justifying? How do you know what they did when you weren't around?"

He acknowledged the point. "But I used to catch them just stopping. If I came into a room, the conversation would stop suddenly, and then it would pick up

about the weather or something equally inane. Then I took to hiding and listening and looking. Adults did not behave the same way in my presence as out of it."

"Your move, I believe. But see here, old man—that was when you were a child. Every child passes through that phase. Now that you are a man, you must see the adult point of view. Children are strange creatures and have to be protected—at least, we do protect them—from many adult interests. There is a whole code of conventions in the matter that—"

"Yes, yes," he interrupted impatiently, "I know all that. Nevertheless, I noticed enough and remembered enough that was never clear to me later. And it put me on my guard to notice the next thing."

"Which was?" He noticed that the doctor's eyes were averted as he adjusted a castle's position.

"The things I saw people doing and heard them talking about were never of any importance. They must be doing something else."

"I don't follow you."

"You don't choose to follow me. I'm telling this to you in exchange for a game of chess."

"Why do you like to play chess so well?"

"Because it is the only thing in the world where I can see all the factors and understand all the rules. Never mind—I saw all around me this enormous plant, cities, farms, factories, churches, schools, homes, railroads, luggage, roller coasters, trees, saxophones, libraries, people and animals. People that looked like me and who should have felt very much like me, if what I was told was the truth. But what did they appear to be doing? 'They went to work to earn the money to buy the food to get the strength to go to work to earn the money to buy the food to get the strength to go to work to get the strength to buy the food to earn the money to go to—' until they fell over dead. Any slight variation in

the basic pattern did not matter, for they always fell over dead. And everybody tried to tell me that I should be doing the same thing. I knew better!"

The doctor gave him a look apparently intended to denote helpless surrender and laughed. "I can't argue with you. Life does look like that, and maybe it is just that futile. But it is the only life we have. Why not make up your mind to enjoy it as much as possible?"

"Oh, no!" He looked both sulky and stubborn. "You can't peddle nonsense to me by claiming to be fresh out of sense. How do I know? Because all this complex stage setting, all these swarms of actors, could not have been put here just to make idiot noises at each other. Some other explanation, but not that one. An insanity as enormous, as complex, as the one around me had to be planned. I've found the plan!"

"Which is?"

He noticed that the doctor's eyes were again averted.

"It is a play intended to divert me, to occupy my mind and confuse me, to keep me so busy with details that I will not have time to think about the meaning. You are all in it, every one of you." He shook his finger in the doctor's face. "Most of them may be helpless automatons, but you're not. You are one of the conspirators. You've been sent in as a troubleshooter to try to force me to go back to playing the role assigned to me!"

He saw that the doctor was waiting for him to quiet down.

"Take it easy," Hayward finally managed to say, "Maybe it is all a conspiracy, but why do you think that you have been singled out for special attention? Maybe it is a joke on all of us. Why couldn't I be one of the victims as well as yourself?"

"Got you!" He pointed a long finger at Hayward. "That is the essence of the plot. All of these creatures have been set up to look like me in order to prevent me

from realizing that I was the center of the arrangements. But I have noticed the key fact, the mathematically inescapable fact, that I am unique. Here am I, sitting on the inside. The world extends outward from me. I am the center—"

"Easy, man, easy! Don't you realize that the world looks that way to me, too. We are each the center of the universe—"

"Not so! That is what you have tried to make me believe, that I am just one of millions more just like me. Wrong! If they were like me, then I could get into communication with them. I can't. I have tried and tried and I can't. I've sent out my inner thoughts, seeking some one other being who has them, too. What have I gotten back? Wrong answers, jarring incongruities, meaningless obscenity. I've tried. I tell you. God! —how I've tried! But there is nothing out there to speak to me—nothing but emptiness and otherness!"

"Wait a minute. Do you mean to say that you think there is nobody home at my end of the line? Don't you believe that I am alive and conscious?"

He regarded the doctor soberly. "Yes, I think you are probably alive, but you are one of the others—my antagonists. But you have set thousands of others around me whose faces are blank, not lived in, and whose speech is a meaningless reflex of noise."

"Well, then, if you concede that I am an ego, why do you insist that I am so very different from yourself?"

"Why? Wait!" He pushed back from the chess table and strode over to the wardrobe, from which he took out a violin case.

While he was playing, the lines of suffering smoothed out of his face and his expression took a relaxed beatitude. For a while he recaptured the emotions, but not the knowledge, which he had possessed in dreams. The melody proceeded easily from proposition to prop-

osition with inescapable, unforced logic. He finished with a triumphant statement of the essential thesis and turned to the doctor. "Well?"

"Hm-m-m." He seemed to detect an even greater degree of caution in the doctor's manner. "It's an odd bit, but remarkable. 'S pity you didn't take up the violin seriously. You could have made quite a reputation. You could even now. Why don't you do it? You could afford to, I believe."

He stood and stared at the doctor for a long moment, then shook his head as if trying to clear it. "It's no use," he said slowly, "no use at all. There is no possibility of communication. I am alone." He replaced the instrument in its case and returned to the chess table. "My move, I believe?"

"Yes. Guard your queen."

He studied the board. "Not necessary. I no longer need my queen. Check."

The doctor interposed a pawn to parry the attack.

He nodded. "You use your pawns well, but I have learned to anticipate your play. Check again—and mate, I think."

The doctor examined the new situation. "No," he decided, "no—not quite." He retreated from the square under attack. "Not checkmate—stalemate at the worst. Yes, another stalemate."

He was upset by the doctor's visit. He couldn't be wrong, basically, yet the doctor had certainly pointed out logical holes in his position. From a logical standpoint the whole world might be a fraud perpetrated on everybody. But logic meant nothing—logic itself was a fraud, starting with unproved assumptions and capable of proving anything. The world is what it is!—and carries its own evidence of trickery.

But does it? What did he have to go on? Could he lay down a line between known facts and everything else

and then make a reasonable interpretation of the world, based on facts alone—an interpretation free from complexities of logic and no hidden assumptions of points not certain. Very well—

First fact, himself. He knew himself directly. He existed.

Second facts, the evidence of his "five senses," everything that he himself saw and heard and smelled and tasted with his physical senses. Subject to their limitations, he must believe his senses. Without them he was entirely solitary, shut up in a locker of bone, blind, deaf, cut off, the only being in the world.

And that was not the case. He knew that he did not invent the information brought to him by his senses. There had to be something else out there, some otherness that produced the things his senses recorded. All philosophies that claimed that the physical world around him did not exist except in his imagination were sheer nonsense.

But beyond that, what? Were there any third facts on which he could rely? No, not at this point. He could not afford to believe anything that he was told, or that he read, or that was implicitly assumed to be true about the world around him. No, he could not believe any of it, for the sum total of what he had been told and read and been taught in school was so contradictory, so senseless, so wildly insane that none of it could be believed unless he personally confirmed it.

Wait a minute— The very telling of these lies, these senseless contradictions, was a fact in itself, known to him directly. To that extent they were data, probably very important data.

The world as it had been shown to him was a piece of unreason, an idiot's dream. Yet it was on too mammoth a scale to be without some reason. He came wearily back to his original point: Since the world could not be

as crazy as it appeared to be, it must necessarily have been arranged to appear crazy in order to deceive him as to the truth.

Why had they done it to him? And what was the truth behind the sham? There must be some clue in the deception itself. What thread ran through it all? Well, in the first place he had been given a superabundance of explanations of the world around him, philosophies, religions, "common sense" explanations. Most of them were so clumsy, so obviously inadequate, or meaningless, that they could hardly have expected him to take them seriously. They must have intended them simply as misdirection.

But there were certain basic assumptions running through all the hundreds of explanations of the craziness around him. It must be these basic assumptions that he was expected to believe. For example, there was the deepseated assumption that he was a "human being," essentially like millions of others around him and billions more in the past and the future.

That was nonsense! He had never once managed to get into real communication with all those things that looked so much like him but were so different. In the agony of his loneliness, he had deceived himself that Alice understood him and was a being like him. He knew now that he had suppressed and refused to examine thousands of little discrepancies because he could not bear the thought of returning to complete loneliness. He had needed to believe that his wife was a living, breathing being of his own kind who understood his inner thoughts. He had refused to consider the possibility that she was simply, a mirror, an echo—or something unthinkably worse.

He had found a mate, and the world was tolerable, even though dull, stupid, and full of petty annoyance. He was moderately happy and had put away his suspicions. He had accepted, quite docilely, the treadmill he

was expected to use, until a slight mischance had momentarily cut through the fraud—then his suspicions had returned with impounded force; the bitter knowledge of his childhood had been confirmed.

He supposed that he had been a fool to make a fuss about it. If he had kept his mouth shut they would not have locked him up. He should have been as subtle and as shrewd as they, kept his eyes and ears open and learned the details of and the reasons for the plot against him. He might have learned how to circumvent it.

But what if they had locked him up—the whole world was an asylum and all of them his keepers.

A key scraped in the lock, and he looked up to see an attendant entering with a tray. "Here's your dinner, sir."

"Thanks, Joe," he said gently. "Just put it down."

"Movies tonight, sir," the attendant went on. "Wouldn't you like to go? Dr. Hayward said you could—"

"No, thank you. I prefer not to."

"I wish you would, sir." He noticed with amusement the persuasive intentness of the attendant's manner. "I think the doctor wants you to. It's a good movie. There's a Mickey Mouse cartoon—"

"You almost persuade me, Joe," he answered with passive agreeableness. "Mickey's trouble is the same as mine, essentially. However, I'm not going. They need not bother to hold movies tonight."

"Oh, there will be movies in any case, sir. Lots of our other guests will attend."

"Really? Is that an example of thoroughness, or are you simply keeping up the pretense in talking to me? It isn't necessary, Joe, if it's any strain on you. I know the game. If I don't attend, there is no point in holding movies."

He liked the grin with which the attendant answered

this thrust. Was it possible that this being was created just as he appeared to be—big muscles, phlegmatic disposition, tolerant, doglike? Or was there nothing going on behind those kind eyes, nothing but robot reflex? No, it was more likely that he was one of them, since he was so closely in attendance on him.

The attendant left and he busied himself at his supper tray, scooping up the already-cut bites of meat with a spoon, the only implement provided. He smiled again at their caution and thoroughness. No danger of that—he would not destroy this body as long as it served him in investigating the truth of the matter. There were still many different avenues of research available before taking that possibily irrevocable step.

After supper he decided to put his thoughts in better order by writing them; he obtained paper. He should start with a general statement of some underlying postulate of the credos that had been drummed into him all his "life." Life? Yes, that was a good one. He wrote:

"I am told that I was born a certain number of years ago and that I will die a similar number of years hence. Various clumsy stories have been offered me to explain to me where I was before birth and what becomes of me after death, but they are rough lies, not intended to deceive, except as misdirection. In every other possible way the world around me assures me that I am mortal, here but a few years, and a few years hence gone completely—nonexistent.

"WRONG—I am immortal. I transcend this little time axis; a seventy-year span on it is but a casual phase in my experience. Second only to the prime datum of my own existence is the emotionally convincing certainty of my own continuity. I may be a closed curve, but, closed or open, I neither have a beginning nor an end. Self-awareness is not relational; it is absolute, and cannot be reached to be destroyed, or created. Memory,

however, being a relational aspect of consciousness, may be tampered with and possibly destroyed.

"It is true that most religions which have been offered me teach immortality, but note the fashion in which they teach it. The surest way to lie convincingly is to tell the truth unconvincingly. They did not wish me to believe.

"Caution: Why have they tried so hard to convince me that I am going to die in a few years? There must be a very important reason. I infer that they are preparing me for some sort of a major change. It may be crucially important for me to figure out their intentions about this—probably I have several years in which to reach a decision. Note: Avoid using the types of reasoning they have taught me."

The attendant was back. "Your wife is here, sir."

"Tell her to go away."

"Please, sir—Dr. Hayward is most anxious that you should see her."

"Tell Dr. Hayward that I said that he is an excellent chess player."

"Yes, sir." The attendant waited for a moment. "Then you won't see her, sir?"

"No, I won't see her."

He wandered around the room for some minutes after the attendant had left, too distrait to return to his recapitulation. By and large they had played very decently with him since they had brought him here. He was glad that they had allowed him to have a room alone, and he certainly had more time free for contemplation than had ever been possible on the outside. To be sure, continuous effort to keep him busy and to distract him was made, but, by being stubborn, he was able to circumvent the rules and gain some hours each day for introspection.

But, damnation!—he did wish they would not persist in using Alice in their attempts to divert his thoughts.

Although the intense terror and revulsion which she had inspired in him when he had first rediscovered the truth had now aged into a simple feeling of repugnance and distaste for her company, nevertheless it was emotionally upsetting to be reminded of her, to be forced into making decisions about her.

After all, she had been his wife for many years. Wife? What was a wife? Another soul like one's own, a complement, the other necessary pole to the couple, a sanctuary of understanding and sympathy in the boundless depths of aloneness. That was what he had thought, what he had needed to believe and had believed fiercely for years. The yearning need for companionship of his own kind had caused him to see himself reflected in those beautiful eyes and had made him quite uncritical of occasional incongruities in her responses.

He sighed. He felt that he had sloughed off most of the typed emotional reactions which they had taught him by precept and example, but Alice had gotten under his skin, way under, and it still hurt. He had been happy—what if it had been a dope dream? They had given him an excellent, a beautiful mirror to play with—the more fool he to have looked behind it!

Wearily he turned back to his summing up:

"The world is explained in either one of two ways; the common-sense way which says that the world is pretty much as it appears to be and that ordinary human conduct and motivations are reasonable, and the religio-mystic solution which states that the world is dream stuff, unreal, insubstantial, with reality somewhere beyond.

"WRONG—both of them. The common-sense scheme has no sense to it of any sort. Life is short and full of trouble. Man born of woman is born to trouble as the sparks fly upward. His days are few and they are

numbered. All is vanity and vexation. Those quotations may be jumbled and incorrect, but that is a fair statement of the common-sense world is-as-it-seems in its only possible evaluation. In such a world, human striving is about as rational as the blind darting of a moth against a light bulb. The common-sense world is a blind insanity, out of nowhere, going nowhere, to no purpose.

"As for the other solution, it appears more rational on the surface, in that it rejects the utterly irrational world of common sense. But it is not a rational solution, it is simply a flight from reality of any sort, for it refuses to believe the results of the only available direct communication between the ego and the Outside. Certainly the 'five senses' are poor enough channels of communication, but they are the only channels."

He crumpled up the paper and flung himself from the chair. Order and logic were no good—his answer was right because it smelled right. But he still did not know all the answer. Why the grand scale to the deception, countless creatures, whole continents, an enormously involved and minutely detailed matrix of insane history, insane tradition, insane culture? Why bother with more than a cell and a strait jacket?

It must be, it had to be, because it was supremely important to deceive him completely, because a lesser deception would not do. Could it be that they dare not let him suspect his real identity no matter how difficult and involved the fraud?

He had to know. In some fashion he must get behind the deception and see what went on when he was not looking. He had had one glimpse; this time he must see the actual workings, catch the puppet masters in their manipulations.

Obviously the first step must be to escape from this asylum, but to do it so craftily that they would never see him, never catch up with him, not have a chance to set

the stage before him. That would be hard to do. He must excel them in shrewdness and subtlety.

Once decided, he spent the rest of the evening in considering the means by which he might accomplish his purpose. It seemed almost impossible—he must get away without once being seen and remain in strict hiding. They must lose track of him completely in order that they would not know where to center their deceptions. That would mean going without food for several days. Very well—he could do it. He must not give them any warning by unusual action or manner.

The lights blinked twice. Docilely he got up and commenced preparations for bed. When the attendant looked through the peephole he was already in bed, with his face turned to the wall.

Gladness! Gladness everywhere! It was good to be with his own kind, to hear the music swelling out of every living thing, as it always had and always would—good to know that everything was living and aware of him, participating in him, as he participated in them. It was good to be, good to know the unity of many and the diversity of one. There had been one bad thought—the details escaped him—but it was gone—it had never been; there was no place for it.

The early-morning sounds from the adjacent ward penetrated the sleepladen body which served him here and gradually recalled him to awareness of the hospital room. The transition was so gentle that he carried over full recollection of what he had been doing and why. He lay still, a gentle smile on his face, and savored the uncouth, but not unpleasant, languor of the body he wore. Strange that he had ever forgotten despite their tricks and stratagems. Well, now that he had recalled the key, he would quickly set things right in this odd

place. He would call them in at once and announce the new order. It would be amusing to see old Glaroon's expression when he realized that the cycle had ended—

The click of the peephole and the rasp of the door being unlocked guillotined his line of thought. The morning attendant pushed briskly in with the breakfast tray and placed it on the tip table. "Morning, sir. Nice, bright day—want it in bed, or will you get up?"

Don't answer! Don't listen! Suppress this distraction! This is part of their plan—But it was too late, too late. He felt himself slipping, falling, wrenched from reality back into the fraud world in which they had kept him. It was gone, gone completely, with no single association around him to which to anchor memory. There was nothing left but the sense of heartbreaking loss and the acute ache of unsatisfied catharsis.

"Leave it where it is. I'll take care of it."

"Okey-doke." The attendant bustled out, slamming the door, and noisily locked it.

He lay quite still for a long time, every nerve end in his body screaming for relief.

At last he got out of bed, still miserably unhappy, and attempted to concentrate on his plans for escape. But the psychic wrench he had received in being recalled so suddenly from his plane of reality had left him bruised and emotionally disturbed. His mind insisted on rechewing its doubts, rather than engage in constructive thought. Was it possible that the doctor was right, that he was not alone in his miserable dilemma? Was he really simply suffering from paranoia, delusions of self-importance?

Could it be that each unit in this yeasty swarm around him was the prison of another lonely ego—helpless, blind, and speechless, condemned to an eternity of miserable loneliness? Was the look of suffering which he had brought to Alice's face a true reflection of

inner torment and not simply a piece of play-acting intended to maneuver him into compliance with their plans?

A knock sounded at the door. He said "Come in," without looking up. Their comings and goings did not matter to him.

"Dearest—" A well-known voice spoke slowly and hesitantly.

"Alice!" He was on his feet at once, and facing her. "Who let you in here?"

"Please, dear, please—I had to see you."

"It isn't fair. It isn't fair." He spoke more to himself than to her. Then: "Why did you come?"

She stood up to him with a dignity he had hardly expected. The beauty of her childlike face had been marred by line and shadow, but it shone with an unexpected courage. "I love you," she answered quietly. "You can tell me to go away, but you can't make me stop loving you and trying to help you."

He turned away from her in an agony of indecision. Could it be possible that he had misjudged her? Was there, behind that barrier of flesh and sound symbols, a spirit that truly yearned toward his? Lovers whispering in the dark—*"You do understand, don't you?"*

"Yes, dear heart, I understand."

"Then nothing that happens to us can matter, as long as we are together and understand—" Words, words, rebounding hollowly from an unbroken wall—

No, he couldn't be wrong! Test her again— "Why did you keep me on that job in Omaha?"

"But I didn't make you keep that job. I simply pointed out that we should think twice before—"

"Never mind. Never mind." Soft hands and a sweet face preventing him with mild stubbornness from ever doing the thing that his heart told him to do. Always with the best of intentions, the best of intentions, but always so that he had never quite managed to do the

silly, unreasonable things that he knew were worth-while. Hurry, hurry, hurry, and strive, with an angelfaced jockey to see that you don't stop long enough to think for youself—

"Why did you try to stop me from going back upstairs that day?"

She managed to smile, although her eyes were already spilling over with tears. "I didn't know it really mattered to you. I didn't want us to miss the train."

It had been a small thing, an unimportant thing. For some reason not clear to him he had insisted on going back upstairs to his study when they were about to leave the house for a short vacation. It was raining, and she had pointed out that there was barely enough time to get to the station. He had surprised himself and her, too, by insisting on his own way in circumstances in which he had never been known to be stubborn.

He had actually pushed her to one side and forced his way up the stairs. Even then nothing might have come of it had he not—quite unnecessarily—raised the shade of the window that faced toward the rear of the house.

It was a very small matter. It had been raining, hard, out in front. From this window the weather was clear and sunny, with no sign of rain.

He had stood there quite a long while, gazing out at the impossible sunshine and rearranging his cosmos in his mind. He reexamined long-suppressed doubts in the light of this one small but totally unexplainable discrepancy. Then he had turned and had found that she was standing behind him.

He had been trying ever since to forget the expression that he had surprised on her face.

"What about the rain?"

"The rain?" she repeated in a small, puzzled voice. "Why, it was raining, of course. What about it?"

"But it was not raining out my study window."

"What? But of course it was. I did notice the sun break through the clouds for a moment, but that was all."

"Nonsense!"

"But darling, what has the weather to do with you and me? What difference does it make whether it rains or not—to us?" She approached him timidly and slid a small hand between his arm and side. "Am I responsible for the weather?"

"I think you are. Now please go."

She withdrew from him, brushed blindly at her eyes, gulped once, then said in a voice held steady: "All right. I'll go. But remember—you can come home if you want to. And I'll be there, if you want me." She waited a moment, then added hesitantly: "Would you . . . would you kiss me good-bye?"

He made no answer of any sort, neither with voice nor eyes. She looked at him, then turned, fumbled blindly for the door, and rushed through it.

The creature he knew as Alice went to the place of assembly without stopping to change form. "It is necessary to adjourn this sequence. I am no longer able to influence his decisions."

They had expected it, nevertheless they stirred with dismay.

The Glaroon addressed the First for Manipulation. "Prepare to graft the selected memory track at once."

Then, turning to the First for Operations, the Glaroon said: "The extrapolation shows that he will tend to escape within two of his days. This sequence degenerated primarily through your failure to extend that rainfall all around him. Be advised."

"It would be simpler if we understood his motives."

"In my capacity as Dr. Hayward, I have often thought so," commented the Glaroon acidly, "but if we understood his motives, we would be part of him. Bear in mind the Treaty! He almost remembered."

The creature known as Alice spoke up. "Could he not have the Taj Mahal next sequence? For some reason he values it."

"You are becoming assimilated!"

"Perhaps. I am not in fear. Will he receive it?"

"It will be considered."

The Glaroon continued with orders: "Leave structures standing until adjournment. New York City and Harvard University are now dismantled. Divert him from those sectors.

"Move!"

H. P. Lovecraft (1890–1937)

At the Mountains of Madness

Howard Phillips Lovecraft is the most important American horror writer since Poe. Like Poe, he was a theoretician, poet and writer. His essay, *Supernatural Horror in Literature*, is, despite its gorgeous prose excesses, the best piece of criticism and history of the genre. Arkham House, the most distinguished publisher of horror fiction of this century, was founded after his death in 1937 by August Derleth and Donald Wandrei, two writers of his circle, specifically to publish Lovecraft's collected works. His influence has been enormous since the initial appearances of his works in *Weird Tales* in the 1920s and 1930s, not only on the circle that gathered around him in his lifetime, including Clark Ashton Smith, Robert E. Howard, Derleth, Wandrei, Robert Bloch, Fritz Leiber and others, but on much of the literature in the English language (and to a certain extent in Europe and elsewhere—in a same manner as Poe, Lovecraft was noticed early in France, where his reputation is perhaps higher than here. Even Jorge Luis Borges wrote a consciously Lovecraftian story or two). It is particularly interesting that he chose, in this novella, the longest work he wrote published during his lifetime, to create what is essentially a sequel to Poe's "unfinished" *Narrative of Arthur Gordon Pym*. This piece was first published in *Astounding*, shortly before the Campbell era, one of the few Lovecraft stories to appear in a magazine other than *Weird Tales* (of which he was a mainstay). It is also one of the crucial links between

science fiction and horror, a work that helped to forge the bond between the two categories that has lasted until the present.

I

I am forced into speech because men of science have refused to follow my advice without knowing why. It is altogether against my will that I tell my reasons for opposing this contemplated invasion of the antarctic— with its vast fossil-hunt and its wholesale boring and melting of the ancient ice-cap—and I am the more reluctant because my warning may be in vain. Doubt of the real facts, as I must reveal them, is inevitable; yet if I suppressed what will seem extravagant and incredible there would be nothing left. The hitherto withheld photographs, both ordinary and aërial, will count in my favour; for they are damnably vivid and graphic. Still, they will be doubted because of the great lengths to which clever fakery can be carried. The ink drawings, of course, will be jeered at as obvious impostures; notwithstanding a strangeness of technique which art experts ought to remark and puzzle over.

In the end I must rely on the judgment and standing of the few scientific leaders who have, on the one hand, sufficient independence of thought to weigh my data on its own hideously convincing merits or in the light of certain primordial and highly baffling mythcycles; and on the other hand, sufficient influence to deter the exploring world in general from any rash and overambitious programme in the region of those mountains of madness. It is an unfortunate fact that relatively obscure men like myself and my associates, connected only with a small university, have little chance of making an impression where matters of a wildly bizarre or highly controversial nature are concerned.

It is further against us that we are not, in the strictest sense, specialists in the fields which came primarily to be concerned. As a geologist my object in leading the Miskatonic University Expedition was wholly that of securing deep-level specimens of rock and soil from various parts of the antarctic continent, aided by the remarkable drill devised by Prof. Frank H. Pabodie of our engineering department. I had no wish to be a pioneer in any other field than this; but I did hope that the use of this new mechanical appliance at different points along previously explored paths would bring to light materials of a sort hitherto unreached by the ordinary methods of collection. Pabodie's drilling apparatus, as the public already knows from our reports, was unique and radical in its lightness, portability, and capacity to combine the ordinary artesian drill principle with the principle of the small circular rock drill in such a way as to cope quickly with strata of varying hardness. Steel head, jointed rods, gasoline motor, collapsible wooden derrick, dynamiting paraphernalia, cording, rubbish-removal auger, and sectional piping for bores five inches wide and up to 1000 feet deep all formed, with needed accessories, no greater load than three seven-dog sledges could carry; this being made possible by the clever aluminum alloy of which most of the metal objects were fashioned. Four large Dornier aëroplanes, designed especially for the tremendous altitude flying necessary on the antarctic plateau and with added fuel-warming and quick-starting devices worked out by Pabodie, could transport our entire expedition from a base at the edge of the great ice barrier to various suitable inland points, and from these points a sufficient quota of dogs would serve us.

We planned to cover as great an area as one antarctic season—or longer, if absolutely necessary—would permit, operating mostly in the mountain-ranges and on the plateau south of Ross Sea; regions explored in

varying degree by Shackleton, Amundsen, Scott, and Byrd. With frequent changes of camp, made by aëroplane and involving distances great enough to be of geological significance, we expected to unearth a quite unprecedented amount of material; especially in the pre-Cambrian strata of which so narrow a range of antarctic specimens had previously been secured. We wished also to obtain as great as possible a variety of the upper fossiliferous rocks, since the primal life-history of this bleak realm of ice and death is of the highest importance to our knowledge of the earth's past. That the antarctic continent was once temperate and even tropical, with a teeming vegetable and animal life of which the lichens, marine fauna, arachnida, and penguins of the northern edge are the only survivals, is a matter of common information; and we hoped to expand that information in variety, accuracy, and detail. When a simple boring revealed fossiliferous signs, we would enlarge the aperture by blasting in order to get specimens of suitable size and condition.

Our borings, of varying depth according to the promise held out by the upper soil or rock, were to be confined to exposed or nearly exposed land surfaces—these inevitably being slopes and ridges because of the mile or two-mile thickness of solid ice overlying the lower levels. We could not afford to waste drilling depth on any considerable amount of mere glaciation, though Pabodie had worked out a plan for sinking copper electrodes in thick clusters of borings and melting off limited areas of ice with current from a gasoline-driven dynamo. It is this plan—which we could not put into effect except experimentally on an expedition such as ours—that the coming Starkweather-Moore Expedition proposes to follow despite the warnings I have issued since our return from the antarctic.

The public knows of the Miskatonic Expedition through our frequent wireless reports to the *Arkham*

Advertiser and Associated Press, and through the later articles of Pabodie and myself. We consisted of four men from the University—Pabodie, Lake of the biology department, Atwood of the physics department (also a meterologist), and I representing geology and having nominal command—besides sixteen assistants; seven graduate students from Miskatonic and nine skilled mechanics. Of these sixteen, twelve were qualified aëroplane pilots, all but two of whom were competent wireless operators. Eight of them understood navigation with compass and sextant, as did Pabodie, Atwood, and I. In addition, of course, our two ships— wooden ex-whalers, reinforced for ice conditions and having auxiliary steam—were fully manned. The Nathaniel Derby Pickman Foundation, aided by a few special contributions, financed the expedition; hence our preparations were extremely thorough despite the absence of great publicity. The dogs, sledges, machines, camp materials, and unassembled parts of our five planes were delivered in Boston, and there our ships were loaded. We were marvellously well-equipped for our specific purposes, and in all matters pertaining to supplies, regimen, transportation, and camp construction we profited by the excellent example of our many recent and exceptionally brilliant predecessors. It was the unusual number and fame of these predecessors which made our own expedition—ample though it was—so little noticed by the world at large.

As the newspapers told, we sailed from Boston Harbour on September 2, 1930; taking a leisurely course down the coast and through the Panama Canal, and stopping at Samoa and Hobart, Tasmania, at which latter place we took on final supplies. None of our exploring party had ever been in the polar regions before, hence we all relied greatly on our ship captains—J. B. Douglas, commanding the brig *Arkham*,

and serving as commander of the sea party, and Georg Thorfinnssen, commanding the barque *Miskatonic*—both veteran whalers in antarctic waters. As we left the inhabited world behind the sun sank lower and lower in the north, and stayed longer and longer above the horizon each day. At about 62° South Latitude we sighted our first icebergs—table-like objects with vertical sides—and just before reaching the Antarctic Circle, which we crossed on October 20 with appropriately quaint ceremonies, we were considerably troubled with field ice. The falling temperature bothered me considerably after our long voyage through the tropics, but I tried to brace up for the worse rigours to come. On many occasions the curious atmospheric effects enchanted me vastly; these including a strikingly vivid mirage—the first I had ever seen—in which distant bergs became the battlements of unimaginable cosmic castles.

Pushing through the ice, which was fortunately neither extensive nor thickly packed, we regained open water at South Latitude 67°, East Longitude 175°. On the morning of October 26 a strong "land blink" appeared on the south, and before noon we all felt a thrill of excitement at beholding a vast, lofty, and snow-clad mountain chain which opened out and covered the whole vista ahead. At last we had encountered an outpost of the great unknown continent and its cryptic world of frozen death. These peaks were obviously the Admiralty Range discovered by Ross, and it would now be our task to round Cape Adare and sail down the east coast of Victoria Land to our contemplated base on the shore of McMurdo Sound at the foot of the volcano Erebus in South Latitude 77° 9′.

The last lap of the voyage was vivid and fancy-stirring, great barren peaks of mystery looming up constantly against the west as the low northern sun of

noon or the still lower horizon-grazing southern sun of midnight poured its hazy reddish rays over the white snow, bluish ice and water lanes, and black bits of exposed granite slope. Through the desolate summits swept raging intermittent gusts of the terrible antarctic wind; whose cadences sometimes held vague suggestions of a wild and half-sentient musical piping, with notes extending over a wide range, and which for some subconscious mnemonic reason seemed to me disquieting and even dimly terrible. Something about the scene reminded me of the strange and disturbing Asian paintings of Nicholas Roerich, and of the still stranger and more disturbing descriptions of the evilly fabled plateau of Leng which occur in the dreaded *Necronomicon* of the mad Arab Abdul Alhazred. I was rather sorry, later on, that I had ever looked into that monstrous book at the college library.

On the seventh of November, sight of the westward range having been temporarily lost, we passed Franklin Island; and the next day descried the cones of Mts. Erebus and Terror on Ross Island ahead, with the long line of the Parry Mountains beyond. There now stretched off to the east the low, white line of the great ice barrier; rising perpendicularly to a height of 200 feet like the rocky cliffs of Quebec, and marking the end of southward navigation. In the afternoon we entered McMurdo Sound and stood off the coast in the lee of smoking Mt. Erebus. The scoriac peak towered up some 12,700 feet against the eastern sky, like a Japanese print of the sacred Fujiyama; while beyond it rose the white, ghost-like height of Mt. Terror, 10,900 feet in altitude, and now extinct as a volcano. Puffs of smoke from Erebus came intermittently, and one of the graduate assistants—a brilliant young fellow named Danforth—pointed out what looked like lava on the snowy slope; remarking that this mountain, discovered

in 1840, had undoubtedly been the source of Poe's image when he wrote seven years later of

> "—the lavas that restlessly roll
> Their sulphurous currents down Yaanek
> In the ultimate climes of the pole—
> That groan as they roll down Mount Yaanek
> In the realms of the boreal pole."

Danforth was a great reader of bizarre material, and had talked a good deal of Poe. I was interested myself because of the antarctic scene of Poe's only long story—the disturbing and enigmatical *Arthur Gordon Pym*. On the barren shore, and on the lofty ice barrier in the background, myriads of grotesque penguins squawked and flapped their fins; while many fat seals were visible on the water, swimming or sprawling across large cakes of slowly drifting ice.

Using small boats, we effected a difficult landing on Ross Island shortly after midnight on the morning of the 9th, carrying a line of cable from each of the ships and preparing to unload supplies by means of a breeches-buoy arrangement. Our sensations on first treading antarctic soil were poignant and complex, even though at this particular point the Scott and Shackleton expeditions had preceded us. Our camp on the frozen shore below the volcano's slope was only a provisional one; headquarters being kept aboard the *Arkham*. We landed all our drilling apparatus, dogs, sledges, tents, provisions, gasoline tanks, experimental ice-melting outfit, cameras both ordinary and aërial, aëroplane parts, and other accessories, including three small portable wireless outfits (besides those in the planes) capable of communicating with the *Arkham*'s large outfit from any part of the antarctic continent that we would be likely to visit. The ship's outfit, communi-

cating with the outside world, was to convey press reports to the *Arkham Advertiser*'s powerful wireless station on Kingsport Head, Mass. We hoped to complete our work during a single antarctic summer; but if this proved impossible we would winter on the *Arkham*, sending the *Miskatonic* north before the freezing of the ice for another summer's supplies.

I need not repeat what the newspapers have already published about our early work: of our ascent of Mt. Erebus; our successful mineral borings at several points on Ross Island and the singular speed with which Pabodie's apparatus accomplished them, even through solid rock layers; our provisional test of the small ice-melting equipment; our perilous ascent of the great barrier with sledges and supplies; and our final assembling of five huge aëroplanes at the camp atop the barrier. The health of our land party—twenty men and 55 Alaskan sledge dogs—was remarkable, though of course we had so far encountered no really destructive temperatures or windstorms. For the most part, the thermometer varied between zero and 20° or 25° above, and our experience with New England winters had accustomed us to rigours of this sort. The barrier camp was semi-permanent, and destined to be a storage cache for gasoline, provisions, dynamite, and other supplies. Only four of our planes were needed to carry the actual exploring material, the fifth being left with a pilot and two men from the ships at the storage cache to form a means of reaching us from the *Arkham* in case all our exploring planes were lost. Later, when not using all the other planes for moving apparatus, we would employ one or two in a shuttle transportation service between this cache and another permanent base on the great plateau from 600 to 700 miles southward, beyond Beardmore Glacier. Despite the almost unanimous accounts of appalling winds and tempests that pour

down from the plateau, we determined to dispense with intermediate bases; taking our chances in the interest of economy and probable efficiency.

Wireless reports have spoken of the breath-taking four-hour nonstop flight of our squadron on November 21 over the lofty shelf ice, with vast peaks rising on the west, and the unfathomed silences echoing to the sound of our engines. Wind troubled us only moderately, and our radio compasses helped us through the one opaque fog we encountered. When the vast rise loomed ahead, between Latitudes 83° and 84°, we knew we had reached Beardmore Glacier, the largest valley glacier in the world, and that the frozen sea was now giving place to a frowning and mountainous coastline. At last we were truly entering the white, aeon-dead world of the ultimate south, and even as we realised it we saw the peak of Mt. Nansen in the eastern distance, towering up to its height of almost 15,000 feet.

The successful establishment of the southern base above the glacier in Latitude 86° 7′, East Longitude 174° 23′, and the phenomenally rapid and effective borings and blastings made at various points reached by our sledge trips and short aëroplane flights, are matters of history; as is the arduous and triumphant ascent of Mt. Nansen by Pabodie and two of the graduate students—Gedney and Carroll—on December 13–15. We were some 8500 feet above sea-level, and when experimental drillings revealed solid ground only twelve feet down through the snow and ice at certain points, we made considerable use of the small melting apparatus and sunk bores and performed dynamiting at many places where no previous explorer had ever thought of securing mineral specimens. The pre-Cambrian granites and beacon sandstones thus obtained confirmed our belief that this plateau was homogeneous with the great bulk of the continent to

the west, but somewhat different from the parts lying eastward below South America—which we then thought to form a separate and smaller continent divided from the larger one by a frozen junction of Ross and Weddell Seas, though Byrd has since disproved the hypothesis.

In certain of the sandstones, dynamited and chiselled after boring revealed their nature, we found some highly interesting fossil markings and fragments— notably ferns, seaweeds, trilobites, crinoids, and such molluscs as lingulellae and gasteropods—all of which seemed of real significance in connexion with the region's primordial history. There was also a queer triangular, striated marking about a foot in greatest diameter which Lake pieced together from three fragments of slate brought up from a deep-blasted aperture. These fragments came from a point to the westward, near the Queen Alexandra Range; and Lake, as a biologist, seemed to find their curious marking unusually puzzling and provocative, though to my geological eye it looked not unlike some of the ripple effects reasonably common in the sedimentary rocks. Since slate is no more than a metamorphic formation into which a sedimentary stratum is pressed, and since the pressure itself produces odd distorting effects on any markings which may exist, I saw no reason for extreme wonder over the striated depression.

On January 6, 1931, Lake, Pabodie, Daniels, all six of the students, four mechanics, and I flew directly over the south pole in two of the great planes, being forced down once by a sudden high wind which fortunately did not develop into a typical storm. This was, as the papers have stated, one of several observation flights; during others of which we tried to discern new topographical features in areas unreached by previous explorers. Our early flights were disappointing in this

latter respect; though they afforded us some magnificent examples of the richly fantastic and deceptive mirages of the polar regions, of which our sea voyage had given us some brief foretastes. Distant mountains floated in the sky as enchanted cities, and often the whole white world would dissolve into a gold, silver, and scarlet land of Dunsanian dreams and adventurous expectancy under the magic of the low midnight sun. On cloudy days we had considerable trouble in flying, owing to the tendency of snowy earth and sky to merge into one mystical opalescent void with no visible horizon to mark the junction of the two.

At length we resolved to carry out our original plan of flying 500 miles eastward with all four exploring planes and establishing a fresh sub-base at a point which would probably be on the smaller continental division, as we mistakenly conceived it. Geological specimens obtained there would be desirable for purposes of comparison. Our health so far had remained excellent; lime-juice well offsetting the steady diet of tinned and salted food, and temperatures generally above zero enabling us to do without our thickest furs. It was now midsummer, and with haste and care we might be able to conclude work by March and avoid a tedious wintering through the long antarctic night. Several savage windstorms had burst upon us from the west, but we had escaped damage through the skill of Atwood in devising rudimentary aëroplane shelters and windbreaks of heavy snow blocks, and reinforcing the principal camp buildings with snow. Our good luck and efficiency had indeed been almost uncanny.

The outside world knew, of course, of our programme, and was told also of Lake's strange and dogged insistence on a westward—or rather, northwestward—prospecting trip before our radical shift to the new base. It seems he had pondered a great

deal, and with alarmingly radical daring, over that triangular striated marking in the slate; reading into it certain contradictions in Nature and geological period which whetted his curiosity to the utmost, and made him avid to sink more borings and blastings in the west-stretching formation to which the exhumed fragments evidently belonged. He was strangely convinced that the marking was the print of some bulky, unknown, and radically unclassifiable organism of considerably advanced evolution, notwithstanding that the rock which bore it was of so vastly ancient a date—Cambrian if not actually pre-Cambrian—as to preclude the probable existence not only of all highly evolved life, but of any life at all above the unicellular or at most the trilobite stage. These fragments, with their odd marking, must have been 500 million to a thousand million years old.

II

Popular imagination, I judge, responded actively to our wireless bulletins of Lake's start northwestward into regions never trodden by human foot or penetrated by human imagination; though we did not mention his wild hopes of revolutionising the entire sciences of biology and geology. His preliminary sledging and boring journey of January 11–18 with Pabodie and five others—marred by the loss of two dogs in an upset when crossing one of the great pressure-ridges in the ice—had brought up more and more of the Archaean slate; and even I was interested by the singular profusion of evident fossil markings in that unbelievably ancient stratum. These markings, however, were of very primitive life-forms involving no great paradox except that any life-forms should occur in rock as

definitely pre-Cambrian as this seemed to be; hence I still failed to see the good sense of Lake's demand for an interlude in our time-saving programme—an interlude requiring the use of all four planes, many men, and the whole of the expedition's mechanical apparatus. I did not, in the end, veto the plan; though I decided not to accompany the northwestward party despite Lake's plea for my geological advice. While they were gone, I would remain at the base with Pabodie and five men and work out final plans for the eastward shift. In preparation for this transfer one of the planes had begun to move up a good gasoline supply from McMurdo Sound; but this could wait temporarily. I kept with me one sledge and nine dogs, since it is unwise to be at any time without possible transportation in an utterly tenantless world of aeon-long death.

Lake's sub-expedition into the unknown, as everyone will recall, sent out its own reports from the short-wave transmitters on the planes; these being simultaneously picked up by our apparatus at the southern base and by the *Arkham* at McMurdo Sound, whence they were relayed to the outside world on wave-lengths up to fifty metres. The start was made January 22 at 4 AM; and the first wireless message we received came only two hours later, when Lake spoke of descending and starting a small-scale ice-melting and bore at a point some 300 miles away from us. Six hours after that a second and very excited message told of the frantic, beaver-like work whereby a shallow shaft had been sunk and blasted; culminating in the discovery of slate fragments with several markings approximately like the one which had caused the original puzzlement.

Three hours later a brief bulletin announced the resumption of the flight in the teeth of a raw and piercing gale; and when I despatched a message of protest against further hazards, Lake replied curtly that

his new specimens made any hazard worth taking. I saw
that his excitement had reached the point of mutiny,
and that I could do nothing to check this headlong risk
of the whole expedition's success; but it was appalling
to think of his plunging deeper and deeper into that
treacherous and sinister white immensity of tempests
and unfathomed mysteries which stretched off for some
1500 miles to the half-known, half-suspected coast-line
of Queen Mary and Knox Lands.

Then, in about an hour and a half more, came that
doubly excited message from Lake's moving plane
which almost reversed my sentiments and made me
wish I had accompanied the party.

"10:05 PM On the wing. After snowstorm, have
spied mountainrange ahead higher than any hitherto seen. May equal Himalayas allowing for
height of plateau. Probable Latitude 76° 15′,
Longitude 113° 10′ E. Reaches far as can see to
right and left. Suspicion of two smoking cones. All
peaks black and bare of snow. Gale blowing off
them impedes navigation."

After that Pabodie, the men, and I hung breathlessly
over the receiver. Thought of this titanic mountain
rampart 700 miles away inflamed our deepest sense of
adventure; and we rejoiced that our expedition, if not
ourselves personally, had been its discoverers. In half
an hour Lake called us again.

"Moulton's plane forced down on plateau in
foothills, but nobody hurt and perhaps can repair.
Shall transfer essentials to other three for return
or further moves if necessary, but no more heavy
plane travel needed just now. Mountains surpass
anything in imagination. Am going up scouting in

Carroll's plane, with all weight out. You can't imagine anything like this. Highest peaks must go over 35,000 feet. Everest out of the running. Atwood to work out height with theodolite while Carroll and I go up. Probably wrong about cones, for formations look stratified. Possibly pre-Cambrian slate with other strata mixed in. Queer skyline effects—regular sections of cubes clinging to highest peaks. Whole thing marvellous in red-gold light of low sun. Like land of mystery in a dream or gateway to forbidden world of untrodden wonder. Wish you were here to study."

Though it was technically sleeping-time, not one of us listeners thought for a moment of retiring. It must have been a good deal the same at McMurdo Sound, where the supply cache and the *Arkham* were also getting the messages; for Capt. Douglas gave out a call congratulating everybody on the important find, and Sherman, the cache operator, seconded his sentiments. We were sorry, of course, about the damaged aëroplane; but hoped it could be easily mended. Then, at 11 PM, came another call from Lake.

"Up with Carroll over highest foothills. Don't dare try really tall peaks in present weather, but shall later. Frightful work climbing, and hard going at this altitude, but worth it. Great range fairly solid, hence can't get any glimpses beyond. Main summits exceed Himalayas, and very queer. Range looks like pre-Cambrian slate, with plain signs of many other upheaved strata. Was wrong about volcanism. Goes farther in either direction than we can see. Swept clear of snow above about 21,000 feet. Odd formations on slopes of highest mountains. Great low square blocks with exactly

vertical sides, and rectangular lines of low vertical ramparts, like the old Asian castles clinging to steep mountains in Roerich's paintings. Impressive from distance. Flew close to some, and Carroll thought they were formed of smaller separate pieces, but that is probably weathering. Most edges crumbled and rounded off as if exposed to storms and climate changes for millions of years. Parts, especially upper parts, seem to be of lighter-coloured rock than any visible strata on slopes proper, hence an evidently crystalline origin. Close flying shews many cave-mouths, some unusually regular in outline, square or semicircular. You must come and investigate. Think I saw rampart squarely on top of one peak. Height seems about 30,000 to 35,000 feet. Am up 21,500 myself, in devilish gnawing cold. Wind whistles and pipes through passes and in and out of caves, but no flying danger so far."

From then on for another half-hour Lake kept up a running fire of comment, and expressed his intention of climbing some of the peaks on foot. I replied that I would join him as soon as he could send a plane, and that Pabodie and I would work out the best gasoline plan—just where and how to concentrate our supply in view of the expedition's altered character. Obviously, Lake's boring operations, as well as his aëroplane activities, would need a great deal delivered for the new base which he was to establish at the foot of the mountains; and it was possible that the eastward flight might not be made after all this season. In connexion with this business I called Capt. Douglas and asked him to get as much as possible out of the ships and up the barrier with the single dog-team we had left there. A direct route across the unknown region between Lake

and McMurdo Sound was what we really ought to establish.

Lake called me later to say that he had decided to let the camp stay where Moulton's plane had been forced down, and where repairs had already progressed somewhat. The ice-sheet was very thin, with dark ground here and there visible, and he would sink some borings and blasts at that very point before making any sledge trips or climbing expeditions. He spoke of the ineffable majesty of the whole scene, and the queer state of his sensations at being in the lee of vast silent pinnacles whose ranks shot up like a wall reaching the sky at the world's rim. Atwood's theodolite observations had placed the height of the five tallest peaks at from 30,000 to 34,000 feet. The windswept nature of the terrain clearly disturbed Lake, for it argued the occasional existence of prodigious gales violent beyond anything we had so far encountered. His camp lay a little more than five miles from where the higher foothills abruptly rose. I could almost trace a note of subconscious alarm in his words—flashed across a glacial void of 700 miles—as he urged that we all hasten with the matter and get the strange new region disposed of as soon as possible. He was about to rest now, after a continuous day's work of almost unparalleled speed, strenuousness, and results.

In the morning I had a three-cornered wireless talk with Lake and Capt. Douglas at their widely separated bases; and it was agreed that one of Lake's planes would come to my base for Pabodie, the five men, and myself, as well as for all the fuel it could carry. The rest of the fuel question, depending on our decision about an easterly trip, could wait for a few days; since Lake had enough for immediate camp heat and borings. Eventually the old southern base ought to be restocked; but if we postponed the easterly trip we would not use it till

the next summer, and meanwhile Lake must send a plane to explore a direct route between his new mountains and McMurdo Sound.

Pabodie and I prepared to close our base for a short or long period, as the case might be. If we wintered in the antarctic we would probably fly straight from Lake's base to the *Arkham* without returning to this spot. Some of our conical tents had already been reinforced by blocks of hard snow, and now we decided to complete the job of making a permanent Esquimau village. Owing to a very liberal tent supply, Lake had with him all that his base would need even after our arrival. I wirelessed that Pabodie and I would be ready for the northwestward move after one day's work and one night's rest.

Our labours, however, were not very steady after 4 PM; for about that time Lake began sending in the most extraordinary and excited messages. His working day had started unpropitiously; since an aëroplane survey of the nearly exposed rock surfaces shewed an entire absence of those Archaean and primordial strata for which he was looking, and which formed so great a part of the colossal peaks that loomed up at a tantalising distance from the camp. Most of the rocks glimpsed were apparently Jurassic and Comanchian sandstones and Permian and Triassic schists, with now and then a glossy black outcropping suggesting a hard and slaty coal. This rather discouraged Lake, whose plans all hinged on unearthing specimens more than 500 million years older. It was clear to him that in order to recover the Archaean slate vein in which he had found the odd markings, he would have to make a long sledge trip from these foothills to the steep slopes of the gigantic mountains themselves.

He had resolved, nevertheless, to do some local boring as part of the expedition's general programme;

hence set up the drill and put five men to work with it while the rest finished settling the camp and repairing the damaged aëroplane. The softest visible rock—a sandstone about a quarter of a mile from the camp—had been chosen for the first sampling; and the drill made excellent progress without much supplementary blasting. It was about three hours afterward, following the first really heavy blast of the operation, that the shouting of the drill crew was heard; and that young Gedney—the acting foreman—rushed into the camp with the startling news.

They had struck a cave. Early in the boring the sandstone had given place to a vein of Comanchian limestone full of minute fossil cephalopods, corals, echini, and spirifera, and with occasional suggestions of siliceous sponges and marine vertebrate bones—the latter probably of teliosts, sharks, and ganoids. This in itself was important enough, as affording the first vertebrate fossils the expedition had yet secured; but when shortly afterward the drill-head dropped through the stratum into apparent vacancy, a wholly new and doubly intense wave of excitement spread among the excavators. A good-sized blast had laid open the subterrene secret; and now, through a jagged aperture perhaps five feet across and three feet thick, there yawned before the avid searchers a section of shallow limestone hollowing worn more than fifty million years ago by the trickling ground waters of a bygone tropic world.

The hollowed layer was not more than seven or eight feet deep, but extended off indefinitely in all directions and had a fresh, slightly moving air which suggested its membership in an extensive subterranean system. Its roof and floor were abundantly equipped with large stalactites and stalagmites, some of which met in columnar form; but important above all else was the vast deposit of shells and bones which in places nearly

choked the passage. Washed down from unknown jungles of Mesozoic tree-ferns and fungi, and forests of Tertiary cycads, fan-palms, and primitive angiosperms, this osseous medley contained representatives of more Cretaceous, Eocene, and other animal species than the greatest palaeontologist could have counted or classified in a year. Molluscs, crustacean armour, fishes, amphibians, reptiles, birds, and early mammals—great and small, known and unknown. No wonder Gedney ran back to the camp shouting, and no wonder everyone else dropped work and rushed headlong through the biting cold to where the tall derrick marked a new-found gateway to secrets of inner earth and vanished aeons.

When Lake had satisfied the first keen edge of his curiosity he scribbled a message in his notebook and had young Moulton run back to the camp to despatch it by wireless. This was my first word of the discovery, and it told of the identification of early shells, bones of ganoids and placoderms, remnants of labyrinthodonts and thecodonts, great mososaur skull fragments, dinosaur vertebrae and armour-plates, pterodactyl teeth and wing-bones, archaeopteryx debris, Miocene sharks' teeth, primitive bird-skulls, and skulls, vertebrae, and other bones of archaic mammals such as palaeotheres, xiphodons, dinocerases, eohippi, oreodons, and titanotheres. There was nothing as recent as a mastodon, elephant, true camel, deer, or bovine animal; hence Lake concluded that the last deposits had occurred during the Oligocene age, and that the hollowed stratum had lain in its present dried, dead, and inaccessible state for at least thirty million years.

On the other hand, the prevalence of very early life-forms was singular in the highest degree. Though the limestone formation was, on the evidence of such typical imbedded fossils as ventriculites, positively and

unmistakably Comanchian and not a particle earlier; the free fragments in the hollow space included a surprising proportion from organisms hitherto considered as peculiar to far older periods—even rudimentary fishes, molluscs, and corals as remote as the Silurian or Ordovician. The inevitable inference was that in this part of the world there had been a remarkable and unique degree of continuity between the life of over 300 million years ago and that of only thirty million years ago. How far this continuity had extended beyond the Oligocene age when the cavern was closed, was of course past all speculation. In any event, the coming of the frightful ice in the Pleistocene some 500,000 years ago—a mere yesterday as compared with the age of this cavity—must have put an end to any of the primal forms which had locally managed to outlive their common terms.

Lake was not content to let his first message stand, but had another bulletin written and despatched across the snow to the camp before Moulton could get back. After that Moulton stayed at the wireless in one of the planes; transmitting to me—and to the *Arkham* for relaying to the outside world—the frequent postscripts which Lake sent him by a succession of messengers. Those who followed the newspapers will remember the excitement created among men of science by that afternoon's reports—reports which have finally led, after all these years, to the organisation of that very Starkweather-Moore Expedition which I am so anxious to dissuade from its purposes. I had better give the messages literally as Lake sent them, and as our base operator McTighe translated them from his pencil shorthand.

"Fowler makes discovery of highest importance in sandstone and limestone fragments from

blasts. Several distinct triangular striated prints like those in Archaean slate, proving that source survived from over 600 million years ago to Comanchian times without more than moderate morphological changes and decrease in average size. Comanchian prints apparently more primitive or decadent, if anything, than older ones. Emphasise importance of discovery in press. Will mean to biology what Einstein has meant to mathematics and physics. Joins up with my previous work and amplifies conclusions. Appears to indicate, as I suspected, that earth has seen whole cycle or cycles of organic life before known one that begins with Archaeozoic cells. Was evolved and specialised not later than thousand million years ago, when planet was young and recently uninhabitable for any life-forms or normal protoplasmic structure. Question arises when, where, and how development took place."

"Later. Examining certain skeletal fragments of large land and marine saurians and primitive mammals, find singular local wounds or injuries to bony structure not attributable to any known predatory or carnivorous animal of any period. Of two sorts—straight, penetrant bores, and apparently hacking incisions. One or two cases of cleanly severed bone. Not many specimens affected. Am sending to camp for electric torches. Will extend search area underground by hacking away stalactites."

"Still later. Have found peculiar soapstone fragment about six inches across and an inch and a

half thick, wholly unlike any visible local formation. Greenish, but no evidences to place its period. Has curious smoothness and regularity. Shaped like five-pointed star with tips broken off, and signs of other cleavage at inward angles and in centre of surface. Small, smooth depression in centre of unbroken surface. Arouses much curiosity as to source and weathering. Probably some freak of water action. Carroll, with magnifier, thinks he can make out additional markings of geologic significance. Groups of tiny dots in regular patterns. Dogs growing uneasy as we work, and seem to hate this soapstone. Must see if it has any peculiar odour. Will report again when Mills gets back with light and we start on underground area."

"10:15 PM Important discovery. Orrendorf and Watkins, working underground at 9:45 with light, found monstrous barrel-shaped fossil of wholly unknown nature; probably vegetable unless overgrown specimen of unknown marine radiata. Tissue evidently preserved by mineral salts. Tough as leather, but astonishing flexibility retained in places. Marks of broken-off parts at ends and around sides. Six feet end to end, 3.5 feet central diameter, tapering to 1 foot at each end. Like a barrel with five bulging ridges in place of staves. Lateral breakages, as of thinnish stalks, are at equator in middle of these ridges. In furrows between ridges are curious growths. Combs or wings that fold up and spread out like fans. All greatly damaged but one, which gives almost seven-foot wing spread. Arrangement reminds one of certain monsters of primal myth, especially

fabled Elder Things in *Necronomicon*. These
wings seem to be membraneous, stretched on
framework of glandular tubing. Apparent minute
orifices in frame tubing at wing tips. Ends of body
shrivelled, giving no clue to interior or to what has
been broken off there. Must dissect when we get
back to camp. Can't decide whether vegetable or
animal. Many features obviously of almost incredible primitiveness. Have set all hands cutting
stalactites and looking for further specimens.
Additional scarred bones found, but these must
wait. Having trouble with dogs. They can't endure
the new specimen, and would probably tear it to
pieces if we didn't keep it at a distance from
them."

———————————

"11:30 PM Attention, Dyer, Pabodie, Douglas.
Matter of highest—I might say transcendent—
importance. *Arkham* must relay to Kingsport
Head Station at once. Strange barrel growth is the
Archaean thing that left prints in rocks. Mills,
Boudreau, and Fowler discover cluster of thirteen
more at underground point forty feet from aperture. Mixed with curiously rounded and config-
ured soapstone fragments smaller than one
previously found—star-shaped but no marks of
breakage except at some of the points. Of organic
specimens, eight apparently perfect, with all appendages. Have brought all to surface, leading off
dogs to distance. They cannot stand the things.
Give close attention to description and repeat
back for accuracy. Papers must get this right.

"Objects are eight feet long all over. Six-foot
five-ridged barrel torso 3.5 feet central diameter,
1 foot end diameters. Dark grey, flexible, and infi-

nitely tough. Seven-foot membraneous wings of same colour, found folded, spread out of furrows between ridges. Wing framework tubular or glandular, of lighter grey, with orifices at wing tips. Spread wings have serrated edge. Around equator, one at central apex of each of the five vertical, stave-like ridges, are five systems of light grey flexible arms or tentacles found tightly folded to torso but expansible to maximum length of over 3 feet. Like arms of primitive crinoid. Single stalks 3 inches diameter branch after 6 inches into five sub-stalks, each of which branches after 8 inches into five small, tapering tentacles or tendrils, giving each stalk a total of 25 tentacles.

"At top of torso blunt bulbous neck of lighter grey with gill-like suggestions holds yellowish five-pointed starfish-shaped apparent head covered with three-inch wiry cilia of various prismatic colours. Head thick and puffy, about 2 feet point to point, with three-inch flexible yellowish tubes projecting from each point. Slit in exact centre of top probably breathing aperture. At end of each tube is spherical expansion where yellowish membrane rolls back on handling to reveal glassy, red-irised globe, evidently an eye. Five slightly longer reddish tubes start from inner angles of starfish-shaped head and end in sac-like swellings of same colour which upon pressure open to bell-shaped orifices 2 inches maximum diameter and lined with sharp white tooth-like projections. Probable mouths. All these tubes, cilia, and points of starfish-head found folded tightly down; tubes and points clinging to bulbous neck and torso. Flexibility surprising despite vast toughness.

"At bottom of torso rough but dissimilarly

functioning counterparts of head arrangements exist. Bulbous light-grey pseudo-neck, without gill suggestions, holds greenish five-pointed starfish-arrangement. Tough, muscular arms 4 feet long and tapering from 7 inches diameter at base to about 2.5 at point. To each point is attached small end of a greenish five-veined membraneous triangle 8 inches long and 6 wide at farther end. This is the paddle, fin, or pseudo-foot which has made prints in rocks from a thousand million to fifty or sixty million years old. From inner angles of starfish-arrangement project two-foot reddish tubes tapering from 3 inches diameter at base to 1 at tip. Orifices at tips. All these parts infinitely tough and leathery, but extremely flexible. Four-foot arms with paddles undoubtedly used for locomotion of some sort, marine or otherwise. When moved, display suggestions of exaggerated muscularity. As found, all these projections tightly folded over pseudo-neck and end of torso, corresponding to projections at other end.

"Cannot yet assign positively to animal or vegetable kingdom, but odds now favour animal. Probably represents incredibly advanced evolution of radiata without loss of certain primitive features. Echinoderm resemblances unmistakable despite local contradictory evidences. Wing structure puzzles in view of probable marine habitat, but may have use in water navigation. Symmetry is curiously vegetable-like, suggesting vegetable's essentially up-and-down structure rather than animal's fore-and-aft structure. Fabulously early date of evolution, preceding even simplest Archaean protozoa hitherto known, baffles all conjecture as to origin.

"Complete specimens have such uncanny re-

semblance to certain creatures of primal myth that suggestion of ancient existence outside antarctic becomes inevitable. Dyer and Pabodie have read *Necronomicon* and seen Clark Ashton Smith's nightmare paintings based on text, and will understand when I speak of Elder Things supposed to have created all earth-life as jest or mistake. Students have always thought conception formed from morbid imaginative treatment of very ancient tropical radiata. Also like prehistoric folklore things Wilmarth has spoken of— Cthulhu cult appendages, etc.

"Vast field of study opened. Deposits probably of late Cretaceous or early Eocene period, judging from associated specimens. Massive stalagmites deposited above them. Hard work hewing out, but toughness prevented damage. State of preservation miraculous, evidently owing to limestone action. No more found so far, but will resume search later. Job now to get fourteen huge specimens to camp without dogs, which bark furiously and can't be trusted near them. With nine men— three left to guard the dogs—we ought to manage the three sledges fairly well, though wind is bad. Must establish plane communication with McMurdo Sound and begin shipping material. But I've got to dissect one of these things before we take any rest. Wish I had a real laboratory here. Dyer better kick himself for having tried to stop my westward trip. First the world's greatest mountains, and then this. If this last isn't the high spot of the expedition, I don't know what is. We're made scientifically. Congrats, Pabodie, on the drill that opened up the cave. Now will *Arkham* please repeat description?"

The sensations of Pabodie and myself at receipt of this report were almost beyond description, nor were our companions much behind us in enthusiasm. McTighe, who had hastily translated a few high spots as they came from the droning receiving set, wrote out the entire message from his shorthand version as soon as Lake's operator signed off. All appreciated the epoch-making significance of the discovery, and I sent Lake congratulations as soon as the *Arkham*'s operator had repeated back the descriptive parts as requested; and my example was followed by Sherman from his station at the McMurdo Sound supply cache, as well as by Capt. Douglas of the *Arkham*. Later, as head of the expedition, I added some remarks to be relayed through the *Arkham* to the outside world. Of course, rest was an absurd thought amidst this excitement; and my only wish was to get to Lake's camp as quickly as I could. It disappointed me when he sent word that a rising mountain gale made early aërial travel impossible.

But within an hour and a half interest again rose to banish disappointment. Lake was sending more messages, and told of the completely successful transportation of the fourteen great specimens to the camp. It had been a hard pull, for the things were surprisingly heavy; but nine men had accomplished it very neatly. Now some of the party were hurriedly building a snow corral at a safe distance from the camp, to which the dogs could be brought for greater convenience in feeding. The specimens were laid out on the hard snow near the camp, save for one on which Lake was making crude attempts at dissection.

This dissection seemed to be a greater task than had been expected; for despite the heat of a gasoline stove in the newly raised laboratory tent, the deceptively flexible tissues of the chosen specimen—a powerful

and intact one—lost nothing of their more than leathery toughness. Lake was puzzled as to how he might make the requisite incisions without violence destructive enough to upset all the structural niceties he was looking for. He had, it is true, seven more perfect specimens; but these were too few to use up recklessly unless the cave might later yield an unlimited supply. Accordingly he removed the specimen and dragged in one which, though having remnants of the starfish-arrangements at both ends, was badly crushed and partly disrupted along one of the great torso furrows.

Results, quickly reported over the wireless, were baffling and provocative indeed. Nothing like delicacy or accuracy was possible with instruments hardly able to cut the anomalous tissue, but the little that was achieved left us all awed and bewildered. Existing biology would have to be wholly revised, for this thing was no product of any cell-growth science knows about. There had been scarcely any mineral replacement, and despite an age of perhaps forty million years the internal organs were wholly intact. The leathery, undeteriorative, and almost indestructible quality was an inherent attribute of the thing's form of organisation; and pertained to some palaeogean cycle of invertebrate evolution utterly beyond our powers of speculation. At first all that Lake found was dry, but as the heated tent produced its thawing effect, organic moisture of pungent and offensive odour was encountered toward the thing's uninjured side. It was not blood, but a thick, dark-green fluid apparently answering the same purpose. By the time Lake reached this stage all 37 dogs had been brought to the still uncompleted corral near the camp; and even at that distance set up a savage barking and show of restlessness at the acrid, diffusive smell.

Far from helping to place the strange entity, this

provisional dissection merely deepened its mystery. All guesses about its external members had been correct, and on the evidence of these one could hardly hesitate to call the thing animal; but internal inspection brought up so many vegetable evidences that Lake was left hopelessly at sea. It had digestion and circulation, and eliminated waste matter through the reddish tubes of its starfish-shaped base. Cursorily, one would say that its respiratory apparatus handled oxygen rather than carbon dioxide; and there were odd evidences of air-storage chambers and methods of shifting respiration from the external orifice to at least two other fully developed breathing-systems—gills and pores. Clearly, it was amphibian and probably adapted to long airless hibernation-periods as well. Vocal organs seemed present in connexion with the main respiratory system, but they presented anomalies beyond immediate solution. Articulate speech, in the sense of syllable-utterance, seemed barely conceivable; but musical piping notes covering a wide range were highly probable. The muscular system was almost preternaturally developed.

The nervous system was so complex and highly developed as to leave Lake aghast. Though excessively primitive and archaic in some respects, the thing had a set of ganglial centres and connectives arguing the very extremes of specialised development. Its five-lobed brain was surprisingly advanced; and there were signs of a sensory equipment, served in part through the wiry cilia of the head, involving factors alien to any other terrestrial organism. Probably it had more than five senses, so that its habits could not be predicted from any existing analogy. It must, Lake thought, have been a creature of keen sensitiveness and delicately differentiated functions in its primal world; much like the ants and bees of today. It reproduced like the vegetable cryptogams, especially the pteridophytes; having spore-

cases at the tips of the wings and evidently developing from a thallus or prothallus.

But to give it a name at this stage was mere folly. It looked like a radiate, but was clearly something more. It was partly vegetable, but had three-fourths of the essentials of animal structure. That it was marine in origin, its symmetrical contour and certain other attributes clearly indicated; yet one could not be exact as to the limit of its later adaptations. The wings, after all, held a persistent suggestion of the aërial. How it could have undergone its tremendously complex evolution on a new-born earth in time to leave prints in Archaean rocks was so far beyond conception as to make Lake whimsically recall the primal myths about Great Old Ones who filtered down from the stars and concocted earth-life as a joke or mistake; and the wild tales of cosmic hill things from Outside told by a folklorist colleague in Miskatonic's English department.

Naturally, he considered the possibility of the pre-Cambrian prints having been made by a less evolved ancestor of the present specimens; but quickly rejected this too facile theory upon considering the advanced structural qualities of the older fossils. If anything, the later contours shewed decadence rather than higher evolution. The size of the pseudo-feet had decreased, and the whole morphology seemed coarsened and simplified. Moreover, the nerves and organs just examined held singular suggestions of retrogression from forms still more complex. Atrophied and vestigial parts were surprisingly prevalent. Altogether, little could be said to have been solved; and Lake fell back on mythology for a provisional name—jocosely dubbing his finds "The Elder Ones."

At about 2:30 AM, having decided to postpone further work and get a little rest, he covered the dissected organism with a tarpaulin, emerged from the laborato-

ry tent, and studied the intact specimens with renewed interest. The ceaseless antarctic sun had begun to limber up their tissues a trifle, so that the head-points and tubes of two or three shewed signs of unfolding; but Lake did not believe there was any danger of immediate decomposition in the almost sub-zero air. He did, however, move all the undissected specimens closer together and throw a spare tent over them in order to keep off the direct solar rays. That would also help to keep their possible scent away from the dogs, whose hostile unrest was really becoming a problem even at their substantial distance and behind the higher and higher snow walls which an increased quota of the men were hastening to raise around their quarters. He had to weight down the corners of the tent-cloth with heavy blocks of snow to hold it in place amidst the rising gale, for the titan mountains seemed about to deliver some gravely severe blasts. Early apprehensions about sudden antarctic winds were revived, and under Atwood's supervision precautions were taken to bank the tents, new dog-corral, and crude aëroplane shelters with snow on the mountainward side. These latter shelters, begun with hard snow blocks during odd moments, were by no means as high as they should have been; and Lake finally detached all hands from other tasks to work on them.

It was after four when Lake at last prepared to sign off and advised us all to share the rest period his outfit would take when the shelter walls were a little higher. He held some friendly chat with Pabodie over the ether, and repeated his praise of the really marvelous drills that had helped him make his discovery. Atwood also sent greetings and praises. I gave Lake a warm word of congratulation, owning up that he was right about the western trip; and we all agreed to get in touch by wireless at ten in the morning. If the gale was then over,

Lake would send a plane for the party at my base. Just before retiring I despatched a final message to the *Arkham* with instructions about toning down the day's news for the outside world, since the full details seemed radical enough to rouse a wave of incredulity until further substantiated.

III

None of us, I imagine, slept very heavily or continuously that morning; for both the excitement of Lake's discovery and the mounting fury of the wind were against such a thing. So savage was the blast, even where we were, that we could not help wondering how much worse it was at Lake's camp, directly under the vast unknown peaks that bred and delivered it. McTighe was awake at ten o'clock and tried to get Lake on the wireless, as agreed, but some electrical condition in the disturbed air to the westward seemed to prevent communication. We did, however, get the *Arkham*, and Douglas told me that he had likewise been vainly trying to reach Lake. He had not known about the wind, for very little was blowing at McMurdo Sound despite its persistent rage where we were.

Throughout the day we all listened anxiously and tried to get Lake at intervals, but invariably without results. About noon a positive frenzy of wind stampeded out of the west, causing us to fear for the safety of our camp; but it eventually died down, with only a moderate relapse at 2 PM. After three o'clock it was very quiet, and we redoubled our efforts to get Lake. Reflecting that he had four planes, each provided with an excellent short-wave outfit, we could not imagine any ordinary accident capable of crippling all his wireless equipment at once. Nevertheless the stony silence

continued; and when we thought of the delirious force the wind must have had in his locality we could not help making the most direful conjectures.

By six o'clock our fears had become intense and definite, and after a wireless consultation with Douglas and Thorfinnssen I resolved to take steps toward investigation. The fifth aëroplane, which we had left at the McMurdo Sound supply cache with Sherman and two sailors, was in good shape and ready for instant use; and it seemed that the very emergency for which it had been saved was now upon us. I got Sherman by wireless and ordered him to join me with the plane and the two sailors at the southern base as quickly as possible; the air conditions being apparently highly favourable. We then talked over the personnel of the coming investigation party; and decided that we would include all hands, together with the sledge and dogs which I had kept with me. Even so great a load would not be too much for one of the huge planes built to our especial orders for heavy machinery transportation. At intervals I still tried to reach Lake with the wireless, but all to no purpose.

Sherman, with the sailors Gunnarsson and Larsen, took off at 7:30; and reported a quiet flight from several points on the wing. They arrived at our base at midnight, and all hands at once discussed the next move. It was risky business sailing over the antarctic in a single aëroplane without any line of bases, but no one drew back from what seemed like the plainest necessity. We turned in at two o'clock for a brief rest after some preliminary loading of the plane, but were up again in four hours to finish the loading and packing.

At 7:15 AM, January 25th, we started flying north-westward under McTighe's pilotage with ten men, seven dogs, a sledge, a fuel and food supply, and other items including the plane's wireless outfit. The atmosphere was clear, fairly quiet, and relatively mild in

temperature; and we anticipated very little trouble in reaching the latitude and longitude designated by Lake as the site of his camp. Our apprehensions were over what we might find, or fail to find, at the end of our journey; for silence continued to answer all calls despatched to the camp.

Every incident of that four-and-a-half-hour flight is burned into my recollection because of its crucial position in my life. It marked my loss, at the age of fifty-four, of all that peace and balance which the normal mind possesses through its accustomed conception of external Nature and Nature's laws. Thence forward the ten of us—but the student Danforth and myself above all others—were to face a hideously amplified world of lurking horrors which nothing can erase from our emotions, and which we would refrain from sharing with mankind in general if we could. The newspapers have printed the bulletins we sent from the moving plane; telling of our nonstop course, our two battles with treacherous upper-air gales, our glimpse of the broken surface where Lake had sunk his mid-journey shaft three days before, and our sight of a group of those strange fluffy snow-cylinders noted by Amundsen and Byrd as rolling in the wind across the endless leagues of frozen plateau. There came a point, though, when our sensations could not be conveyed in any words the press would understand; and a later point when we had to adopt an actual rule of strict censorship.

The sailor Larsen was first to spy the jagged line of witch-like cones and pinnacles ahead, and his shouts sent everyone to the windows of the great cabined plane. Despite our speed, they were very slow in gaining prominence; hence we knew that they must be infinitely far off, and visible only because of their abnormal height. Little by little, however, they rose grimly into the western sky; allowing us to distinguish

various bare, bleak, blackish summits, and to catch the curious sense of phantasy which they inspired as seen in the reddish antarctic light against the provocative background of iridescent ice-dust clouds. In the whole spectacle there was a persistent, pervasive hint of stupendous secrecy and potential revelation; as if these stark, nightmare spires marked the pylons of a frightful gateway into forbidden spheres of dream, and complex gulfs of remote time, space, and ultra-dimensionality. I could not help feeling that they were evil things—mountains of madness whose farther slopes looked out over some accursed ultimate abyss. That seething, half-luminous cloud-background held ineffable suggestions of a vague, ethereal *beyondness* far more than terrestrially spatial; and gave appalling reminders of the utter remoteness, separateness, desolation, and aeon-long death of this untrodden and unfathomed austral world.

It was young Danforth who drew our notice to the curious regularities of the higher mountain skyline—regularities like clinging fragments of perfect cubes, which Lake had mentioned in his messages, and which indeed justified his comparison with the dream-like suggestions of primordial temple-ruins on cloudy Asian mountain-tops so subtly and strangely painted by Roerich. There was indeed something hauntingly Roerich-like about this whole unearthly continent of mountainous mystery. I had felt it in October when we first caught sight of Victoria Land, and I felt it afresh now. I felt, too, another wave of uneasy consciousness of Archaean mythical resemblances; of how disturbingly this lethal realm corresponded to the evilly famed plateau of Leng in the primal writings. Mythologists have placed Leng in Central Asia; but the racial memory of man—or of his predecessors—is long, and it may well be that certain tales have come down from

lands and mountains and temples of horror earlier than Asia and earlier than any human world we know. A few daring mystics have hinted at a pre-Pleistocene origin for the fragmentary Pnakotic Manuscripts, and have suggested that the devotees of Tsathoggua were as alien to mankind as Tsathoggua itself. Leng, wherever in space or time it might brood, was not a region I would care to be in or near; nor did I relish the proximity of a world that had ever bred such ambiguous and Archaean monstrosities as those Lake had just mentioned. At the moment I felt sorry that I had ever read the abhorred *Necronomicon,* or talked so much with that unpleasant- ly erudite folklorist Wilmarth at the university.

This mood undoubtedly served to aggravate my reaction to the bizarre mirage which burst upon us from the increasingly opalescent zenith as we drew near the mountains and began to make out the cumulative undulations of the foothills. I had seen dozens of polar mirages during the preceding weeks, some of them quite as uncanny and fantastically vivid as the present sample; but this one had a wholly novel and obscure quality of menacing symbolism, and I shuddered as the seething labyrinth of fabulous walls and towers and minarets loomed out of the troubled ice-vapours above our heads.

The effect was that of a Cyclopean city of no architec- ture known to man or to human imagination, with vast aggregations of night-black masonry embodying mon- strous perversions of geometrical laws and attaining the most grotesque extremes of sinister bizarrerie. There were truncated cones, sometimes terraced or fluted, surmounted by tall cylindrical shafts here and there bulbously enlarged and often capped with tiers of thinnish scalloped discs; and strange, beetling, table- like constructions suggesting piles of multitudinous rectangular slabs or circular plates or five-pointed stars

with each one overlapping the one beneath. There were composite cones and pyramids either alone or surmounting cylinders or cubes or flatter truncated cones and pyramids, and occasional needle-like spires in curious clusters of five. All of these febrile structures seemed knit together by tubular bridges crossing from one to the other at various dizzy heights, and the implied scale of the whole as terrifying and oppressive in its sheer giganticism. The general type of mirage was not unlike some of the wilder forms observed and drawn by the Arctic whaler Scoresby in 1820; but at this time and place, with those dark, unknown mountain peaks soaring stupendously ahead, that anomalous elder-world discovery in our minds, and the pall of probable disaster enveloping the greater part of our expedition, we all seemed to find in it a taint of latent malignity and infinitely evil portent.

I was glad when the mirage began to break up, though in the process the various nightmare turrets and cones assumed distorted temporary forms of even vaster hideousness. As the whole illusion dissolved to churning opalescence we began to look earthward again, and saw that our journey's end was not far off. The unknown mountains ahead rose dizzingly up like a fearsome rampart of giants, their curious regularities shewing with startling clearness even without a field-glass. We were over the lowest foothills now, and could see amidst the snow, ice, and bare patches of their main plateau a couple of darkish spots which we took to be Lake's camp and boring. The higher foothills shot up between five and six miles away, forming a range almost distinct from the terrifying line of more than Himalayan peaks beyond them. At length Ropes—the student who had relieved McTighe at the controls—began to head downward toward the left-hand dark spot whose size marked it as the camp. As he did so, McTighe sent

out the last uncensored wireless message the world was to receive from our expedition.

Everyone, of course, has read the brief and unsatisfying bulletins of the rest of our antarctic sojourn. Some hours after our landing we sent a guarded report of the tragedy we found, and reluctantly announced the wiping out of the whole Lake party by the frightful wind of the preceding day, or of the night before that. Eleven known dead, young Gedney missing. People pardoned our hazy lack of details through realisation of the shock the sad event must have caused us, and believed us when we explained that the mangling action of the wind had rendered all eleven bodies unsuitable for transportation outside. Indeed, I flatter myself that even in the midst of our distress, utter bewilderment, and soul-clutching horror, we scarcely went beyond the truth in any specific instance. The tremendous significance lies in what we dared not tell—what I would not tell now but for the need of warning others off from nameless terrors.

It is a fact that the wind had wrought dreadful havoc. Whether all could have lived through it, even without the other thing, is gravely open to doubt. The storm, with its fury of madly driven ice-particles, must have been beyond anything our expedition had encountered before. One aëroplane shelter—all, it seems, had been left in a far too flimsy and inadequate state—was nearly pulverised; and the derrick at the distant boring was entirely shaken to pieces. The exposed metal of the grounded planes and drilling machinery was bruised into a high polish, and two of the small tents were flattened despite their snow banking. Wooden surfaces left out in the blast were pitted and denuded of paint, and all signs of tracks in the snow were completely obliterated. It is also true that we found none of the Archaean biological objects in a condition to take

outside as a whole. We did gather some minerals from a vast tumbled pile, including several of the greenish soapstone fragments whose odd five-pointed rounding and faint patterns of grouped dots caused so many doubtful comparisons; and some fossil bones, among which were the most typical of the curiously injured specimens.

None of the dogs survived, their hurriedly built snow enclosure near the camp being almost wholly destroyed. The wind may have done that, though the greater breakage on the side next the camp, which was not the windward one, suggests an outward leap or break of the frantic beasts themselves. All three sledges were gone, and we have tried to explain that the wind may have blown them off into the unknown. The drill and ice-melting machinery at the boring were too badly damaged to warrant salvage, so we used them to choke up that subtly disturbing gateway to the past which Lake had blasted. We likewise left at the camp the two most shaken-up of the planes; since our surviving party had only four real pilots—Sherman, Danforth, McTighe, and Ropes—in all, with Danforth in a poor nervous shape to navigate. We brought back all the books, scientific equipment, and other incidentals we could find, though much was rather unaccountably blown away. Spare tents and furs were either missing or badly out of condition.

It was approximately 4 PM, after wide plane cruising had forced us to give Gedney up for lost, that we sent our guarded message to the *Arkham* for relaying; and I think we did well to keep it as calm and non-committal as we succeeded in doing. The most we said about agitation concerned our dogs, whose frantic uneasiness near the biological specimens was to be expected from poor Lake's accounts. We did not mention, I think, their display of the same uneasiness when sniffing

around the queer greenish soapstones and certain other objects in the disordered region; objects including scientific instruments, aëroplanes, and machinery both at the camp and at the boring, whose parts had been loosened, moved, or otherwise tampered with by winds that must have harboured singular curiosity and investigativeness.

About the fourteen biological specimens we were pardonably indefinite. We said that the only ones we discovered were damaged, but that enough was left of them to prove Lake's description wholly and impressively accurate. It was hard work keeping our personal emotions out of this matter—and we did not mention numbers or say exactly how we had found those which we did find. We had by that time agreed not to transmit anything suggesting madness on the part of Lake's men, and it surely looked like madness to find six imperfect monstrosities carefully buried upright in nine-foot snow graves under five-pointed mounds punched over with groups of dots in patterns exactly like those on the queer greenish soapstones dug up from Mesozoic or Tertiary times. The eight perfect specimens mentioned by Lake seemed to have been completely blown away.

We were careful, too, about the public's general peace of mind; hence Danforth and I said little about that frightful trip over the mountains the next day. It was the fact that only a radically lightened plane could possibly cross a range of such height which mercifully limited that scouting tour to the two of us. On our return at 1 AM Danforth was close to hysterics, but kept an admirably stiff upper lip. It took no persuasion to make him promise not to shew our sketches and the other things we brought away in our pockets, not to say anything more to the others than what we had agreed to relay outside, and to hide our camera films for private development later on; so that part of my present story

will be as new to Pabodie, McTighe, Ropes, Sherman, and the rest as it will be to the world in general. Indeed—Danforth is closer mouthed than I; for he saw—or thinks he saw—one thing he will not tell even me.

As all know, our report included a tale of a hard ascent; a confirmation of Lake's opinion that the great peaks are of Archaean slate and other very primal crumpled strata unchanged since at least middle Comanchian times; a conventional comment on the regularity of the clinging cube and rampart formations; a decision that the cave-mouths indicate dissolved calcareous veins; a conjecture that certain slopes and passes would permit of the scaling and crossing of the entire range by seasoned mountaineers; and a remark that the mysterious other side holds a lofty and immense super-plateau as ancient and unchanging as the mountains themselves—20,000 feet in elevation, with grotesque rock formations protruding through a thin glacial layer and with low gradual foothills between the general plateau surface and the sheer precipices of the highest peaks.

This body of data is in every respect true so far as it goes, and it completely satisfied the men at the camp. We laid our absence of sixteen hours—a longer time than our announced flying, landing, reconnoitring, and rock-collecting programme called for—to a long mythical spell of adverse wind conditions; and told truly of our landing on the farther foothills. Fortunately our tale sounded realistic and prosaic enough not to tempt any of the others into emulating our flight. Had any tried to do that, I would have used every ounce of my persuasion to stop them—and I do not know what Danforth would have done. While we were gone, Pabodie, Sherman, Ropes, McTighe, and Williamson had worked like beavers over Lake's two best planes;

fitting them again for use despite the altogether unaccountable juggling of their operative mechanism.

We decided to load all the planes the next morning and start back for our old base as soon as possible. Even though indirect, that was the safest way to work toward McMurdo Sound; for a straight-line flight across the most utterly unknown stretches of the aeon-dead continent would involve many additional hazards. Further exploration was hardly feasible in view of our tragic decimation and the ruin of our drilling machinery; and the doubts and horrors around us—which we did not reveal—made us wish only to escape from this austral world of desolation and brooding madness as swiftly as we could.

As the public knows, our return to the world was accomplished without further disasters. All planes reached the old base on the evening of the next day—January 27th—after a swift nonstop flight; and on the 28th we made McMurdo Sound in two laps, the one pause being very brief, and occasioned by a faulty rudder in the furious wind over the ice-shelf after we had cleared the great plateau. In five days more the *Arkham* and *Miskatonic,* with all hands and equipment on board, were shaking clear of the thickening field ice and working up Ross Sea with the mocking mountains of Victoria Land looming westward against a troubled antarctic sky and twisting the wind's wails into a wide-ranged musical piping which chilled my soul to the quick. Less than a fortnight later we left the last hint of polar land behind us, and thanked heaven that we were clear of a haunted, accursed realm where life and death, space and time, have made black and blasphemous alliances in the unknown epochs since matter first writhed and swam on the planet's scarce-cooled crust.

Since our return we have all constantly worked to

discourage antarctic exploration, and have kept certain doubts and guesses to ourselves with splendid unity and faithfulness. Even young Danforth, with his nervous breakdown, has not flinched or babbled to his doctors—indeed, as I have said, there is one thing he thinks he alone saw which he will not tell even me, though I think it would help his psychological state if he would consent to do so. It might explain and relieve much, though perhaps the thing was no more than the delusive aftermath of an earlier shock. That is the impression I gather after those rare irresponsible moments when he whispers disjointed things to me—things which he repudiates vehemently as soon as he gets a grip on himself again.

It will be hard work deterring others from the great white south, and some of our efforts may directly harm our cause by drawing inquiring notice. We might have known from the first that human curiosity is undying, and that the results we announced would be enough to spur others ahead on the same age-long pursuit of the unknown. Lake's reports of those biological monstrosities had aroused naturalists and palaeontologists to the highest pitch; though we were sensible enough not to shew the detached parts we had taken from the actual buried specimens, or our photographs of those specimens as they were found. We also refrained from shewing the more puzzling of the scarred bones and greenish soapstones; while Danforth and I have closely guarded the pictures we took or drew on the superplateau across the range, and the crumpled things we smoothed, studied in terror, and brought away in our pockets. But now that Starkweather-Moore party is organising, and with a thoroughness far beyond anything our outfit attempted. If not dissuaded, they will get to the innermost nucleus of the antarctic and melt and bore till they bring up that which may end the world we know. So I must break through all reticences

at last—even about that ultimate nameless thing beyond the mountains of madness.

IV

It is only with vast hesitancy and repugnance that I let my mind go back to Lake's camp and what we really found there—and to that other thing beyond the frightened mountain wall. I am constantly tempted to shirk the details, and to let hints stand for actual facts and ineluctable deductions. I hope I have said enough already to let me glide briefly over the rest; the rest, that is, of the horror at the camp. I have told of the wind-ravaged terrain, the damaged shelters, the disarranged machinery, the varied uneasiness of our dogs, the missing sledges and other items, the deaths of men and dogs, the absence of Gedney, and the six insanely buried biological specimens, strangely sound in texture for all their structural injuries, from a world forty million years dead. I do not recall whether I mentioned that upon checking up the canine bodies we found one dog missing. We did not think much about that till later—indeed, only Danforth and I have thought of it at all.

The principal things I have been keeping back relate to the bodies, and to certain subtle points which may or may not lend a hideous and incredible kind of rationale to the apparent chaos. At the time I tried to keep the men's minds off those points; for it was so much simpler—so much more normal—to lay everything to an outbreak of madness on the part of some of Lake's party. From the look of things, that daemon mountain wind must have been enough to drive any man mad in the midst of this centre of all earthly mystery and desolation.

The crowning abnormality, of course, was the condi-

tion of the bodies—men and dogs alike. They had all been in some terrible kind of conflict, and were torn and mangled in fiendish and altogether inexplicable ways. Death, so far as we could judge, had in each case come from strangulation or laceration. The dogs had evidently started the trouble, for the state of their ill-built corral bore witness to its forcible breakage from within. It had been set some distance from the camp because of the hatred of the animals for those hellish Archaean organisms, but the precaution seemed to have been taken in vain. When left alone in that monstrous wind behind flimsy walls of insufficient height they must have stampeded—whether from the wind itself, or from some subtle, increasing odour emitted by the nightmare specimens, one could not say. Those specimens, of course, had been covered with a tent-cloth; yet the low antarctic sun had beat steadily upon that cloth, and Lake had mentioned that solar heat tended to make the strangely sound and tough tissues of the things relax and expand. Perhaps the wind had whipped the cloth from over them, and jostled them about in such a way that their more pungent olfactory qualities became manifest despite their unbelievable antiquity.

But whatever had happened, it was hideous and revolting enough. Perhaps I had better put squeamishness aside and tell the worst at last—though with a categorical statement of opinion, based on the firsthand observations and most rigid deductions of both Danforth and myself, that the then missing Gedney was in no way responsible for the loathsome horrors we found. I have said that the bodies were frightfully mangled. Now I must add that some were incised and subtracted from in the most curious, cold-blooded, and inhuman fashion. It was the same with dogs and men. All the healthier, fatter bodies, quadrupedal or bipedal,

had had their most solid masses of tissue cut out and removed, as by a careful butcher; and around them was a strange sprinkling of salt—taken from the ravaged provision-chests on the planes—which conjured up the most horrible associations. The thing had occurred in one of the crude aëroplane shelters from which the plane had been dragged out, and subsequent winds had effaced all tracks which could have supplied any plausible theory. Scattered bits of clothing, roughly slashed from the human incision-subjects, hinted no clues. It is useless to bring up the half-impression of certain faint snow-prints in one shielded corner of the ruined enclosure—because that impression did not concern human prints at all, but was clearly mixed up with all the talk of fossil prints which poor Lake had been giving throughout the preceding weeks. One had to be careful of one's imagination in the lee of those overshadowing mountains of madness.

As I have indicated, Gedney and one dog turned out to be missing in the end. When we came on that terrible shelter we had missed two dogs and two men; but the fairly unharmed dissecting tent, which we entered after investigating the monstrous graves, had something to reveal. It was not as Lake had left it, for the covered parts of the primal monstrosity had been removed from the improvised table. Indeed, we had already realised that one of the six imperfect and insanely buried things we had found—the one with the trace of a peculiarly hateful odour—must represent the collected sections of the entity which Lake had tried to analyse. On and around that laboratory table were strown other things, and it did not take long for us to guess that those things were the carefully though oddly and inexpertly dissected parts of one man and one dog. I shall spare the feelings of survivors by omitting mention of the man's identity. Lake's anatomical in-

struments were missing, but there were evidences of their careful cleansing. The gasoline stove was also gone, though around it we found a curious litter of matches. We buried the human parts beside the other ten men, and the canine parts with the other 35 dogs. Concerning the bizarre smudges on the laboratory table, and on the jumble of roughly handled illustrated books scattered near it, we were much too bewildered to speculate.

This formed the worst of the camp horror, but other things were equally perplexing. The disappearance of Gedney, the one dog, the eight uninjured biological specimens, the three sledges, and certain instruments, illustrated technical and scientific books, writing materials, electric torches and batteries, food and fuel, heating apparatus, spare tents, fur suits, and the like, was utterly beyond sane conjecture; as were likewise the spatter-fringed ink-blots on certain pieces of paper, and the evidences of curious alien fumbling and experimentation around the planes and all other mechanical devices both at the camp and at the boring. The dogs seemed to abhor this oddly disordered machinery. Then, too, there was the upsetting of the larder, the disappearance of certain staples, and the jarringly comical heap of tin cans pried open in the most unlikely ways and at the most unlikely places. The profusion of scattered matches, intact, broken, or spent, formed another minor enigma; as did the two or three tent-cloths and fur suits which we found lying about with peculiar and unorthodox slashings conceivably due to clumsy efforts at unimaginable adaptations. The maltreatment of the human and canine bodies, and the crazy burial of the damaged Archaean specimens, were all of a piece with this apparent disintegrative madness. In view of just such an eventuality as the present one, we carefully photographed all the main evidences of insane disorder at the camp; and shall use

the prints to buttress our pleas against the departure of the proposed Starkweather-Moore Expedition.

Our first act after finding the bodies in the shelter was to photograph and open the row of insane graves with the five-pointed snow mounds. We could not help noticing the resemblance of these monstrous mounds, with their clusters of grouped dots, to poor Lake's descriptions of the strange greenish soapstones; and when we came on some of the soapstones themselves in the great mineral pile we found the likeness very close indeed. The whole general formation, it must be made clear, seemed abominably suggestive of the starfish-head of the Archaean entities; and we agreed that the suggestion must have worked potently upon the sensitised minds of Lake's overwrought party. Our own first sight of the actual buried entities formed a horrible moment, and sent the imaginations of Pabodie and myself back to some of the shocking primal myths we had read and heard. We all agreed that the mere sight and continued presence of the things must have coöperated with the oppressive polar solitude and daemon mountain wind in driving Lake's party mad.

For madness—centring in Gedney as the only possible surviving agent—was the explanation spontaneously adopted by everybody so far as spoken utterance was concerned; though I will not be so naive as to deny that each of us may have harboured wild guesses which sanity forbade him to formulate completely. Sherman, Pabodie, and McTighe made an exhaustive aëroplane cruise over all the surrounding territory in the afternoon, sweeping the horizon with field-glasses in quest of Gedney and of the various missing things; but nothing came to light. The party reported that the titan barrier range extended endlessly to right and left alike, without any diminution in height or essential structure. On some of the peaks, though, the regular cube and rampart formations were bolder and plainer; having

doubly fantastic similitudes to Roerich-painted Asian hill ruins. The distribution of cryptical cave-mouths on the black snow-denuded summits seemed roughly even as far as the range could be traced.

In spite of all the prevailing horrors we were left with enough sheer scientific zeal and adventurousness to wonder about the unknown realm beyond those mysterious mountains. As our guarded messages stated, we rested at midnight after our day of terror and bafflement; but not without a tentative plan for one or more range-crossing altitude flights in a lightened plane with aërial camera and geologist's outfit, beginning the following morning. It was decided that Danforth and I try it first, and we awaked at 7 AM intending an early trip; though heavy winds—mentioned in our brief bulletin to the outside world—delayed our start till nearly nine o'clock.

I have already repeated the non-committal story we told the men at camp—and relayed outside—after our return sixteen hours later. It is now my terrible duty to amplify this account by filling in the merciful blanks with hints of what we really saw in the hidden transmontane world—hints of the revelations which have finally driven Danforth to a nervous collapse. I wish he would add a really frank word about the thing which he thinks he alone saw—even though it was probably a nervous delusion—and which was perhaps the last straw that put him where he is; but he is firm against that. All I can do is to repeat his later disjointed whispers about what set him shrieking as the plane soared back through the wind-tortured mountain pass after that real and tangible shock which I shared. This will form my last word. If the plain signs of surviving elder horrors in what I disclose be not enough to keep others from meddling with the inner antarctic—or at least from prying too deeply beneath the surface of that

ultimate waste of forbidden secrets and unhuman, aeon-cursed desolation—the responsibility for unnamable and perhaps immensurable evils will not be mine.

Danforth and I, studying the notes made by Pabodie in his afternoon flight and checking up with a sextant, had calculated that the lowest available pass in the range lay somewhat to the right of us, within sight of camp, and about 23,000 or 24,000 feet above sea-level. For this point, then, we first headed in the lightened plane as we embarked on our flight of discovery. The camp itself, on foothills which sprang from a high continental plateau, was some 12,000 feet in altitude; hence the actual height increase necessary was not so vast as it might seem. Nevertheless we were acutely conscious of the rarefied air and intense cold as we rose; for on account of visibility conditions we had to leave the cabin windows open. We were dressed, of course, in our heaviest furs.

As we drew near the forbidding peaks, dark and sinister above the line of crevasse-riven snow and interstitial glaciers, we noticed more and more the curiously regular formations clinging to the slopes; and thought again of the strange Asian paintings of Nicholas Roerich. The ancient and wind-weathered rock strata fully verified all of Lake's bulletins, and proved that these hoary pinnacles had been towering up in exactly the same way since a surprisingly early time in earth's history—perhaps over fifty million years. How much higher they had once been, it was futile to guess; but everything about this strange region pointed to obscure atmospheric influences unfavourable to change, and calculated to retard the usual climatic processes of rock disintegration.

But it was the mountainside tangle of regular cubes, ramparts, and cave-mouths which fascinated and disturbed us most. I studied them with a field-glass and

took aërial photographs whilst Danforth drove; and at times relieved him at the controls—though my aviation knowledge was purely an amateur's—in order to let him use the binoculars. We could easily see that much of the material of the things was a lightish Archaean quartzite, unlike any formation visible over broad areas of the general surface; and that their regularity was extreme and uncanny to an extent which poor Lake had scarcely hinted.

As he had said, their edges were crumbled and rounded from untold aeons of savage weathering; but their preternatural solidity and tough material had saved them from obliteration. Many parts, especially those closest to the slopes, seemed identical in substance with the surrounding rock surface. The whole arrangement looked like the ruins of Machu Picchu in the Andes, or the primal foundation-walls of Kish as dug up by the Oxford–Field Museum Expedition in 1929; and both Danforth and I obtained that occasional impression of *separate Cyclopean blocks* which Lake had attributed to his flight-companion Carroll. How to account for such things in this place was frankly beyond me, and I felt queerly humbled as a geologist. Igneous formations often have strange regularities— like the famous Giants' Causeway in Ireland—but this stupendous range, despite Lake's original suspicion of smoking cones, was above all else non-volcanic in evident structure.

The curious cave-mouths, near which the odd formations seemed most abundant, presented another albeit a lesser puzzle because of their regularity of outline. They were, as Lake's bulletin had said, often approximately square or semicircular; as if the natural orifices had been shaped to greater symmetry by some magic hand. Their numerousness and wide distribution were remarkable, and suggested that the whole region was

honeycombed with tunnels dissolved out of limestone strata. Such glimpses as we secured did not extend far within the caverns, but we saw that they were apparently clear of stalactites and stalagmites. Outside, those parts of the mountain slopes adjoining the apertures seemed invariably smooth and regular; and Danforth thought that the slight cracks and pittings of the weathering tended toward unusual patterns. Filled as he was with the horrors and strangenesses discovered at the camp, he hinted that the pittings vaguely resembled those baffling groups of dots sprinkled over the prime-val greenish soapstones, so hideously duplicated on the madly conceived snow mounds above those six buried monstrosities.

We had risen gradually in flying over the higher foothills and along toward the relatively low pass we had selected. As we advanced we occasionally looked down at the snow and ice of the land route, wondering whether we could have attempted the trip with the simpler equipment of earlier days. Somewhat to our surprise we saw that the terrain was far from difficult as such things go; and that despite the crevasses and other bad spots it would not have been likely to deter the sledges of a Scott, a Shackleton, or an Amundsen. Some of the glaciers appeared to lead up to wind-bared passes with unusual continuity, and upon reaching our chosen pass we found that its case formed no exception.

Our sensations of tense expectancy as we prepared to round the crest and peer out over an untrodden world can hardly be described on paper; even though we had no cause to think the regions beyond the range essen-tially different from those already seen and traversed. The tough of evil mystery in these barrier mountains, and in the beckoning sea of opalescent sky glimpsed betwixt their summits, was a highly subtle and attenu-ated matter not to be explained in literal words. Rather

was it an affair of vague psychological symbolism and aesthetic association—a thing mixed up with exotic poetry and paintings, and with archaic myths lurking in shunned and forbidden volumes. Even the wind's burden held a peculiar strain of conscious malignity; and for a second it seemed that the composite sound included a bizarre musical whistling or piping over a wide range as the blast swept in and out of the omnipresent and resonant cave-mouths. There was a cloudy note of reminiscent repulsion in this sound, as complex and unplaceable as any of the other dark impressions.

We were now, after a slow ascent, at a height of 23,570 feet according to the aneroid; and had left the region of clinging snow definitely below us. Up here were only dark, bare rock slopes and the start of rough-ribbed glaciers—but with those provocative cubes, ramparts, and echoing cave-mouths to add a portent of the unnatural, the fantastic, and the dream-like. Looking along the line of high peaks, I thought I could see the one mentioned by poor Lake, with a rampart exactly on top. It seemed to be half-lost in a queer antarctic haze; such a haze, perhaps, as had been responsible for Lake's early notion of volcanism. The pass loomed directly before us, smooth and windswept between its jagged and malignly frowning pylons. Beyond it was a sky fretted with swirling vapours and lighted by the low polar sun—the sky of that mysterious farther realm upon which we felt no human eye had ever gazed.

A few more feet of altitude and we would behold that realm. Danforth and I, unable to speak except in shouts amidst the howling, piping wind that raced through the pass and added to the noise of the unmuffled engines, exchanged eloquent glances. And then, having gained those last few feet, we did indeed stare across the

momentous divide and over the unsampled secrets of an elder and utterly alien earth.

V

I think that both of us simultaneously cried out in mixed awe, wonder, terror, and disbelief in our own senses as we finally cleared the pass and saw what lay beyond. Of course we must have had some natural theory in the back of our heads to steady our faculties for the moment. Probably we thought of such things as the grotesquely weathered stones of the Garden of the Gods in Colorado, or the fantastically symmetrical wind-carved rocks of the Arizona desert. Perhaps we even half thought the sight a mirage like that we had seen the morning before on first approaching those mountains of madness. We must have had some such normal notions to fall back upon as our eyes swept that limitless, tempest-scarred plateau and grasped the almost endless labyrinth of colossal, regular, and geometrically eurhythmic stone masses which reared their crumbled and pitted crests above a glacial sheet not more than forty or fifty feet deep at its thickest, and in places obviously thinner.

The effect of the monstrous sight was indescribable, for some fiendish violation of known natural law seemed certain at the outset. Here, on a hellishly ancient table-land fully 20,000 feet high, and in a climate deadly to habitation since a pre-human age not less than 500,000 years ago, there stretched nearly to the vision's limit a tangle of orderly stone which only the desperation of mental self-defence could possibly attribute to any but a conscious and artificial cause. We had previously dismissed, so far as serious thought was concerned, any theory that the cubes and ramparts of

the mountainsides were other than natural in origin. How could they be otherwise, when man himself could scarcely have been differentiated from the great apes at the time when this region succumbed to the present unbroken reign of glacial death?

Yet now the sway of reason seemed irrefutably shaken, for this Cyclopean maze of squared, curved, and angled blocks had features which cut off all comfortable refuge. It was, very clearly, the blasphemous city of the mirage in stark, objective, and ineluctable reality. That damnable portent had had a material basis after all—there had been some horizontal stratum of ice-dust in the upper air, and this shocking stone survival had projected its image across the mountains according to the simple laws of reflection. Of course the phantom had been twisted and exaggerated, and had contained things which the real source did not contain; yet now, as we saw that real source, we thought it even more hideous and menacing than its distant image.

Only the incredible, unhuman massiveness of these vast stone towers and ramparts had saved the frightful thing from utter annihilation in the hundreds of thousands—perhaps millions—of years it had brooded there amidst the blasts of a bleak upland. "Corona Mundi . . . Roof of the World . . ." All sorts of fantastic phrases sprang to our lips as we looked dizzily down at the unbelievable spectacle. I thought again of the eldritch primal myths that had so persistently haunted me since my first sight of this dead antarctic world—of the daemoniac plateau of Leng, of the Mi-Go, or Abominable Snow-Men of the Himalayas, of the Pnakotic Manuscripts with their pre-human implications, of the Cthulhu cult, of the *Necronomicon*, and of the Hyperborean legends of formless Tsathoggua and the worse than formless star-spawn associated with that semi-entity.

For boundless miles in every direction the thing stretched off with very little thinning; indeed, as our eyes followed it to the right and left along the base of the low, gradual foothills which separated it from the actual mountain rim, we decided that we could see no thinning at all except for an interruption at the left of the pass through which we had come. We had merely struck, at random, a limited part of something of incalculable extent. The foothills were more sparsely sprinkled with grotesque stone structures, linking the terrible city to the already familiar cubes and ramparts which evidently formed its mountain outposts. These latter, as well as the queer cave-mouths, were as thick on the inner as on the outer sides of the mountains.

The nameless stone labyrinth consisted, for the most part, of walls from 10 to 150 feet in ice-clear height, and of a thickness varying from five to ten feet. It was composed mostly of prodigious blocks of dark primordial slate, schist, and sandstone—blocks in many cases as large as $4 \times 6 \times 8$ feet—though in several places it seemed to be carved out of a solid, uneven bed-rock of pre-Cambrian slate. The buildings were far from equal in size; there being innumerable honeycomb-arrangements of enormous extent as well as smaller separate structures. The general shape of these things tended to be conical, pyramidal, or terraced; though there were many perfect cylinders, perfect cubes, clusters of cubes, and other rectangular forms, and a peculiar sprinkling of angled edifices whose five-pointed ground plan roughly suggested modern fortifications. The builders had made constant and expert use of the principle of the arch, and domes had probably existed in the city's heyday.

The whole tangle was monstrously weathered, and the glacial surface from which the towers projected was strown with fallen blocks and immemorial debris.

Where the glaciation was transparent we could see the lower parts of the gigantic piles, and noticed the ice-preserved stone bridges which connected the different towers at varying distances above the ground. On the exposed walls we could detect the scarred places where other and higher bridges of the same sort had existed. Closer inspection revealed countless largish windows; some of which were closed with shutters of a petrified material originally wood, though most gaped open in a sinister and menacing fashion. Many of the ruins, of course, were roofless, and with uneven though wind-rounded upper edges; whilst others, of a more sharply conical or pyramidal model or else protected by higher surrounding structures, preserved intact outlines despite the omnipresent crumbling and pitting. With the field-glass we could barely make out what seemed to be sculptural decorations in horizontal bands—decorations including those curious groups of dots whose presence on the ancient soapstones now assumed a vastly larger significance.

In many places the buildings were totally ruined and the ice-sheet deeply riven from various geologic causes. In other places the stonework was worn down to the very level of the glaciation. One broad swath, extending from the plateau's interior to a cleft in the foothills about a mile to the left of the pass we had traversed, was wholly free from buildings; and probably represented, we concluded, the course of some great river which in Tertiary times—millions of years ago—had poured through the city and into some prodigious subterranean abyss of the great barrier range. Certainly, this was above all a region of caves, gulfs, and underground secrets beyond human penetration.

Looking back to our sensations, and recalling our dazedness at viewing this monstrous survival from aeons we had thought pre-human, I can only wonder

that we preserved the semblance of equilibrium which we did. Of course we knew that something—chronology, scientific theory, or our own consciousness—was woefully awry; yet we kept enough poise to guide the plane, observe many things quite minutely, and take a careful series of photographs which may yet serve both us and the world in good stead. In my case, ingrained scientific habit may have helped; for above all my bewilderment and sense of menace there burned a dominant curiosity to fathom more of this age-old secret—to know what sort of beings had built and lived in this incalculably gigantic place, and what relation to the general world of its time or of other times so unique a concentration of life could have had.

For this place could be no ordinary city. It must have formed the primary nucleus and centre of some archaic and unbelievable chapter of earth's history whose outward ramifications, recalled only dimly in the most obscure and distorted myths, had vanished utterly amidst the chaos of terrene convulsions long before any human race we know had shambled out of apedom. Here sprawled a palaeogean megalopolis compared with which the fabled Atlantis and Lemuria, Commoriom and Uzuldaroum, and Olathoë in the land of Lomar are recent things of today—not even of yesterday; a megalopolis ranking with such whispered pre-human blasphemies as Valusia, R'lyeh, Ib in the land of Mnar, and the Nameless City of Arabia Deserta. As we flew above that tangle of stark titan towers my imagination sometimes escaped all bounds and roved aimlessly in realms of fantastic associations—even weaving links betwixt this lost world and some of my own wildest dreams concerning the mad horror at the camp.

The plane's fuel-tank, in the interest of greater lightness, had been only partly filled; hence we now had to

exert caution in our explorations. Even so, however, we covered an enormous extent of ground—or rather, air—after swooping down to a level where the wind became virtually negligible. There seemed to be no limit to the mountain-range, or to the length of the frightful stone city which bordered its inner foothills. Fifty miles of flight in each direction shewed no major change in the labyrinth of rock and masonry that clawed up corpse-like through the eternal ice. There were, though, some highly absorbing diversifications; such as the carvings on the canyon where that broad river had once pierced the foothills and approached its sinking-place in the great range. The headlands at the stream's entrance had been boldly carved into Cyclopean pylons; and something about the ridgy, barrel-shaped designs stirred up oddly vague, hateful, and confusing semi-remembrances in both Danforth and me.

We also came upon several star-shaped open spaces, evidently public squares; and noted various undulations in the terrain. Where a sharp hill rose, it was generally hollowed out into some sort of rambling stone edifice; but there were at least two exceptions. Of these latter, one was too badly weathered to disclose what had been on the jutting eminence, while the other still bore a fantastic conical monument carved out of the solid rock and roughly resembling such things as the well-known Snake Tomb in the ancient valley of Petra.

Flying inland from the mountains, we discovered that the city was not of infinite width, even though its length along the foothills seemed endless. After about thirty miles the grotesque stone buildings began to thin out, and in ten more miles we came to an unbroken waste virtually without signs of sentient artifice. The course of the river beyond the city seemed marked by a broad depressed line; while the land assumed a some-

what greater ruggedness, seeming to slope slightly upward as it receded in the mist-hazed west.

So far we had made no landing, yet to leave the plateau without an attempt at entering some of the monstrous structures would have been inconceivable. Accordingly we decided to find a smooth place on the foothills near our navigable pass, there grounding the plane and preparing to do some exploration on foot. Though these gradual slopes were partly covered with a scattering of ruins, low flying soon disclosed an ample number of possible landing-places. Selecting that nearest to the pass, since our next flight would be across the great range and back to camp, we succeeded about 12:30 PM in coming down on a smooth, hard snowfield wholly devoid of obstacles and well adapted to a swift and favourable takeoff later on.

It did not seem necessary to protect the plane with a snow banking for so brief a time and in so comfortable an absence of high winds at this level; hence we merely saw that the landing skis were safely lodged, and that the vital parts of the mechanism were guarded against the cold. For our foot journey we discarded the heaviest of our flying furs, and took with us a small outfit consisting of pocket compass, hand camera, light provisions, voluminous notebooks and paper, geologist's hammer and chisel, specimen-bags, coil of climbing rope, and powerful electric torches with extra batteries; this equipment having been carried in the plane on the chance that we might be able to effect a landing, take ground pictures, make drawings and topographical sketches, and obtain rock specimens from some bare slope, outcropping, or mountain cave. Fortunately we had a supply of extra paper to tear up, place in a spare specimen-bag, and use on the ancient principle of hare-and-hounds for marking our course in any interior mazes we might be able to penetrate. This had been

brought in case we found some cave system with air quiet enough to allow such a rapid and easy method in place of the usual rock-chipping method of trail-blazing.

Walking cautiously downhill over the crusted snow toward the stupendous stone labyrinth that loomed against the opalescent west, we felt almost as keen a sense of imminent marvels as we had felt on approaching the unfathomed mountain pass four hours previously. True, we had become visually familiar with the incredible secret concealed by the barrier peaks; yet the prospect of actually entering primordial walls reared by conscious beings perhaps millions of years ago—before any known race of men could have existed—was none the less awesome and potentially terrible in its implications of cosmic abnormality. Though the thinness of the air at this prodigious altitude made exertion somewhat more difficult than usual, both Danforth and I found ourselves bearing up very well, and felt equal to almost any task which might fall to our lot. It took only a few steps to bring us to a shapeless ruin worn level with the snow, while ten or fifteen rods farther on there was a huge roofless rampart still complete in its gigantic five-pointed outline and rising to an irregular height of ten or eleven feet. For this latter we headed; and when at last we were able actually to touch its weathered Cyclopean blocks, we felt that we had established an unprecedented and almost blasphemous link with forgotten aeons normally closed to our species.

This rampart, shaped like a star and perhaps 300 feet from point to point, was built of Jurassic sandstone blocks of irregular size, averaging 6 × 8 feet in surface. There was a row of arched loopholes or windows about four feet wide and five feet high; spaced quite symmetrically along the points of the star and at its inner angles, and with the bottoms about four feet from the

glaciated surface. Looking through these, we could see that the masonry was fully five feet thick, that there were no partitions remaining within, and that there were traces of banded carvings or bas-reliefs on the interior walls; facts we had indeed guessed before, when flying low over this rampart and others like it. Though lower parts must have originally existed, all traces of such things were now wholly obscured by the deep layer of ice and snow at this point.

We crawled through one of the windows and vainly tried to decipher the nearly effaced mural designs, but did not attempt to disturb the glaciated floor. Our orientation flights had indicated that many buildings in the city proper were less ice-choked, and that we might perhaps find wholly clear interiors leading down to the true ground level if we entered those structures still roofed at the top. Before we left the rampart we photographed it carefully, and studied its mortarless Cyclopean masonry with complete bewilderment. We wished that Pabodie were present, for his engineering knowledge might have helped us guess how such titanic blocks could have been handled in that unbelievably remote age when the city and its outskirts were built up.

The half-mile walk downhill to the actual city, with the upper wind shrieking vainly and savagely through the skyward peaks in the background, was something whose smallest details will always remain engraved on my mind. Only in fantastic nightmares could any human beings but Danforth and me conceive such optical effects. Between us and the churning vapours of the west lay that monstrous tangle of dark stone towers; its outré and incredible forms impressing us afresh at every new angle of vision. It was a mirage in solid stone, and were it not for the photographs I would still doubt that such a thing could be. The general type of masonry was identical with that of the rampart we had

examined; but the extravagant shapes which this masonry took in its urban manifestations were past all description.

Even the pictures illustrate only one or two phases of its infinite bizarrerie, endless variety, preternatural massiveness, and utterly alien exoticism. There were geometrical forms for which an Euclid could scarcely find a name—cones of all degrees of irregularity and truncation; terraces of every sort of provocative disproportion; shafts with odd bulbous enlargements; broken columns in curious groups; and five-pointed or five-ridged arrangements of mad grotesqueness. As we drew nearer we could see beneath certain transparent parts of the ice-sheet, and detect some of the tubular stone bridges that connected the crazily sprinkled structures at various heights. Of orderly streets there seemed to be none, the only broad open swath being a mile to the left, where the ancient river had doubtless flowed through the town into the mountains.

Our field-glasses shewed the external horizontal bands of nearly effaced sculptures and dot-groups to be very prevalent, and we could half imagine what the city must once have looked like—even though most of the roofs and tower-tops had necessarily perished. As a whole, it had been a complex tangle of twisted lanes and alleys; all of them deep canyons, and some little better than tunnels because of the overhanging masonry or overarching bridges. Now, outspread below us, it loomed like a dream-phantasy against a westward mist through whose northern end the low, reddish antarctic sun of early afternoon was struggling to shine; and when for a moment that sun encountered a denser obstruction and plunged the scene into temporary shadow, the effect was subtly menacing in a way I can never hope to depict. Even the faint howling and piping of the unfelt wind in the great mountain passes behind us took on a wilder note of purposeful malignity. The

last stage of our descent to the town was unusually steep and abrupt, and a rock outcropping at the edge where the grade changed led us to think that an artificial terrace had once existed there. Under the glaciation, we believed, there must be a flight of steps or its equivalent.

When at last we plunged into the labyrinthine town itself, clambering over fallen masonry and shrinking from the oppressive nearness and dwarfing height of omnipresent crumbling and pitted walls, our sensations again became such that I marvel at the amount of self-control we retained. Danforth was frankly jumpy, and began making some offensively irrelevant speculations about the horror at the camp—which I resented all the more because I could not help sharing certain conclusions forced upon us by many features of this morbid survival from nightmare antiquity. The speculations worked on his imagination, too; for in one place—where a debris-littered alley turned a sharp corner—he insisted that he saw faint traces of ground markings which he did not like; whilst elsewhere he stopped to listen to a subtle imaginary sound from some undefined point—a muffled musical piping, he said, not unlike that of the wind in the mountain caves yet somehow disturbingly different. The ceaseless *five-pointedness* of the surrounding architecture and of the few distinguishable mural arabesques had a dimly sinister suggestiveness we could not escape; and gave us a touch of terrible subconscious certainty concerning the primal entities which had reared and dwelt in this unhallowed place.

Nevertheless our scientific and adventurous souls were not wholly dead; and we mechanically carried out our programme of chipping specimens from all the different rock types represented in the masonry. We wished a rather full set in order to draw better conclusions regarding the age of the place. Nothing in the

great outer walls seemed to date from later than the Jurassic and Comanchian periods, nor was any piece of stone in the entire place of a greater recency than the Pliocene age. In stark certainty, we were wandering amidst a death which had reigned at least 500,000 years, and in all probability even longer.

As we proceeded through this maze of stone-shadowed twilight we stopped at all available apertures to study interiors and investigate entrance possibilities. Some were above our reach, whilst others led only into ice-choked ruins as unroofed and barren as the rampart on the hill. One, though spacious and inviting, opened on a seemingly bottomless abyss without visible means of descent. Now and then we had a chance to study the petrified wood of a surviving shutter, and were impressed by the fabulous antiquity implied in the still discernible grain. These things had come from Mesozoic gymnosperms and conifers—especially Cretaceous cycads—and from fan-palms and early angiosperms of plainly Tertiary date. Nothing definitely later than the Pliocene could be discovered. In the placing of these shutters—whose edges shewed the former presence of queer and long-vanished hinges—usage seemed to be varied; some being on the outer and some on the inner side of the deep embrasures. They seemed to have become wedged in place, thus surviving the rusting of their former and probably metallic fixtures and fastenings.

After a time we came across a row of windows—in the bulges of a colossal five-ridged cone of undamaged apex—which led into a vast, well-preserved room with stone flooring; but these were too high in the room to permit of descent without a rope. We had a rope with us, but did not wish to bother with this twenty-foot drop unless obliged to—especially in this thin plateau air where great demands were made upon the heart

action. This enormous room was probably a hall or concourse of some sort, and our electric torches shewed bold, distinct, and potentially startling sculptures arranged round the walls in broad, horizontal bands separated by equally broad strips of conventional arabesques. We took careful note of this spot, planning to enter here unless a more easily gained interior were encountered.

Finally, though, we did encounter exactly the opening we wished; an archway about six feet wide and ten feet high, marking the former end of an aërial bridge which had spanned an alley about five feet above the present level of glaciation. These archways, of course, were flush with upper-story floors; and in this case one of the floors still existed. The building thus accessible was a series of rectangular terraces on our left facing westward. That across the alley, where the other archway yawned, was a decrepit cylinder with no windows and with a curious bulge about ten feet above the aperture. It was totally dark inside, and the archway seemed to open on a well of illimitable emptiness.

Heaped debris made the entrance to the vast left-hand building doubly easy, yet for a moment we hesitated before taking advantage of the long-wished chance. For though we had penetrated into this tangle of archaic mystery, it required fresh resolution to carry us actually inside a complete and surviving building of a fabulous elder world whose nature was becoming more and more hideously plain to us. In the end, however, we made the plunge; and scrambled up over the rubble into the gaping embrasure. The floor beyond was of great slate slabs, and seemed to form the outlet of a long, high corridor with sculptured walls.

Observing the many inner archways which led off from it, and realising the probable complexity of the nest of apartments within, we decided that we must

begin our system of hare-and-hound trail-blazing. Hitherto our compasses, together with frequent glimpses of the vast mountain-range between the towers in our rear, had been enough to prevent our losing our way; but from now on, the artificial substitute would be necessary. Accordingly we reduced our extra paper to shreds of suitable size, placed these in a bag to be carried by Danforth, and prepared to use them as economically as safety would allow. This method would probably gain us immunity from straying, since there did not appear to be any strong air-currents inside the primordial masonry. If such should develop, or if our paper supply should give out, we could of course fall back on the more secure though more tedious and retarding method of rock-chipping.

Just how extensive a territory we had opened up, it was impossible to guess without a trial. The close and frequent connexion of the different buildings made it likely that we might cross from one to another on bridges underneath the ice except where impeded by local collapses and geologic rifts, for very little glaciation seemed to have entered the massive constructions. Almost all the areas of transparent ice had revealed the submerged windows as tightly shuttered, as if the town had been left in that uniform state until the glacial sheet came to crystallise the lower part for all succeeding time. Indeed, one gained a curious impression that this place had been deliberately closed and deserted in some dim, bygone aeon, rather than overwhelmed by any sudden calamity or even gradual decay. Had the coming of the ice been foreseen, and had a nameless population left en masse to seek a less doomed abode? The precise physiographic conditions attending the formation of the ice-sheet at this point would have to wait for later solution. It had not, very plainly, been a grinding drive. Perhaps the pressure of accumulated

snows had been responsible; and perhaps some flood from the river, or from the bursting of some ancient glacial dam in the great range, had helped to create the special state now observable. Imagination could conceive almost anything in connexion with this place.

VI

It would be cumbrous to give a detailed, consecutive account of our wanderings inside that cavernous, aeon-dead honeycomb of primal masonry; that monstrous lair of elder secrets which now echoed for the first time, after uncounted epochs, to the tread of human feet. This is especially true because so much of the horrible drama and revelation came from a mere study of the omnipresent mural carvings. Our flashlight photographs of those carvings will do much toward proving the truth of what we are now disclosing, and it is lamentable that we had not a larger film supply with us. As it was, we made crude notebook sketches of certain salient features after all our films were used up.

The building which we had entered was one of great size and elaborateness, and gave us an impressive notion of the architecture of that nameless geologic past. The inner partitions were less massive than the outer walls, but on the lower levels were excellently preserved. Labyrinthine complexity, involving curiously irregular differences in floor levels, characterised the entire arrangement; and we should certainly have been lost at the very outset but for the trail of torn paper left behind us. We decided to explore the more decrepit upper parts first of all, hence climbed aloft in the maze for a distance of some 100 feet, to where the topmost tier of chambers yawned snowily and ruinously open to the polar sky. Ascent was effected over the steep,

transversely ribbed stone ramps or inclined planes which everywhere served in lieu of stairs. The rooms we encountered were of all imaginable shapes and proportions, ranging from five-pointed stars to triangles and perfect cubes. It might be safe to say that their general average was about 30 × 30 feet in floor area, and 20 feet in height; though many larger apartments existed. After thoroughly examining the upper regions and the glacial level we descended story by story into the submerged part, where indeed we soon saw we were in a continuous maze of connected chambers and passages probably leading over unlimited areas outside this particular building. The Cyclopean massiveness and giganticism of everything about us became curiously oppressive; and there was something vaguely but deeply unhuman in all the contours, dimensions, proportions, decorations, and constructional nuances of the blasphemously archive stonework. We soon realised from what the carvings revealed that this monstrous city was many million years old.

We cannot yet explain the engineering principles used in the anomalous balancing and adjustment of the vast rock masses though the function of the arch was clearly much relied on. The rooms we visited were wholly bare of all portable contents, a circumstance which sustained our belief in the city's deliberate desertion. The prime decorative feature was the almost universal system of mural sculpture; which tended to run in continuous horizontal bands three feet wide and arranged from floor to ceiling in alternation with bands of equal width given over to geometrical arabesques. There were exceptions to this rule of arrangement, but its preponderance was overwhelming. Often, however, a series of smooth cartouches containing oddly patterned groups of dots would be sunk along one of the arabesque bands.

The technique, we soon saw, was mature, accomplished, and aesthetically evolved to the highest degree of civilised mastery though utterly alien in every detail to any known art tradition of the human race. In delicacy of execution no sculpture I have ever seen could approach it. The minutest details of elaborate vegetation, or of animal life, were rendered with astonishing vividness despite the bold scale of the carvings; whilst the conventional designs were marvels of skilful intricacy. The arabesques displayed a profound use of mathematical principles, and were made up of obscurely symmetrical curves and angles based on the quantity of five. The pictorial bands followed a highly formalised tradition, and involved a peculiar treatment of perspective; but had an artistic force that moved us profoundly notwithstanding the intervening gulf of vast geologic periods. Their method of design hinged on a singular juxtaposition of the cross-section with the two-dimensional silhouette, and embodied an analytical psychology beyond that of any known race of antiquity. It is useless to try to compare this art with any represented in our museums. Those who see our photographs will probably find its closest analogue in certain grotesque conceptions of the most daring futurists.

The arabesque tracery consisted altogether of depressed lines whose depth on unweathered walls varied from one to two inches. When cartouches with dot-groups appeared—evidently as inscriptions in some unknown and primordial language and alphabet—the depression of the smooth surface was perhaps an inch and a half, and of the dots perhaps a half-inch more. The pictorial bands were in counter-sunk low relief, their background being depressed about two inches from the original wall surface. In some specimens marks of former colouration could be detected, though

for the most part untold aeons had disintegrated and banished any pigments which may have been applied. The more one studied the marvellous technique the more one admired the things. Beneath their strict conventionalisation one could grasp the minute and accurate observation and graphic skill of the artists; and indeed, the very conventions themselves served to symbolise and accentuate the real essence of vital differentiation of every object delineated. We felt, too, that besides these recognisable excellences there were others lurking beyond the reach of our perceptions. Certain touches here and there gave vague hints of latent symbols and stimuli which another mental and emotional background, and a fuller or different sensory equipment, might have made of profound and poignant significance to us.

The subject-matter of the sculptures obviously came from the life of the vanished epoch of their creation, and contained a large proportion of evident history. It is this abnormal historic-mindedness of the primal race—a chance circumstance operating, through coincidence, miraculously in our favour—which made the carvings so awesomely informative to us, and which caused us to place their photography and transcription above all other considerations. In certain rooms the dominant arrangement was varied by the presence of maps, astronomical charts, and other scientific designs on an enlarged scale—these things giving a naive and terrible corroboration to what we gathered from the pictorial friezes and dadoes. In hinting at what the whole revealed, I can only hope that my account will not arouse a curiosity greater than sane caution on the part of those who believe me at all. It would be tragic if any were to be allured to that realm of death and horror by the very warning meant to discourage them.

Interrupting these sculptured walls were high win-

dows and massive twelve-foot doorways; both now and then retaining the petrified wooden planks—elaborately carved and polished—of the actual shutters and doors. All metal fixtures had long ago vanished, but some of the doors remained in place and had to be forced aside as we progressed from room to room. Window-frames with odd transparent panes—mostly elliptical—survived here and there, though in no considerable quantity. There were also frequent niches of great magnitude, generally empty, but once in a while containing some bizarre object carved from green soapstone which was either broken or perhaps held too inferior to warrant removal. Other apertures were undoubtedly connected with bygone mechanical facilities—heating, lighting, and the like—of a sort suggested in many of the carvings. Ceilings tended to be plain, but had sometimes been inlaid with green soapstone or other tiles, mostly fallen now. Floors were also paved with such tiles, though plain stonework predominated.

As I have said, all furniture and other moveables were absent; but the sculptures gave a clear idea of the strange devices which had once filled these tomb-like, echoing rooms. Above the glacial sheet the floors were generally thick with detritus, litter, and debris; but farther down this condition decreased. In some of the lower chambers and corridors there was little more than gritty dust or ancient incrustations, while occasional areas had an uncanny air of newly swept immaculateness. Of course, where rifts or collapses had occurred, the lower levels were as littered as the upper ones. A central court—as in other structures we had seen from the air—saved the inner regions from total darkness; so that we seldom had to use our electric torches in the upper rooms except when studying sculptured details. Below the ice-cap, however, the

twilight deepened; and in many parts of the tangled ground level there was an approach to absolute blackness.

To form even a rudimentary idea of our thoughts and feelings as we penetrated this aeon-silent maze of unhuman masonry one must correlate a hopelessly bewildering chaos of fugitive moods, memories, and impressions. The sheer appalling antiquity and lethal desolation of the place were enough to overwhelm almost any sensitive person, but added to these elements were the recent unexplained horror at the camp, and the revelations all too soon effected by the terrible mural sculptures around us. The moment we came upon a perfect section of carving, where no ambiguity of interpretation could exist, it took only a brief study to give us the hideous truth—a truth which it would be naive to claim Danforth and I had not independently suspected before, though we had carefully refrained from even hinting it to each other. There could now be no further merciful doubt about the nature of the beings which had built and inhabited this monstrous dead city millions of years ago, when man's ancestors were primitive archaic mammals, and vast dinosaurs roamed the tropical steppes of Europe and Asia.

We had previously clung to a desperate alternative and insisted—each to himself—that the omnipresence of the five-pointed motif meant only some cultural or religious exaltation of the Archaean natural object which had so patently embodied the quality of five-pointedness; as the decorative motifs of Minoan Crete exalted the sacred bull, those of Egypt the scarabaeus, those of Rome the wolf and the eagle, and those of various savage tribes some chosen totem-animal. But this lone refuge was now stripped from us, and we were forced to face definitely the reason-shaking realisation which the reader of these pages has doubtless long ago

anticipated. I can scarcely bear to write it down in black and white even now, but perhaps that will not be necessary.

The things once rearing and dwelling in this frightful masonry in the age of dinosaurs were not indeed dinosaurs, but far worse. Mere dinosaurs were new and almost brainless objects—but the builders of the city were wise and old, and had left certain traces in rocks even then laid down well-nigh a thousand million years . . . rocks laid down before the true life of earth had advanced beyond plastic groups of cells . . . rocks laid down before the true life of earth had existed at all. They were the makers and enslavers of that life, and above all doubt the originals of the fiendish elder myths which things like the Pnakotic Manuscripts and the *Necronomicon* affrightedly hint about. They were the Great Old Ones that had filtered down from the stars when earth was young—the beings whose substance an alien evolution had shaped, and whose powers were such as this planet had never bred. And to think that only the day before Danforth and I had actually looked upon fragments of their millennially fossilised substance . . . and that poor Lake and his party had seen their complete outlines. . . .

It is of course impossible for me to relate in proper order the stages by which we picked up what we know of that monstrous chapter of pre-human life. After the first shock of the certain revelation we had to pause a while to recuperate, and it was fully three o'clock before we got started on our actual tour of systematic research. The sculptures in the building we entered were of relatively late date—perhaps two million years ago—as checked up by geological, biological, and astronomical features; and embodied an art which would be called decadent in comparison with that of specimens we found in older buildings after crossing bridges

under the glacial sheet. One edifice hewn from the solid rock seemed to go back forty or possibly even fifty million years—to the lower Eocene or upper Cretaceous—and contained bas-reliefs of an artistry surpassing anything else, with one tremendous exception, that we encountered. That was, we have since agreed, the oldest domestic structure we traversed.

Were it not for the support of those snapshots soon to be made public, I would refrain from telling what I found and inferred, lest I be confined as a madman. Of course, the infinitely early parts of the patchwork tale—representing the pre-terrestrial life of the star-headed beings on other planets, in other galaxies, and in other universes—can readily be interpreted as the fantastic mythology of those beings themselves; yet such parts sometimes involved designs and diagrams so uncannily close to the latest findings of mathematics and astrophysics that I scarcely know what to think. Let others judge when they see the photographs I shall publish.

Naturally, no one set of carvings which we encountered told more than a fraction of any connected story; nor did we even begin to come upon the various stages of that story in their proper order. Some of the vast rooms were independent units so far as their designs were concerned, whilst in other cases a continuous chronicle would be carried through a series of rooms and corridors. The best of the maps and diagrams were on the walls of a frightful abyss below even the ancient ground level—a cavern perhaps 200 feet square and sixty feet high, which had almost undoubtedly been an educational centre of some sort. There were many provoking repetitions of the same material in different rooms and buildings; since certain chapters of experience, and certain summaries or phases of racial history, had evidently been favourites with different decorators

or dwellers. Sometimes, though, variant versions of the same theme proved useful in settling debatable points and filling in gaps.

I still wonder that we deduced so much in the short time at our disposal. Of course, we even now have only the barest outline; and much of that was obtained later on from a study of the photographs and sketches we made. It may be the effect of this later study—the revived memories and vague impressions acting in conjunction with his general sensitiveness and with that final supposed horror-glimpse whose essence he will not reveal even to me—which has been the immediate source of Danforth's present breakdown. But it had to be; for we could not issue our warning intelligently without the fullest possible information, and the issuance of that warning is a prime necessity. Certain lingering influences in that unknown antarctic world of disordered time and alien natural law make it imperative that further exploration be discouraged.

VII

The full story, so far as deciphered, will shortly appear in an official bulletin of Miskatonic University. Here I shall sketch only the salient highlights in a formless, rambling way. Myth or otherwise, the sculptures told of the coming of those star-headed things to the nascent, lifeless earth out of cosmic space—their coming, and the coming of many other alien entities such as at certain times embark upon spatial pioneering. They seemed able to traverse the interstellar ether on their vast membraneous wings—thus oddly confirming some curious hill folklore long ago told me by an antiquarian colleague. They had lived under the sea a good deal, building fantastic cities and fighting terrific

battles with nameless adversaries by means of intricate devices employing unknown principles of energy. Evidently their scientific and mechanical knowledge far surpassed man's today, though they made use of its more widespread and elaborate forms only when obliged to. Some of the sculptures suggested that they had passed through a stage of mechanised life on other planets, but had receded upon finding its effects emotionally unsatisfying. Their preternatural toughness of organisation and simplicity of natural wants made them peculiarly able to live on a high plane without the more specialised fruits of artificial manufacture, and even without garments except for occasional protection against the elements.

It was under the sea, at first for food and later for other purposes, that they first created earth-life—using available substances according to long-known methods. The more elaborate experiments came after the annihilation of various cosmic enemies. They had done the same thing on other planets; having manufactured not only necessary foods, but certain multicellular protoplasmic masses capable of moulding their tissues into all sorts of temporary organs under hypnotic influence and thereby forming ideal slaves to perform the heavy work of the community. These viscous masses were without doubt what Abdul Alhazred whispered about as the "shoggoths" in his frightful *Necronomicon,* though even that mad Arab had not hinted that any existed on earth except in the dreams of those who had chewed a certain alkaloidal herb. When the star-headed Old Ones on this planet had synthesised their simple food forms and bred a good supply of shoggoths, they allowed other cell-groups to develop into other forms of animal and vegetable life for sundry purposes; extirpating any whose presence became troublesome.

With the aid of the shoggoths, whose expansions

could be made to lift prodigious weights, the small, low cities under the sea grew to vast and imposing labyrinths of stone not unlike those which later rose on land. Indeed, the highly adaptable Old Ones had lived much on land in other parts of the universe, and probably retained many traditions of land construction. As we studied the architecture of all these sculptured palaeogean cities, including that whose aeon-dead corridors we were even then traversing, we were impressed by a curious coincidence which we have not yet tried to explain, even to ourselves. The tops of the buildings, which in the actual city around us had of course been weathered into shapeless ruins ages ago, were clearly displayed in the bas-reliefs; and shewed vast clusters of needle-like spires, delicate finials on certain cone and pyramid apexes, and tiers of thin, horizontal scalloped discs capping cylindrical shafts. This was exactly what we had seen in that monstrous and portentous mirage, cast by a dead city whence such skyline features had been absent for thousands and tens of thousands of years, which loomed on our ignorant eyes across the unfathomed mountains of madness as we first approached poor Lake's ill-fated camp.

Of the life of the Old Ones, both under the sea and after part of them migrated to land, volumes could be written. Those in shallow water had continued the fullest use of the eyes at the ends of their five main head tentacles, and had practiced the arts of sculpture and of writing in quite the usual way—the writing accomplished with a stylus on waterproof waxen surfaces. Those lower down in the ocean depths, though they used a curious phosphorescent organism to furnish light, pieced out their vision with obscure special senses operating through the prismatic cilia on their heads— senses which rendered all the Old Ones partly independent of light in emergencies. Their forms of sculpture

and writing had changed curiously during the descent, embodying certain apparently chemical coating processes—probably to secure phosphorescence—which the bas-reliefs could not make clear to us. The beings moved in the sea partly by swimming—using the lateral crinoid arms—and partly by wriggling with the lower tier of tentacles containing the pseudo-feet. Occasionally they accomplished long swoops with the auxiliary use of two or more sets of their fan-like folding wings. On land they locally used the pseudo-feet, but now and then flew to great heights or over long distances with their wings. The many slender tentacles into which the crinoid arms branched were infinitely delicate, flexible, strong, and accurate in muscular-nervous coördination; ensuring the utmost skill and dexterity in all artistic and other manual operations.

The toughness of the things was almost incredible. Even the terrific pressures of the deepest sea-bottoms appeared powerless to harm them. Very few seemed to die at all except by violence, and their burial-places were very limited. The fact that they covered their vertically inhumed dead with five-pointed inscribed mounds set up thoughts in Danforth and me which made a fresh pause and recuperation necessary after the sculptures revealed it. The beings multiplied by means of spores—like vegetable pteridophytes as Lake had suspected—but owing to their prodigious tough-ness and longevity, and consequent lack of replacement needs, they did not encourage the large-scale develop-ment of new prothalli except when they had new regions to colonise. The young matured swiftly, and received an education evidently beyond any standard we can imagine. The prevailing intellectual and aesthet-ic life was highly evolved, and produced a tenaciously enduring set of customs and institutions which I shall describe more fully in my coming monograph. These

varied slightly according to sea or land residence, but had the same foundations and essentials.

Though able, like vegetables, to derive nourishment from inorganic substances; they vastly preferred organic and especially animal food. They ate uncooked marine life under the sea, but cooked their viands on land. They hunted game and raised meat herds— slaughtering with sharp weapons whose odd marks on certain fossil bones our expedition had noted. They resisted all ordinary temperatures marvellously; and in their natural state could live in water down to freezing. When the great chill of the Pleistocene drew on, however—nearly a million years ago—the land dwellers had to resort to special measures including artificial heating; until at last the deadly cold appears to have driven them back into the sea. For their prehistoric flights through cosmic space, legend said, they had absorbed certain chemicals and became almost independent of eating, breathing, or heat conditions; but by the time of the great cold they had lost track of the method. In any case they could not have prolonged the artificial state indefinitely without harm.

Being non-pairing and semi-vegetable in structure, the Old Ones had no biological basis for the family phase of mammal life; but seemed to organise large households on the principles of comfortable space-utility and—as we deduced from the pictured occupations and diversions of co-dwellers—congenial mental association. In furnishing their homes they kept everything in the centre of the huge rooms, leaving all the wall spaces free for decorative treatment. Lighting, in the case of the land inhabitants, was accomplished by a device probably electro-chemical in nature. Both on land and under water they used curious tables, chairs, and couches like cylindrical frames—for they rested and slept upright with folded-down tentacles—and

racks for the hinged sets of dotted surfaces forming their books.

Government was evidently complex and probably socialistic, though no certainties in this regard could be deduced from the sculptures we saw. There was extensive commerce, both local and between different cities; certain small, flat counters, five-pointed and inscribed, serving as money. Probably the smaller of the various greenish soapstones found by our expedition were pieces of such currency. Though the culture was mainly urban, some agriculture and much stock-raising existed. Mining and a limited amount of manufacturing were also practiced. Travel was very frequent, but permanent migration seemed relatively rare except for the vast colonising movements by which the race expanded. For personal locomotion no external aid was used; since in land, air, and water movement alike the Old Ones seemed to possess excessively vast capacities for speed. Loads, however, were drawn by beasts of burden—shoggoths under the sea, and a curious variety of primitive vertebrates in the later years of land existence.

These vertebrates, as well as an infinity of other life-forms—animal and vegetable, marine, terrestrial, and aërial—were the products of unguided evolution acting on life-cells made by the Old Ones but escaping beyond their radius of attention. They had been suffered to develop unchecked because they had not come in conflict with the dominant beings. Bothersome forms, of course, were mechanically exterminated. It interested us to see in some of the very last and most decadent sculptures a shambling primitive mammal, used sometimes for food and sometimes as an amusing buffoon by the land dwellers, whose vaguely simian and human foreshadowings were unmistakable. In the building of land cities the huge stone blocks of the high

towers were generally lifted by vastwinged pterodactyls of a species heretofore unknown to palaeontology.

The persistence with which the Old Ones survived various geologic changes and convulsions of the earth's crust was little short of miraculous. Though few or none of their first cities seem to have remained beyond the Archaean age, there was no interruption in their civilisation or in the transmission of their records. Their original place of advent to the planet was the Antarctic Ocean, and it is likely that they came not long after the matter forming the moon was wrenched from the neighbouring South Pacific. According to one of the sculptured maps, the whole globe was then under water, with stone cities scattered farther and farther from the antarctic as aeons passed. Another map shews a vast bulk of dry land around the south pole, where it is evident that some of the beings made experimental settlements though their main centres were transferred to the nearest sea-bottom. Later maps, which display this land mass as cracking and drifting, and sending certain detached parts northward, uphold in a striking way the theories of continental drift lately advanced by Taylor, Wegener, and Joly.

With the upheaval of new land in the South Pacific tremendous events began. Some of the marine cities were hopelessly shattered, yet that was not the worst misfortune. Another race—a land race of beings shaped like octopi and probably corresponding to the fabulous pre-human spawn of Cthulhu—soon began filtering down from cosmic infinity and precipitated a monstrous war which for a time drove the Old Ones wholly back to the sea—a colossal blow in view of the increasing land settlements. Later peace was made, and the new lands were given to the Cthulhu spawn whilst the Old Ones held the sea and the older lands. New land cities were founded—the greatest of them in the ant-

arctic, for this region of first arrival was sacred. From then on, as before, the antarctic remained the centre of the Old Ones' civilisation, and all the discoverable cities built there by the Cthulhu spawn were blotted out. Then suddenly the lands of the Pacific sank again, taking with them the frightful stone city of R'lyeh and all the cosmic octopi, so that the Old Ones were again supreme on the planet except for one shadowy fear about which they did not like to speak. At a rather later age their cities dotted all the land and water areas of the globe—hence the recommendation in my coming monograph that some archaeologist make systematic borings with Pabodie's type of apparatus in certain widely separated regions.

The steady trend down the ages was from water to land; a movement encouraged by the rise of new land masses, though the ocean was never wholly deserted. Another cause of the landward movement was the new difficulty in breeding and managing the shoggoths upon which successful sea-life depended. With the march of time, as the sculptures sadly confessed, the art of creating new life from inorganic matter had been lost; so that the Old Ones had to depend on the moulding of forms already in existence. On land the great reptiles proved highly tractable; but the shoggoths of the sea, reproducing by fission and acquiring a dangerous degree of accidental intelligence, presented for a time a formidable problem.

They had always been controlled through the hypnotic suggestion of the Old Ones, and had modelled their tough plasticity into various useful temporary limbs and organs; but now their self-modelling powers were sometimes exercised independently, and in various imitative forms implanted by past suggestion. They had, it seems, developed a semi-stable brain whose separate and occasionally stubborn volition echoed the

will of the Old Ones without always obeying it. Sculptured images of these shoggoths filled Danforth and me with horror and loathing. They were normally shapeless entities composed of a viscous jelly which looked like an agglutination of bubbles; and each averaged about fifteen feet in diameter when a sphere. They had, however, a constantly shifting shape and volume; throwing out temporary developments or forming apparent organs of sight, hearing, and speech in imitation of their masters, either spontaneously or according to suggestion.

They seem to have become peculiarly intractable toward the middle of the Permian age, perhaps 150 million years ago, when a veritable war of resubjugation was waged upon them by the marine Old Ones. Pictures of this war, and of the headless, slime-coated fashion in which the shoggoths typically left their slain victims, held a marvellously fearsome quality despite the intervening abyss of untold ages. The Old Ones had used curious weapons of molecular disturbance against the rebel entities, and in the end had achieved a complete victory. Thereafter the sculptures shewed a period in which shoggoths were tamed and broken by armed Old Ones as the wild horses of the American west were tamed by cowboys. Though during the rebellion the shoggoths had shewn an ability to live out of water, this transition was not encouraged; since their usefulness on land would hardly have been commensurate with the trouble of their management.

During the Jurassic age the Old Ones met fresh adversity in the form of a new invasion from outer space—this time by half-fungous, half-crustacean creatures from a planet identifiable as the remote and recently discovered Pluto; creatures undoubtedly the same as those figuring in certain whispered hill legends of the north, and remembered in the Himalayas as the

Mi-Go, or Abominable Snow-Men. To fight these beings the Old Ones attempted, for the first time since their terrene advent, to sally forth again into the planetary ether; but despite all traditional preparations found it no longer possible to leave the earth's atmosphere. Whatever the old secret of interstellar travel had been, it was now definitely lost to the race. In the end the Mi-Go drove the Old Ones out of all the northern lands, though they were powerless to disturb those in the sea. Little by little the slow retreat of the elder race to their original antarctic habitat was beginning.

It was curious to note from the pictured battles that both the Cthulhu spawn and the Mi-Go seem to have been composed of matter more widely different from that which we know than was the substance of the Old Ones. They were able to undergo transformations and reintegrations impossible for their adversaries, and seem therefore to have originally come from even remoter gulfs of cosmic space. The Old Ones, but for their abnormal toughness and peculiar vital properties, were strictly material, and must have had their absolute origin within the known space-time continuum; whereas the first sources of the other beings can only be guessed at with bated breath. All this, of course, assuming that the non-terrestrial linkages and the anomalies ascribed to the invading foes are not pure mythology. Conceivably, the Old Ones might have invented a cosmic framework to account for their occasional defeats; since historical interest and pride obviously formed their chief psychological element. It is significant that their annals failed to mention many advanced and potent races of beings whose mighty cultures and towering cities figure persistently in certain obscure legends.

The changing state of the world through long geologic ages appeared with startling vividness in many of the

sculptured maps and scenes. In certain cases existing science will require revision, while in other cases its bold deductions are magnificently confirmed. As I have said, the hypothesis of Taylor, Wegener, and Joly that all the continents are fragments of an original antarctic land mass which cracked from centrifugal force and drifted apart over a technically viscous lower surface— an hypothesis suggested by such things as the complementary outlines of Africa and South America, and the way the great mountain chains are rolled and shoved up—receives striking support from this uncanny source.

Maps evidently shewing the Carboniferous world of an hundred million or more years ago displayed significant rifts and chasms destined later to separate Africa from the once continuous realms of Europe (then the Valusia of hellish primal legend), Asia, the Americas, and the antarctic continent. Other charts—and most significantly one in connexion with the founding fifty million years ago of the vast dead city around us— shewed all the present continents well differentiated. And in the latest discoverable specimen—dating perhaps from the Pliocene age—the approximate world of today appeared quite clearly despite the linkage of Alaska with Siberia, of North America with Europe through Greenland, and of South America with the antarctic continent through Graham Land. In the Carboniferous map the whole globe—ocean floor and rifted land mass alike—bore symbols of the Old Ones' vast stone cities, but in the later charts the gradual recession toward the antarctic became very plain. The final Pliocene specimen shewed no land cities except on the antarctic continent and the tip of South America, nor any ocean cities north of the fiftieth parallel of South Latitude. Knowledge and interest in the northern world, save for a study of coast-lines probably made

during long exploration flights on those fan-like membraneous wings, had evidently declined to zero among the Old Ones.

Destruction of cities through the upthrust of mountains, the centrifugal rending of continents, the seismic convulsions of land or sea-bottom, and other natural causes was a matter of common record; and it was curious to observe how fewer and fewer replacements were made as the ages wore on. The vast dead megalopolis that yawned around us seemed to be the last general centre of the race; built early in the Cretaceous age after a titanic earth-buckling had obliterated a still vaster predecessor not far distant. It appeared that this general region was the most sacred spot of all, where reputedly the first Old Ones had settled on a primal sea-bottom. In the new city—many of whose features we could recognise in the sculptures, but which stretched fully an hundred miles along the mountain-range in each direction beyond the farthest limits of our aërial survey—there were reputed to be preserved certain sacred stones forming part of the first sea-bottom city, which were thrust up to light after long epochs in the course of the general crumpling of strata.

VIII

Naturally, Danforth and I studied with especial interest and a peculiarly personal sense of awe everything pertaining to the immediate district in which we were. Of this local material there was naturally a vast abundance; and on the tangled ground level of the city we were lucky enough to find a house of very late date whose walls, though somewhat damaged by a neighbouring rift, contained sculptures of decadent workmanship carrying the story of the region much beyond

the period of the Pliocene map whence we derived our last general glimpse of the pre-human world. This was the last place we examined in detail, since what we found there gave us a fresh immediate objective.

Certainly, we were in one of the strangest, weirdest, and most terrible of all the corners of earth's globe. Of all existing lands it was infinitely the most ancient; and the conviction grew upon us that this hideous upland must indeed be the fabled nightmare plateau of Leng which even the mad author of the *Necronomicon* was reluctant to discuss. The great mountain chain was tremendously long—starting as a low range at Luitpold Land on the coast of Weddell Sea and virtually crossing the entire continent. The really high part stretched in a mighty arc from about Latitude 82°, E. Longitude 60° to Latitude 70°, E. Longitude 115°, with its concave side toward our camp and its seaward end in the region of that long, ice-locked coast whose hills were glimpsed by Wilkes and Mawson at the Antarctic Circle.

Yet even more monstrous exaggerations of Nature seemed disturbingly close at hand. I have said that these peaks are higher than the Himalayas, but the sculptures forbid me to say that they are earth's highest. That grim honour is beyond doubt reserved for something which half the sculptures hesitated to record at all, whilst others approached it with obvious repugnance and trepidation. It seems that there was one part of the ancient land—the first part that ever rose from the waters after the earth had flung off the moon and the Old Ones had seeped down from the stars—which had come to be shunned as vaguely and namelessly evil. Cities built there had crumbled before their time, and had been found suddenly deserted. Then when the first great earth-buckling had convulsed the region in the Comanchian age, a frightful line of peaks had shot suddenly up amidst the most appalling din and chaos

—and earth had received her loftiest and most terrible mountains.

If the scale of the carvings was correct, these abhorred things must have been much over 40,000 feet high—radically vaster than even the shocking mountains of madness we had crossed. They extended, it appeared, from about Latitude 77°, E. Longitude 70° to Latitude 70°, E. Longitude 100°—less than 300 miles away from the dead city, so that we would have spied their dreaded summits in the dim western distance had it not been for that vague opalescent haze. Their northern end must likewise be visible from the long Antarctic Circle coast-line at Queen Mary Land.

Some of the Old Ones, in the decadent days, had made strange prayers to those mountains; but none ever went near them or dared to guess what lay beyond. No human eye had ever seen them, and as I studied the emotions conveyed in the carvings I prayed that none ever might. There are protecting hills along the coast beyond them—Queen Mary and Kaiser Wilhelm Lands—and I thank heaven no one has been able to land and climb those hills. I am not as sceptical about old tales and fears as I used to be, and I do not laugh now at the pre-human sculptor's notion that lightning paused meaningfully now and then at each of the brooding crests, and that an unexplained glow shone from one of those terrible pinnacles all through the long polar night. There may be a very real and very monstrous meaning in the old Pnakotic whispers about Kadath in the Cold Waste.

But the terrain close at hand was hardly less strange, even if less namelessly accursed. Soon after the founding of the city the great mountain-range became the seat of the principal temples, and many carvings shewed what grotesque and fantastic towers had pierced the sky where now we saw only the curiously

clinging cubes and ramparts. In the course of ages the caves had appeared, and had been shaped into adjuncts of the temples. With the advance of still later epochs all the limestone veins of the region were hollowed out by ground waters, so that the mountains, the foothills, and the plains below them were a veritable network of connected caverns and galleries. Many graphic sculptures told of explorations deep underground, and of the final discovery of the Stygian sunless sea that lurked at earth's bowels.

This vast nighted gulf had undoubtedly been worn by the great river which flowed down from the nameless and horrible westward mountains, and which had formerly turned at the base of the Old Ones' range and flowed beside that chain into the Indian Ocean between Budd and Totten Lands on Wilkes's coast-line. Little by little it had eaten away the limestone hill base at its turning, till at last its sapping currents reached the caverns of the ground waters and joined with them in digging a deeper abyss. Finally its whole bulk emptied into the hollow hills and left the old bed toward the ocean dry. Much of the later city as we now found it had been built over that former bed. The Old Ones, understanding what had happened, and exercising their always keen artistic sense, had carved into ornate pylons those headlands of the foothills where the great stream began its descent into eternal darkness.

This river, once crossed by scores of noble stone bridges, was plainly the one whose extinct course we had seen in our aëroplane survey. Its position in different carvings of the city helped us to orient ourselves to the scene as it had been at various stages of the region's age-long, aeon-dead history; so that we were able to sketch a hasty but careful map of the salient features—squares, important buildings, and the like—for guidance in further explorations. We could soon

reconstruct in fancy the whole stupendous thing as it was a million or ten million or fifty million years ago, for the sculptures told us exactly what the buildings and mountains and squares and suburbs and landscape setting and luxuriant Tertiary vegetation had looked like. It must have had a marvellous and mystic beauty, and as I thought of it I almost forgot the clammy sense of sinister oppression with which the city's inhuman age and massiveness and deadness and remoteness and glacial twilight had choked and weighed on my spirit. Yet according to certain carvings the denizens of that city had themselves known the clutch of oppressive terror; for there was a sombre and recurrent type of scene in which the Old Ones were shewn in the act of recoiling affrightedly from some object—never allowed to appear in the design—found in the great river and indicated as having been washed down through waving, vine-draped cycad-forests from those horrible westward mountains.

It was only in the one late-built house with the decadent carvings that we obtained any foreshadowing of the final calamity leading to the city's desertion. Undoubtedly there must have been many sculptures of the same age elsewhere, even allowing for the slackened energies and aspirations of a stressful and uncertain period; indeed, very certain evidence of the existence of others came to us shortly afterward. But this was the first and only set we directly encountered. We meant to look farther later on; but as I have said, immediate conditions dictated another present objective. There would, though, have been a limit—for after all hope of a long future occupancy of the place had perished among the Old Ones, there could not but have been a complete cessation of mural decoration. The ultimate blow, of course, was the coming of the great cold which once held most of the earth in thrall, and which has

never departed from the ill-fated poles—the great cold that, at the world's other extremity, put an end to the fabled lands of Lomar and Hyperborea.

Just when this tendency began in the antarctic it would be hard to say in terms of exact years. Nowadays we set the beginning of the general glacial periods at a distance of about 500,000 years from the present, but at the poles the terrible scourge must have commenced much earlier. All quantitative estimates are partly guesswork; but it is quite likely that the decadent sculptures were made considerably less than a million years ago, and that the actual desertion of the city was complete long before the conventional opening of the Pleistocene—500,000 years ago—as reckoned in terms of the earth's whole surface.

In the decadent sculptures there were signs of thinner vegetation everywhere, and of a decreased country life on the part of the Old Ones. Heating devices were shewn in the houses, and winter travellers were represented as muffled in protective fabrics. Then we saw a series of cartouches (the continuous band arrangement being frequently interrupted in these late carvings) depicting a constantly growing migration to the nearest refuges of greater warmth—some fleeing to cities under the sea off the far-away coast, and some clambering down through networks of limestone caverns in the hollow hills to the neighbouring black abyss of subterrene waters.

In the end it seems to have been the neighbouring abyss which received the greatest colonisation. This was partly due, no doubt, to the traditional sacredness of this especial region; but may have been more conclusively determined by the opportunities it gave for continuing the use of the great temples on the honeycombed mountains, and for retaining the vast land city as a place of summer residence and base of

communication with various mines. The linkage of old and new abodes was made more effective by means of several gradings and improvements along the connecting routes, including the chiselling of numerous direct tunnels from the ancient metropolis to the black abyss —sharply down-pointing tunnels whose mouths we carefully drew, according to our most thoughtful estimates, on the guide map we were compiling. It was obvious that at least two of these tunnels lay within a reasonable exploring distance of where we were; both being on the mountainward edge of the city, one less than a quarter-mile toward the ancient river-course, and the other perhaps twice that distance in the opposite direction.

The abyss, it seems, had shelving shores of dry land at certain places; but the Old Ones built their new city under water—no doubt because of its greater certainty of uniform warmth. The depth of the hidden sea appears to have been very great, so that the earth's internal heat could ensure its habitability for an indefinite period. The beings seem to have had no trouble in adapting themselves to part-time—and eventually, of course, whole-time—residence under water; since they had never allowed their gill systems to atrophy. There were many sculptures which shewed how they had always frequently visited their submarine kinsfolk elsewhere, and how they had habitually bathed on the deep bottom of their great river. The darkness of inner earth could likewise have been no deterrent to a race accustomed to long antarctic nights.

Decadent though their style undoubtedly was, these latest carvings had a truly epic quality where they told of the building of the new city in the cavern sea. The Old Ones had gone about it scientifically; quarrying insoluble rocks from the heart of the honeycombed mountains, and employing expert workers from the

nearest submarine city to perform the construction according to the best methods. These workers brought with them all that was necessary to establish the new venture—shoggoth-tissue from which to breed stone-lifters and subsequent beasts of burden for the cavern city, and other protoplasmic matter to mould into phosphorescent organisms for lighting purposes.

At last a mighty metropolis rose on the bottom of that Stygian sea; its architecture much like that of the city above, and its workmanship displaying relatively little decadence because of the precise mathematical element inherent in building operations. The newly bred shoggoths grew to enormous size and singular intelligence, and were represented as taking and executing orders with marvellous quickness. They seemed to converse with the Old Ones by mimicking their voices—a sort of musical piping over a wide range, if poor Lake's dissection had indicated aright—and to work more from spoken commands than from hypnotic suggestions as in earlier times. They were, however, kept in admirable control. The phosphorescent organisms supplied light with vast effectiveness, and doubtless atoned for the loss of the familiar polar auroras of the outer-world night.

Art and decoration were pursued, though of course with a certain decadence. The Old Ones seemed to realise this falling off themselves; and in many cases anticipated the policy of Constantine the Great by transplanting especially fine blocks of ancient carving from their land city, just as the emperor, in a similar age of decline, stripped Greece and Asia of their finest art to give his new Byzantine capital greater splendours than its own people could create. That the transfer of sculptured blocks had not been more extensive, was doubtless owing to the fact that the land city was not at first wholly abandoned. By the time total abandonment

did occur—and it surely must have occurred before the polar Pleistocene was far advanced—the Old Ones had perhaps become satisfied with their decadent art—or had ceased to recognise the superior merit of the older carvings. At any rate, the aeon-silent ruins around us had certainly undergone no wholesale sculptural denudation; though all the best separate statues, like other moveables, had been taken away.

The decadent cartouches and dadoes telling this story were, as I have said, the latest we could find in our limited search. They left us with a picture of the Old Ones shuttling back and forth betwixt the land city in summer and the sea-cavern city in winter, and sometimes trading with the sea-bottom cities off the antarctic coast. By this time the ultimate doom of the land city must have been recognised, for the sculptures shewed many signs of the cold's malign encroachments. Vegetation was declining, and the terrible snows of the winter no longer melted completely even in midsummer. The saurian livestock were nearly all dead, and the mammals were standing it none too well. To keep on with the work of the upper world it had become necessary to adapt some of the amorphous and curiously cold-resistant shoggoths to land life; a thing the Old Ones had formerly been reluctant to do. The great river was now lifeless, and the upper sea had lost most of its denizens except the seals and whales. All the birds had flown away, save only the great, grotesque penguins.

What had happened afterward we could only guess. How long had the new sea-cavern city survived? Was it still down there, a stony corpse in eternal blackness? Had the subterranean waters frozen at last? To what fate had the ocean-bottom cities of the outer world been delivered? Had any of the Old Ones shifted north ahead of the creeping ice-cap? Existing geology shews no trace of their presence. Had the frightful Mi-Go been still a menace in the outer land world of the north?

Could one be sure of what might or might not linger even to this day in the lightless and unplumbed abysses of earth's deepest waters? Those things had seemingly been able to withstand any amount of pressure—and men of the sea have fished up curious objects at times. And has the killer-whale theory really explained the savage and mysterious scars on antarctic seals noticed a generation ago by Borchgrevingk?

The specimens found by poor Lake did not enter into these guesses, for their geologic setting proved them to have lived at what must have been a very early date in the land city's history. They were, according to their location, certainly not less than thirty million years old; and we reflected that in their day the sea-cavern city, and indeed the cavern itself, had had no existence. They would have remembered an older scene, with lush Tertiary vegetation everywhere, a younger land city of flourishing arts around them, and a great river sweeping northward along the base of the mighty mountains toward a far-away tropic ocean.

And yet we could not help thinking about these specimens—especially about the eight perfect ones that were missing from Lake's hideously ravaged camp. There was something abnormal about that whole business—the strange things we had tried so hard to lay to somebody's madness—those frightful graves—the amount *and nature* of the missing material—Gedney—the unearthly toughness of those archaic monstrosities, and the queer vital freaks the sculptures now shewed the race to have. . . . Danforth and I had seen a good deal in the last few hours, and were prepared to believe and keep silent about many appalling and incredible secrets of primal Nature.

IX

I have said that our study of the decadent sculptures brought about a change in our immediate objective. This of course had to do with the chiselled avenues to the black inner world, of whose existence we had not known before, but which we were now eager to find and traverse. From the evident scale of the carvings we deduced that a steeply descending walk of about a mile through either of the neighbouring tunnels would bring us to the brink of the dizzy sunless cliffs above the great abyss; down whose side adequate paths, improved by the Old Ones, led to the rocky shore of the hidden and nighted ocean. To behold this fabulous gulf in stark reality was a lure which seemed impossible of resistance once we knew of the thing—yet we realised we must begin the quest at once if we expected to include it on our present flight.

It was now 8 PM, and we had not enough battery replacements to let our torches burn on forever. We had done so much of our studying and copying below the glacial level that our battery supply had had at least five hours of nearly continuous use; and despite the special dry cell formula would obviously be good for only about four more—though by keeping one torch unused, except for especially interesting or difficult places, we might manage to eke out a safe margin beyond that. It would not do to be without a light in these Cyclopean catacombs, hence in order to make the abyss trip we must give up all further mural deciphering. Of course we intended to revisit the place for days and perhaps weeks of intensive study and photography—curiosity having long ago got the better of horror—but just now we must hasten. Our supply of trail-blazing paper was far from unlimited, and we were reluctant to sacrifice spare notebooks or sketching paper to augment it; but

we did let one large notebook go. If worst came to worst, we could resort to rock-chipping—and of course it would be possible, even in case of really lost direction, to work up to full daylight by one channel or another if granted sufficient time for plentiful trial and error. So at last we set off eagerly in the indicated direction of the nearest tunnel.

According to the carvings from which we had made our map, the desired tunnel-mouth could not be much more than a quarter-mile from where we stood; the intervening space shewing solid-looking buildings quite likely to be penetrable still at a sub-glacial level. The opening itself would be in the basement—on the angle nearest the foothills—of a vast five-pointed structure of evidently public and perhaps ceremonial nature, which we tried to identify from our aërial survey of the ruins. No such structure came to our minds as we recalled our flight, hence we concluded that its upper parts had been greatly damaged, or that it had been totally shattered in an ice-rift we had noticed. In the latter case the tunnel would probably turn out to be choked, so that we would have to try the next nearest one—the one less than a mile to the north. The intervening river-course prevented our trying any of the more southerly tunnels on this trip; and indeed, if both of the neighbouring ones were choked it was doubtful whether our batteries would warrant an attempt on the next northerly one—about a mile beyond our second choice.

As we threaded our dim way through the labyrinth with the aid of map and compass—traversing rooms and corridors in every stage of ruin or preservation, clambering up ramps, crossing upper floors and bridges and clambering down again, encountering choked doorways and piles of debris, hastening now and then along finely preserved and uncannily immaculate

stretches, taking false leads and retracing our way (in such cases removing the blind paper trail we had left), and once in a while striking the bottom of an open shaft through which daylight poured or trickled down—we were repeatedly tantalised by the sculptured walls along our route. Many must have told tales of immense historical importance, and only the prospect of later visits reconciled us to the need of passing them by. As it was, we slowed down once in a while and turned on our second torch. If we had had more films we would certainly have paused briefly to photograph certain bas-reliefs, but time-consuming hand copying was clearly out of the question.

I come now once more to a place where the temptation to hesitate, or to hint rather than state, is very strong. It is necessary, however, to reveal the rest in order to justify my course in discouraging further exploration. We had wormed our way very close to the computed site of the tunnel's mouth—having crossed a second-story bridge to what seemed plainly the tip of a pointed wall, and descended to a ruinous corridor especially rich in decadently elaborate and apparently ritualistic sculptures of late workmanship—when, about 8:30 PM, Danforth's keen young nostrils gave us the first hint of something unusual. If we had had a dog with us, I suppose we would have been warned before. At first we could not precisely say what was wrong with the formerly crystal-pure air, but after a few seconds our memories reacted only too definitely. Let me try to state the thing without flinching. There was an odour— and that odour was vaguely, subtly, and unmistakably akin to what had nauseated us upon opening the insane grave of the horror poor Lake had dissected.

Of course the revelation was not as clearly cut at the time as it sounds now. There were several conceivable explanations, and we did a good deal of indecisive whispering. Most important of all, we did not retreat

without further investigation; for having come this far, we were loath to be balked by anything short of certain disaster. Anyway, what we must have suspected was altogether too wild to believe. Such things did not happen in any normal world. It was probably sheer irrational instinct which made us dim our single torch —tempted no longer by the decadent and sinister sculptures that leered menacingly from the oppressive walls—and which softened our progress to a cautious tiptoeing and crawling over the increasingly littered floor and heaps of debris.

Danforth's eyes as well as nose proved better than mine, for it was likewise he who first noticed the queer aspect of the debris after we had passed many half-choked arches leading to chambers and corridors on the ground level. It did not look quite as it ought after countless thousands of years of desertion, and when we cautiously turned on more light we saw that a kind of swath seemed to have been lately tracked through it. The irregular nature of the litter precluded any definite marks, but in the smoother places there were suggestions of the dragging of heavy objects. Once we thought there was a hint of parallel tracks, as if of runners. This was what made us pause again.

It was during that pause that we caught— simultaneously this time—the other odour ahead. Paradoxically, it was both a less frightful and a more frightful odour—less frightful intrinsically, but infinitely appalling in this place under the known circumstances . . . unless, of course, Gedney. . . . For the odour was the plain and familiar one of common petrol—every-day gasoline.

Our motivation after that is something I will leave to psychologists. We knew now that some terrible extension of the camp horrors must have crawled into this nighted burial-place of the aeons, hence could not doubt any longer the existence of nameless conditions

—present or at least recent—just ahead. Yet in the end
we did let sheer burning curiosity—or anxiety—or
auto-hypnotism—or vague thoughts of responsibility
toward Gedney—or what not—drive us on. Danforth
whispered again of the print he thought he had seen at
the alley-turning in the ruins above; and of the faint
musical piping—potentially of tremendous significance in the light of Lake's dissection report despite its
close resemblance to the cave-mouth echoes of the
windy peaks—which he thought he had shortly afterward half heard from unknown depths below. I, in my
turn, whispered of how the camp was left—of what had
disappeared, and of how the madness of a lone survivor
might have conceived the inconceivable—a wild trip
across the monstrous mountains and a descent into the
unknown primal masonry—

But we could not convince each other, or even
ourselves, of anything definite. We had turned off all
light as we stood still, and vaguely noticed that a trace
of deeply filtered upper day kept the blackness from
being absolute. Having automatically begun to move
ahead, we guided ourselves by occasional flashes from
our torch. The disturbed debris formed an impression
we could not shake off, and the smell of gasoline grew
stronger. More and more ruin met our eyes and ham-
pered our feet, until very soon we saw that the forward
way was about to cease. We had been all too correct in
our pessimistic guess about that rift glimpsed from the
air. Our tunnel quest was a blind one, and we were not
even going to be able to reach the basement out of
which the abyssward aperture opened.

The torch, flashing over the grotesquely carven walls
of the blocked corridor in which we stood, shewed
several doorways in various states of obstruction; and
from one of them the gasoline odour—quite submerg-
ing that other hint of odour—came with especial

distinctness. As we looked more steadily, we saw that beyond a doubt there had been a slight and recent clearing away of debris from that particular opening. Whatever the lurking horror might be, we believed the direct avenue toward it was now plainly manifest. I do not think anyone will wonder that we waited an appreciable time before making any further motion.

And yet, when we did venture inside that black arch, our first impression was one of anticlimax. For amidst the littered expanse of that sculptured crypt—a perfect cube with sides of about twenty feet—there remained no recent object of instantly discernible size; so that we looked instinctively, though in vain, for a farther doorway. In another moment, however, Danforth's sharp vision had descried a place where the floor debris had been disturbed; and we turned on both torches full strength. Though what we saw in that light was actually simple and trifling, I am none the less reluctant to tell of it because of what it implied. It was a rough levelling of the debris, upon which several small objects lay carelessly scattered, and at one corner of which a considerable amount of gasoline must have been spilled lately enough to leave a strong odour even at this extreme super-plateau altitude. In other words, it could not be other than a sort of camp—a camp made by questing beings who like us had been turned back by the unexpectedly choked way to the abyss.

Let me be plain. The scattered objects were, so far as substance was concerned, all from Lake's camp; and consisted of tin cans as queerly opened as those we had seen at that ravaged place, many spent matches, three illustrated books more or less curiously smudged, an empty ink bottle with its pictorial and instructional carton, a broken fountain pen, some oddly snipped fragments of fur and tent-cloth, a used electric battery with circular of directions, a folder that came with our

type of tent heater, and a sprinkling of crumpled papers. It was all bad enough, but when we smoothed out the papers and looked at what was on them we felt we had come to the worst. We had found certain inexplicably blotted papers at the camp which might have prepared us, yet the effect of the sight down there in the pre-human vaults of a nightmare city was almost too much to bear.

A mad Gedney might have made the groups of dots in imitation of those found on the greenish soapstones, just as the dots on those insane five-pointed grave-mounds might have been made; and he might conceivably have prepared rough, hasty sketches—varying in their accuracy or lack of it—which outlined the neighbouring parts of the city and traced the way from a circularly represented place outside our previous route—a place we identified as a great cylindrical tower in the carvings and as a vast circular gulf glimpsed in our aërial survey—to the present five-pointed structure and the tunnel-mouth therein. He might, I repeat, have prepared such sketches; for those before us were quite obviously compiled as our own had been from late sculptures somewhere in the glacial labyrinth, though not from the ones which we had seen and used. But what this art-blind bungler could never have done was to execute those sketches in a strange and assured technique perhaps superior, despite haste and careless-ness, to any of the decadent carvings from which they were taken—the characteristic and unmistakable tech-nique of the Old Ones themselves in the dead city's heyday.

There are those who will say Danforth and I were utterly mad not to flee for our lives after that; since our conclusions were now—notwithstanding their wild-ness—completely fixed, and of a nature I need not even mention to those who have read my account as far

as this. Perhaps we were mad—for have I not said those horrible peaks were mountains of madness? But I think I can detect something of the same spirit—albeit in a less extreme form—in the men who stalk deadly beasts through African jungles to photograph them or study their habits. Half-paralysed with terror though we were, there was nevertheless fanned within us a blazing flame of awe and curiosity which triumphed in the end.

Of course we did not mean to face that—or those—which we knew had been there, but we felt that they must be gone by now. They would by this time have found the other neighbouring entrance to the abyss, and have passed within to whatever night-black fragments of the past might await them in the ultimate gulf—the ultimate gulf they had never seen. Or if that entrance, too, was blocked, they would have gone on to the north seeking another. They were, we remembered, partly independent of light.

Looking back to that moment, I can scarcely recall just what precise form our new emotions took—just what change of immediate objective it was that so sharpened our sense of expectancy. We certainly did not mean to face what we feared—yet I will not deny that we may have had a lurking, unconscious wish to spy certain things from some hidden vantage-point. Probably we had not given up our zeal to glimpse the abyss itself, though there was interposed a new goal in the form of that great circular place shewn on the crumpled sketches we had found. We had at once recognised it as a monstrous cylindrical tower figuring in the very earliest carvings, but appearing only as a prodigious round aperture from above. Something about the impressiveness of its rendering, even in these hasty diagrams, made us think that its sub-glacial levels must still form a feature of peculiar importance. Perhaps it embodied architectural marvels as yet

unencountered by us. It was certainly of incredible age according to the sculptures in which it figured—being indeed among the first things built in the city. Its carvings, if preserved, could not but be highly significant. Moreover, it might form a good present link with the upper world—a shorter route than the one we were so carefully blazing, and probably that by which those others had descended.

At any rate, the thing we did was to study the terrible sketches—which quite perfectly confirmed our own—and start back over the indicated course to the circular place; the course which our nameless predecessors must have traversed twice before us. The other neighbouring gate to the abyss would lie beyond that. I need not speak of our journey—during which we continued to leave an economical trail of paper—for it was precisely the same in kind as that by which we had reached the cul de sac; except that it tended to adhere more closely to the ground level and even descend to basement corridors. Every now and then we could trace certain disturbing marks in the debris or litter under foot; and after we had passed outside the radius of the gasoline scent we were again faintly conscious—spasmodically—of that more hideous and more persistent scent. After the way had branched from our former course we sometimes gave the rays of our single torch a furtive sweep along the walls; noting in almost every case the well-nigh omnipresent sculptures, which indeed seem to have formed a main aesthetic outlet for the Old Ones.

About 9:30 PM, while traversing a vaulted corridor whose increasingly glaciated floor seemed somewhat below the ground level and whose roof grew lower as we advanced, we began to see strong daylight ahead and were able to turn off our torch. It appeared that we were coming to the vast circular place, and that our distance

from the upper air could not be very great. The corridor ended in an arch surprisingly low for these megalithic ruins, but we could see much through it even before we emerged. Beyond there stretched a prodigious round space—fully 200 feet in diameter—strown with debris and containing many choked archways corresponding to the one we were about to cross. The walls were—in available spaces—boldly sculptured into a spiral band of heroic proportions; and displayed, despite the destructive weathering caused by the openness of the spot, an artistic splendour far beyond anything we had encountered before. The littered floor was quite heavily glaciated, and we fancied that the true bottom lay at a considerably lower depth.

But the salient object of the place was the titanic stone ramp which, eluding the archways by a sharp turn outward into the open floor, wound spirally up the stupendous cylindrical wall like an inside counterpart of those once climbing outside the monstrous towers or ziggurats of antique Babylon. Only the rapidity of our flight, and the perspective which confounded the descent with the tower's inner wall, had prevented our noticing this feature from the air, and thus caused us to seek another avenue to the sub-glacial level. Pabodie might have been able to tell what sort of engineering held it in place, but Danforth and I could merely admire and marvel. We could see mighty stone corbels and pillars here and there, but what we saw seemed inadequate to the function performed. The thing was excellently preserved up to the present top of the tower—a highly remarkable circumstance in view of its exposure—and its shelter had done much to protect the bizarre and disturbing cosmic sculptures on the walls.

As we stepped out into the awesome half-daylight of this monstrous cylinder-bottom—fifty million years

old, and without doubt the most primally ancient structure ever to meet our eyes—we saw that the ramp-traversed sides stretched dizzily up to a height of fully sixty feet. This, we recalled from our aërial survey, meant an outside glaciation of some forty feet; since the yawning gulf we had seen from the plane had been at the top of an approximately twenty-foot mound of crumbled masonry, somewhat sheltered for three-fourths of its circumference by the massive curving walls of a line of higher ruins. According to the sculptures the original tower had stood in the centre of an immense circular plaza; and had been perhaps 500 or 600 feet high, with tiers of horizontal discs near the top, and a row of needle-like spires along the upper rim. Most of the masonry had obviously toppled outward rather than inward—a fortunate happening, since otherwise the ramp might have been shattered and the whole interior choked. As it was, the ramp shewed sad battering; whilst the choking was such that all the archways at the bottom seemed to have been recently half-cleared.

It took us only a moment to conclude that this was indeed the route by which those others had descended, and that this would be the logical route for our own ascent despite the long trail of paper we had left elsewhere. The tower's mouth was no farther from the foothills and our waiting plane than was the great terraced building we had entered, and any further sub-glacial exploration we might make on this trip would lie in this general region. Oddly, we were still thinking about possible later trips—even after all we had seen and guessed. Then as we picked our way cautiously over the debris of the great floor, there came a sight which for the time excluded all other matters.

It was the neatly huddled array of three sledges in that farther angle of the ramp's lower and outward-

projecting course which had hitherto been screened from our view. There they were—the three sledges missing from Lake's camp—shaken by a hard usage which must have included forcible dragging along great reaches of snowless masonry and debris, as well as much hand portage over utterly unnavigable places. They were carefully and intelligently packed and strapped, and contained things memorably familiar enough—the gasoline stove, fuel cans, instrument cases, provision tins, tarpaulins obviously bulging with books, and some bulging with less obvious contents— everything derived from Lake's equipment. After what we had found in that other room, we were in a measure prepared for this encounter. The really great shock came when we stepped over and undid one tarpaulin whose outlines had peculiarly disquieted us. It seems that others as well as Lake had been interested in collecting typical specimens; for there were two here, both stiffly frozen, perfectly preserved, patched with adhesive plaster where some wounds around the neck had occurred, and wrapped with patent care to prevent further damage. They were the bodies of young Gedney and the missing dog.

X

Many people will probably judge us callous as well as mad for thinking about the northward tunnel and the abyss so soon after our sombre discovery, and I am not prepared to say that we would have immediately re- vived such thoughts but for a specific circumstance which broke in upon us and set up a whole new train of speculations. We had replaced the tarpaulin over poor Gedney and were standing in a kind of mute be- wilderment when the sounds finally reached our

consciousness—the first sounds we had heard since descending out of the open where the mountain wind whined faintly from its unearthly heights. Well known and mundane though they were, their presence in this remote world of death was more unexpected and unnerving than any grotesque or fabulous tones could possibly have been—since they gave a fresh upsetting to all our notions of cosmic harmony.

Had it been some trace of that bizarre musical piping over a wide range which Lake's dissection report had led us to expect in those others—and which, indeed, our overwrought fancies had been reading into every wind-howl we had heard since coming on the camp horror—it would have had a kind of hellish congruity with the aeon-dead region around us. A voice from other epochs belongs in a graveyard of other epochs. As it was, however, the noise shattered all our profoundly seated adjustments—all our tacit acceptance of the inner antarctic as a waste as utterly and irrevocably void of every vestige of normal life as the sterile disc of the moon. What we heard was not the fabulous note of any buried blasphemy of elder earth from whose supernal toughness an age-denied polar sun had evoked a monstrous response. Instead, it was a thing so mockingly normal and so unerringly familiarised by our sea days off Victoria Land and our camp days at McMurdo Sound that we shuddered to think of it here, where such things ought not to be. To be brief—it was simply the raucous squawking of a penguin.

The muffled sound floated from sub-glacial recesses nearly opposite to the corridor whence we had come—regions manifestly in the direction of that other tunnel to the vast abyss. The presence of a living water-bird in such a direction—in a world whose surface was one of age-long and uniform lifelessness—could lead to only one conclusion; hence our first thought was to verify the

objective reality of the sound. It was, indeed, repeated; and seemed at times to come from more than one throat. Seeking its source, we entered an archway from which much debris had been cleared; resuming our trail-blazing—with an added paper-supply taken with curious repugnance from one of the tarpaulin bundles on the sledges—when we left daylight behind.

As the glaciated floor gave place to a litter of detritus, we plainly discerned some curious dragging tracks; and once Danforth found a distinct print of a sort whose description would be only too superfluous. The course indicated by the penguin cries was precisely what our map and compass prescribed as an approach to the more northerly tunnel-mouth, and we were glad to find that a bridgeless thoroughfare on the ground and basement levels seemed open. The tunnel, according to the chart, ought to start from the basement of a large pyramidal structure which we seemed vaguely to recall from our aërial survey as remarkably well preserved. Along our path the single torch shewed a customary profusion of carvings, but we did not pause to examine any of these.

Suddenly a bulky white shape loomed up ahead of us, and we flashed on the second torch. It is odd how wholly this new quest had turned our minds from earlier fears of what might lurk near. Those other ones, having left their supplies in the great circular place, must have planned to return after their scouting trip toward or into the abyss; yet we had now discarded all caution concerning them as completely as if they had never existed. This white, waddling thing was fully six feet high, yet we seemed to realise at once that it was not one of those others. They were larger and dark, and according to the sculptures their motion over land surfaces was a swift, assured matter despite the queerness of their sea-born tentacle equipment. But to say

that the white thing did not profoundly frighten us would be vain. We were indeed clutched for an instant by a primitive dread almost sharper than the worst of our reasoned fears regarding those others. Then came a flash of anticlimax as the white shape sidled into a lateral archway to our left to join two others of its kind which had summoned it in raucous tones. For it was only a penguin—albeit of a huge, unknown species larger than the greatest of the known king penguins, and monstrous in its combined albinism and virtual eyelessness.

When we had followed the thing into the archway and turned both our torches on the indifferent and unheeding group of three we saw that they were all eyeless albinos of the same unknown and gigantic species. Their size reminded us of some of the archaic penguins depicted in the Old Ones' sculptures, and it did not take us long to conclude that they were descended from the same stock—undoubtedly surviving through a retreat to some warmer inner region whose perpetual blackness had destroyed their pigmentation and atrophied their eyes to mere useless slits. That their present habitat was the vast abyss we sought, was not for a moment to be doubted; and this evidence of the gulf's continued warmth and habitability filled us with the most curious and subtly perturbing fancies.

We wondered, too, what had caused these three birds to venture out of their usual domain. The state and silence of the great dead city made it clear that it had at no time been an habitual seasonal rookery, whilst the manifest indifference of the trio to our presence made it seem odd that any passing party of those others should have startled them. Was it possible that those others had taken some aggressive action or tried to increase their meat supply? We doubted whether that pungent odour which the dogs had hated could cause an equal

antipathy in these penguins; since their ancestors had obviously lived on excellent terms with the Old Ones— an amicable relationship which must have survived in the abyss below as long as any of the Old Ones remained. Regretting—in a flareup of the old spirit of pure science—that we could not photograph these anomalous creatures, we shortly left them to their squawking and pushed on toward the abyss whose openness was now so positively proved to us, and whose exact direction occasional penguin tracks made clear.

Not long afterward a steep descent in a long, low, doorless, and peculiarly sculptureless corridor led us to believe that we were approaching the tunnel-mouth at last. We had passed two more penguins, and heard others immediately ahead. Then the corridor ended in a prodigious open space which made us gasp involuntarily—a perfect inverted hemisphere, obviously deep underground; fully an hundred feet in diameter and fifty feet high, with low archways opening around all parts of the circumference but one, and that one yawning cavernously with a black arched aperture which broke the symmetry of the vault to a height of nearly fifteen feet. It was the entrance to the great abyss.

In this vast hemisphere, whose concave roof was impressively though decadently carved to a likeness of the primordial celestial dome, a few albino penguins waddled—aliens there, but indifferent and unseeing. The black tunnel yawned indefinitely off at a steep descending grade, its aperture adorned with grotesquely chiselled jambs and lintel. From that cryptical mouth we fancied a current of slightly warmer air and perhaps even a suspicion of vapour proceeded; and we wondered what living entities other than penguins the limitless void below, and the contiguous honeycombings of the land and the titan mountains,

might conceal. We wondered, too, whether the trace of mountain-top smoke at first suspected by poor Lake, as well as the odd haze we had ourselves perceived around the rampart-crowned peak, might not be caused by the tortuous-channelled rising of some such vapour from the unfathomed regions of earth's core.

Entering the tunnel, we saw that its outline was—at least at the start—about fifteen feet each way; sides, floor, and arched roof composed of the usual megalithic masonry. The sides were sparsely decorated with cartouches of conventional designs in a late, decadent style; and all the construction and carving were marvellously well preserved. The floor was quite clear, except for a slight detritus bearing outgoing penguin tracks and the inward tracks of those others. The farther one advanced, the warmer it became; so that we were soon unbuttoning our heavy garments. We wondered whether there were any actually igneous manifestations below, and whether the waters of that sunless sea were hot. After a short distance the masonry gave place to solid rock, though the tunnel kept the same proportions and presented the same aspect of carved regularity. Occasionally its varying grade became so steep that grooves were cut in the floor. Several times we noted the mouths of small lateral galleries not recorded in our diagrams; none of them such as to complicate the problem of our return, and all of them welcome as possible refuges in case we met unwelcome entities on their way back from the abyss. The nameless scent of such things was very distinct. Doubtless it was suicidally foolish to venture into that tunnel under the known conditions, but the lure of the unplumbed is stronger in certain persons than most suspect—indeed, it was just such a lure which had brought us to this unearthly polar waste in the first place. We saw several penguins as we passed along, and speculated on the distance we would

doubtless ⬚⬚⬚
temperature was rapidly ⬚⬚⬚
surprised to come upon a careless ⬚⬚⬚
shudderingly familiar to us. It was composed of furs
and tent-cloth taken from Lake's camp, and we did not
pause to study the bizarre forms into which the fabrics
had been slashed. Slightly beyond this point we noticed
a decided increase in the size and number of the
side-galleries, and concluded that the densely honeycombed region beneath the higher foothills must now
have been reached. The nameless scent was now curiously mixed with another and scarcely less offensive
odour—of what nature we could not guess, though we
thought of decaying organisms and perhaps unknown
subterrene fungi. Then came a startling expansion of
the tunnel for which the carvings had not prepared
us—a broadening and rising into a lofty, natural-
looking elliptical cavern with a level floor; some 75 feet
long and 50 broad, and with many immense side-
passages leading away into cryptical darkness.

Though this cavern was natural in appearance, an
inspection with both torches suggested that it had been
formed by the artificial destruction of several walls
between adjacent honeycombings. The walls were
rough, and the high vaulted roof was thick with
stalactites; but the solid rock floor had been smoothed
off, and was free from all debris, detritus, or even dust
to a positively abnormal extent. Except for the avenue

ㅡ ㅡㅡ passage immediately ahead, as ㅡㅡ ㅡ ㅡㅡ larger proportion of penguin-droppings there, prevented all confusion as to the right course amidst this plethora of equally great cave-mouths. Nevertheless we resolved to resume our paper trail-blazing if any further complexity should develop; for dust tracks, of course, could no longer be expected. Upon resuming our direct progress we cast a beam of torchlight over the tunnel walls—and stopped short in amazement at the supremely radical change which had come over the carvings in this part of the passage. We realised, of course, the great decadence of the Old Ones' sculpture at the time of the tunnelling; and had indeed noticed the inferior workmanship of the arabesques in the stretches behind us. But now, in this deeper section beyond the cavern, there was a sudden difference wholly transcending explanation—a difference in basic nature as well as in mere quality, and involving so profound and calamitous a degradation of skill that nothing in the hitherto observed rate of decline could have led one to expect it.

This new and degenerate work was coarse, bold, and wholly lacking in delicacy of detail. It was counter-sunk with exaggerated depth in bands following the same general line as the sparse cartouches of the earlier sections, but the height of the reliefs did not reach the

level of the general surface. Danforth had the idea that it was a second carving—a sort of palimpsest formed after the obliteration of a previous design. In nature it was wholly decorative and conventional; and consisted of crude spirals and angles roughly following the quintile mathematical tradition of the Old Ones, yet seeming more like a parody than a perpetuation of that tradition. We could not get it out of our minds that some subtly but profoundly alien element had been added to the aesthetic feeling behind the technique—an alien element, Danforth guessed, that was responsible for the manifestly laborious substitution. It was like, yet disturbingly unlike, what we had come to recognise as the Old Ones' art; and I was persistently reminded of such hybrid things as the ungainly Palmyrene sculptures fashioned in the Roman manner. That others had recently noticed this belt of carving was hinted by the presence of a used torch battery on the floor in front of one of the most characteristic designs.

Since we could not afford to spend any considerable time in study, we resumed our advance after a cursory look; though frequently casting beams over the walls to see if any further decorative changes developed. Nothing of the sort was perceived, though the carvings were in places rather sparse because of the numerous mouths of smooth-floored lateral tunnels. We saw and heard fewer penguins, but thought we caught a vague suspicion of an infinitely distant chorus of them somewhere deep within the earth. The new and inexplicable odour was abominably strong, and we could detect scarcely a sign of that other nameless scent. Puffs of visible vapour ahead bespoke increasing contrasts in temperature, and the relative nearness of the sunless sea-cliffs of the great abyss. Then, quite unexpectedly, we saw certain obstructions on the polished floor ahead—

through which we had come, this was true of t of all the great galleries opening off from it; singularity of the condition was such as to set us puzzling. The curious new foetor which supplemented the nameless scent was excessively gent here; so much so that it destroyed all trace o other. Something about this whole place, with polished and almost glistening floor, struck us as m vaguely baffling and horrible than any of the m things we had previously encountered

The regularity of the
well as th

ve to traverse. The carvings had led us to expect a
eep downhill walk of about a mile to the abyss, but
ur previous wanderings had shewn us that matters of
cale were not wholly to be depended on.

After about a quarter of a mile that nameless scent
became greatly accentuated, and we kept very careful
track of the various lateral openings we passed. There
was no visible vapour as at the mouth, but this was
⋯ due to the lack of contrasting cooler air. The
⋯ ⋯idly ascending, and we were not
⋯ ⋯ heap of material

obstructions which were quite definitely not penguins
—and turned on our second torch after making sure
that the objects were quite stationary.

XI

Still another time have I come to a place where it is very
difficult to proceed. I ought to be hardened by this
stage; but there are some experiences and intimations
which scar too deeply to permit of healing, and leave
only such an added sensitiveness that memory re-
inspires all the original horror. We saw, as I have said,
certain obstructions on the polished floor ahead; and I
may add that our nostrils were assailed almost simultaneously by a very curious intensification of the strange
prevailing foetor, now quite plainly mixed with the
nameless stench of those others which had gone before
us. The light of the second torch left no doubt of what
the obstructions were, and we dared approach them
only because we could see, even from a distance, that
they were quite as past all harming power as had been
the six similar specimens unearthed from the monstrous star-mounded graves at poor Lake's camp.

They were, indeed, as lacking in completeness as
most of those we had unearthed—though it grew plain
from the thick, dark-green pool gathering around them
that their incompleteness was of infinitely greater recency. There seemed to be only four of them, whereas
Lake's bulletins would have suggested no less than eight
as forming the group which had preceded us. To find
them in this state was wholly unexpected, and we
wondered what sort of monstrous struggle had occurred down here in the dark.

Penguins, attacked in a body, retaliate savagely with
their beaks; and our ears now made certain the existence of a rookery far beyond. Had those others dis-

turbed such a place and aroused murderous pursuit? The obstructions did not suggest it, for penguin beaks against the tough tissues Lake had dissected could hardly account for the terrible damage our approaching glance was beginning to make out. Besides, the huge blind birds we had seen appeared to be singularly peaceful.

Had there, then, been a struggle among those others, and were the absent four responsible? If so, where were they? Were they close at hand and likely to form an immediate menace to us? We glanced anxiously at some of the smooth-floored lateral passages as we continued our slow and frankly reluctant approach. Whatever the conflict was, it had clearly been that which had frightened the penguins into their unaccustomed wandering. It must, then, have arisen near that faintly heard rookery in the incalculable gulf beyond, since there were no signs that any birds had normally dwelt here. Perhaps, we reflected, there had been a hideous running fight, with the weaker party seeking to get back to the cached sledges when their pursuers finished them. One could picture the daemoniac fray between namelessly monstrous entities as it surged out of the black abyss with great clouds of frantic penguins squawking and scurrying ahead.

I say that we approached those sprawling and incomplete obstructions slowly and reluctantly. Would to heaven we had never approached them at all, but had run back at top speed out of that blasphemous tunnel with the greasily smooth floors and the degenerate murals aping and mocking the things they had superseded—run back, before we had seen what we did see, and before our minds were burned with something which will never let us breathe easily again!

Both of our torches were turned on the prostrate objects, so that we soon realised the dominant factor in their incompleteness. Mauled, compressed, twisted,

and ruptured as they were, their chief common injury was total decapitation. From each one the tentacled starfish-head had been removed; and as we drew near we saw that the manner of removal looked more like some hellish tearing or suction than like any ordinary form of cleavage. Their noisome dark-green ichor formed a large, spreading pool; but its stench was half overshadowed by that newer and stranger stench, here more pungent than at any other point along our route. Only when we had come very close to the sprawling obstructions could we trace that second, unexplainable foetor to any immediate source—and the instant we did so Danforth, remembering certain very vivid sculptures of the Old Ones' history in the Permian age 150 million years ago, gave vent to a nerve-tortured cry which echoed hysterically through that vaulted and archaic passage with the evil palimpsest carvings.

I came only just short of echoing his cry myself; for I had seen those primal sculptures, too, and had shudderingly admired the way the nameless artist had suggested that hideous slime-coating found on certain incomplete and prostrate Old Ones—those whom the frightful shoggoths had characteristically slain and sucked to a ghastly headlessness in the great war of re-subjugation. They were infamous, nightmare sculptures even when telling of age-old, bygone things; for shoggoths and their work ought not to be seen by human beings or portrayed by any beings. The mad author of the *Necronomicon* had nervously tried to swear that none had been bred on this planet, and that only drugged dreamers had ever conceived them. Formless protoplasm able to mock and reflect all forms and organs and processes—viscous agglutinations of bubbling cells—rubbery fifteen-foot spheroids infinitely plastic and ductile—slaves of suggestion, builders of cities—more and more sullen, more and more intelli-

gent, more and more amphibious, more and more imitative—Great God! What madness made even those blasphemous Old Ones willing to use and to carve such things?

And now, when Danforth and I saw the freshly glistening and reflectively iridescent black slime which clung thickly to those headless bodies and stank obscenely with that new unknown odour whose cause only a diseased fancy could envisage—clung to those bodies and sparkled less voluminously on a smooth part of the accursedly re-sculptured wall *in a series of grouped dots*—we understood the quality of cosmic fear to its uttermost depths. It was not fear of those four missing others—for all too well did we suspect they would do no harm again. Poor devils! After all, they were not evil things of their kind. They were the men of another age and another order of being. Nature had played a hellish jest on them—as it will on any others that human madness, callousness, or cruelty may hereafter drag up in that hideously dead or sleeping polar waste—and this was their tragic homecoming.

They had not been even savages—for what indeed had they done? That awful awakening in the cold of an unknown epoch—perhaps an attack by the furry, frantically barking quadrupeds, and a dazed defence against them and the equally frantic white simians with the queer wrappings and paraphernalia . . . poor Lake, poor Gedney . . . and poor Old Ones! Scientists to the last—what had they done that we would not have done in their place? God, what intelligence and persistence! What a facing of the incredible, just as those carven kinsmen and forbears had faced things only a little less incredible! Radiates, vegetables, monstrosities, starspawn—whatever they had been, they were men!

They had crossed the icy peaks on whose templed slopes they had once worshipped and roamed among

the tree-ferns. They had found their dead city brooding under its curse, and had read its carven latter days as we had done. They had tried to reach their living fellows in fabled depths of blackness they had never seen—and what had they found? All this flashed in unison through the thoughts of Danforth and me as we looked from those headless, slime-coated shapes to the loathsome palimpsest sculptures and the diabolical dot-groups of fresh slime on the wall beside them—looked and understood what must have triumphed and survived down there in the Cyclopean water-city of that nighted, penguin-fringed abyss, whence even now a sinister curling mist had begun to belch pallidly as if in answer to Danforth's hysterical scream.

The shock of recognising that monstrous slime and headlessness had frozen us into mute, motionless statues, and it is only through later conversations that we have learned of the complete identity of our thoughts at that moment. It seemed aeons that we stood there, but actually it could not have been more than ten or fifteen seconds. That hateful, pallid mist curled forward as if veritably driven by some remoter advancing bulk—and then came a sound which upset much of what we had just decided, and in so doing broke the spell and enabled us to run like mad past squawking, confused penguins over our former trail back to the city, along ice-sunken megalithic corridors to the great open circle, and up that archaic spiral ramp in a frenzied automatic plunge for the sane outer air and light of day.

The new sound, as I have intimated, upset much that we had decided; because it was what poor Lake's dissection had led us to attribute to those we had just judged dead. It was, Danforth later told me, precisely what he had caught in infinitely muffled form when at that spot beyond the alley-corner above the glacial level; and it certainly had a shocking resemblance to

the wind-pipings we had both heard around the lofty mountain caves. At the risk of seeming puerile I will add another thing, too; if only because of the surprising way Danforth's impression chimed with mine. Of course common reading is what prepared us both to make the interpretation, though Danforth has hinted at queer notions about unsuspected and forbidden sources to which Poe may have had access when writing his *Arthur Gordon Pym* a century ago. It will be remembered that in that fantastic tale there is a word of unknown but terrible and prodigious significance connected with the antarctic and screamed eternally by the gigantic, spectrally snowy birds of that malign region's core. *"Tekeli-li! Tekeli-li!"* That, I may admit, is exactly what we thought we heard conveyed by that sudden sound behind the advancing white mist—that insidious musical piping over a singularly wide range.

We were in full flight before three notes or syllables had been uttered, though we knew that the swiftness of the Old Ones would enable any scream-roused and pursuing survivor of the slaughter to overtake us in a moment if it really wished to do so. We had a vague hope, however, that non-aggressive conduct and a display of kindred reason might cause such a being to spare us in case of capture; if only from scientific curiosity. After all, if such an one had nothing to fear for itself it would have no motive in harming us. Concealment being futile at this juncture, we used our torch for a running glance behind, and perceived that the mist was thinning. Would we see, at last, a complete and living specimen of those others? Again came that insidious musical piping—*"Tekeli-li! Tekeli-li!"*

Then, noting that we were actually gaining on our pursuer, it occurred to us that the entity might be wounded. We could take no chances, however, since it was very obviously approaching in answer to Dan-

forth's scream rather than in flight from any other entity. The timing was too close to admit of doubt. Of the whereabouts of that less conceivable and less mentionable nightmare—that foetid, unglimpsed mountain of slime-spewing protoplasm whose race had conquered the abyss and sent land pioneers to recarve and squirm through the burrows of the hills—we could form no guess; and it cost us a genuine pang to leave this probably crippled Old One—perhaps a lone survivor—to the peril of recapture and a nameless fate.

Thank heaven we did not slacken our run. The curling mist had thickened again, and was driving ahead with increased speed; whilst the straying penguins in our rear were squawking and screaming and displaying signs of a panic really surprising in view of their relatively minor confusion when we had passed them. Once more came that sinister, wide-ranged piping—*"Tekeli-li! Tekeli-li!"* We had been wrong. The thing was not wounded, but had merely paused on encountering the bodies of its fallen kindred and the hellish slime inscription above them. We could never know what that daemon message was—but those burials at Lake's camp had shewn how much importance the beings attached to their dead. Our recklessly used torch now revealed ahead of us the large open cavern where various ways converged, and we were glad to be leaving those morbid palimpsest sculptures—almost felt even when scarcely seen—behind.

Another thought which the advent of the cave inspired was the possibility of losing our pursuer at this bewildering focus of large galleries. There were several of the blind albino penguins in the open space, and it seemed clear that their fear of the oncoming entity was extreme to the point of unaccountability. If at that point we dimmed our torch to the very lowest limit of travelling need, keeping it strictly in front of us, the

frightened squawking motions of the huge birds in the mist might muffle our footfalls, screen our true course, and somehow set up a false lead. Amidst the churning, spiralling fog the littered and unglistening floor of the main tunnel beyond this point, as differing from the other morbidly polished burrows, could hardly form a highly distinguishing feature; even, so far as we could conjecture, for those indicated special senses which made the Old Ones partly though imperfectly independent of light in emergencies. In fact, we were somewhat apprehensive lest we go astray ourselves in our haste. For we had, of course, decided to keep straight on toward the dead city; since the consequences of loss in those unknown foothill honeycombings would be unthinkable.

The fact that we survived and emerged is sufficient proof that the thing did take a wrong gallery whilst we providentially hit on the right one. The penguins alone could not have saved us, but in conjunction with the mist they seem to have done so. Only a benign fate kept the curling vapours thick enough at the right moment, for they were constantly shifting and threatening to vanish. Indeed, they did lift for a second just before we emerged from the nauseously re-sculptured tunnel into the cave; so that we actually caught one first and only half-glimpse of the oncoming entity as we cast a final, desperately fearful glance backward before dimming the torch and mixing with the penguins in the hope of dodging pursuit. If the fate which screened us was benign, that which gave us the half-glimpse was infinitely the opposite; for to that flash of semi-vision can be traced a full half of the horror which has ever since haunted us.

Our exact motive in looking back again was perhaps no more than the immemorial instinct of the pursued to gauge the nature and course of its pursuer; or

perhaps it was an automatic attempt to answer a subconscious question raised by one of our senses. In the midst of our flight, with all our faculties centred on the problem of escape, we were in no condition to observe and analyse details; yet even so our latent brain-cells must have wondered at the message brought them by our nostrils. Afterward we realised what it was—that our retreat from the foetid slime-coating on those headless obstructions, and the coincident approach of the pursuing entity, had not brought us the exchange of stenches which logic called for. In the neighbourhood of the prostrate things that new and lately unexplainable foetor had been wholly dominant; but by this time it ought to have largely given place to the nameless stench associated with those others. This it had not done—for instead, the newer and less bearable smell was now virtually undiluted, and growing more and more poisonously insistent each second.

So we glanced back—simultaneously, it would appear; though no doubt the incipient motion of one prompted the imitation of the other. As we did so we flashed both torches full strength at the momentarily thinned mist; either from sheer primitive anxiety to see all we could, or in a less primitive but equally unconscious effort to dazzle the entity before we dimmed our light and dodged among the penguins of the labyrinth-centre ahead. Unhappy act! Not Orpheus himself, or Lot's wife, paid much more dearly for a backward glance. And again came that shocking, wide-ranged piping—*"Tekeli-li! Tekeli-li!"*

I might as well be frank—even if I cannot bear to be quite direct—in stating what we saw; though at the time we felt that it was not to be admitted even to each other. The words reaching the reader can never even suggest the awfulness of the sight itself. It crippled our consciousness so completely that I wonder we had the

residual sense to dim our torches as planned, and to strike the right tunnel toward the dead city. Instinct alone must have carried us through—perhaps better than reason could have done; though if that was what saved us, we paid a high price. Of reason we certainly had little enough left. Danforth was totally unstrung, and the first thing I remember of the rest of the journey was hearing him light-headedly chant an hysterical formula in which I alone of mankind could have found anything but insane irrelevance. It reverberated in falsetto echoes among the squawks of the penguins; reverberated through the vaultings ahead, and—thank God—through the now empty vaultings behind. He could not have begun it at once—else we would not have been alive and blindly racing. I shudder to think of what a shade of difference in his nervous reactions might have brought.

"South Station Under—Washington Under—Park Street Under—Kendall—Central—Harvard. . . ." The poor fellow was chanting the familiar stations of the Boston–Cambridge tunnel that burrowed through our peaceful native soil thousands of miles away in New England, yet to me the ritual had neither irrelevance nor home-feeling. It had only horror, because I knew unerringly the monstrous, nefandous analogy that had suggested it. We had expected, upon looking back, to see a terrible and incredibly moving entity if the mists were thin enough; but of that entity we had formed a clear idea. What we did see—for the mists were indeed all too malignly thinned—was something altogether different, and immeasurably more hideous and detestable. It was the utter, objective embodiment of the fantastic novelist's 'thing that should not be'; and its nearest comprehensible analogue is a vast, onrushing subway train as one sees it from a station platform— the great black front looming colossally out of infinite

subterraneous distance, constellated with strangely col-
oured lights and filling the prodigious burrow as a
piston fills a cylinder.

But we were not on a station platform. We were on
the track ahead as the nightmare plastic column of
foetid black iridescence oozed tightly onward through
its fifteen-foot sinus; gathering unholy speed and driving before it a spiral, re-thickening cloud of the pallid
abyss-vapour. It was a terrible, indescribable thing
vaster than any subway train—a shapeless congeries of
protoplasmic bubbles, faintly self-luminous, and with
myriads of temporary eyes forming and unforming as
pustules of greenish light all over the tunnel-filling front
that bore down upon us, crushing the frantic penguins
and slithering over the glistening floor that it and its
kind had swept so evilly free of all litter. Still came that
eldritch, mocking cry—*"Tekeli-li! Tekeli-li!"* And at
last we remembered that the daemoniac shoggoths—
given life, thought, and plastic organ patterns solely by
the Old Ones, and having no language save that which
the dot-groups expressed—*had likewise no voice save
the imitated accents of their bygone masters.*

XII

Danforth and I have recollections of emerging into the
great sculptured hemisphere and of threading our back
trail through the Cyclopean rooms and corridors of the
dead city; yet these are purely dream-fragments involving no memory of volition, details, or physical exertion.
It was as if we floated in a nebulous world or dimension
without time, causation, or orientation. The grey half-
daylight of the vast circular space sobered us somewhat;
but we did not go near those cached sledges or look
again at poor Gedney and the dog. They have a strange

and titanic mausoleum, and I hope the end of this planet will find them still undisturbed.

It was while struggling up the colossal spiral incline that we first felt the terrible fatigue and short breath which our race through the thin plateau air had produced; but not even the fear of collapse could make us pause before reaching the normal outer realm of sun and sky. There was something vaguely appropriate about our departure from those buried epochs; for as we wound our panting way up the sixty-foot cylinder of primal masonry we glimpsed beside us a continuous procession of heroic sculptures in the dead race's early and undecayed technique—a farewell from the Old Ones, written fifty million years ago.

Finally scrambling out at the top, we found ourselves on a great mound of tumbled blocks; with the curved walls of higher stonework rising westward, and the brooding peaks of the great mountains shewing beyond the more crumbled structures toward the east. The low antarctic sun of midnight peered redly from the southern horizon through rifts in the jagged ruins, and the terrible age and deadness of the nightmare city seemed all the starker by contrast with such relatively known and accustomed things as the features of the polar landscape. The sky above was a churning and opalescent mass of tenuous ice-vapours, and the cold clutched at our vitals. Wearily resting the outfit-bags to which we had instinctively clung throughout our desperate flight, we rebuttoned our heavy garments for the stumbling climb down the mound and the walk through the aeon-old stone maze to the foothills where our aëroplane waited. Of what had set us fleeing from the darkness of earth's secret and archaic gulfs we said nothing at all.

In less than a quarter of an hour we had found the steep grade to the foothills—the probable ancient

terrace—by which we had descended, and could see the dark bulk of our great plane amidst the sparse ruins on the rising slope ahead. Half way uphill toward our goal we paused for a momentary breathing-spell, and turned to look again at the fantastic palaeogean tangle of incredible stone shapes below us—once more outlined mystically against an unknown west. As we did so we saw that the sky beyond had lost its morning haziness; the restless ice-vapours having moved up to the zenith, where their mocking outlines seemed on the point of settling into some bizarre pattern which they feared to make quite definite or conclusive.

There now lay revealed on the ultimate white horizon behind the grotesque city a dim, elfin line of pinnacled violet whose needle-pointed heights loomed dream-like against the beckoning rose-colour of the western sky. Up toward this shimmering rim sloped the ancient table-land, the depressed course of the bygone river traversing it as an irregular ribbon of shadow. For a second we gasped in admiration of the scene's unearthly cosmic beauty, and then vague horror began to creep into our souls. For this far violet line could be nothing else than the terrible mountains of the forbidden land—highest of earth's peaks and focus of earth's evil; harbourers of nameless horrors and Archaean secrets; shunned and prayed to by those who feared to carve their meaning; untrodden by any living thing of earth, but visited by the sinister lightnings and sending strange beams across the plains in the polar night—beyond doubt the unknown archetype of that dreaded Kadath in the Cold Waste beyond abhorrent Leng, whereof unholy primal legends hint evasively. We were the first human beings ever to see them—and I hope to God we may be the last.

If the sculptured maps and pictures in that pre-human city had told truly, these cryptic violet moun-

tains could not be much less than 300 miles away; yet none the less sharply did their dim elfin essence jut above that remote and snowy rim, like the serrated edge of a monstrous alien planet about to rise into unaccustomed heavens. Their height, then, must have been tremendous beyond all known comparison—carrying them up into tenuous atmospheric strata peopled by such gaseous wraiths as rash flyers have barely lived to whisper of after unexplainable falls. Looking at them, I thought nervously of certain sculptured hints of what the great bygone river had washed down into the city from their accursed slopes—and wondered how much sense and how much folly had lain in the fears of those Old Ones who carved them so reticently. I recalled how their northerly end must come near the coast at Queen Mary Land, where even at that moment Sir Douglas Mawson's expedition was doubtless working less than a thousand miles away; and hoped that no evil fate would give Sir Douglas and his men a glimpse of what might lie beyond the protecting coastal range. Such thoughts formed a measure of my overwrought condition at the time—and Danforth seemed to be even worse.

Yet long before we had passed the great star-shaped ruin and reached our plane our fears had become transferred to the lesser but vast enough range whose re-crossing lay ahead of us. From these foothills the black, ruin-crusted slopes reared up starkly and hideously against the east, again reminding us of those strange Asian paintings of Nicholas Roerich; and when we thought of the damnable honeycombs inside them, and of the frightful amorphous entities that might have pushed their foetidly squirming way even to the topmost hollow pinnacles, we could not face without panic the prospect of again sailing by those suggestive sky-

ward cave-mouths where the wind made sounds like an evil musical piping over a wide range. To make matters worse, we saw distinct traces of local mist around several of the summits—as poor Lake must have done when he made that early mistake about volcanism—and thought shiveringly of that kindred mist from which we had just escaped; of that, and of the blasphemous, horror-fostering abyss whence all such vapours came.

All was well with the plane, and we clumsily hauled on our heavy flying furs. Danforth got the engine started without trouble, and we made a very smooth takeoff over the nightmare city. Below us the primal Cyclopean masonry spread out as it had done when first we saw it—so short, yet infinitely long, a time ago—and we began rising and turning to test the wind for our crossing through the pass. At a very high level there must have been great disturbance, since the ice-dust clouds of the zenith were doing all sorts of fantastic things; but at 24,000 feet, the height we needed for the pass, we found navigation quite practicable. As we drew close to the jutting peaks the wind's strange piping again became manifest, and I could see Danforth's hands trembling at the controls. Rank amateur though I was, I thought at that moment that I might be a better navigator than he in effecting the dangerous crossing between pinnacles; and when I made motions to change seats and take over his duties he did not protest. I tried to keep all my skill and self-possession about me, and stared at the sector of reddish farther sky betwixt the walls of the pass—resolutely refusing to pay attention to the puffs of mountain-top vapour, and wishing that I had wax-stopped ears like Ulysses' men off the Sirens' coast to keep that disturbing wind-piping from my consciousness.

But Danforth, released from his piloting and keyed up to a dangerous nervous pitch, could not keep quiet. I felt him turning and wriggling about as he looked back at the terrible receding city, ahead at the cave-riddled, cube-barnacled peaks, sidewise at the bleak sea of snowy, rampart-strown foothills, and upward at the seething, grotesquely clouded sky. It was then, just as I was trying to steer safely through the pass, that his mad shrieking brought us so close to disaster by shattering my tight hold on myself and causing me to fumble helplessly with the controls for a moment. A second afterward my resolution triumphed and we made the crossing safely—yet I am afraid that Danforth will never be the same again.

I have said that Danforth refused to tell me what final horror made him scream out so insanely—a horror which, I feel sadly sure, is mainly responsible for his present breakdown. We had snatches of shouted conversation above the wind's piping and the engine's buzzing as we reached the safe side of the range and swooped slowly down toward the camp, but that had mostly to do with the pledges of secrecy we had made as we prepared to leave the nightmare city. Certain things, we had agreed, were not for people to know and discuss lightly—and I would not speak of them now but for the need of heading off that Starkweather-Moore Expedition, and others, at any cost. It is absolutely necessary, for the peace and safety of mankind, that some of earth's dark, dead corners and unplumbed depths be let alone; lest sleeping abnormalities wake to resurgent life, and blasphemously surviving nightmares squirm and splash out of their black lairs to newer and wider conquests.

All that Danforth has ever hinted is that the final horror was a mirage. It was not, he declares, anything

connected with the cubes and caves of echoing, vaporous, wormily honeycombed mountains of madness which we crossed; but a single fantastic, daemoniac glimpse, among the churning zenith-clouds, of what lay back of those other violet westward mountains which the Old Ones had shunned and feared. It is very probable that the thing was a sheer delusion born of the previous stresses we had passed through, and of the actual though unrecognised mirage of the dead transmontane city experienced near Lake's camp the day before; but it was so real to Danforth that he suffers from it still.

He has on rare occasions whispered disjointed and irresponsible things about "the black pit," "the carven rim," "the proto-shoggoths," "the windowless solids with five dimensions," "the nameless cylinder," "the elder pharos," "Yog-Sothoth," "the primal white jelly," "the colour out of space," "the wings," "the eyes in darkness," "the moon-ladder," "the original, the eternal, the undying," and other bizarre conceptions; but when he is fully himself he repudiates all this and attributes it to his curious and macabre reading of earlier years. Danforth, indeed, is known to be among the few who have ever dared go completely through that worm-riddled copy of the *Necronomicon* kept under lock and key in the college library.

The higher sky, as we crossed the range, was surely vaporous and disturbed enough; and although I did not see the zenith I can well imagine that its swirls of ice-dust may have taken strange forms. Imagination, knowing how vividly distant scenes can sometimes be reflected, refracted, and magnified by such layers of restless cloud, might easily have supplied the rest—and of course Danforth did not hint any of those specific horrors till after his memory had

had a chance to draw on his bygone reading. He could never have seen so much in one instantaneous glance.

At the time his shrieks were confined to the repetition of a single mad word of all too obvious source:

"Tekeli-li! Tekeli-li!"

Madeline Yale Wynne (1847–1918)

THE LITTLE ROOM

Madeline Yale Wynne was an American artist, poet, and short story writer, the daughter of the inventor of the Yale lock. She is remembered for her early contributions to the arts-and-crafts movement, especially in jewelry and enamelling long before the crafts became fashionable. The *Encyclopedia of Arts and Crafts* says, "she learned about metal in the workshops of her father. . . . The ideas for her jewels grew out of the metal itself, from what happened when she hit a coil of silver with a hammer or drove a blunt punch into sheet copper—a similar approach to that of Alexander Calder half a century later," and praises her work as "witty and intuitive." Alfred Bendixen reports that she was known for her attempts to interest other women in this art form. Her writing, however, has been substantially forgotten. Although apparently "The Little Room" received much praise and attention upon its original appearance in *Harper's Magazine*, no mention of it or her appears in most standard reference books. Her collection, *The Little Room and Other Stories* (1895), is a little known book. But in fact "The Little Room" is a minor masterpiece, on a par with Charlotte Perkins Gilman's "The Yellow Wall-Paper," which it predates. It is not only a subtle feminist work but also a mysterious meditation upon the nature of reality, the more powerful for its ambiguity. A unique haunted house story, it achieves considerable psychological depth through attention to nuance and detail, and careful use of allusion

to events outside the story in the past. One wonders how many other stories of this quality have been forgotten.

How would it do for a smoking-room?"

"Just the very place! Only, you know, Roger, you must not think of smoking in the house. I am almost afraid that having just a plain, common man around, let alone a smoking man, will upset Aunt Hannah. She is New England—Vermont, New England —boiled down."

"You leave Aunt Hannah to me; I'll find her tender side. I'm going to ask her about the old sea-captain and the yellow calico."

"Not yellow calico—blue chintz."

"Well, yellow *shell* then."

"No, no! don't mix it up so; you won't know yourself what to expect, and that's half the fun."

"Now you tell me again exactly what to expect; to tell the truth, I didn't half hear about it the other day; I was wool-gathering. It was something queer that happened when you were a child, wasn't it?"

"Something that began to happen long before that, and kept happening, and may happen again—but I hope not."

"What was it?"

"I wonder if the other people in the car can hear us?"

"I fancy not; we don't hear them—not consecutively, at least."

"Well, mother was born in Vermont, you know; she was the only child by a second marriage. Aunt Hannah and Aunt Maria are only half-aunts to me, you know."

"I hope they are half as nice as you are."

"Roger, be still—they certainly will hear us."

"Well, don't you want them to know we are married?"

"Yes, but not just married. There's all the difference in the world."

"You are afraid we look too happy!"

"No, only I want my happiness all to myself."

"Well, the little room?"

"My aunts brought mother up; they were nearly twenty years older than she. I might say Hiram and they brought her up. You see, Hiram was bound out to my grandfather when he was a boy, and when grandfather died Hiram said he 's'posed he went with the farm, 'long o' the critters,' and he has been there ever since. He was my mother's only refuge from the decorum of my aunts. They are simply workers. They make me think of the Maine woman who wanted her epitaph to be: 'She was a *hard*-working woman.'"

"They must be almost beyond their working-days. How old are they?"

"Seventy, or thereabouts; but they will die standing; or, at least, on a Saturday night, after all the housework is done up. They were rather strict with mother, and I think she had a lonely childhood. The house is almost a mile away from any neighbours, and off on top of what they call Stony Hill. It is bleak enough up there, even in summer.

"When mamma was about ten years old they sent her to cousins in Brooklyn, who had children of their own, and knew more about bringing them up. She stayed there till she was married; she didn't go to Vermont in all that time, and of course hadn't seen her sisters, for they never would leave home for a day. They couldn't even be induced to go to Brooklyn for her wedding, so she and father took their wedding trip up there."

"And that's why we are going up there on our own?"

"Don't, Roger; you have no idea how loud you speak."

"You never say so except when I am going to say that one little word."

"Well, don't say it, then, or say it very, very quietly."

"Well, what was the queer thing?"

"When they got to the house, mother wanted to take father right off into the little room; she had been telling him about it, just as I am going to tell you, and she had said that of all the rooms, that one was the only one that seemed pleasant to her. She described the furniture and the books and paper and everything, and said it was on the north side, between the front and back rooms. Well, when they went to look for it, there was no little room there; there was only a shallow china-closet. She asked her sisters when the house had been altered and a closet made of the room that used to be there. They both said the house was exactly as it had been built—that they had never made any changes, except to tear down the old wood-shed and build a smaller one.

"Father and mother laughed a good deal over it, and when anything was lost they would always say it must be in the little room, and any exaggerated statement was called 'little-roomy.' When I was a child I thought that was a regular English phrase, I heard it so often.

"Well, they talked it over, and finally they concluded that my mother had been a very imaginative sort of a child, and had read in some book about such a little room, or perhaps even dreamed it, and then had 'made believe,' as children do, till she herself had really thought the room was there."

"Why, of course, that might easily happen."

"Yes, but you haven't heard the queer part yet; you wait and see if you can explain the rest as easily.

"They stayed at the farm two weeks, and then went to New York to live. When I was eight years old my father was killed in the war, and mother was broken-hearted. She never was quite strong afterwards, and that summer we decided to go up to the farm for three months.

"I was a restless sort of a child, and the journey seemed very long to me; and finally, to pass the time, mamma told me the story of the little room, and how it was all in her own imagination, and how there really was only a china-closet there.

"She told it with all the particulars; and even to me, who knew beforehand that the room wasn't there, it seemed just as real as could be. She said it was on the north side, between the front and back rooms; that it was very small, and they sometimes called it an entry. There was a door also that opened out-of-doors, and that one was painted green, and was cut in the middle like the old Dutch doors, so that it could be used for a window by opening the top part only. Directly opposite the door was a lounge or couch; it was covered with blue chintz—India chintz—some that had been brought over by an old Salem sea-captain as a 'venture.' He had given it to Hannah when she was a young girl. She was sent to Salem for two years to school. Grandfather originally came from Salem."

"I thought there wasn't any room or chintz."

"That is just it. They had decided that mother had imagined it all, and yet you see how exactly everything was painted in her mind, for she had even remembered that Hiram had told her that Hannah could have married the sea-captain if she had wanted to!

"The India cotton was the regular blue stamped chintz, with the peacock figure on it. The head and body of the bird were in profile, while the tail was full front view behind it. It had seemed to take mamma's fancy, and she drew it for me on a piece of paper as she talked. Doesn't it seem strange to you that she could have made all that up, or even dreamed it?

"At the foot of the lounge were some hanging shelves with some old books on them. All the books were leather-coloured except one; that was bright red, and

was called the *Ladies' Album*. It made a bright break between the other thicker books.

"On the lower shelf was a beautiful pink sea-shell, lying on a mat made of balls of red shaded worsted. This shell was greatly coveted by mother, but she was only allowed to play with it when she had been particularly good. Hiram had shown her how to hold it close to her ear and hear the roar of the sea in it.

"I know you will like Hiram, Roger; he is quite a character in his way.

"Mamma said she remembered, or *thought* she remembered, having been sick once, and she had to lie quietly for some days on the lounge; then was the time she had become so familiar with everything in the room, and she had been allowed to have the shell to play with all the time. She had had her toast brought to her in there, with make-believe tea. It was one of her pleasant memories of her childhood; it was the first time she had been of any importance to anybody, even herself.

"Right at the head of the lounge was a light-stand, as they called it, and on it was a very brightly-polished brass candlestick and a brass tray with snuffers. That is all I remember of her describing, except that there was a braided rag rug on the floor, and on the wall was a beautiful flowered paper—roses and morning-glories in a wreath on a light blue ground. The same paper was in the front room."

"And all this never existed except in her imagination?"

"She said that when she and father went up there, there wasn't any little room at all like it anywhere in the house; there was a china-closet where she had believed the room to be."

"And your aunts said there had never been any such room?"

"That is what they said."

"Wasn't there any blue chintz in the house with a peacock figure?"

"Not a scrap, and Aunt Hannah said there had never been any that she could remember; and Aunt Maria just echoed her—she always does that. You see, Aunt Hannah is an up-and-down New England woman. She looks just like herself; I mean, just like her character. Her joints move up and down or backward and forward in a plain square fashion. I don't believe she ever leaned on anything in her life or sat in an easy chair. But Maria is different; she is rounder and softer—she hasn't any ideas of her own, she never had any. I don't believe she would think it right or becoming to have one that differed from Aunt Hannah's, so what would be the use of having any? She is an echo, that's all.

"When mamma and I got there, of course I was all excitement to see the china-closet, and I had a sort of feeling that it would be the little room after all. So I ran ahead and threw open the door, crying, 'Come and see the little room.'

"And, Roger," said Mrs. Grant, laying her hand in his, "there really was a little room there, exactly as mother had remembered it. There was the lounge, the peacock chintz, the green door, the shell, the morning-glory, and the rose paper, *everything exactly as she had described it to me.*"

"What in the world did the sisters say about it?"

"Wait a minute and I will tell you. My mother was in the front hall still talking with Aunt Hannah. She didn't hear me at first, but I ran out there and dragged her through the front room, saying, 'The room *is* here—it's all right.'

"It seemed for a minute as if my mother would faint. She clung to me in terror. I can remember now how strained her eyes looked and how pale she was.

"I called out to Aunt Hannah and asked her when they had had the closet taken away and the little room built; for in my excitement I thought that was what had been done.

"'That little room has always been there,' said Aunt Hannah, 'ever since the house was built.'

"'But mamma said there wasn't any little room here, only a china-closet, when she was here with papa,' said I.

"'No, there has never been any china-closet there; it has always been just as it is now,' said Aunt Hannah.

"Then mother spoke; her voice sounded weak and far off. She said, slowly and with an effort, 'Maria, don't you remember that you told me that there had *never been any little room here,* and Hannah said so too, and then I said I must have dreamed it?'

"'No, I don't remember anything of the kind,' said Maria, without the slightest emotion. 'I don't remember you ever said anything about any china-closet. The house has never been altered; you used to play in this room when you were a child, don't you remember?'

"'I know it,' said mother, in that queer slow voice that made me feel frightened. 'Hannah, don't you remember my finding the china-closet here, with the gilt-edged china on the shelves, and then you said the *china-closet* had always been here?'

"'No,' said Hannah, pleasantly but unemotionally, 'no, I don't think you ever asked me about any china-closet, and we haven't any gilt-edged china that I know of.'

"And that was the strangest thing about it. We never could make them remember that there had ever been any question about it. You would think they could remember how surprised mother had been before, unless she had imagined the whole thing. Oh, it was so queer! They were always pleasant about it, but they

didn't seem to feel any interest or curiosity. It was always this answer: 'The house is just as it was built; there have never been any changes, so far as we know.'

"And my mother was in an agony of perplexity. How cold their grey eyes looked to me! There was no reading anything in them. It just seemed to break my mother down, this queer thing. Many times that summer, in the middle of the night, I have seen her get up and take a candle and creep softly downstairs. I could hear the steps creak under her weight. Then she would go through the front room and peer into the darkness, holding her thin hand between the candle and her eyes. She seemed to think the little room might vanish. Then she would come back to bed and toss about all night, or lie still and shiver; it used to frighten me.

"She grew pale and thin, and she had a little cough; then she did not like to be left alone. Sometimes she would make errands in order to send me to the little room for something—a book, or her fan, or her handkerchief; but she would never sit there or let me stay in there long, and sometimes she wouldn't let me go in there for days together. Oh, it was pitiful!"

"Well, don't talk any more about it, Margaret, if it makes you feel so," said Mr. Grant.

"Oh yes, I want you to know all about it, and there isn't much more—no more about the room.

"Mother never got well, and she died that autumn. She used often to sigh, and say, with a wan little laugh, 'There is one thing I am glad of, Margaret; your father knows now all about the little room.' I think she was afraid I distrusted her. Of course, in a child's way, I thought there was something queer about it, but I did not brood over it. I was too young then, and took it as a part of her illness. But, Roger, do you know, it really did affect me. I almost hate to go there after talking about it; I somehow feel as if it might, you know, be a china-closet again."

"That's an absurd idea."

"I know it; of course it can't be. I saw the room, and there isn't any china-closet there, and no gilt-edged china in the house, either."

And then she whispered, "But, Roger, you may hold my hand as you do now, if you will, when we go to look for the little room."

"And you won't mind Aunt Hannah's grey eyes?"

"I won't mind *anything*."

It was dusk when Mr. and Mrs. Grant went into the gate under the two old Lombardy poplars and walked up the narrow path to the door, where they were met by the two aunts.

Hannah gave Mrs. Grant a frigid but not unfriendly kiss; and Maria seemed for a moment to tremble on the verge of an emotion, but she glanced at Hannah, and then gave her greeting in exactly the same repressed and non-committal way.

Supper was waiting for them. On the table was the *gilt-edged* china. Mrs. Grant didn't notice it immediately, till she saw her husband smiling at her over his teacup; then she felt fidgety, and couldn't eat. She was nervous, and kept wondering what was behind her, whether it would be a little room or a closet.

After supper she offered to help about the dishes, but, mercy! she might as well have offered to help bring the seasons round; Maria and Hannah couldn't be helped.

So she and her husband went to find the little room, or closet, or whatever was to be there.

Aunt Maria followed them, carrying the lamp, which she set down, and then went back to the dish-washing.

Margaret looked at her husband. He kissed her, for she seemed troubled; and then, hand in hand, they opened the door. It opened into a *china-closet*. The shelves were neatly draped with scalloped paper; on them was the gilt-edged china, with the dishes missing that had been used at the supper, and which at that

moment were being carefully washed and wiped by the two aunts.

Margaret's husband dropped her hand and looked at her. She was trembling a little, and turned to him for help, for some explanation, but in an instant she knew that something was wrong. A cloud had come between them; he was hurt, he was antagonised.

He paused for an appreciable instant, and then said, kindly enough, but in a voice that cut her deeply:

"I am glad this ridiculous thing is ended; don't let us speak of it again."

"Ended!" said she. "How ended?" And somehow her voice sounded to her as her mother's voice had when she stood there and questioned her sisters about the little room. She seemed to have to drag her words out. She spoke slowly: "It seems to me to have only begun in my case. It was just so with mother when she—"

"I really wish, Margaret, you would let it drop. I don't like to hear you speak of your mother in connection with it. It—" He hesitated, for was not this their wedding-day? "It doesn't seem quite the thing, quite delicate, you know, to use her name in the matter."

She saw it all now; *he didn't believe her.* She felt a chill sense of withering under his glance.

"Come," he added, "let us go out, or into the dining-room, somewhere, anywhere, only drop this nonsense."

He went out; he did not take her hand now—he was vexed, baffled, hurt. Had he not given her his sympathy, his attention, his belief—and his hand?—and she was fooling him. What did it mean? She so truthful, so free from morbidness—a thing he hated. He walked up and down under the poplars, trying to get into the mood to go and join her in the house.

Margaret heard him go out; then she turned and shook the shelves; she reached her hand behind them

and tried to push the boards away; she ran out of the house on to the north side and tried to find in the darkness, with her hands, a door, or some steps leading to one. She tore her dress on the old rose-trees, she fell and rose and stumbled, then she sat down on the ground and tried to think. What could she think—was she dreaming?

She went into the house and out into the kitchen, and begged Aunt Maria to tell her about the little room— what had become of it, when they had built the closet, when they had bought the gilt-edged china?

They went on washing dishes and drying them on the spotless towels with methodical exactness; and as they worked they said that there had never been any little room, so far as they knew; the china-closet had always been there, and the gilt-edged china had belonged to their mother, it had always been in the house.

"No, I don't remember that your mother ever asked about any little room," said Hannah. "She didn't seem very well that summer, but she never asked about any changes in the house; there hadn't ever been any changes."

There it was again: not a sign of interest, curiosity, or annoyance, not a spark of memory.

She went out to Hiram. He was telling Mr. Grant about the farm. She had meant to ask him about the room, but her lips were sealed before her husband.

Months afterwards, when time had lessened the sharpness of their feelings, they learned to speculate reasonably about the phenomenon, which Mr. Grant had accepted as something not to be scoffed away, not to be treated as a poor joke, but to be put aside as something inexplicable on any ordinary theory.

Margaret alone in her heart knew that her mother's words carried a deeper significance than she had dreamed of at that time. "One thing I am glad of, your

father knows now," and she wondered if Roger or she would ever know.

Five years later they were going to Europe. The packing was done; the children were lying asleep, with their travelling things ready to be shipped on for an early start.

Roger had a foreign appointment. They were not to be back in America for some years. She had meant to go up to say good-bye to her aunts; but a mother of three children intends to do a great many things that never get done. One thing she had done that very day, and as she paused for a moment between the writing of two notes that must be posted before she went to bed, she said:

"Roger, you remember Rita Lash? Well, she and Cousin Nan go up to the Adirondacks every autumn. They are clever girls, and I have entrusted to them something I want done very much."

"They are the girls to do it, then, every inch of them."

"I know it, and they are going to."

"Well?"

"Why, you see, Roger, that little room—"

"Oh—"

"Yes, I was a coward not to go myself, but I didn't find time, because I hadn't the courage."

"Oh! *that* was it, was it?"

"Yes, just that. They are going, and they will write us about it."

"Want to get—?"

"No; I only want to know."

Rita Lash and Cousin Nan planned to go to Vermont on their way to the Adirondacks. They found they would have three hours between trains, which would give them time to drive up to the Keys farm, and they could still get to the camp that night. But, at the last minute, Rita was prevented from going. Nan had to go

to meet the Adirondack party, and she promised to telegraph Rita when she arrived at the camp. Imagine Rita's amusement when she received this message: "Safely arrived; went to Keys farm; it is a little room."

Rita was amused, because she did not in the least think Nan had been there. She thought it was a hoax; but it put it into her mind to carry the joke further by really stopping herself when she went up, as she meant to do the next week. She did stop over. She introduced herself to the two maiden ladies, who seemed familiar, as they had been described by Mrs. Grant.

They were, if not cordial, at least not disconcerted at her visit, and willingly showed her over the house. As they did not speak of any other stranger's having been to see them lately, she became confirmed in her belief that Nan had not been there.

In the north room she saw the roses and morning-glory paper on the wall, and also the door that should open into—what?

She asked if she might open it.

"Certainly," said Hannah; and Maria echoed, "Certainly."

She opened it, and found the china-closet. She experienced a certain relief; she at least was not under any spell. Mrs. Grant left it a china-closet; she found it the same. Good.

But she tried to induce the old sisters to remember that there had at various times been certain questions relating to a confusion as to whether the closet had always been a closet. It was no use: their stony eyes gave no sign.

Then she thought of the story of the sea-captain, and said, "Miss Keys, did you ever have a lounge covered with India chintz, with a figure of a peacock on it, given to you in Salem by a sea-captain, who brought it from India?"

"I dunno as I ever did," said Hannah. That was all. She thought Maria's cheeks were a little flushed, but her eyes were like a stone wall.

She went on that night to the Adirondacks. When Nan and she were alone in their room, she said: "By the way, Nan, what did you see at the farmhouse, and how did you like Maria and Hannah?"

Nan didn't mistrust that Rita had been there, and she began excitedly to tell her all about her visit. Rita could almost have believed Nan had been there if she hadn't known it was not so. She let her go on for some time, enjoying her enthusiasm, and the impressive way in which she described her opening the door and finding the "little room." Then Rita said: "Now, Nan, that is enough fibbing. I went to the farm myself on my way up yesterday, and there is *no* little room, and there *never* has been any; it is a china-closet, just as Mrs. Grant saw it last."

She was pretending to be busy unpacking her trunk, and did not look up for a moment; but as Nan did not say anything, she glanced at her over her shoulder. Nan was actually pale, and it was hard to say whether she was more angry or frightened. There was something of both in her look. And then Rita began to explain how her telegram had put her in the spirit of going up there alone. She hadn't meant to cut Nan out. She only thought—Then Nan broke in: "It isn't that; I am sure you can't think it is that. But I went myself, and you did not go; you can't have been there, for *it is a little room*."

Oh, what a night they had! They couldn't sleep. They talked and argued, and then kept still for a while, only to break out again, it was so absurd. They both maintained that they had been there, but both sure the other one was either crazy or obstinate beyond reason. They were wretched; it was perfectly ridiculous, two friends at odds over such a thing; but there it was—"little room," "china-closet," "china-closet," "little room."

The next morning Nan was tacking up some tarlatan at a window to keep the midges out. Rita offered to help her, as she had done for the past ten years. Nan's "No, thanks," cut her to the heart.

"Nan," said she, "come right down from that stepladder and pack your satchel. The stage leaves in just twenty minutes. We can catch the afternoon express train, and we will go together to the farm. I am either going there or going home. You had better go with me."

Nan didn't say a word. She gathered up the hammer and tacks, and was ready to start when the stage came round.

It meant for them thirty miles of staging and six hours of train, besides crossing the lake; but what of that, compared to having a lie lying round loose between them! Europe would have seemed easy to accomplish, if it would settle the question.

At the little junction in Vermont they found a farmer with a wagon full of meal-bags. They asked him if he could not take them up to the old Keys farm and bring them back in time for the return train, due in two hours.

They had planned to call it a sketching trip, so they said: "We have been there before, we are artists, and we might find some views worth taking; and we want also to make a short call upon the Misses Keys."

"Did ye calculate to paint the old *house* in the picture?"

They said it was possible they might do so. They wanted to see it, anyway.

"Waal, I guess you are too late. The *house* burnt down last night, and everything in it."

Jean Ray (1887–1964)

THE SHADOWY STREET

Raymundus Joannes Maria De Kremer (1887–1964), who wrote under the pseudonym "Jean Ray," was a Belgian journalist and European pulp writer sometimes called "The Belgian Poe." Significantly, at least four of his stories were translated and published in the 1930s in *Weird Tales*. It was not until 1965, however, that a collection of his work appeared in English, in a garish paperback original entitled *Ghouls in my Grave*, at the dying end of the mass market horror boomlet of the early 1960s. It contains several of his better stories, including "The Shadowy Street," which is perhaps his masterpiece. The influence of Lovecraft and Poe is clear, particularly in the pseudoscientific mentions of Einstein and the Lorenz-Fitzgerald contraction. But one must also look back to the earlier Hoffmanesque tales of the Romantic period for characters fascinated by golden riches, which suggest a folktale morality at work. Still, this tale is firmly in the horror genre and deserves a wider audience.

On a Rotterdam dock, winches were fishing bales of old paper from the hold of a freighter. The wind was fluttering the multicolored streamers that hung from the bales when one of them burst open like a cask in a roaring fire. The longshoremen hastily scooped up

some of the rustling mass, but a large part of it was abandoned to the joy of the little children who gleaned in the eternal autumn of the waterfront.

There were beautiful Pearsons engravings, cut in half by order of Customs; green and pink bundles of stocks and bonds, the last echoes of resounding bankruptcies; pitiful books whose pages were still joined like desperate hands. My cane explored that vast residue of thought, in which neither shame nor hope was now alive.

Amid all that English and German prose I found a few pages of France: copies of *Le Magasin Pittoresque,* solidly bound and somewhat scorched by fire.

It was in looking through those magazines, so adorably illustrated and so dismally written, that I found the two manuscripts, one in German, the other in French. Their authors had apparently been unaware of each other, and yet the French manuscript seemed to cast a little light on the black anguish that rose from the German one like a noxious vapor—insofar as any light can be shed on that story which appears to be haunted by such sinister and hostile forces!

The cover bore the name Alphonse Archipetre, followed by the word *Lehrer.* I shall translate the German pages:

The German Manuscript

I am writing this for Hermann, when he comes back from sea.

If he does not find me here, if I, along with my poor friends, have been swallowed up by the savage mystery that surrounds us, I want him to know our days of horror through this little notebook. It will be the best proof of my affection that I can give him, because it takes real courage for a woman to keep a journal in such

hours of madness. I am also writing so that he will pray for me, if he believes my soul to be in peril. . . .

After the death of my Aunt Hedwige, I did not want to go on living in our sad Holzdamm house. The Rückhardt sisters offered to let me stay with them. They lived in a big apartment on the Deichstrasse, in the spacious house of Councillor Hühnebein, an old bachelor who never left the first floor, which was littered with books, paintings, and engravings.

Lotte, Eleonore, and Meta Rückhardt were adorable old maids who used all their ingenuity in trying to make life pleasant for me. Frida, our maid, came with me; she found favor in the eyes of the ancient Frau Pilz, the Rückhardts' inspired cook, who was said to have turned down ducal offers in order to remain in the humble service of her mistresses.

That evening . . .

On that evening, which was to bring unspeakable terror into our calm lives, we had decided against going to a celebration in Tempelhof, because it was raining in torrents. Frau Pilz, who liked to have us stay home, had made us an outstanding supper: grilled trout and a guinea-hen pie. Lotte had searched the cellar and come up with a bottle of Cape brandy that had been aging there for over twenty years. When the table had been cleared, the beautiful dark liquor was poured into glasses of Bohemian crystal. Eleonore served the Lapsang Souchong tea that an old Bremen sailor brought back to us from his voyages.

Through the sound of the rain we heard the clock of Saint Peter's strike eight. Frida was sitting beside the fire. Her head drooped over her illustrated Bible; she was unable to read it, but she liked to look at the pictures. She asked for permission to go to bed. The four of us who remained went on sorting colored silks for Meta's embroidery.

Downstairs, the councillor noisily locked his bedroom door. Frau Pilz went up to her room, bade us good night through the door, and added that the bad weather would no doubt prevent us from having fresh fish for dinner the next day. A small cascade was splattering loudly on the pavement from a broken rain gutter on the house next door. A strong wind came thundering down the street; the cascade was dispersed into a silvery mist, and a window slammed shut on one of the upper stories.

"That's the attic window," said Lotte. "It won't stay closed." She raised the garnet-red curtain and looked down at the street. "I've never seen it so dark before. I'm not sleepy, and I certainly have no desire to go to bed. I feel as though the darkness of the street would follow me, along with the wind and the rain."

"You're talking like a fool," said Eleonore, who was not very gentle. "Well, since no one is going to bed, let's do as men do and fill our glasses again."

She went off to get three of those beautiful Sieme candles that burn with a pink flame and give off a delightful smell of flowers and incense.

I felt that we all wanted to give a festive tone to that bleak evening, and that for some reason we were unsuccessful. I saw Eleonore's energetic face darkened by a sudden shadow of ill-humor. Lotte seemed to be having difficulty in breathing. Only Meta was leaning placidly over her embroidery, and yet I sensed that she was attentive, as though she were trying to detect a sound in the depths of the silence.

Just then the door opened and Frida came in. She staggered over to the armchair beside the fire and sank into it, staring wild-eyed at each of us in turn.

"Frida!" I cried. "What's the matter?"

She sighed deeply, then murmured a few indistinct words.

"She's still asleep," said Eleonore.

Frida shook her head forcefully and made violent efforts to speak. I handed her my glass of brandy and she emptied it in one gulp, like a coachman or a porter. Under other circumstances we would have been offended by this vulgarity, but she seemed so unhappy, and the atmosphere in the room had been so depressing for the past few minutes, that it passed unnoticed.

"Fräulein," said Frida, "there's . . ." Her eyes, which softened for a moment, resumed their wild expression. "I don't know. . . ."

Eleonore uttered an impatient exclamation.

"What have you seen or heard? What's wrong with you, Frida?"

"Fräulein, there's . . ." Frida seemed to reflect deeply. "I don't know how to say it. . . . There's a great fear in my room."

"Oh!" said all three of us, reassured and apprehensive at the same time.

"You've had a nightmare," said Meta. "I know how it is: you hide your head under the covers when you wake up."

"No, that's not it," said Frida. "I hadn't been dreaming. I just woke up, that's all, and then . . . How can I make you understand? There's a great fear in my room. . . ."

"Good heavens, that doesn't explain anything!" I said.

Frida shook her head in despair:

"I'd rather sit outside in the rain all night than go back to that room. No, I won't go back!"

"I'm going to see what's happening up there, you fool!" said Eleonore, throwing a shawl over her shoulders.

She hesitated for a moment before her father's old rapier, hanging among some university insignia. Then she shrugged, picked up the candlestick with its pink

candles, and walked out, leaving a perfumed wake behind her.

"Oh, don't let her go there alone!" cried Frida, alarmed.

We slowly went to the staircase. The flickering glow of Eleonore's candlestick was already vanishing on the attic landing.

We stood in the semidarkness at the foot of the stairs. We heard Eleonore open a door. There was a minute of oppressive silence. I felt Frida's hand tighten on my waist.

"Don't leave her alone," she moaned.

Just then there was a loud laugh, so horrible that I would rather die than hear it again. Almost at the same time, Meta raised her hand and cried out, "There! . . . There! . . . A face. . . . There. . . ."

The house became filled with sounds. The councillor and Frau Pilz appeared in the yellow haloes of the candles they were holding.

"Fräulein Eleonore!" sobbed Frida. "Dear God, how are we going to find her?"

It was a frightening question, and I can now answer it: *We never found her.*

Frida's room was empty. The candlestick was standing on the floor and its candles were still burning peacefully, with their delicate pink flames.

We searched the whole house and even went out on the roof. We never saw Eleonore again.

We could not count on the help of the police, as will soon be seen. When we went to the police station, we found that it had been invaded by a frenzied crowd; some of the furniture had been overturned, the windows were covered with dust, and the clerks were being pushed around like puppets. Eighty people had vanished that night, some from their homes, others while they were on their way home!

The world of ordinary conjectures was closed to us; only supernatural apprehensions remained.

Several days went by. We led a bleak life of tears and terror.

Councillor Hühnebein had the attic sealed off from the rest of the house by a thick oak partition.

One day I went in search of Meta. We were beginning to fear another tragedy when we found her squatting in front of the partition with her eyes dry and an expression of anger on her usually gentle face. She was holding her father's rapier in her hand, and seemed annoyed at having been disturbed.

We tried to question her about the face she had glimpsed, but she looked at us as though she did not understand. She remained completely silent. She did not answer us, and even seemed unaware of our presence.

All sorts of wild stories were being repeated in the town. There was talk of a secret criminal league; the police were accused of negligence, and worse; public officials had been dismissed. All this, of course, was useless.

Strange crimes had been committed: savagely mutilated corpses were found at dawn. Wild animals could not have shown more ardent lust for carnage than the mysterious attackers. Some of the victims had been robbed, but most of them had not, and this surprised everyone.

But I do not want to dwell on what was happening in the town; it will be easy to find enough people to tell about it. I will limit myself to the framework of our house and our life, which, though narrow, still enclosed enough fear and despair.

The days passed and April came, colder and windier than the worst month of winter. We remained huddled beside the fire. Sometimes Councillor Hühnebein came to keep us company and give us what he called courage.

This consisted in trembling in all his limbs, holding his hands out toward the fire, drinking big mugs of punch, starting at every sound, and crying out five or six times an hour, "Did you hear that? Did you hear? . . ."

Frida tore some of the pages out of her Bible, and we found them pinned or pasted on every door and curtain, in every nook and cranny. She hoped that this would ward off the spirits of evil. We did not interfere, and since we spent several days in peace we were far from thinking it a bad idea.

We soon saw how terribly mistaken we were. The day had been so dark, and the clouds so low, that evening had come early. I was walking out of the living room to put a lamp on the broad landing—for ever since the terrifying night we had placed lights all over the house, and even the halls and stairs remained lighted till dawn—when I heard voices murmuring on the top floor.

It was not yet completely dark. I bravely climbed the stairs and found myself before the frightened faces of Frida and Frau Pilz, who motioned me to be silent and pointed to the newly-built partition.

I stood beside them, adopting their silence and attention. It was then that I heard an indefinable sound from behind the wooden wall, something like the faint roar of giant conch shells, or the tumult of a faraway crowd.

"Fräulein Eleonore, . . ." moaned Frida.

The answer came immediately and hurled us screaming down the stairs: a long shriek of terror rang out, not from the partition above us, but from downstairs, from the councillor's apartment. Then he called for help at the top of his lungs. Lotte and Meta had hurried out onto the landing.

"We must go there," I said courageously.

We had not taken three steps when there was another cry of distress, this time from above us.

"Help! Help!"

We recognized Frau Pilz's voice. We heard her call again, feebly.

Meta picked up the lamp I had placed on the landing. Halfway up the stairs we found Frida alone. Frau Pilz had disappeared.

At this point I must express my admiration of Meta Rückhardt's calm courage.

"There's nothing more we can do here," she said, breaking the silence she had stubbornly maintained for several days. "Let's go downstairs. . . ."

She was holding her father's rapier, and she did not look at all ridiculous, for we sensed that she would use it as effectively as a man.

We followed her, subjugated by her cold strength.

The councillor's study was as brightly lighted as a traveling carnival. The poor man had given the darkness no chance to get in. Two enormous lamps with white porcelain globes stood at either end of the mantelpiece, looking like two placid moons. A small Louis XV chandelier hung from the ceiling, its prisms flashing like handfuls of precious stones. Copper and stone candlesticks stood on the floor in every corner of the room. On the table, a row of tall candles seemed to be illuminating an invisible catafalque.

We stopped, dazzled, and looked around for the councillor.

"Oh!" Frida exclaimed suddenly. "Look, there he is! He's hiding behind the window curtain."

Lotte abruptly pulled back the heavy curtain. Herr Hühnebein was there, leaning out the open window, motionless.

Lotte went over to him, then leapt back with a cry of horror.

"Don't look! For the love of heaven, don't look! He . . . he . . . his head is gone!"

I saw Frida stagger, ready to faint. Meta's voice called us back to reason:

"Be careful! There's danger here!"

We pressed up close to her, feeling protected by her presence of mind. Suddenly something blinked on the ceiling, and we saw with alarm that darkness had invaded two opposite corners of the room, where the lights had just been extinguished.

"Hurry, protect the lights!" panted Meta. "Oh! . . . There! . . . There he is!"

At that moment the white moons on the mantelpiece burst, spat out streaks of smoky flame, and vanished.

Meta stood motionless, but she looked all around the room with a cold rage that I had never seen in her before.

The candles on the table were blown out. Only the little chandelier continued to shed its calm light. I saw that Meta was keeping her eyes on it. Suddenly her rapier flashed and she lunged forward into empty space.

"Protect the light!" she cried. "I see him! I've got him! . . . Ah! . . ."

We saw the rapier make strange, violent movements in her hand, as though an invisible force were trying to take it away from her.

It was Frida who had the odd but fortunate inspiration that saved us that evening. She uttered a fierce cry, picked up one of the heavy copper candlesticks, leapt to Meta's side, and began striking the air with her gleaming club. The rapier stopped moving; something very light seemed to brush against the floor, then the door opened by itself, and a heartrending clamor arose.

"That takes care of one of them," said Meta.

One might wonder why we stubbornly went on living in that murderously haunted house.

At least a hundred other houses were in the same situation. People had stopped counting the murders and disappearances, and had become almost indifferent to them. The town was gloomy. There were dozens of suicides, for some people preferred to die by their own hands rather than be killed by the phantom executioners. And then, too, Meta wanted to take vengeance. She was now waiting for the invisible beings to return.

She had relapsed into her grim silence; she spoke to us only to order us to lock the doors and shutters at nightfall. As soon as darkness fell, the four of us went into the living room, which was now a dormitory and dining room as well. We did not leave it until morning.

I questioned Frida about her strange armed intervention. She was able to give me only a confused answer.

"I don't know," she said. "It seemed to me I saw something. . . . A face. . . . I don't know how to say what it was. . . . Yes, it was the great fear that was in my room the first night."

That was all I could get out of her.

One evening toward the middle of April, Lotte and Frida were lingering in the kitchen. Meta opened the living-room door and told them to hurry. I saw that the shadows of night had already invaded the landings and the hall.

"We're coming," they replied in unison.

Meta came back into the living room and closed the door. She was horribly pale. No sound came from downstairs. I waited vainly to hear the footsteps of the two women. The silence was like a threatening flood rising on the other side of the wall.

Meta locked the door.

"What are you doing?" I asked. "What about Lotte and Frida?"

"It's no use," she said dully.

Her eyes, motionless and terrible, stared at the rapier. The sinister darkness arrived.

It was thus that Lotte and Frida vanished into mystery.

Dear God, what was it? There was a presence in the house, a suffering, wounded presence that was seeking help. I did not know whether Meta was aware of it or not. She was more taciturn than ever, but she barricaded the doors and windows in a way that seemed designed more to prevent an escape than an intrusion. My life had become a fearful solitude. Meta herself was like a sneering specter.

During the day, I sometimes came upon her unexpectedly in one of the halls; in one hand she held the rapier, and in the other she held a powerful lantern with a reflector and a lens that she shone into all the dark corners.

During one of these encounters, she told me rather impolitely that I had better go back to the living room, and when I obeyed her too slowly she shouted furiously at me that I must never interfere with her plans.

Her face no longer had the placid look it had worn as she leaned over her embroidery only a few days before. It was now a savage face, and she sometimes glared at me with a flame of hatred in her eyes. For I had a secret. . . .

Was it curiosity, perversity, or pity that made me act as I did? I pray to God that I was moved by nothing more than pity and kindness.

I had just drawn some fresh water from the fountain in the wash-house when I heard a muffled moan: "Moh. . . . Moh. . . ."

I thought of our vanished friends and looked around me. I saw a well-concealed door that led into a storeroom in which poor Hühnebein had kept stacks of books and paintings, amid dust and cobwebs.

"Moh. . . . Moh. . . ."

It was coming from inside the storeroom. I opened the door and looked into the gray semidarkness. Everything seemed normal. The lamentation had stopped. I stepped inside. Suddenly I felt something seize my dress. I cried out. I immediately heard the moaning very close to me, plaintive, supplicating, and something tapped on my pitcher.

I put it down. There was a slight splashing sound, like that of a dog lapping, and the level of the water in my pitcher began to sink. The thing, the being, was drinking!

"Moh! . . . Moh! . . ."

Something caressed my hair more softly than a breath.

"Moh. . . . Moh. . . ."

Then the moaning changed to a sound of human weeping, almost like the sobbing of a child, and I felt pity for the suffering invisible monster. But there were footsteps in the hall; I put my hands over my lips and the being fell silent.

Without a sound, I closed the door of the secret storeroom. Meta was coming toward me in the hall.

"Did I hear your voice just now?" she asked.

"Yes. My foot slipped and I was startled. . . ."

I was an accomplice of the phantoms.

I brought milk, wine, and apples. Nothing manifested itself. When I returned, the milk had been drunk to the last drop, but the wine and the apples were intact. Then a kind of breeze surrounded me and passed over my hair for a long time. . . .

I went back, bringing more fresh milk. The soft voice was no longer weeping, but the caress of the breeze was longer and seemed to be more ardent.

Meta began looking at me suspiciously and prowling around the storeroom.

I found a safer refuge for my mysterious protégé. I explained it to him by signs. How strange it was to make gestures to empty space! But he understood me. He was following me along the hall like a breath of air when I suddenly had to hide in a corner.

A pale light slid across the floor. I saw Meta coming down the spiral staircase at the end of the hall. She was walking quietly, partially hiding the glow of her lantern. The rapier glittered. I sensed that the being beside me was afraid. The breeze stirred around me, feverishly, abruptly, and I heard that plaintive "Moh! . . . Moh! . . ."

Meta's footsteps faded away in the distance. I made a reassuring gesture and went to the new refuge: a large closet that was never opened.

The breeze touched my lips and remained there a moment. I felt a strange shame.

May came.

The twenty square feet of the miniature garden, which poor, dear Hühnebein had spattered with his blood, were dotted with little white flowers.

Under a magnificent blue sky, the town was almost silent. The cries of the swallows were answered only by the peevish sounds of closing doors, sliding bolts, and turning keys.

The being had become imprudent. He sought me out. All at once I would feel him around me. I cannot describe the feeling; it was like a great tenderness surrounding me. I would make him understand that I was afraid of Meta, and then I would feel him vanish like a dying wind.

I could not bear the look in Meta's fiery eyes.

On May 4, the end came abruptly.

We were in the living room, with all the lamps lighted. I was closing the shutters. Suddenly I sensed his

presence. I made a desperate gesture, turned around, and met Meta's terrible gaze in a mirror.

"Traitress!" she cried.

She quickly closed the door. He was imprisoned with us.

"I knew it!" she said vehemently. "I've seen you carrying pitchers of milk, daughter of the devil! You gave him strength when he was dying from the wound I gave him on the night of Hühnebein's death. Yes, your phantom is vulnerable! He's going to die now, and I think that dying is much more horrible for him than it is for us. Then your turn will come, you wretch! Do you hear me?"

She had shrieked this in short phrases. She uncovered her lantern. A beam of white light shot across the room, and I saw it strike something like thin, gray smoke. She plunged her rapier into it.

"Moh! . . . Moh! . . ." cried the heartrending voice, and then suddenly, awkwardly, but in a loving tone, my name was spoken. I leapt forward and knocked over the lantern with my fist. It went out.

"Meta, listen to me," I begged, "have pity. . . ."

Her face was contorted into a mask of demoniac fury.

"Traitress!" she screamed.

The rapier flashed before my eyes. It struck me below the left breast and I fell to my knees.

Someone was weeping violently beside me, strangely beseeching Meta. She raised her rapier again. I tried to find the words of supreme contrition that reconcile us with God forever, but then I saw Meta's face freeze and the sword fell from her hand.

Something murmured near us. I saw a thin flame stretch out like a ribbon and greedily attack the curtains.

"We're burning!" cried Meta. "All of us together!"

At that moment, when everything was about to sink

into death, the door opened. An immensely tall old woman came in. I saw only her terrible green eyes glowing in her unimaginable face.

A flame licked my left hand. I stepped back as much as my strength allowed. I saw Meta still standing motionless with a strange grimace on her face, and I realized that her soul, too, had flown away. Then the monstrous old woman's eyes, without pupils, slowly looked around the flame-filled room and came to rest on me.

I am writing this in a strange little house. Where am I? Alone. And yet all this is full of tumult, an invisible but unrestrained presence is everywhere. He has come back. I have again heard my name spoken in that awkward, gentle way. . . .

* * * * * *

Here ends the German manuscript, as though cut off with a knife.

* * * * * *

The French Manuscript

The town's oldest coachman was pointed out to me in the smoky inn where he was drinking heady, fragrant October beer.

I bought him a drink and gave him some tobacco. He swore I was a prince. I pointed to his droshky outside the inn and said, "And now, take me to Saint Beregonne's Lane."

He gave me a bewildered look, then laughed.

"Ah, you're very clever!"

"Why?"

"You're testing me. I know every street in this

town—I can almost say I know every paving-stone! There's no Saint Bere. . . . What did you say?"

"Beregonne. Are you sure? Isn't it near the Mohlenstrasse?"

"No," he said decisely. "There's no such street here, no more than Mount Vesuvius is in Saint Petersburg."

No one knew the town, in all its twisting byways, better than that splendid beer-drinker.

A student sitting at a nearby table looked up from the love letter he had been writing and said to me, "There's no saint by that name, either."

And the innkeeper's wife added, with a touch of anger, "You can't manufacture saints like sausages!"

I calmed everyone with wine and beer. There was great joy in my heart.

The policeman who paced up and down the Mohlenstrasse from dawn till dark had a face like a bulldog, but he was obviously a man who knew his job.

"No," he said slowly, coming back from a long journey among his thoughts and memories, "there's no such street here or anywhere else in town."

Over his shoulder I saw the beginning of Saint Beregonne's Lane, between the Klingbom distillery and the shop of an anonymous seed merchant.

I had to turn away with impolite abruptness in order not to show my elation. Saint Beregonne's Lane did not exist for the coachman, the student, the policeman, or anyone else: it existed only for me!

How did I make that amazing discovery? By an almost scientific observation, as some of my pompous fellow-teachers would have said. My colleague Seifert, who taught natural science by bursting balloons filled with strange gases in his pupils' faces, would not have been able to find any fault with my procedure.

When I walked along the Mohlenstrasse, it took me

two or three seconds to cover the distance between the distillery and the seed merchant's shop. I noticed, however, that when other people passed by the same place they went immediately from the distillery to the shop, without visibly crossing the entrance of Saint Beregonne's Lane.

By adroitly questioning various people, and by consulting the town's cadastral map, I learned that only a wall separated the distillery from the shop.

I concluded that, for everyone in the world except myself, that street existed outside of time and space.

I knew that mysterious street for several years without ever venturing into it, and I think that even a more courageous man would have hesitated. What laws governed that unknown space? Once it had drawn me into its mystery, would it ever return me to my own world?

I finally invented various reasons to convince myself that that world was inhospitable to human beings, and my curiosity surrendered to my fear. And yet what I could see of that opening into the incomprehensible was so ordinary, so commonplace! I must admit, however, that the view was cut off after ten paces by a sharp bend in the street. All I could see was two high, badly whitewashed walls with the name of the street painted on one of them in black letters, and a stretch of worn, greenish pavement with a gap in which a viburnum bush was growing. That sickly bush seemed to live in accordance with our seasons, for I sometimes saw a little tender green and a few lumps of·snow among its twigs.

I might have made some curious observations concerning the insertion of that slice of an alien cosmos into ours, but to do so I would have had to spend a considerable amount of time standing on the Mohlenstrasse; and Klingbom, who often saw me staring at some of his windows, became suspicious of his wife and gave me hostile looks.

I wondered why, of all the people in the world, I was the only one to whom that strange privilege had been given. This led me to think of my maternal grandmother. She was a tall, somber woman, and her big green eyes seemed to be following the happenings of another life on the wall in front of her.

Her background was obscure. My grandfather, a sailor, was supposed to have rescued her from some Algerian pirates. She sometimes stroked my hair with her long, white hands and murmured, "Maybe he . . . Why not? After all . . ." She repeated it on the night of her death, and while the pale fire of her gaze wandered among the shadows she added, "Maybe he'll go where I wasn't able to return. . . ."

A black storm was blowing that night. Just after my grandmother died, while the candles were being lit, a big stormy petrel shattered the window and lay dying, bloody and threatening, on her bed.

That was the only odd thing I remembered in my life; but did it have any connection with Saint Beregonne's Lane?

It was a sprig of the viburnum bush that set off the adventure.

But am I sincere in looking there for the initial tap that set events in motion? Perhaps I should speak of Anita.

Several years ago, in the Hanseatic ports one could see the arrival of little lateen-rigged ships creeping out of the mist like crestfallen animals.

Colossal laughter would immediately shake the port, down to the deepest beer cellars.

"Aha! Here come the dream ships!"

I always felt heartbroken at the sight of those heroic dreams dying in formidable Germanic laughter.

It was said that the sad crews of those ships lived on the golden shores of the Adriatic and the Tyrrhenian Sea in a mad dream, for they believed in a fantastic

land of plenty, related to the Thule of the ancients, lying somewhere in our cruel North. Not having much more knowledge than their forefathers of a thousand years ago, they had carefully nurtured a heritage of legends about islands of diamonds and emeralds, legends that had been born when their forefathers encountered the glittering vanguard of an ice floe.

The compass was one of the few items of progress that their minds had seized upon in the course of the centuries. Its enigmatic needle, always pointing in the same direction, was for them a final proof of the mysteries of the North.

One day when a dream was walking like a new Messiah on the choppy waters of the Mediterranean, when the nets had brought up only fish poisoned by the coral on the bottom, and when Lombardy had sent neither grain nor flour to the poverty-stricken lands of the South, they had hoisted their sails in the offshore wind.

Their flotilla had dotted the sea with its hard wings; then, one by one, their ships had melted into the storms of the Atlantic. The Bay of Biscay had nibbled the flotilla and passed the remainder on to the granite teeth of Brittany. Some of the hulls were sold to firewood merchants in Germany and Denmark; one of the ships died in its dream, killed by an iceberg blazing in the sun off the Lofoten Islands.

But the North adorned the grave of that flotilla with a sweet name: "the dream ships." Although it made coarse sailors laugh, I was deeply moved by it, and I might well have been willing to set sail with those dreamers.

Anita was their daughter.

She came from the Mediterranean when she was still a baby in her mother's arms, aboard a tartan. The ship was sold. Her mother died, and so did her little sisters. Her father set out for America on a sailing ship that

never returned. Anita was left all alone, but the dream that had brought the tartan to those moldering wooden docks never left her: she still believed in the fortune of the North, and she wanted it fiercely, almost with hatred.

In Tempelhof, with its clusters of white lights, she sang, danced, and threw red flowers that either fell on her like a rain of blood or were burned in the short flames of the Argand lamps. She would then pass among the crowd, holding out a pink conch shell. Silver was dropped into it, or sometimes gold, and only then did her eyes smile as they rested for a second, like a caress, on the generous man.

I gave gold—I, a humble teacher of French grammar in the Gymnasium, gave gold for one look from Anita.

Brief notes:

I sold my Voltaire. I had sometimes read my pupils extracts from his correspondence with the King of Prussia; it pleased the principal.

I owed two months' room and board to Frau Holz, my landlady. She told me she was poor. . . .

I asked the bursar of the school for another advance on my salary. He told me with embarrassment that it was difficult, that it was against regulations. . . . I did not listen any longer. My colleague Seifert curtly refused to lend me a few thalers.

I dropped a heavy gold coin into the conch shell. Anita's eyes burned my soul. Then I heard someone laughing in the laurel thickets of Tempelhof. I recognized two servants of the Gymnasium. They ran away into the darkness.

It was my last gold coin. I had no more money, none at all. . . .

As I was walking past the distillery on the Mohlenstrasse, I was nearly run over by a carriage. I made a frightened leap into Saint Beregonne's Lane.

My hand clutched the viburnum bush and broke off a sprig of it.

I took the sprig home with me and laid it on my table. It had opened up an immense new world to me, like a magician's wand.

Let us reason, as my stingy colleague Seifert would say.

First of all, my leap into Saint Beregonne's Lane and my subsequent return to the Mohlenstrasse had shown that the mysterious street was as easy to enter and leave as any ordinary thoroughfare.

But the viburnum sprig had enormous philosophical significance. It was "in excess" in our world. If I had taken a branch from any forest in America and brought it here, I would not have changed the number of branches on earth. But in bringing that sprig of viburnum from Saint Beregonne's Lane I had made an intrinsic addition that could not have been made by all the tropical growths in the world, because I had taken it from a plane of existence that was real only for me.

I was therefore able to take an object from that plane and bring it into the world of men, where no one could contest my ownership of it. Ownership could never be more absolute, in fact, because the object would owe nothing to any industry, and it would augment the normally immutable patrimony of the earth. . . .

My reasoning flowed on, wide as a river, carrying fleets of words, encircling islands of appeals to philosophy; it was swollen by a vast system of logical tributaries until it reached a conclusive demonstration that a theft committed in Saint Beregonne's Lane was not a theft in the Mohlenstrasse.

Fortified by this nonsense, I judged that the matter was settled. My only concern would be to avoid the reprisals of the mysterious inhabitants of the street, or of the world to which it led.

When the Spanish conquistadores spent the gold they

had brought back from the new India, I think they cared very little about the anger of the faraway peoples they had despoiled.

I decided to enter the unknown the following day.

Klingbom made me waste some time. I think he had been waiting for me in the little square vestibule that opened into his shop on one side and his office on the other. As I walked past, clenching my teeth, ready to plunge into my adventure, he grabbed me by my coat.

"Ah, professor," he said, "how I misjudged you! It wasn't you! I must have been blind to suspect you! She's left me, professor, but not with you. Oh, no, you're a man of honor! She's gone off with a postmaster, a man who's half coachman and half scribe. What a disgrace for the House of Klingbom!"

He had dragged me into the shadowy back room of his shop. He poured me a glass of orange-flavored brandy.

"And to think that I mistrusted you, professor! I always saw you looking at my wife's windows, but I know now that it was the seed merchant's wife you had your eye on."

I masked my embarrassment by raising my glass.

"To tell you the truth," said Klingbom, pouring me out some more of the reddish liquid, "I'd be glad to see you put one over on that malicious seed merchant: he's delighted by my misfortune."

He added, with a smile, "I'll do you a favor: the lady of your dreams is in her garden right now. Why don't you go and see her?"

He led me up a spiral staircase to a window. I saw the poisonous sheds of the Klingbom distillery smoking among a tangled array of little courtyards, miniature gardens, and muddy streams narrow enough to step across. It was through that landscape that the secret

street ought to run, but I saw nothing except the smoky activity of the Klingbom buildings and the seed merchant's nearby garden, where a thin form was leaning over some arid flower beds.

One last swallow of brandy gave me a great deal of courage. After leaving Klingbom, I walked straight into Saint Beregonne's Lane.

Three little yellow doors in the white wall . . .

Beyond the bend in the street, the viburnum bushes continued to place spots of green and black among the paving stones; then the three little doors appeared, almost touching each other. They gave the aspect of a Flemish Beguine convent to what should have been singular and terrible.

My footsteps resounded clearly in the silence.

I knocked on the first of the doors. Only the futile life of an echo was stirred behind it.

Fifty paces away, the street made another bend.

I was discovering the unknown parsimoniously. So far I had found only two thinly whitewashed walls and those three doors. But is not any closed door a powerful mystery in itself?

I knocked on all three doors, more violently this time. The echoes departed loudly and shattered the silence lurking in the depths of prodigious corridors. Sometimes their dying murmurs seemed to imitate the sound of light footsteps, but that was the only reply from the enclosed world.

The doors had locks on them, the same as all the other doors I was used to seeing. Two nights before, I had spent an hour picking the lock on my bedroom door with a piece of bent wire, and it had been as easy as a game.

There was a little sweat on my temples, a little shame in my heart. I took the same piece of wire from my

pocket and slipped it into the lock of the first little door.
And very simply, just like my bedroom door, it opened.

Later, when I was back in my bedroom among my
books, in front of the table on which lay a red ribbon
that had fallen from Anita's dress, I sat clutching three
silver thalers in my hand.

Three thalers!

I had destroyed my finest destiny with my own hand.
That new world had opened for me alone. What had it
expected of me, that universe more mysterious than
those that gravitate toward the bottom of Infinity?
Mystery had made advances to me, had smiled at me
like a pretty girl, and I had entered it as a thief. I had
been petty, vile, absurd.

Three thalers!

My adventure should have been so prodigious, and it
had become so paltry!

Three thalers reluctantly given to me by Gockel, the
antique dealer, for that engraved metal dish. Three
thalers. . . . But they would buy one of Anita's smiles.

I abruptly threw them into a drawer: someone was
knocking on my door.

It was Gockel. It was difficult for me to believe that
this was the same malevolent man who had contemptuously put down the metal dish on his counter cluttered
with barbarous and shabby trinkets. He was smiling
now, and he constantly mingled my name—which he
mispronounced—with the title of "Herr Doktor" or
"Herr Lehrer."

"I think I did you a great injustice, Herr Doktor," he
said. "That dish is certainly worth more."

He took out a leather purse and I saw the bright
yellow smile of gold.

"It may be," he went on, "that you have other objects
from the same source . . . or rather, of the same kind."

The distinction did not escape me. Beneath the urbanity of the antique dealer was the spirit of a receiver of stolen goods.

"The fact is," I said, "that a friend of mine, an erudite collector, is in a difficult situation and needs to pay off certain debts, so he wants to sell part of his collection. He prefers to remain unknown: he's a shy scholar. He's already unhappy enough over having to part with some of the treasures in his showcases. I want to spare him any further sadness, so I'm helping him to sell them."

Gockel nodded enthusiastically. He seemed overwhelmed with admiration for me.

"That's my idea of true friendship!" he said. "Ach, Herr Doktor, I'll reread Cicero's *De Amicitia* this evening with renewed pleasure. How I wish that I had a friend like your unfortunate scholar has found in you! But I'll contribute a little to your good deed by buying everything your friend is willing to part with, and by paying very good prices. . . ."

I had a slight stirring of curiosity:

"I didn't look at the dish very closely," I said loftily. "It didn't concern me, and besides, I don't know anything about such things. What kind of work is it? Byzantine?"

Gockel scratched his chin in embarrassment.

"Uh . . . I couldn't say for sure. Byzantine, yes, maybe. . . . I'll have to study it more carefully. . . . But," he went on, suddenly recovering his serenity, "in any case it's sure to find a buyer." Then, in a tone that cut short all further discussion: "That's the most important thing to us . . . and to your friend, too, of course."

Late that night I accompanied Anita in the moonlight to the street where her house stood half-hidden in a clump of tall lilacs.

But I must go back in my story to the tray I sold for thalers and gold, which gave me for one evening the friendship of the most beautiful girl in the world.

The door opened onto a long hall with a blue stone floor. A frosted window pane cast light into it and broke up the shadows. My first impression of being in a Flemish Beguine convent became stronger, especially when an open door at the end of the hall led me into a broad kitchen with a vaulted ceiling and rustic furniture, gleaming with wax and polish.

This innocuous scene was so reassuring that I called aloud:

"Hello! Is there anyone upstairs?"

A powerful resonance rumbled, but no presence cared to manifest itself.

I must admit that at no time did the silence and absence of life surprise me; it was as though I had expected it. In fact, from the time when I first perceived the existence of the enigmatic street, I had not thought for one moment of any possible inhabitants. And yet I had just entered it like a nocturnal thief.

I took no precautions when I ransacked the drawers containing silverware and table linen. My footsteps clattered freely in the adjoining rooms furnished like convent visiting-rooms, and on a magnificent oak staircase that. . . . Ah, there *was* something surprising in my visit! That staircase led nowhere! It ran into the drab wall as though it continued on the other side of it.

All this was bathed in the whitish glow of the frosted glass that formed the ceiling. I saw, or thought I saw, a vaguely hideous shape on the rough plaster wall, but when I looked at it attentively I realized that it was composed of thin cracks and was of the same order as those monsters that we distinguish in clouds and the lace of curtains. Furthermore, it did not trouble me,

because when I looked a second time I no longer saw it in the network of cracks in the plaster.

I went back to the kitchen. Through a barred window, I saw a shadowy little courtyard that was like a pit surrounded by four big, mossy walls.

On a sideboard there was a heavy tray that looked as though it ought to have some value. I slipped it under my coat. I was deeply disappointed: I felt as though I had just stolen a few coins from a child's piggy bank, or from an old-maid aunt's shabby woolen stocking.

I went to Gockel, the antique dealer.

The three little houses were identical. In all of them, I found the same clean, tidy kitchen, the same sparse, gleaming furniture, the same dim, unreal light, the same serene quietness, the same senseless wall that ended the staircase. And in all three houses, I found identical candlesticks and the same heavy tray.

I took them away, and . . . and the next day I always found them in their places again. I took them to Gockel, who smiled broadly as he paid me for them.

It was enough to drive me mad; I felt my soul becoming monotonous, like that of a whirling dervish. Over and over again, I stole the same objects from the same house, under the same circumstances. I wondered whether this might not be the first vengeance of that unknown without mystery. Might not damnation be the unvarying repetition of sin for all eternity?

One day I did not go. I had resolved to space out my wretched incursions. I had a reserve of gold; Anita was happy and was showing wonderful tenderness toward me.

That same evening, Gockel came to see me, asked me if I had anything to sell, and, to my surprise, offered to pay me even more than he had been paying. He scowled when I told him of my decision.

"You've found a regular buyer, haven't you?" I said to him as he was leaving.

He slowly turned around and looked me straight in the eyes.

"Yes, Herr Doktor. I won't tell you anything about him, just as you never speak to me of . . . your friend, the seller." His voice became lower: "Bring me objects every day; tell me how much gold you want for them, and I'll give it to you, without bargaining. We're both tied to the same wheel, Herr Doktor. Perhaps we'll have to pay later. In the meantime, let's live the kind of life we like: you with a pretty girl, I with a fortune."

We never broached the subject again. But Anita suddenly became very demanding, and Gockel's gold slipped between her little fingers like water.

Then the atmosphere of the street changed, if I may express it that way. I heard melodies. At least it seemed to me that it was marvelous, faraway music. Summoning up my courage again, I decided to explore the street beyond the bend and go on toward the song that vibrated in the distance.

When I passed the third door and entered a part of the street where I had never gone before, I felt a terrible tightening in my heart. I took only three or four hesitant steps.

I turned around. I could still see the first part of the street, but it looked much smaller. It seemed to me that I had moved dangerously far away from my world. Nevertheless, in a surge of irrational temerity, I ran a short distance, then knelt, and, like a boy peering over a hedge, ventured to look down the unknown part of the street.

Disappointment struck me like a slap. The street continued its winding way, but again I saw nothing except three little doors in a white wall, and some viburnum bushes.

I would surely have gone back then if the wind of

song had not passed by, like a distant tide of billowing sound. . . . I surmounted an inexplicable terror and listened to it, hoping to analyze it if possible.

I have called it a tide: it was a sound that came from a considerable distance, but it was enormous, like the sound of the sea.

As I listened to it, I no longer heard the harmonies I had thought I discerned in it at first; instead, I heard a harsh dissonance, a furious clamor of wails and hatred.

Have you ever noticed that the first whiffs of a repulsive smell are sometimes soft and even pleasant? I remember that when I left my house one day I was greeted in the street by an appetizing aroma of roast beef. "Someone's doing some good cooking early in the morning," I thought. But when I had walked a hundred paces, this aroma changed into the sharp, sickening smell of burning cloth: a draper's shop was on fire, filling the air with sparks and smoky flames. In the same way, I may have been deceived by my first perception of the melodious clamor.

"Why don't I go beyond the next bend?" I said to myself. My apprehensive inertia had almost disappeared. Walking calmly now, I covered the space before me in a few seconds—and once again I found exactly the same scene that I had left behind.

I was overwhelmed by a kind of bitter fury that engulfed my broken curiosity. Three identical houses, then three more identical houses. I had plumbed the mystery merely by opening the first door.

Gloomy courage took possession of me. I walked forward along the street, and my disappointment grew at an incredible rate.

A bend, three little yellow doors, a clump of virburnum bushes, then another bend, the same three little doors in the white wall, and the shadow of spindle trees. This repetition continued obsessively while I walked furiously, with loud footsteps.

Suddenly, when I had turned one more bend in the street, this terrible symmetry was broken. There were again three little doors and some viburnum bushes, but there was also a big wooden portal, darkened and worn smooth by time. I was afraid of it.

I now heard the clamor from much closer, hostile and threatening. I began walking back toward the Mohlenstrasse. The scenes went by like the quatrains of a ballad: three little doors and viburnum bushes, three little doors and viburnum bushes. . . .

Finally I saw the first lights of the real world twinkling before me. But the clamor had pursued me to the edge of the Mohlenstrasse. There it stopped abruptly, adapting itself to the joyous evening sounds of the populous streets, so that the mysterious and terrible shouting ended in a chorus of children's voices singing a roundelay.

The whole town is in the grip of an unspeakable terror.

I would not have spoken of it in these brief memoirs, which concern only myself, if I had not found a link between the shadowy street and the crimes that steep the town in blood every night.

Over a hundred people have suddenly disappeared, a hundred others have been savagely murdered.

I recently took a map of the town and drew on it the winding line that must represent Saint Beregonne's Lane, that incomprehensible street that overlaps our terrestrial world. I was horrified to see that *all the crimes have been committed along that line*.

Thus poor Klingbom was one of the first to disappear. According to his clerk, he vanished like a puff of smoke just as he was entering the room containing his stills. The seed merchant's wife was next, snatched away while she was in her sad garden. Her husband was found in his drying-room with his skull smashed.

As I traced the fateful line on the map, my idea

became a certainty. I can explain the victims' disappearance only by their passage into an unknown plane; as for the murders, they are easy for invisible beings.

All the inhabitants of a house on Old Purse Street have disappeared. On Church Street, six corpses have been found. On Post Street, there have been five disappearances and four deaths. This goes on and on, apparently limited by the Deichstrasse, where more murders and disappearances are taking place.

I now realize that to talk about what I know would be to place myself in the Kirchhaus insane asylum, a tomb from which no Lazarus ever arises; or else it would give free rein to a superstitious crowd that is exasperated enough to tear me to pieces as a sorcerer.

And yet, ever since the beginning of my monotonous daily thefts, anger has been welling up inside me, driving me to vague plans of vengeance.

"Gockel knows more about this than I do," I thought. "I'm going to tell him what I know: that will make him more inclined to confide in me."

But that evening, while Gockel was emptying his heavy purse into my hands, I said nothing, and he left as usual with polite words that made no allusion to the strange bargain that had attached us to the same chain.

I had a feeling that events were about to leap forward and rush like a torrent through my tranquil life. I was becoming more and more aware that Saint Beregonne's Lane and its little houses were only a mask concealing some sort of horrible face.

So far, fortunately for me, I had gone there only in broad daylight, because for some reason I dreaded to encounter the shadows of evening there. But one day I lingered later than usual, stubbornly pushing furniture around, turning drawers inside out, determined to discover something new. And the "new" came of itself, in the form of a dull rumble, like that of heavy doors moving on rollers. I looked up and saw that the

opalescent light had changed into an ashy semidarkness. The panes of glass above the staircase were livid; the little courtyards were already filled with shadow.

My heart tightened, but when the rumbling continued, reinforced by the powerful resonance of the house, my curiosity became stronger than my fear, and I began climbing the stairs to see where the noise was coming from.

It was growing darker and darker, but before leaping back down the stairs like a madman and running out of the house, I was able to see. . . . There was no more wall! The staircase ended at the edge of an abyss dug out of the night, from which vague monstrosities were rising.

I reached the door; behind me, something was furiously knocked over.

The Mohlenstrasse gleamed before me like a haven. I ran faster. Something suddenly seized me with extreme savagery.

"What's the matter with you? Can't you see where you're going?"

I found myself sitting on the pavement of the Mohlenstrasse, before a sailor who was rubbing his sore skull and looking at me in bewilderment. My coat was torn, my neck was bleeding.

I immediately hurried away without wasting any time on apologies, to the supreme indignation of the sailor, who shouted after me that after colliding with him so brutally I should at least buy him a drink.

Anita is gone, vanished!

My heart is broken; I collapse, sobbing, on my useless gold.

And yet her house is far from the zone of danger. Good God! I failed through an excess of prudence and love! One day, without mentioning the street, I showed

her the line I had drawn on the map and told her that all the danger seemed to be concentrated along that sinuous trail. Her eyes glowed strangely at that moment. I should have known that the great spirit of adventure that animated her ancestors was not dead in her.

Perhaps, in a flash of feminine intuition, she made a connection between that line and my sudden fortune. . . . Oh, how my life is disintegrating!

There have been more murders and disappearances. And my Anita has been carried off in the bloody, inexplicable whirlwind!

The case of Hans Mendell has given me a mad idea: those vaporous beings, as he described them, may not be invulnerable.

Although Hans Mendell was not a distinguished man, I see no reason not to believe his story. He was a scoundrel who made his living as a mountebank and a cutthroat. When he was found, he had in his pocket the purses and watches of two unfortunate men whose corpses lay bleeding on the ground a few paces away from him.

It would have been assumed that he was guilty of murder if he himself had not been found moaning with both arms torn from his body.

Being a man with a powerful constitution, he was able to live long enough to answer the feverish questions of the magistrates and priests.

He confessed that for several days he had followed a shadow, a kind of black mist, and robbed the bodies of the people it killed. On the night of his misfortune, he saw the black mist waiting in the middle of Post Street in the moonlight. He hid in an empty sentry-box and watched it. He saw other dark, vaporous, awkward forms that bounced like rubber balls, then disappeared.

Soon he heard voices and saw two young men coming up the street. The black mist was no longer in sight, but

he suddenly saw the two men writhe on their backs, then lie still.

Mendell added that he had already observed the same sequence in those nocturnal murders on seven other occasions. He had always waited for the shadow to leave, then robbed the bodies. This shows that he had remarkable self-control, worthy of being put to a better use.

As he was robbing the two bodies, he saw with alarm that the shadow had not left, but had only risen off the ground, interposing itself between him and the moon. He then saw that it had a roughly human shape. He tried to go back to the sentry-box but did not have time: the figure pounced on him.

Mendell was an extraordinarily strong man. He struck an enormous blow and encountered a slight resistance, as though he were pushing his hand through a strong current of air.

That was all he was able to say. His horrible wound allowed him to live only another hour after telling his story.

The idea of avenging Anita has now taken root in my brain. I said to Gockel, "Don't come any more. I need revenge and hatred, and your gold can no longer do anything for me."

He looked at me with that profound expression that was familiar to me by now.

"Gockel," I said, "I'm going to take vengeance."

His face suddenly brightened, as though with great joy:

"And . . . do you believe . . . Herr Doktor, that they will disappear?"

I harshly ordered him to have a cart filled with fagots and casks of oil, raw alcohol and gunpowder, and to leave it without a driver early in the morning on the Mohlenstrasse. He bowed low like a servant, and as he

was leaving he said to me, "May the Lord help you! May the Lord come to your aid!"

I feel that these are the last lines I shall write in this journal.

I piled up the fagots, streaming with oil and alcohol, against the big door. I laid down trails of gunpowder connecting the nearby small doors with other oil-soaked fagots. I placed charges of powder in all the cracks in the walls.

The mysterious clamor continued all around me. This time I discerned in it abominable lamentations, human wails, echoes of horrible torments of the flesh. But my heart was agitated by tumultuous joy, because I felt around me a wild apprehension that came from *them*. They saw my terrible preparations and were unable to prevent them, for, as I had come to realize, only night released their frightful power.

I calmly struck a light with my tinderbox. A moan passed, and the viburnum bushes quivered as though blown by a sudden stiff breeze. A long blue flame rose into the air, the fagots began crackling, fire crept along the trails of gunpowder. . . .

I ran down the winding street, from bend to bend, feeling a little dizzy, as though I were going too fast down a spiral staircase that descended deep into the earth.

The Deichstrasse and the whole surrounding neighborhood were in flames. From my window, I could see the sky turning yellow above the rooftops. The weather was dry and the town's water supply was nearly exhausted. A red band of sparks and flames hovered high above the street.

The fire had been burning for a day and a night, but it was still far from the Mohlenstrasse. Saint Beregonne's

Lane was there, calm with its quivering viburnum bushes. Explosions rumbled in the distance.

Another cart was there, loaded and left by Gockel. Not a soul was in sight: everyone had been drawn toward the formidable spectacle of the fire. *It was not expected here.*

I walked from bend to bend to bend, sowing fagots, pools of oil and alcohol, and the dark frost of gunpowder. Suddenly, just as I had turned another bend, I stopped and stared. Three little houses, the everlasting three little houses, were burning calmly with pretty yellow flames in the peaceful air. It was as though even the fire respected their serenity, for it was doing its work without noise or ferocity. I realized that I was at the red edge of the conflagration that was destroying the town.

With anguish in my soul, I moved back from that mystery that was about to die.

I was near the Mohlenstrasse. I stopped in front of the first of the little doors, the one I had opened, trembling, a few weeks earlier. It was there that I would start the new fire.

For the last time, I saw the kitchen, the austere parlor, and the staircase, which now ended at the wall, as before; and I felt that all this had become familiar, almost dear to me.

On the big tray, the one I had stolen so many times before only to find it waiting for me again the next day, I saw some sheets of paper covered with elegant feminine handwriting.

I picked them up. This was going to be my last theft on the shadowy street.

Vampires! Vampires! Vampires!

* * * * * *

So ends the French manuscript. The last words, evoking the impure spirits of the night, are written

across the page in sharp letters that cry out terror and despair. Thus must write those who, on a sinking ship, want to convey a last farewell to the families they hope will survive them.

It was last year in Hamburg. I was strolling through the old city, with its good smell of fresh beer. It was dear to my heart, because it reminded me of the cities I had loved in my youth. And there, on an empty, echoing street, I saw a name on the front of an antique shop: Lockmann Gockel.

I bought an old Bavarian pipe with truculent decorations. The shopkeeper seemed friendly. I asked him if the name of Archipetre meant anything to him. His face had been the color of gray earth; in the twilight it now turned so white that it stood out from the shadows as though illuminated by an inner flame.

"Archipetre," he murmured slowly. "Oh! What are you saying? What do you know?"

I had no reason to conceal the story I had found on the dock. I told it to him.

He lit an archaic gaslight. Its flame danced and hissed foolishly.

I saw that his eyes were weary.

"He was my grandfather," he said, when I mentioned Gockel the antique dealer.

When I had finished my story I heard a great sigh from a dark corner.

"That's my sister," he said.

I nodded to her. She was young and pretty, but very pale. She had been listening to me, motionless among grotesque shadows.

"Our grandfather talked to our father about it nearly every evening," he said in a faltering voice, "and our father used to discuss it with us. Now that he's dead too, we talk about it with each other."

"And now," I said nervously, "thanks to you, we're

going to be able to do some research on the subject of that mysterious street, aren't we?"

He slowly raised his hand.

"Alphonse Archipetre taught French in the Gymnasium until 1842."

"Oh!" I said, disappointed. "That's a long time ago!"

"It was the year of the great fire that nearly destroyed Hamburg. The Mohlenstrasse and the vast section of the city between it and the Deichstrasse were a sea of flames."

"And Archipetre?"

"He lived rather far from there, toward Bleichen. The fire didn't reach his street, but in the middle of the second night, on May 6—a terrible night, dry and without water—his house burned down, all alone among the others that were miraculously spared. He died in the flames; or at least he was never found."

"The story . . ." I began.

Lockmann Gockel did not let me finish. He was so happy to have found an outlet that he seized upon the subject greedily. Fortunately he told me more or less what I wanted to hear.

"The story compressed time, just as space was compressed at the fateful location of Saint Beregonne's Lane. In the Hamburg archives, there are accounts of atrocities committed *during the fire* by a band of mysterious evil-doers. Fantastic crimes, looting, riots, red hallucinations on the part of whole crowds—all those things are precisely described, and yet they took place *before the fire*. Do you understand my reference to the contraction of space and time?"

His face became a little calmer.

"Isn't modern science driven back to Euclidean weakness by the theory of that admirable Einstein for whom the whole world envies us? And isn't it forced to accept, with horror and despair, that fantastic

Fitzgerald-Lorentz law of contraction? Contraction! Ah, there's a word that's heavy with meaning!"

The conversation seemed to be going off on an insidious tangent.

The young woman silently brought tall glasses filled with yellow wine. Gockel raised his toward the flame and marvelous colors flowed onto his frail hand like a silver river of gems.

He abandoned his scientific dissertation and returned to the story of the conflagration:

"My grandfather, and other people of the time, reported that enormous green flames shot up from the debris. There were hallucinated people who claimed to see figures of indescribably ferocious women in them."

The wine had a soul. I emptied the glass and smiled at Gockel's terrified words.

"Those same green flames," he went on, "rose from Archipetre's house and roared so horribly that people were said to have died of fear in the street."

"Mr. Gockel," I said, "did your grandfather ever speak of the mysterious purchaser who came every evening to buy the same trays and the same candlesticks?"

A weary voice replied for him, in words that were almost identical with those that ended the German manuscript:

"A tall old woman, an immense old woman with fishy eyes in an incredible face. She brought bags of gold so heavy that our grandfather had to divide them into four parts to carry them to his coffers."

The young woman continued:

"When Professor Archipetre came to my grandfather, the Gockel firm was about to go bankrupt. It became rich, and we're still enormously rich, from the gold of the . . . yes, from the gold of those beings of the night!"

"They're gone now," murmured her brother, refilling our glasses.

"Don't say that! They can't have forgotten us. Remember our nights, our horrible nights! All I can hope for now is that there is, or was, a human presence with them that they cherish and that may intercede for us."

Her lovely eyes opened wide before the black abyss of her thoughts.

"Kathie!" exclaimed Gockel. "Have you again seen? . . ."

"You know the things are here every night," she said in a voice as low as a moan. "They assail our thoughts as soon as sleep comes over us. Ah, to sleep no more! . . ."

"To sleep no more," repeated her brother in an echo of terror.

"They come out of their gold, which we keep, and which we love in spite of everything; they rise from everything we've acquired with that infernal fortune. . . . They'll always come back, as long as we exist, and as long as this wretched earth endures!"

—*translated by Lowell Bair*

Robert Silverberg (b. 1935)

PASSENGERS

Robert Silverberg is one of the dominant figures in science fiction of the last thirty years. Enormously prolific in his younger years, he became one of the leading craftsmen in the field by the end of the 1960s and then, perhaps the leading master of the science fiction short story of the 1970s. During an enormously creative period beginning in the late sixties and ending in the mid-seventies, he wrote a majority of the work upon which his reputation rests. He has won the Nebula Award several times for best story (in 1969 for "Passengers") and for best novella of the year. While his science fiction is often dark and atmospheric, most of his work is far from the horror mode. "Passengers" is a notable exception. It was Silverberg's first award-winner and was one of the works that distinguish the career transition noted above. It is a monster story in which the ambiguous alien invaders function as a psychological metaphor in an unusually foregrounded manner. The only evidence for them is human behavior—and we do not know how far to trust the point-of-view character. Altogether, "Passengers" is a virtuoso performance.

There are only fragments of me left now. Chunks of memory have broken free and drifted away like

calved glaciers. It is always like that when a Passenger leaves us. We can never be sure of all the things our borrowed bodies did. We have only the lingering traces, the imprints.

Like sand clinging to an ocean-tossed bottle. Like the throbbings of amputated legs.

I rise. I collect myself. My hair is rumpled; I comb it. My face is creased from too little sleep. There is sourness in my mouth. Has my Passenger been eating dung with my mouth? They do that. They do anything.

It is morning.

A gray, uncertain morning. I stare at it awhile, and then, shuddering, I opaque the window and confront instead the gray, uncertain surface of the inner panel. My room looks untidy. Did I have a woman here? There are ashes in the trays. Searching for butts, I find several with lipstick stains. Yes, a woman was here.

I touch the bedsheets. Still warm with shared warmth. Both pillows tousled. She has gone, though, and the Passenger is gone, and I am alone.

How long did it last, this time?

I pick up the phone and ring Central. "What is the date?"

The computer's bland feminine voice replies, "Friday, December fourth, nineteen eighty-seven."

"The time?"

"Nine fifty-one, Eastern Standard Time."

"The weather forecast?"

"Predicted temperature range for today thirty to thirty-eight. Current temperature, thirty-one. Wind from the north, sixteen miles an hour. Chances of precipitation slight."

"What do you recommend for a hangover?"

"Food or medication?"

"Anything you like," I say.

The computer mulls that one over for a while. Then it decides on both, and activates my kitchen. The spigot

yields cold tomato juice. Eggs begin to fry. From the medicine slot comes a purplish liquid. The Central Computer is always so thoughtful. Do the Passengers ever ride it, I wonder? What thrills could that hold for them? Surely it must be more exciting to borrow the million minds of Central than to live a while in the faulty, short-circuited soul of a corroding human being!

December 4, Central said. Friday. So the Passenger had me for three nights.

I drink the purplish stuff and probe my memories in a gingerly way, as one might probe a festering sore.

I remember Tuesday morning. A bad time at work. None of the charts will come out right. The section manager irritable; he has been taken by Passengers three times in five weeks, and his section is in disarray as a result, and his Christmas bonus is jeopardized. Even though it is customary not to penalize a person for lapses due to Passengers, according to the system, the section manager seems to feel he will be treated unfairly. So he treats us unfairly. We have a hard time. Revise the charts, fiddle with the program, check the fundamentals ten times over. Out they come: the detailed forecasts for price variations of public utility securities, February–April 1988. That afternoon we are to meet and discuss the charts and what they tell us.

I do not remember Tuesday afternoon.

That must have been when the Passenger took me. Perhaps at work; perhaps in the mahogany-paneled boardroom itself, during the conference. Pink concerned faces all about me; I cough, I lurch, I stumble from my seat. They shake their heads sadly. No one reaches for me. No one stops me. It is too dangerous to interfere with one who has a Passenger. The chances are great that a second Passenger lurks nearby in the discorporate state, looking for a mount. So I am avoided. I leave the building.

After that, what?

Sitting in my room on bleak Friday morning, I eat my scrambled eggs and try to reconstruct the three lost nights.

Of course it is impossible. The conscious mind functions during the period of captivity, but upon withdrawal of the Passenger nearly every recollection goes too. There is only a slight residue, a gritty film of faint and ghostly memories. The mount is never precisely the same person afterwards; though he cannot recall the details of his experience, he is subtly changed by it.

I try to recall.

A girl? Yes: lipstick on the butts. Sex, then, here in my room. Young? Old? Blonde? Dark? Everything is hazy. How did my borrowed body behave? Was I a good lover? I try to be, when I am myself. I keep in shape. At 38, I can handle three sets of tennis on a summer afternoon without collapsing. I can make a woman glow as a woman is meant to glow. Not boasting: just categorizing. We have our skills. These are mine.

But Passengers, I am told, take wry amusement in controverting our skills. So would it have given my rider a kind of delight to find me a woman and force me to fail repeatedly with her?

I dislike that thought.

The fog is going from my mind now. The medicine prescribed by Central works rapidly. I eat, I shave, I stand under the vibrator until my skin is clean. I do my exercises. Did the Passenger exercise my body Wednesday and Thursday mornings? Probably not. I must make up for that. I am close to middle age, now; tonus lost is not easily regained.

I touch my toes twenty times, knees stiff.

I kick my legs in the air.

I lie flat and lift myself on pumping elbows.

The body responds, maltreated though it has been. It

is the first bright moment of my awakening: to feel the
inner tingling, to know that I still have vigor.

Fresh air is what I want next. Quickly I slip into my
clothes and leave. There is no need for me to report to
work today. They are aware that since Tuesday afternoon I have had a Passenger; they need not be aware
that before dawn on Friday the Passenger departed. I
will have a free day. I will walk the city's streets,
stretching my limbs, repaying my body for the abuse it
has suffered.

I enter the elevator. I drop fifty stories to the ground.
I step out into the December dreariness.

The towers of New York rise about me.

In the street the cars stream forward. Drivers sit
edgily at their wheels. One never knows when the driver
of a nearby car will be borrowed, and there is always a
moment of lapsed coordination as the Passenger takes
over. Many lives are lost that way on our streets and
highways; but never the life of a Passenger.

I begin to walk without purpose. I cross Fourteenth
Street, heading north, listening to the soft violent purr
of the electric engines. I see a boy jigging in the street
and know he is being ridden. At Fifth and Twenty-
second a prosperous-looking paunchy man approaches,
his necktie askew, this morning's *Wall Street Journal*
jutting from an overcoat pocket. He giggles. He thrusts
out his tongue. Ridden. Ridden. I avoid him. Moving
briskly, I come to the underpass that carries traffic
below Thirty-fourth Street toward Queens, and pause
for a moment to watch two adolescent girls quarreling
at the rim of the pedestrian walk. One is a Negro. Her
eyes are rolling in terror. The other pushes her closer to
the railing. Ridden. But the Passenger does not have
murder on its mind, merely pleasure. The Negro girl is
released and falls in a huddled heap, trembling. Then
she rises and runs. The other girl draws a long strand of

gleaming hair into her mouth, chews on it, seems to awaken. She looks dazed.

I avert my eyes. One does not watch while a fellow sufferer is awakening. There is a morality of the ridden; we have so many new tribal mores in these dark days.

I hurry on.

Where am I going so hurriedly? Already I have walked more than a mile. I seem to be moving toward some goal, as though my Passenger still hunches in my skull, urging me about. But I know that is not so. For the moment, at least, I am free.

Can I be sure of that?

Cogito ergo sum no longer applies. We go on thinking even while we are ridden, and we live in quiet desperation, unable to halt our courses no matter how ghastly, no matter how self-destructive. I am certain that I can distinguish between the condition of bearing a Passenger and the condition of being free. But perhaps not. Perhaps I bear a particularly devilish Passenger which has not quitted me at all, but which merely has receded to the cerebellum, leaving me the illusion of freedom while all the time surreptitiously driving me onward to some purpose of its own.

Did we ever have more than that: the illusion of freedom?

But this is disturbing, the thought that I may be ridden without realizing it. I burst out in heavy perspiration, not merely from the exertion of walking. Stop. Stop here. Why must you walk? You are at Forty-second Street. There is the library. Nothing forces you onward. Stop a while, I tell myself. Rest on the library steps.

I sit on the cold stone and tell myself that I have made this decision for myself.

Have I? It is the old problem, free will versus determinism, translated into the foulest of forms. Determinism is no longer a philosopher's abstraction; it is

cold alien tendrils sliding between the cranial sutures. The Passengers arrived three years ago. I have been ridden five times since then. Our world is quite different now. But we have adjusted even to this. We have adjusted. We have our mores. Life goes on. Our governments rule, our legislatures meet, our stock exchanges transact business as usual, and we have methods for compensating for the random havoc. It is the only way. What else can we do? Shrivel in defeat? We have an enemy we cannot fight; at best we can resist through endurance. So we endure.

The stone steps are cold against my body. In December few people sit here.

I tell myself that I made this long walk of my own free will, that I halted of my own free will, that no Passenger rides my brain now. Perhaps. Perhaps. I cannot let myself believe that I am not free.

Can it be, I wonder, that the Passenger left some lingering command in me? Walk to this place, halt at this place? That is possible too.

I look about me at the others on the library steps.

An old man, eyes vacant, sitting on newspaper. A boy of thirteen or so with flaring nostrils. A plump woman. Are all of them ridden? Passengers seem to cluster about me today. The more I study the ridden ones, the more convinced I become that I am, for the moment, free. The last time, I had three months of freedom between rides. Some people, they say, are scarcely ever free. Their bodies are in great demand, and they know only scattered bursts of freedom, a day here, a week there, an hour. We have never been able to determine how many Passengers infest our world. Millions, maybe. Or maybe five. Who can tell?

A wisp of snow curls down out of the gray sky. Central had said the chance of precipitation was slight. Are they riding Central this morning too?

I see the girl.

She sits diagonally across from me, five steps up and a hundred feet away, her black skirt pulled up on her knees to reveal handsome legs. She is young. Her hair is deep, rich auburn. Her eyes are pale; at this distance, I cannot make out the precise color. She is dressed simply. She is younger than thirty. She wears a dark green coat and her lipstick has a purplish tinge. Her lips are full, her nose slender, high-bridged, her eyebrows carefully plucked.

I know her.

I have spent the past three nights with her in my room. She is the one. Ridden, she came to me, and ridden, I slept with her. I am certain of this. The veil of memory opens; I see her slim body naked on my bed.

How can it be that I remember this?

It is too strong to be an illusion. Clearly this is something that I have been *permitted* to remember for reasons I cannot comprehend. And I remember more. I remember her soft gasping sounds of pleasure. I know that my own body did not betray me those three nights, nor did I fail her need.

And there is more. A memory of sinuous music; a scent of youth in her hair; the rustle of winter trees. Somehow she brings back to me a time of innocence, a time when I am young and girls are mysterious, a time of parties and dances and warmth and secrets.

I am drawn to her now.

There is an etiquette about such things, too. It is in poor taste to approach someone you have met while being ridden. Such an encounter gives you no privilege; a stranger remains a stranger, no matter what you and she may have done and said during your involuntary time together.

Yet I am drawn to her.

Why this violation of taboo? Why this raw breach of etiquette? I have never done this before. I have been scrupulous.

But I get to my feet and walk along the step on which I have been sitting, until I am below her, and I look up, and automatically she folds her ankles together and angles her knees as if in awareness that her position is not a modest one. I know from the gesture that she is not ridden now. My eyes meet hers. Her eyes are hazy green. She is beautiful, and I rack my memory for more details of our passion.

I climb step by step until I stand before her.

"Hello," I say.

She gives me a neutral look. She does not seem to recognize me. Her eyes are veiled, as one's eyes often are, just after the Passenger has gone. She purses her lips and appraises me in a distant way.

"Hello," she replies coolly. "I don't think I know you."

"No. You don't. But I have the feeling you don't want to be alone just now. And I know I don't." I try to persuade her with my eyes that my motives are decent. "There's snow in the air," I say. "We can find a warmer place. I'd like to talk to you."

"About what?"

"Let's go elsewhere, and I'll tell you. I'm Charles Roth."

"Helen Martin."

She gets to her feet. She still has not cast aside her cool neutrality; she is suspicious, ill at ease. But at least she is willing to go with me. A good sign.

"Is it too early in the day for a drink?" I ask.

"I'm not sure. I hardly know what time it is."

"Before noon."

"Let's have a drink anyway," she says, and we both smile.

We go to a cocktail lounge across the street. Sitting face to face in the darkness, we sip drinks, daiquiri for her, bloody mary for me. She relaxes a little. I ask myself what it is I want from her. The pleasure of her

company, yes. Her company in bed? But I have already had that pleasure, three nights of it, though she does not know that. I want something more. Something more. What?

Her eyes are bloodshot. She has had little sleep these past three nights.

I say, "Was it very unpleasant for you?"

"What?"

"The Passenger."

A whiplash of reaction crosses her face. "How did you know I've had a Passenger?"

"I know."

"We aren't supposed to talk about it."

"I'm broadminded," I tell her. "My Passenger left me some time during the night. I was ridden since Tuesday afternoon."

"Mine left me about two hours ago, I think." Her cheeks color. She is doing something daring, talking like this. "I was ridden since Monday night. This was my fifth time."

"Mine also."

We toy with our drinks. Rapport is growing, almost without the need of words. Our recent experiences with Passengers give us something in common, although Helen does not realize how intimately we shared those experiences.

We talk. She is a designer of display windows. She has a small apartment several blocks from here. She lives alone. She asks me what I do. "Securities analyst," I tell her. She smiles. Her teeth are flawless. We have a second round of drinks. I am positive, now, that this is the girl who was in my room when I was ridden.

A seed of hope grows in me. It was a happy chance that brought us together again, so soon after we parted as dreamers. A happy chance, too, that some vestige of the dream lingered in my mind.

We have shared something, who knows what, and it

must have been good to leave such a vivid imprint on me, and now I want to come to her conscious, aware, my own master, and renew that relationship, making it a real one this time. It is not proper, for I am trespassing on a privilege that is not mine except by virtue of our Passengers' brief presence in us. Yet I need her. I want her.

She seems to need me, too, without realizing who I am. But fear holds her back.

I am frightened of frightening her, and I do not try to press my advantage too quickly. Perhaps she would take me to her apartment with her now, perhaps not, but I do not ask. We finish our drinks. We arrange to meet by the library steps again tomorrow. My hand momentarily brushes hers. Then she is gone.

I fill three ashtrays that night. Over and over I debate the wisdom of what I am doing. But why not leave her alone? I have no right to follow her. In the place our world has become, we are wisest to remain apart.

And yet—there is that stab of half-memory when I think of her. The blurred lights of lost chances behind the stairs, of girlish laughter in second-floor corridors, of stolen kisses, of tea and cake. I remember the girl with the orchid in her hair, and the one in the spangled dress, and the one with the child's face and the woman's eyes, all so long ago, all lost, all gone, and I tell myself that this one I will not lose, I will not permit her to be taken from me.

Morning comes, a quiet Saturday. I return to the library, hardly expecting to find her there, but she is there, on the steps, and the sight of her is like a reprieve. She looks wary, troubled; obviously she has done much thinking, little sleeping. Together we walk along Fifth Avenue. She is quite close to me, but she does not take my arm. Her steps are brisk, short, nervous.

I want to suggest that we go to her apartment instead of to the cocktail lounge. In these days we must move

swiftly while we are free. But I know it would be a mistake to think of this as a matter of tactics. Coarse haste would be fatal, bringing me perhaps an ordinary victory, a numbing defeat within it. In any event her mood hardly seems promising. I look at her, thinking of string music and new snowfalls, and she looks toward the gray sky.

She says, "I can feel them watching me all the time. Like vultures swooping overhead, waiting, waiting. Ready to pounce."

"But there's a way of beating them. We can grab little scraps of life when they're not looking."

"They're *always* looking."

"No," I tell her. "There can't be enough of them for that. Sometimes they're looking the other way. And while they are, two people can come together and try to share warmth."

"But what's the use?"

"You're too pessimistic, Helen. They ignore us for months at a time. We have a chance. We have a chance."

But I cannot break through her shell of fear. She is paralyzed by the nearness of the Passengers, unwilling to begin anything for fear it will be snatched away by our tormentors. We reach the building where she lives, and I hope she will relent and invite me in. For an instant she wavers, but only for an instant: she takes my hand in both of hers, and smiles, and the smile fades, and she is gone, leaving me only with the words, "Let's meet at the library again tomorrow. Noon."

I make the long chilling walk home alone.

Some of her pessimism seeps into me that night. It seems futile for us to try to salvage anything. More than that: wicked for me to seek her out, shameful to offer a hesitant love when I am not free. In this world, I tell myself, we should keep well clear of others, so that we do not harm anyone when we are seized and ridden.

I do not go to meet her in the morning.

It is best this way, I insist. I have no business trifling with her. I imagine her at the library, wondering why I am late, growing tense, impatient, then annoyed. She will be angry with me for breaking our date, but her anger will ebb, and she will forget me quickly enough.

Monday comes. I return to work.

Naturally, no one discusses my absence. It is as though I have never been away. The market is strong that morning. The work is challenging; it is mid-morning before I think of Helen at all. But once I think of her, I can think of nothing else. My cowardice in standing her up. The childishness of Saturday night's dark thoughts. Why accept fate so passively? Why give in? I want to fight, now, to carve out a pocket of security despite the odds. I feel a deep conviction that it can be done. The Passengers may never bother the two of us again, after all. And that flickering smile of hers outside her building Saturday, that momentary glow— it should have told me that behind her wall of fear she felt the same hopes. She was waiting for me to lead the way. And I stayed home instead.

At lunchtime I go to the library, convinced it is futile.

But she is there. She paces along the steps; the wind slices at her slender figure. I go to her.

She is silent a moment. "Hello," she says finally.

"I'm sorry about yesterday."

"I waited a long time for you."

I shrug. "I made up my mind that it was no use to come. But then I changed my mind again."

She tried to look angry. But I know she is pleased to see me again—else why did she come here today? She cannot hide her inner pleasure. Nor can I. I point across the street to the cocktail lounge.

"A daiquiri?" I say. "As a peace offering?"

"All right."

Today the lounge is crowded, but we find a booth

somehow. There is a brightness in her eyes that I have not seen before. I sense that a barrier is crumbling within her.

"You're less afraid of me, Helen," I say.

"I've never been afraid of you. I'm afraid of what could happen if we take the risks."

"Don't be. Don't be."

"I'm trying not to be afraid. But sometimes it seems so hopeless. Since *they* came here—"

"We can still try to live our own lives."

"Maybe."

"We have to. Let's make a pact, Helen. No more gloom. No more worrying about the terrible things that might just maybe happen. All right?"

A pause. Then a cool hand against mine.

"All right."

We finished our drinks, and I present my Credit Central to pay for them, and we go outside. I want her to tell me to forget about this afternoon's work and come home with her. It is inevitable, now, that she will ask me, and better sooner than later.

We walk a block. She does not offer the invitation. I sense the struggle inside her, and I wait, letting that struggle reach its own resolution without interference from me. We walk a second block. Her arm is through mine, but she talks only of her work, of the weather, and it is a remote, arm's-length conversation. At the next corner she swings around, away from her apartment, back toward the cocktail lounge. I try to be patient with her.

I have no need to rush things now, I tell myself. Her body is not a secret tome. We have begun our relationship topsy-turvy, with the physical part first; now it will take time to work backward to the more difficult part that some people call love.

But of course she is not aware that we have known

each other that way. The wind blows swirling snow-flakes in our faces, and somehow the cold sting awakens honesty in me. I know what I must say. I must relinquish my unfair advantage.

I tell her, "While I was ridden last week, Helen, I had a girl in my room."

"Why talk of such things now?"

"I have to, Helen. You were the girl."

She halts. She turns to me. People hurry past us in the street. Her face is very pale, with dark red spots growing in her cheeks.

"That's not funny, Charles."

"It wasn't meant to be. You were with me from Tuesday night to early Friday morning."

"How can you possibly know that?"

"I do. I do. The memory is clear. Somehow it remains, Helen. I see your whole body."

"Stop it, Charles."

"We were very good together," I say. "We must have pleased our Passengers because we were so good. To see you again—it was like waking from a dream, and finding that the dream was real, the girl right there—"

"No!"

"Let's go to your apartment and begin again."

She says, "You're being deliberately filthy, and I don't know why, but there wasn't any reason for you to spoil things. Maybe I was with you and maybe I wasn't, but you wouldn't know it, and if you did know it you should keep your mouth shut about it, and—"

"You have a birthmark the size of a dime," I say, "about three inches below your left breast."

She sobs and hurls herself at me, there in the street. Her long silvery nails rake my cheeks. She pummels me. I seize her. Her knees assail me. No one pays attention; those who pass by assume we are ridden, and turn their heads. She is all fury, but I have my arms

around hers like metal bands, so that she can only stamp and snort, and her body is close against mine. She is rigid, anguished.

In a low, urgent voice I say, "We'll defeat them, Helen. We'll finish what they started. Don't fight me. There's no reason to fight me. I know, it's a fluke that I remember you, but let me go with you and I'll prove that we belong together."

"Let—go—"

"Please. Please. Why should we be enemies? I don't mean you any harm. I love you, Helen. Do you remember, when we were kids, we could play at being in love? I did; you must have done it too. Sixteen, seventeen years old. The whispers, the conspiracies—all a big game and we knew it. But the game's over. We can't afford to tease and run. We have so little time, when we're free—we have to trust, to open ourselves—"

"It's wrong."

"No. Just because it's the stupid custom for two people brought together by Passengers to avoid one another, that doesn't mean we have to follow it. Helen —Helen—"

Something in my tone registers with her. She ceases to struggle. Her rigid body softens. She looks up at me, her tearstreaked face thawing, her eyes blurred.

"Trust me," I say. "Trust me, Helen!"

She hesitates. Then she smiles.

In that moment I feel the chill at the back of my skull, the sensation as of a steel needle driven deep through bone. I stiffen. My arms drop away from her. For an instant, I lose touch, and when the mists clear all is different.

"Charles?" she says. *"Charles?"*

Her knuckles are against her teeth. I turn, ignoring her, and go back into the cocktail lounge. A young man sits in one of the front booths. His dark hair gleams

with pomade; his cheeks are smooth. His eyes meet mine.

I sit down. He orders drinks. We do not talk.

My hand falls on his wrist, and remains there. The bartender, serving the drinks, scowls but says nothing. We sip our cocktails and put the drained glasses down.

"Let's go," the young man says.

I follow him out.

Harriet Prescott Spofford
(1835–1921)

THE MOONSTONE MASS

Harriet Prescott Spofford is, according to Alfred Bendixen, "the major female practitioner of a mode of symbolic romance which many have asserted to be the mainstream of American fiction." She established a reputation as the female heir to Poe and Hawthorne, and especially in supernatural fiction, is one of the most important conduits between Poe and the twentieth century. Her first novel, in the Gothic mode, *Sir Rohan's Ghost* (1859) was praised by James Russell Lowell, who said that no American had ever written a first novel with such "genuine poetic power," and her collection, *The Amber Gods and other stories* (1863), was praised in a review by Henry James, who, although objecting to her "morbid and unhealthful" fascination with the "diseased side of human nature," admired the "united strength and brilliancy of her descriptions." A prolific and sometimes hasty magazine writer, Spofford published hundreds of stories, but her best work was in the supernatural. "The Moonstone Mass" (1868), a symbolic romance in her major mode, shows the clear influence of Poe's *Narrative of Arthur Gordon Pym*, and echoes of poetry from Coleridge's *The Rime of the Ancient Mariner* and "Kubla Khan" to Dante's *Inferno*. It is interesting to compare Spofford's treatment to Lovecraft's "At the Mountains of Madness." Both, it seems to me, reach the heights of poetic frenzy, awe and wonder and fear.

There was a certain weakness possessed by my ancestors, though in nowise peculiar to them, and of which, in common with other more or less undesirable traits, I have come into the inheritance.

It was the fear of dying in poverty. That, too, in the face of a goodly share of pelf stored in stocks, and lands, and copper-bottomed clippers, or what stood for copper-bottomed clippers, or rather sailed for them, in the clumsy commerce of their times.

There was one old fellow in particular—his portrait is hanging over the hall stove today, leaning forward, somewhat blistered by the profuse heat and wasted fuel there, and as if as long as such an outrageous expenditure of caloric was going on he meant to have the full benefit of it—who is said to have frequently shed tears over the probable price of his dinner, and on the next day to have sent home a silver dish to eat it from at a hundred times the cost. I find the inconsistencies of this individual constantly cropping out in myself; and although I could by no possibility be called a niggard, yet I confess that even now my prodigalities make me shiver.

Some years ago I was the proprietor of the old family estate, unencumbered by any thing except timber, that is worth its weight in gold yet, as you might say; alone in the world, save for an unloved relative; and with a sufficiently comfortable income, as I have since discovered, to meet all reasonable wants. I had, moreover, promised me in marriage the hand of a woman without a peer, and which, I believe now, might have been mine on any day when I saw fit to claim it.

That I loved Eleanor tenderly and truly you can not doubt; that I desired to bring her home, to see her flitting here and there in my dark old house, illuminating it with her youth and beauty, sitting at the head of my table that sparkled with its gold and silver heir-

looms, making my days and nights like one delightful dream, was just as true.

And yet I hesitated. I looked over my bankbook—I cast up my accounts. I have enough for one, I said; I am not sure that it is enough for two. Eleanor, daintily nurtured, requires as dainty care for all time to come; moreover, it is not two alone to be considered, for should children come, there is their education, their maintenance, their future provision and portion to be found. All this would impoverish us, and unless we ended by becoming mere dependents, we had, to my excited vision, only the cold charity of the world and the work-house to which to look forward. I do not believe that Eleanor thought me right in so much of the matter as I saw fit to explain, but in maiden pride her lips perforce were sealed. She laughed though, when I confessed my work-house fear, and said that for her part she was thankful there was such a refuge at all, standing as it did on its knoll in the midst of green fields, and shaded by broad-limbed oaks—she had always envied the old women sitting there by their evening fireside, and mumbling over their small affairs to one another. But all her words seemed merely idle badinage—so I delayed. I said—when this ship sails in, when that dividend is declared, when I see how this speculation turns out—the days were long that added up the count of years, the nights were dreary; but I believed that I was actuated by principle, and took pride to myself for my strength and self-denial.

Moreover, old Paul, my great-uncle on my mother's side, and the millionaire of the family, was a bitter misogynist, and regarded women and marriage and household cares as the three remediless mistakes of an over-ruling Providence. He knew of my engagement to Eleanor, but so long as it remained in that stage he had nothing to say. Let me once marry, and my share of his million would be best represented by a cipher. Howev-

er, he was not a man to adore, and he could not live forever.

Still, with all my own effort, I amassed wealth but slowly, according to my standard; my various ventures had various luck; and one day my old Uncle Paul, always intensely interested in the subject, both scientifically and from a commercial point of view, too old and feeble to go himself, but fain to send a proxy, and desirous of money in the family, made me an offer of that portion of his wealth on my return which would be mine on his demise, funded safely subject to my order, provided I made one of those who sought the discovery of the Northwest Passage.

I went to town, canvassed the matter with the experts—I had always an adventurous streak, as old Paul well knew—and having given many hours to the pursuit of the smaller sciences, had a turn for danger and discovery as well. And when the *Albatross* sailed— in spite of Eleanor's shivering remonstrance and prayers and tears, in spite of the grave looks of my friends—I was one of those that clustered on her deck, prepared for either fate. They—my companions—it is true, were led by nobler lights; but as for me, it was much as I told Eleanor—my affairs were so regulated that they would go on uninterruptedly in my absence; I should be no worse off for going, and if I returned, letting alone the renown of the thing, my Uncle Paul's donation was to be appropriated; every thing then was assured, and we stood possessed of lucky lives. If I had any keen or eager desire of search, any purpose to aid the growth of the world or to penetrate the secrets of its formation; as indeed I think I must have had, I did not at that time know any thing about it. But I was to learn that death and stillness have no kingdom on this globe, and that even in the extremest bitterness of cold and ice perpetual interchange and motion is taking place. So we went, all sails set on favorable winds, bounding over

blue sea, skirting frowning coasts, and ever pushing our way up into the dark mystery of the North.

I shall not delay here to tell of Danish posts and the hospitality of summer settlements in their long afternoon of arctic daylight; nor will I weary you with any description of the succulence of the radishes that grew under the panes of glass in the Governor's scrap of moss and soil, scarcely of more size than a lady's parlor fernery, and which seemed to our dry mouths full of all the earth's cool juices—but advance, as we ourselves hastened to do, while that chill and crystalline sun shone, up into the ice-cased dens and caverns of the Pole. By the time that the long, blue twilight fell, when the rough and rasping cold sheathed all the atmosphere, and the great stars pricked themselves out on the heavens like spears' points, the *Albatross* was hauled up for winter-quarters, banked and boarded, heaved high on fields of ice; and all her inmates, during the wintry dark, led the life that prepared them for further exploits in higher latitudes the coming year, learning the dialects of the Esquimaux, the tricks of the seal and walrus, making long explorations with the dogs and Glipnu, their master, breaking ourselves in for business that had no play about it.

Then, at last, the August suns set us free again; inlets of tumultuous water traversed the great ice-floes; the *Albatross*, refitted, ruffled all her plumage and spread her wings once more for the North—for the secret that sat there domineering all its substance.

It was a year since we had heard from home; but who staid to think of that while our keel spurned into foam the sheets of steely seas, and day by day brought us nearer to the hidden things we sought? For myself I confess that, now so close to the end as it seemed, curiosity and research absorbed every other faculty; Eleanor might be mouldering back to the parent earth—I could not stay to meditate on such a possibili-

ty; my Uncle Paul's donation might enrich itself with gold-dust instead of the gathered dust of idle days—it was nothing to me. I had but one thought, one ambition, one desire in those days—the discovery of the clear seas and open passage. I endured all our hardships as if they had been luxuries: I made light of scurvy, banqueted off train-oil, and met that cold for which there is no language framed, and which might be a new element; or which, rather, had seemed in that long night like the vast void of ether beyond the uttermost star, where was neither air nor light nor heat, but only bitter negation and emptiness. I was hardly conscious of my body; I was only a concentrated search in myself.

The recent explorers had announced here, in the neighborhood of where our third summer at last found us, the existence of an immense space of clear water. One even declared that he had seen it.

My Uncle Paul had pronounced the declaration false, and the sight an impossibility. The North he believed to be the breeder of icebergs, an ever-welling fountain of cold; the great glaciers there forever form, forever fall; the ice-packs line the gorges from year to year unchanging; peaks of volcanic rock drop their frozen mantles like a scale only to display the fresher one beneath. The whole region, said he, is Plutonic, blasted by a primordial convulsion of the great forces of creation; and though it may be a few miles nearer to the central fires of the earth, allowing that there are such things, yet that would not in itself detract from the frigid power of its sunless solitudes, the more especially when it is remembered that the spinning of the earth, while in its first plastic material, which gave it greater circumference and thinness of shell at its equator, must have thickened the shell correspondingly at the poles; and the character of all the waste and wilderness there only signifies the impenetrable wall between its surface and centre, through which wall no heat could enter or

escape. The great rivers, like the White and the Mac-kenzie, emptying to the north of the continents, so far from being enough in themselves to form any body of ever fresh and flowing water, can only pierce the opposing ice-fields in narrow streams and bays and inlets as they seek the Atlantic and the Pacific seas. And as for the theory of the currents of water heated in the tropics and carried by the rotary motion of the planet to the Pole, where they rise and melt the ice-floes into this great supposititious sea, it is simply an absurdity on the face of it, he argued, when you remember that warm water being in its nature specifically lighter than cold it would have risen to the surface long before it reached there. No, thought my Uncle Paul, who took nothing for granted; it is as I said, an absurdity on the face of it; my nephew shall prove it, and I stake half the earnings of my life upon it.

To tell the truth, I thought much the same as he did; and now that such a mere trifle of distance intervened between me and the proof, I was full of a feverish impatience that almost amounted to insanity.

We had proceeded but a few days, coasting the crushing capes of rock that every where seemed to run out in a diablerie of tusks and horns to drive us from the region that they warded, now cruising through a runlet of blue water just wide enough for our keel, with silver reaches of frost stretching away into a ghastly horizon—now plunging upon tossing seas, the sun wheeling round and round, and never sinking from the strange, weird sky above us, when again to our look-out a glimmer in the low horizon told its awful tale—a sort of smoky lustre like that which might ascend from an army of spirits—the fierce and fatal spirits tented on the terrible field of the ice-floe.

We were alone, our single little ship speeding ever upward in the midst of that untraveled desolation. We spoke seldom to one another, oppressed with the sense

of our situation. It was a loneliness that seemed more than a death in life, a solitude that was supernatural. Here and now it was clear water; ten hours later and we were caught in the teeth of the cold, wedged in the ice that had advanced upon us and surrounded us, fettered by another winter in latitudes where human life had never before been supported.

We found, before the hands of the dial had taught us the lapse of a week, that this would be something not to be endured. The sun sank lower every day behind the crags and silvery horns; the heavens grew to wear a hue of violet, almost black, and yet unbearably dazzling; as the notes of our voices fell upon the atmosphere they assumed a metallic tone, as if the air itself had become frozen from the beginning of the world and they tinkled against it; our sufferings had mounted in their intensity till they were too great to be resisted.

It was decided at length—when the one long day had given place to its answering night, and in the jet-black heavens the stars, like knobs of silver, sparkled so large and close upon us that we might have grasped them in our hands—that I should take a sledge with Glipnu and his dogs, and see if there were any path to the westward by which, if the *Albatross* were forsaken, those of her crew that remained might follow it, and find an escape to safety. Our path was on a frozen sea; if we discovered land we did not know that the foot of man had ever trodden it; we could hope to find no *caché* of snow-buried food—neither fish nor game lived in this desert of ice that was so devoid of life in any shape as to seem dead itself. But, well provisioned, furred to the eyes, and essaying to nurse some hopefulness of heart, we set out on our way through this Valley of Death, relieving one another, and traveling day and night.

Still night and day to the west rose the black coast, one interminable height; to the east extended the sheets of unbroken ice; sometimes a huge glacier hung pendu-

lous from the precipice; once we saw, by the starlight, a white, foaming, rushing river arrested and transformed to ice in its flight down that steep. A south wind began to blow behind us; we traveled on the ice; three days, perhaps, as days are measured among men, had passed, when we found that we made double progress, for the ice traveled too; the whole field, carried by some northward-bearing current, was afloat; it began to be crossed and cut by a thousand crevasses; the cakes, an acre each, tilted up and down, and made wide waves with their ponderous plashing in the black body of the sea; we could hear them grinding distantly in the clear dark against the coast, against each other. There was no retreat—there was no advance; we were on the ice, and the ice was breaking up. Suddenly we rounded a tongue of the primeval rock, and recoiled before a narrow gulf—one sharp shadow, as deep as despair, as full of aguish fears. It was just wide enough for the sledge to span. Glipnu made the dogs leap; we could be no worse off if they drowned. They touched the opposite block; it careened; it went under; the sledge went with it; I was left alone where I had stood. Two dogs broke loose, and scrambled up beside me; Glipnu and the others I never saw again. I sank upon the ice; the dogs crouched beside me; sometimes I think they saved my brain from total ruin, for without them I could not have withstood the enormity of that loneliness, a loneliness that it was impossible should be broken—floating on and on with that vast journeying company of spectral ice. I had food enough to support life for several days to come, in the pouch at my belt; the dogs and I shared it—for, last as long as it would, when it should be gone there was only death before us—no reprieve—sooner or later that; as well sooner as later—the living terrors of this icy hell were all about us, and death could be no worse.

Still the south wind blew, the rapid current carried us, the dark skies grew deep and darker, the lanes and

avenues between the stars were crowded with forebodings—for the air seemed full of a new power, a strange and invisible influence, as if a king of unknown terrors here held his awful state. Sometimes the dogs stood up and growled and bristled their shaggy hides; I, prostrate on the ice, in all my frame was stung with a universal tingle. I was no longer myself. At this moment my blood seemed to sing and bubble in my veins; I grew giddy with a sort of delirious and inexplicable ecstasy; with another moment unutterable horror seized me; I was plunged and weighed down with a black and suffocating load, while evil things seemed to flap their wings in my face, to breathe in my mouth, to draw my soul out of my body and carry it careering through the frozen realm of that murky heaven, to restore it with a shock of agony. Once as I lay there, still floating, floating northward, out of the dim dark rim of the water-world, a lance of piercing light shot up the zenith; it divided the heavens like a knife; they opened out in one blaze, and the fire fell sheetingly down before my face—cold fire, curdlingly cold—light robbed of heat, and set free in a preternatural anarchy of the elements; its fringes swung to and fro before my face, pricked it with flaming spiculæ, dissolving in a thousand colors that spread every where over the low field, flashing, flickering, creeping, reflecting, gathering again in one long serpentine line of glory that wavered in slow convolutions across the cuts and crevasses of the ice, wreathed ever nearer, and, lifting its head at last, became nothing in the darkness but two great eyes like glowing coals, with which it stared me to a stound, till I threw myself face down to hide me in the ice; and the whining, bristling dogs cowered backward, and were dead.

I should have supposed myself to be in the region of the magnetic pole of the sphere, if I did not know that I had long since left it behind me. My pocket-compass

had become entirely useless, and every scrap of metal that I had about me had become a loadstone. The very ice, as if it were congealed from water that held large quantities of iron in solution; iron escaping from whatever solid land there was beneath or around, the Plutonic rock that such a region could have alone veined and seamed with metal. The very ice appeared to have a magnetic quality; it held me so that I changed my position upon it with difficulty, and, as if it established a battery by the aid of the singular atmosphere above it, frequently sent thrills quivering through and through me till my flesh seemed about to resolve into all the jarring atoms of its original constitution; and again soothed me, with a velvet touch, into a state which, if it were not sleep, was at least haunted by visions that I dare not believe to have been realities, and from which I always awoke with a start to find myself still floating, floating. My watch had long since ceased to beat. I felt an odd persuasion that I had died when that stood still, and only this slavery of the magnet, of the cold, this power that locked every thing in invisible fetters and let nothing loose again, held my soul still in the bonds of my body. Another idea, also, took possession of me, for my mind was open to whatever visitant chose to enter, since utter despair of safety or release had left it vacant of a hope or fear. These enormous days and nights, swinging in their arc six months long, were the pendulum that dealt time in another measure than that dealt by the sunlight of lower zones; they told the time of what interminable years, the years of what vast generations far beyond the span that covered the age of the primeval men of Scripture—they measured time on this gigantic and enduring scale for what wonderful and mighty beings, old as the everlasting hills, as destitute as they of mortal sympathy, cold and inscrutable, handling the two-edged javelins of frost and magnetism, and served by all

the unknown polar agencies. I fancied that I saw their far-reaching cohorts, marshaling and manœuvring at times in the field of an horizon that was boundless, the glitter of their spears and casques, the sheen of their white banners; and again, sitting in fearful circle with their phantasmagoria they shut and hemmed me in and watched me write like a worm before them.

I had a fancy that the perpetual play of magnetic impulses here gradually disintegrated the expanse of ice, as sunbeams might have done. If it succeeded in unseating me from my cold station I should drown, and there would be an end of me; it would be all one; for though I clung to life I did not cling to suffering. Something of the wild beast seemed to spring up in my nature; that ignorance of any moment but the present. I felt a certain kinship to the bear in her comfortable snowiness whom I had left in the parallels far below this unreal tract of horrors. I remembered traditions of such metempsychoses; the thought gave me a pang that none of these fierce and subtle elements had known how to give before. But all the time my groaning, cracking ice was moving with me, splitting now through all its leagues of length along the darkness, with an explosion like a cannon's shot, that echoed again and again in every gap and chasm of its depth, and seemed to be caught up and repeated by a thousand airy sprites, and snatched on from one to another till it fell dead through the frozen thickness of the air.

It was at about this time that I noticed another species of motion than that which had hitherto governed it seizing this journeying ice. It bent and bent, as a glacier does in its viscous flow between mountains; it crowded, and loosened, and rent apart, and at last it broke in every direction, and every fragment was crushed and jammed together again; and the whole mass was following, as I divined, the curve of some enormous whirlpool that swept it from beneath. It

might have been a day and night, it might have been an hour, that we traveled on this vast curve—I had no more means of knowing than if I had veritably done with time. We were one expanse of shadow; not a star above us, only a sky of impenetrable gloom received the shimmering that now and again the circling ice cast off. It was a strange slow motion, yet with such a steadiness and strength about it that it had the effect of swiftness. It was long since any water, or the suspicion of any, had been visible; we might have been grinding through some gigantic hollow for all I could have told; snow had never fallen here; the mass moved you knew as if you felt the prodigious hand that grasped and impelled it from beneath. Whither was it tending, in the eddy of what huge stream that went, with the smoke of its fall hovering on the brink, to plunge a tremendous cataract over the limits of the earth into the unknown abyss of space? Far in advance there was a faint glimmering, a sort of powdery light glancing here and there. As we approached it—the ice and I—it grew fainter, and was, by-and-by, lost in a vast twilight that surrounded us on all sides; at the same time it became evident that we had passed under a roof, an immense and vaulted roof. As crowding, stretching, rending, we passed on, uncanny gleams were playing distantly above us and around us, now and then overlaying all things with a sheeted illumination as deathly as a grave-light, now and then shooting up in spires of blood-red radiance that disclosed the terrible aurora. I was in a cavern of ice, as wide and as high as the heavens; these flashes of glory, alternated with equal flashes of darkness, as you might say, taught me to perceive. Perhaps tremendous tide after tide had hollowed it with all its fantastic recesses; or had that Titantic race of the interminable years built it as a palace for their monarch, a temple for their deity, with its domes that sprung far up immeasurable heights and hung palely shining like mock heavens of hazy

stars; its aisles that stretched away down colonnades of crystal columns into unguessed darkness; its high-heaved arches, its pierced and open sides? Now an aurora burned up like a blue-light, and went skimming under all the vaults far off into far and farther hollows, revealing, as it went, still loftier heights and colder answering radiances. Then these great arches glowed like blocks of beryl. Wondrous tracery of delicate vines and leaves, greener than the greenest moss, wandered over them, wreathed the great pillars, and spread round them in capitals of flowers; roses crimson as a carbuncle; hyacinths like bedded cubes of amethyst; violets bluer than sapphires—all as if the flowers had been turned to flame, yet all so cruelly cold, as if the power that wrought such wonders could simulate a sparkle beyond even the lustre of light, but could not give it heat, that principle of life, that fountain of first being. Yonder a stalactite of clustered ruby—that kept the aurora and glinted faintly, and more faintly, till the thing came again, when it grasped a whole body-full of splendor—hung downward and dropped a thread-like stem and a blossom of palest pink, like a transfigured Linnæa, to meet the snow-drop in its sheath of green that shot up from a spire of aqua marine below. Here living rainbows flew from buttress to buttress and frolicked in the domes—the only things that dared to live and sport where beauty was frozen into horror. It seemed as if that shifting death-light of the aurora photographed all these things upon my memory, for I noted none of them at the time. I only wondered idly whither we were tending as we drove in deeper and deeper under that ice-roof, and curved more and more circlingly upon our course while the silent flashes sped on overhead. Now we were in the dark again crashing onward; now a cold blue radiance burst from every icicle, from every crevice, and I saw that the whole enormous mass of our motion bent and swept around a

single point—a dark yet glittering form that sat as if
upon the apex of the world. Was it one of those mightier
than the Anakim, more than the sons of God, to whom
all the currents of this frozen world converged? Sooth I
know not—for presently I imagined that my vision
made only an exaggeration of some brown Esquimaux
sealed up and left in his snow-house to die. A thin
sheathing of ice appeared to clothe him and give the
glister to his duskiness. Insensible as I had thought
myself to any further fear, I cowered beneath the stare
of those dead and icy eyes. Slowly we rounded, and ever
rounded; the inside, on which my place was, moving
less slowly than the outer circle of the sheeted mass in
its viscid flow; and as we moved, by some fate my eye
was caught by the substance on which this figure sat. It
was no figure at all now, but a bare jag of rock rising in
the centre of this solid whirlpool, and carrying on its
summit something which held a light that not one of
these icy freaks, pranking in the dress of gems and
flowers, had found it possible to assume. It was a thing
so real, so genuine, my breath became suspended; my
heart ceased to beat; my brain, that had been a lump of
ice, seemed to move in its skull; hope, that had deserted
me, suddenly sprung up like a second life within me;
the old passion was not dead, if I was. It rose stronger
than life or death or than myself. If I could but snatch
that mass of moonstone, that inestimable wealth! It was
nothing deceptive, I declared to myself. What more
natural home could it have than this region, thrown up
here by the old Plutonic powers of the planet, as the
same substance in smaller shape was thrown up on the
peaks of the Mount St. Gothard, when the Alpine
aiguilles first sprang into the day? There it rested,
limpid with its milky pearl, casting out flakes of flame
and azure, of red and leaf-green light, and holding yet a
sparkle of silver in the reflections and refractions of its
inner axis—the splendid Turk's-eye of the lapidaries,

the cousin of the water-opal and the girasole, the precious essence of feldspar. Could I break it, I would find clusters of great hemitrope crystals. Could I obtain it, I should have a jewel in that mass of moonstone such as the world never saw! The throne of Jemschid could not cast a shadow beside it.

Then the bitterness of my fate overwhelmed me. Here, with this treasure of a kingdom, this jewel that could not be priced, this wealth beyond an Emperor's —and here only to die! My stolid apathy vanished, old thoughts dominated once more, old habits, old desires. I thought of Eleanor then in her warm, sunny home, the blossoms that bloomed around her, the birds that sang, the cheerful evening fires, the longing thoughts for one who never came, who never was to come. But I would! I cried, where human voice had never cried before. I would return! I would take this treasure with me! I would not be defrauded! Should not I, a man, conquer this inanimate blind matter? I reached out my hands to seize it. Slowly it receded—slowly, and less slowly; or was the motion of the ice still carrying me onward? Had we encircled this apex? and were we driving out into the open and uncovered North, and so down the seas and out to the open main of black water again? If so—if I could live through it—I must have this thing!

I rose, and as well as I could, with my cramped and stiffened limbs, I moved to go back for it. It was useless; the current that carried us was growing invincible, the gaping gulfs of the outer seas were sucking us toward them. I fell; I scrambled to my feet; I would still have gone back, but, as I attempted it, the ice whereon I was inclined ever so slightly, tipped more boldly, gave way, and rose in a billow, broke, and piled over on another mass beneath. Then the cavern was behind us, and I comprehended that this ice-stream, having doubled its central point, now in its outward movement encountered the still incoming body, and was to pile above and

pass over it, the whole expanse bending, cracking, breaking, crowding, and compressing, till its rearing tumult made bergs more mountainous than the offshot glaciers of the Greenland continent, that should ride safely down to crumble in the surging seas below. As block after block of the rent ice rose in the air, lighted by the blue and bristling aurora-points, toppled and mounted higher, it seemed to me that now indeed I was battling with those elemental agencies in the dreadful fight I had desired—one man against the might of matter. I sprang from that block to another; I gained my balance on a third, climbing, shouldering, leaping, struggling, holding with my hands, catching with my feet, crawling, stumbling, tottering, rising high and higher with the mountain ever making underneath; a power unknown to my foes coming to my aid, a blessed rushing warmth that glowed on all the surface of my skin, that set the blood to racing in my veins, that made my heart beat with newer hope, sink with newer despair, rise buoyant with new determination. Except when the shaft of light pierced the shivering sky I could not see or guess the height that I had gained. I was vaguely aware of chasms that were bottomless, of precipices that opened on them, of pinnacles rising round me in aerial spires, when suddenly the shelf, on which I must have stood, yielded, as if it were pushed by great hands, swept down a steep incline like an avalanche, stopped half-way, but sent me flying on, sliding, glancing, like a shooting-star, down, down the slippery side, breathless, dizzy, smitten with blistering pain by awful winds that whistled by me, far out upon the level ice below that tilted up and down again with the great resonant plash of open water, and conscious for a moment that I lay at last upon a fragment that the mass behind urged on, I knew and I remembered nothing more.

Faces were bending over me when I opened my eyes again, rough, uncouth, and bearded faces, but no monsters of the pole. Whalemen rather, smelling richly of train-oil, but I could recall nothing in all my life one fraction so beautiful as they; the angels on whom I hope to open my eyes when Death has really taken me will scarcely seem sights more blest than did those rude whalers of the North Pacific Sea. The North Pacific Sea—for it was there that I was found, explain it how you may—whether the *Albatross* had pierced farther to the west than her sailing-master knew, and had lost her reckoning with a disordered compass-needle under new stars—or whether I had really been the sport of the demoniac beings of the ice, tossed by them from zone to zone in a dozen hours. The whalers, real creatures enough, had discovered me on a block of ice, they said; nor could I, in their opinion, have been many days undergoing my dreadful experience, for there was still food in my wallet when they opened it. They would never believe a word of my story, and so far from regarding me as one who had proved the Northwest Passage in my own person, they considered me a mere idle maniac, as uncomfortable a thing to have on ship-board as a ghost or a dead body, wrecked and unable to account for myself, and gladly transferred me to a homeward-bound Russian man-of-war, whose officers afforded me more polite but quite as decided skepticism. I have never to this day found any one who believed my story when I told it—so you can take it for what it is worth. Even my Uncle Paul flouted it, and absolutely refused to surrender the sum on whose expectation I had taken ship; while my old ancestor, who hung peeling over the hall fire, dropped from his frame in disgust at the idea of one of his hard-cash descendants turning romancer. But all I know is that the *Albatross* never sailed into port again, and that if I

open my knife today and lay it on the table it will wheel about till the tip of its blade points full at the North Star.

I have never found any one to believe me, did I say? Yes, there is one—Eleanor never doubted a word of my narration, never asked me if cold and suffering had not shaken my reason. But then, after the first recital, she has never been willing to hear another word about it, and if I ever allude to my lost treasure or the possibility of instituting search for it, she asks me if I need more lessons to be content with the treasure that I have, and gathers up her work and gently leaves the room. So that, now I speak of it so seldom, if I had not told the thing to you it might come to pass that I should forget altogether the existence of my mass of moonstone. My mass of moonshine, old Paul calls it. I let him have his say; he can not have that nor any thing else much longer; but when all is done I recall Galileo and I mutter to myself, *"Per si muove*—it *was* a mass of moonstone! With these eyes I saw it, with these hands I touched it, with this heart I longed for it, with this will I mean to have it yet!"

Peter Straub (b. 1943)

Blue Rose

Peter Straub is a poet and novelist who began writing horror without wide reading in the genre. His novel, *Julia* (1975) sparked a friendship between Straub, then living in England, and the visiting Stephen King, who told Straub that his talents lay in the direction of the horror genre and encouraged him to read more of it. The impressive results of Straub's successful integration of his already deep knowledge of contemporary literature with newfound depth in nineteenth and twentieth century horror were the novels *Ghost Story* (1979) and *Shadowland* (1980), two of the finest horror novels of recent decades. Straub and King collaborated on the best-seller, *The Talisman* (1983). He won the World Fantasy Award for best novel of the year in 1989 for his thriller, *Koko*. He is a central figure in the horror novel renaissance of the 1970s, and in the British-American social group of writers discussing the strengths and problems of long-form horror. He began writing novellas in the 1980s, resulting in his recent collection of four novellas, *Houses Without Doors* (1990). "Blue Rose" was his first novella and, while perhaps evincing the influence of King, is very much in Straub's characteristic mode, showing a commitment to character and in this case a kind of dark nostalgia reminiscent of Ray Bradbury's *Something Wicked This Way Comes* (1962), transmuted into grim realism.

I

(for Rosemary Clooney)

On a stifling summer day the two youngest of the five Beevers children, Harry and Little Eddie, were sitting on cane-backed chairs in the attic of their house on South Sixth Street in Palmyra, New York. Their father called it "the upstairs junk room," as this large irregular space was reserved for the boxes of tablecloths, stacks of diminishingly sized girl's winter coats, and musty old dresses Maryrose Beevers had mummified as testimony to the superiority of her past to her present.

A tall mirror that could be tilted in its frame, an artifact of their mother's onetime glory, now revealed to Harry the rear of Little Eddie's head. This object, looking more malleable than a head should be, an elongated wad of Play-Doh covered with straggling feathers, was just peeking above the back of the chair. Even the back of Little Eddie's head looked tense to Harry.

"Listen to me," Harry said. Little Eddie squirmed in his chair, and the wobbly chair squirmed with him. "You think I'm kidding you? I had her last year."

"Well, she didn't kill *you,*" Little Eddie said.

"Course not, she liked me, you little dummy. She only hit me a couple of times. She hit some of those kids every single day."

"But teachers can't *kill* people," Little Eddie said.

At nine, Little Eddie was only a year younger than he, but Harry knew that his undersized fretful brother saw him as much a part of the world of big people as their older brothers.

"Most teachers can't," Harry said. "But what if they live right in the same building as the principal? What if

they won *teaching awards,* hey, and what if every other teacher in the place is scared stiff of them? Don't you think they can get away with murder? Do you think anybody really misses a snot-faced little brat—a little brat like you? Mrs. Franken took this kid, this runty little Tommy Golz, into the cloakroom, and she killed him right there. I heard him scream. At the end, it sounded just like bubbles. He was trying to yell, but there was too much blood in his throat. He never came back, and nobody ever said boo about it. She killed him, and next year she's going to be your teacher. I hope you're afraid, Little Eddie, because you ought to be." Harry leaned forward. "Tommy Golz even looked sort of like you, Little Eddie."

Little Eddie's entire face twitched as if a lightning bolt had crossed it.

In fact, the young Golz boy had suffered an epileptic fit and been removed from school, as Harry knew.

"Mrs. Franken especially hates selfish little brats that don't share their toys."

"I do share my toys," Little Eddie wailed, tears beginning to run down through the delicate smears of dust on his cheeks. "Everybody *takes* my toys, that's why."

"So give me your Ultraglide Roadster," Harry said. This had been Little Eddie's birthday present, given three days previous by a beaming father and a scowling mother. "Or I'll tell Mrs. Franken as soon as I get inside that school, this fall."

Under its layer of grime, Little Eddie's face went nearly the same white-gray shade as his hair.

An ominous slamming sound came up the stairs.

"Children? Are you messing around up there in the attic? Get down here!"

"We're just sitting in the chairs, Mom," Harry called out.

"Don't you bust those chairs! Get down here this minute!"

Little Eddie slid out of his chair and prepared to bolt.

"I want that car," Harry whispered. "And if you don't give it to me, I'll tell Mom you were foolin' around with her old clothes."

"I didn't do nothin'!" Little Eddie wailed, and broke for the stairs.

"Hey, Mom, we didn't break any stuff, honest!" Harry yelled. He bought a few minutes more by adding, "I'm coming right now," and stood up and went toward a cardboard box filled with interesting books he had noticed the day before his brother's birthday, and which had been his goal before he had remembered the Roadster and coaxed Little Eddie upstairs.

When, a short time later, Harry came through the door to the attic steps, he was carrying a tattered paperback book. Little Eddie stood quivering with misery and rage just outside the bedroom the two boys shared with their older brother Albert. He held out a small blue metal car, which Harry instantly took and eased into a front pocket of his jeans.

"When do I get it back?" Little Eddie asked.

"Never," Harry said. "Only selfish people want to get presents back. Don't you know anything at all?" When Eddie pursed his face up to wail, Harry tapped the book in his hands and said, "I got something here that's going to help you with Mrs. Franken, so don't complain."

His mother intercepted him as he came down the stairs to the main floor of the little house—here were the kitchen and living room, both floored with faded linoleum, the actual "junk room" separated by a stiff brown woolen curtain from the little makeshift room where Edgar Beevers slept, and the larger bedroom reserved for Maryrose. Children were never permitted

more than a few steps within this awful chamber, for they might disarrange Maryrose's mysterious "papers" or interfere with the rows of antique dolls on the window seat, which was the sole, much-revered architectural distinction of the Beevers house.

Maryrose Beevers stood at the bottom of the stairs, glaring suspiciously up at her fourth son. She did not ever look like a woman who played with dolls, and she did not look that way now. Her hair was twisted into a knot at the back of her head. Smoke from her cigarette curled up past the big glasses like bird's wings which magnified her eyes.

Harry thrust his hand into his pocket and curled his fingers protectively around the Ultraglide Roadster.

"Those things up there are the possessions of my family," she said. "Show me what you took."

Harry shrugged and held out the paperback as he came down within striking range.

His mother snatched it from him, and tilted her head to see its cover through the cigarette smoke. "Oh. This is from that little box of books up there? Your father used to pretend to read books." She squinted at the print on the cover: *"Hypnosis Made Easy.* Some drugstore trash. You want to read this?"

Harry nodded.

"I don't suppose it can hurt you much." She negligently passed the book back to him. "People in society read books, you know—I used to read a lot, back before I got stuck here with a bunch of dummies. *My* father had a lot of books."

Maryrose nearly touched the top of Harry's head, then snatched back her hand. "You're my scholar, Harry. You're the one who's going places."

"I'm gonna do good in school next year," he said.

"Well. You're going to do well. As long as you don't ruin every chance you have by speaking like your father."

Harry felt that particular pain composed of scorn, shame, and terror that filled him when Maryrose spoke of his father in this way. He mumbled something that sounded like acquiescence, and moved a few steps sideways and around her.

II

The porch of the Beevers house extended six feet on either side of the front door, and was the repository for furniture either too large to be crammed into the junk room or too humble to be enshrined in the attic. A sagging porch swing sat beneath the living-room window, to the left of an ancient couch whose imitation green leather had been repaired with black duct tape; on the other side of the front door, through which Harry Beevers now emerged, stood a useless icebox dating from the earliest days of the Beeverses' marriage and two unsteady camp chairs Edgar Beevers had won in a card game. These had never been allowed into the house. Unofficially, this side of the porch was Harry's father's, and thereby had an entirely different atmosphere, defeated, lawless, and shameful, from the side with the swing and couch.

Harry knelt down in neutral territory directly before the front door and fished the Ultraglide Roadster from his pocket. He placed the hypnotism book on the porch and rolled the little metal car across its top. Then he gave the car a hard shove and watched it clunk nose-down onto the wood. He repeated this several times before moving the book aside, flattening himself out on his stomach, and giving the little car a decisive push toward the swing and the couch.

The Roadster rolled a few feet before an irregular board tilted it over on its side and stopped it.

"You dumb car," Harry said, and retrieved it. He gave it another push deeper into his mother's realm. A stiff, brittle section of paint which had separated from its board cracked in half and rested atop the stalled Roadster like a miniature mattress.

Harry knocked off the chip of paint and sent the car backwards down the porch, where it flipped over again and skidded into the side of the icebox. The boy ran down the porch and this time simply hurled the little car back in the direction of the swing. It bounced off the swing's padding and fell heavily to the wood. Harry knelt before the icebox, panting.

His whole head felt funny, as if wet hot towels had been stuffed inside it. Harry picked himself up and walked across to where the car lay before the swing. He hated the way it looked, small and helpless. He experimentally stepped on the car and felt it pressing into the undersole of his moccasin. Harry raised his other foot and stood on the car, but nothing happened. He jumped on the car, but the moccasin was no better than his bare foot. Harry bent down to pick up the Roadster.

"You dumb little car," he said. "You're no good anyhow, you low-class little jerky thing." He turned it over in his hands. Then he inserted his thumbs between the frame and one of the little tires. When he pushed, the tire moved. His face heated. He mashed his thumbs against the tire, and the little black doughnut popped into the tall thick weeds before the porch. Breathing hard more from emotion than exertion, Harry popped the other front tire into the weeds. Harry whirled around, and ground the car into the wall beside his father's bedroom window. Long deep scratches appeared in the paint. When Harry peered at the top of the car, it too was scratched. He found a nailhead which protruded a quarter of an inch out from the front of the house, and scraped a long paring of blue paint off the

driver's side of the Roadster. Gray metal shone through. Harry slammed the car several times against the edge of the nailhead, chipping off small quantities of paint. Panting, he popped off the two small rear tires and put them in his pocket because he liked the way they looked.

Without tires, well scratched and dented, the Ultraglide Roadster had lost most of its power. Harry looked it over with a bitter, deep satisfaction and walked across the porch and shoved it far into the nest of weeds. Gray metal and blue paint shone at him from within the stalks and leaves. Harry thrust his hands into their midst and swept his arms back and forth. The car tumbled away and fell into invisibility.

When Maryrose appeared scowling on the porch, Harry was seated serenely on the squeaking swing, looking at the first few pages of the paperback book.

"What are you doing? What was all that banging?"

"I'm just reading, I didn't hear anything," Harry said.

III

"Well, if it isn't the shitbird," Albert said, jumping up the porch steps thirty minutes later. His face and T-shirt bore broad black stripes of grease. Short, muscular, and thirteen, Albert spent every possible minute hanging around the gas station two blocks from their house. Harry knew that Albert despised him. Albert raised a fist and made a jerky, threatening motion toward Harry, who flinched. Albert had often beaten him bloody, as had their two older brothers, Sonny and George, now at Army bases in Oklahoma and Germany. Like Albert, his two oldest brothers had seriously disappointed their mother.

Albert laughed, and this time swung his fist within a couple of inches of Harry's face. On the backswing he knocked the book from Harry's hands.

"Thanks," Harry said.

Albert smirked and disappeared around the front door. Almost immediately Harry could hear his mother beginning to shout about the grease on Albert's face and clothes. Albert thumped up the stairs.

Harry opened his clenched fingers and spread them wide, closed his hands into fists, then spread them wide again. When he heard the bedroom door slam shut upstairs, he was able to get off the swing and pick up the book. Being around Albert made him feel like a spring coiled up in a box. From the upper rear of the house, Little Eddie emitted a ghostly wail. Maryrose screamed that she was going to start smacking him if he didn't shut up, and that was that. The three unhappy lives within the house fell back into silence. Harry sat down, found his page, and began reading again.

A man named Dr. Roland Mentaine had written *Hypnosis Made Easy,* and his vocabulary was much larger than Harry's. Dr. Mentaine used words like "orchestrate" and "ineffable" and "enhance," and some of his sentences wound their way through so many subordinate clauses that Harry lost his way. Yet Harry, who had begun the book only half expecting that he would comprehend anything in it at all, found it a wonderful book. He had made it most of the way through the chapter called "Mind Power."

Harry thought it was neat that hypnosis could cure smoking, stuttering, and bedwetting. (He himself had wet the bed almost nightly until months after his ninth birthday. The bedwetting stopped the night a certain lovely dream came to Harry. In the dream he had to urinate terribly, and was hurrying down a stony castle corridor past suits of armor and torches guttering on

the walls. At last Harry reached an open door, through which he saw the most splendid bathroom of his life. The floors were of polished marble, the walls white-tiled. As soon as he entered the gleaming bathroom, a uniformed butler waved him toward the rank of urinals. Harry began pulling down his zipper, fumbled with himself, and got his penis out of his underpants just in time. As the dream-urine gushed out of him, Harry had blessedly awakened.) Hypnotism could get you right inside someone's mind and let you do things there. You could make a person speak in any foreign language they'd ever heard, even if they'd only heard it once, and you could make them act like a baby. Harry considered how pleasurable it would be to make his brother Albert lie squalling and red-faced on the floor, unable to walk or speak as he pissed all over himself.

Also, and this was a new thought to Harry, you could take a person back to a whole row of lives they had led before they were born as the person they were now. This process of rebirth was called reincarnation. Some of Dr. Mentaine's patients had been kings in Egypt and pirates in the Caribbean, some had been murderers, novelists, and artists. They remembered the houses they'd lived in, the names of their mothers and servants and children, the locations of shops where they'd bought cake and wine. Neat stuff, Harry thought. He wondered if someone who had been a famous murderer a long time ago could remember pushing in the knife or bringing down the hammer. A lot of the books remaining in the little cardboard box upstairs, Harry had noticed, seemed to be about murderers. It would not be any use to take Albert back to a previous life, however. If Albert had any previous lives, he had spent them as inanimate objects on the order of boulders and anvils.

Maybe in another life Albert was a murder weapon, Harry thought.

"Hey, college boy! Joe College!"

Harry looked toward the sidewalk and saw the baseball cap and T-shirted gut of Mr. Petrosian, who lived in a tiny house next to the tavern on the corner of South Sixth and Livermore Street. Mr. Petrosian was always shouting genial things at kids, but Maryrose wouldn't let Harry or Little Eddie talk to him. She said Mr. Petrosian was common as dirt. He worked as a janitor in the telephone building and drank a case of beer every night while he sat on his porch.

"Me?" Harry said.

"Yeah! Keep reading books, and you could go to college, right?"

Harry smiled noncommittally. Mr. Petrosian lifted a wide arm and continued to toil down the street toward his house next to the Idle Hour.

In seconds Maryrose burst through the door, folding an old white dish towel in her hands. "Who was that? I heard a man's voice."

"Him," Harry said, pointing at the substantial back of Mr. Petrosian, now half of the way home.

"What did he say? As if it could possibly be interesting, coming from an Armenian janitor."

"He called me Joe College."

Maryrose startled him by smiling.

"Albert says he wants to go back to the station tonight, and I have to go to work soon." Maryrose worked the night shift as a secretary at St. Joseph's Hospital. "God knows when your father'll show up. Get something to eat for Little Eddie and yourself, will you, Harry? I've just got too many things to take care of, as usual."

"I'll get something at Big John's." This was a hamburger stand, a magical place to Harry, erected the summer before in a vacant lot on Livermore Street two blocks down from the Idle Hour.

His mother handed him two carefully folded dollar bills, and he pushed them into his pocket. "Don't let Little Eddie stay in the house alone," his mother said before going back inside. "Take him with you. You know how scared he gets."

"Sure," Harry said, and went back to his book. He finished the chapter on "Mind Power" while first Maryrose left to stand up at the bus stop on the corner and then Albert noisily departed. Little Eddie sat frozen before his soap operas in the living room. Harry turned a page and started reading "Techniques of Hypnosis."

IV

At eight-thirty that night the two boys sat alone in the kitchen, on opposite sides of the table covered in yellow bamboo Formica. From the living room came the sound of Sid Caesar babbling in fake German to Imogene Coca on *Your Show of Shows*. Little Eddie claimed to be scared of Sid Caesar, but when Harry had returned from the hamburger stand with a Big Johnburger (with "the works") for himself and a Mama Marydog for Eddie, double fries, and two chocolate shakes, he had been sitting in front of the television, his face moist with tears of moral outrage. Eddie usually liked Mama Marydogs, but he had taken only a couple of meager bites from the one before him now, and was disconsolately pushing a french fry through a blob of ketchup. Every now and then he wiped at his eyes, leaving nearly symmetrical smears of ketchup to dry on his cheeks.

"Mom *said* not to leave me alone in the house," said Little Eddie. "I heard. It was during *The Edge of Night* and you were on the porch. I think I'm gonna tell on

you." He peeped across at Harry, then quickly looked back at the french fry and drew it out of the puddle of ketchup. "I'm ascared to be alone in the house." Sometimes Eddie's voice was like a queer speeded-up mechanical version of Maryrose's.

"Don't be so dumb," Harry said, almost kindly. "How can you be scared in your own house? You live here, don't you?"

"I'm ascared of the attic," Eddie said. He held the dripping french fry before his mouth and pushed it in. "The attic makes noise." A little squirm of red appeared at the corner of his mouth. "You were supposed to take me with you."

"Oh jeez, Eddie, you slow everything down. I wanted to just get the food and come back. I got you your dinner, didn't I? Didn't I get you what you like?"

In truth, Harry liked hanging around Big John's by himself because then he could talk to Big John and listen to his theories. Big John called himself a "renegade Papist" and considered Hitler the greatest man of the twentieth century, followed closely by Paul VI, Padre Pio who bled from the palms of his hands, and Elvis Presley.

All these events occurred in what is usually but wrongly called a simpler time, before Kennedy and feminism and ecology, before the Nixon presidency and Watergate, and before American soldiers, among them a twenty-one-year-old Harry Beevers, journeyed to Vietnam.

"I'm still going to tell," said Little Eddie. He pushed another french fry into the puddle of ketchup. "And that car was my birthday present." He began to snuffle. "Albert hit me, and you stole my car, and you left me alone, and I was scared. And I don't wanna have Mrs. Franken next year, cuz I think she's gonna hurt me."

Harry had nearly forgotten telling his brother about

Mrs. Franken and Tommy Golz, and this reminder brought back very sharply the memory of destroying Eddie's birthday present.

Eddie twisted his head sideways and dared another quick look at his brother. "Can I have my Ultraglide Roadster back, Harry? You're going to give it back to me, aren'cha? I won't tell Mom you left me alone if you give it back."

"Your car is okay," Harry said. "It's in a sort of a secret place I know."

"You hurt my car!" Eddie squalled. "You did!"

"Shut up!" Harry shouted, and Little Eddie flinched. "You're driving me crazy!" Harry yelled. He realized that he was leaning over the table, and that Little Eddie was getting ready to cry again. He sat down. "Just don't scream at me like that, Eddie."

"You did something to my car," Eddie said with a stunned certainty. "I knew it."

"Look, I'll prove your car is okay," Harry said, and took the two rear tires from his pocket and displayed them on his palm.

Little Eddie stared. He blinked, then reached out tentatively for the tires.

Harry closed his fist around them. "Do they look like I did anything to them?"

"You took them *off*!"

"But don't they look okay, don't they look fine?" Harry opened his fist, closed it again, and returned the tires to his pocket. "I didn't want to show you the whole car, Eddie, because you'd get all worked up, and you gave it to me. Remember? I wanted to show you the tires so you'd see everything was all right. Okay? Got it?"

Eddie miserably shook his head.

"Anyway, I'm going to help you, just like I said."

"With Mrs. Franken?" A fraction of his misery left Little Eddie's smeary face.

"Sure. You ever hear of something called hypnotism?"

"I heard a hypmotism." Little Eddie was sulking. "Everybody in the whole world heard a that."

"Hypnotism, stupid, not hypmotism."

"Sure, hypmotism. I saw it on the TV. They did it on *As the World Turns*. A man made a lady go to sleep and think she was going to have a baby."

Harry smiled. "That's just TV, Little Eddie. Real hypnotism is a lot better than that. I read all about it in one of the books from the attic."

Little Eddie was still sulky because of the car. "So what makes it better?"

"Because it lets you do amazing things," Harry said. He called on Dr. Mentaine. "Hypnosis unlocks your mind and lets you use all the power you really have. If you start now, you'll really knock those books when school starts up again. You'll pass every test Mrs. Franken gives you, just like the way I did." He reached across the table and grasped Little Eddie's wrist, stalling a fat brown french fry on its way to the puddle. "But it won't just make you good in school. If you let me try it on you, I'm pretty sure I can show you that you're a lot stronger than you think you are."

Eddie blinked.

"And I bet I can make you so you're not scared of anything anymore. Hypnotism is real good for that. I read in this book, there was this guy who was afraid of bridges. Whenever he even *thought* about crossing a bridge he got all dizzy and sweaty. Terrible stuff happened to him, like he lost his job and once he just had to ride in a car across a bridge and he dumped a load in his pants. He went to see Dr. Mentaine, and Dr. Mentaine hypnotized him and said he would never be afraid of bridges again, and he wasn't."

Harry pulled the paperback from his hip pocket. He opened it flat on the table and bent over the pages.

"Here. Listen to this. 'Benefits of the course of treatment were found in all areas of the patient's life, and results were obtained for which he would have paid any price.'" Harry read these words haltingly, but with complete understanding.

"Hypmotism can make me strong?" Little Eddie asked, evidently having saved this point in his head.

"Strong as a bull."

"Strong as Albert?"

"A lot stronger than Albert. A lot stronger than me, too."

"And I can beat up on big guys that hurt me?"

"You just have to learn how."

Eddie sprang up from the chair, yelling nonsense. He flexed his stringlike biceps and for some time twisted his body into a series of muscleman poses.

"You want to do it?" Harry finally asked.

Little Eddie popped into his chair and stared at Harry. His T-shirt's neckband sagged all the way to his breastbone without ever actually touching his chest. "I wanna start."

"Okay, Eddie, good man." Harry stood up and put his hand on the book. "Up to the attic."

"Only, I don't wanna go in the attic," Eddie said. He was still staring at Harry, but his head was tilted over like a weird little echo of Maryrose, and his eyes had filled with suspicion.

"I'm not gonna *take* anything from you, Little Eddie," Harry said. "It's just, we should be out of everybody's way. The attic's real quiet."

Little Eddie stuck his hand inside his T-shirt and let his arm dangle from the wrist.

"You turned your shirt into an armrest," Harry said.

Eddie jerked his hand out of its sling.

"Albert might come waltzing in and wreck everything if we do it in the bedroom."

"If you go up first and turn on the lights," Eddie said.

V

Harry held the book open on his lap, and glanced from it to Little Eddie's tense smeary face. He had read these pages over many times while he sat on the porch. Hypnotism boiled down to a few simple steps, each of which led to the next. The first thing he had to do was to get his brother started right, "relaxed and receptive," according to Dr. Mentaine.

Little Eddie stirred in his cane-backed chair and kneaded his hands together. His shadow, cast by the bulb dangling overhead, imitated him like a black little chair-bound monkey. "I wanna get started, I wanna get to be strong," he said.

"Right here in this book it says you have to be relaxed," Harry said. "Just put your hands on top of your legs, nice and easy, with your fingers pointing forward. Then close your eyes and breathe in and out a couple of times. Think about being nice and tired and ready to go to sleep."

"I don't wanna go to sleep!"

"It's not really sleep, Little Eddie, it's just sort of like it. You'll still really be awake, but nice and relaxed. Or else it won't work. You have to do everything I tell you. Otherwise everybody'll still be able to beat up on you, like they do now. I want you to pay attention to everything I say."

"Okay." Little Eddie made a visible effort to relax. He placed his hands on his thighs and twice inhaled and exhaled.

"Now close your eyes."

Eddie closed his eyes.

Harry suddenly knew that it was going to work—if he did everything the book said, he would really be able to hypnotize his brother.

"Little Eddie, I want you just to listen to the sound of my voice," he said, forcing himself to be calm. "You are already getting nice and relaxed, as easy and peaceful as if you were lying in bed, and the more you listen to my voice, the more relaxed and tired you are going to get. Nothing can bother you. Everything bad is far away, and you're just sitting here, breathing in and out, getting nice and sleepy."

He checked his page to make sure he was doing it right, and then went on.

"It's like lying in bed, Eddie, and the more you hear my voice, the more tired and sleepy you're getting, a little more sleepy the more you hear me. Everything else is sort of fading away, and all you can hear is my voice. You feel tired but good, just like the way you do right before you fall asleep. Everything is fine, and you're drifting a little bit, drifting and drifting, and you're getting ready to raise your right hand."

He leaned over and very lightly stroked the back of Little Eddie's grimy right hand. Eddie sat slumped in the chair with his eyes closed, breathing shallowly. Harry spoke very slowly.

"I'm going to count backwards from ten, and every time I get to another number, your hand is going to get lighter and lighter. When I count, your right hand is going to get so light it floats up and finally touches your nose when you hear me say 'one.' And then you'll be in a deep sleep. Now I'm starting. Ten. Your hand is already feeling light. Nine. It wants to float up. Eight. Your hand really feels light now. It's going to start to go up now. Seven."

Little Eddie's hand obediently floated an inch up from his thigh.

"Six." The grimy little hand rose another few inches.

"It's getting lighter and lighter now, and every time I say another number it gets closer and closer to your nose, and you get sleepier and sleepier. Five."

The hand ascended several inches nearer Eddie's face.

"Four."

The hand now dangled like a sleeping bird half of the way between Eddie's knee and his nose.

"Three."

It rose nearly to Eddie's chin.

"Two."

Eddie's hand hung a few inches from his mouth.

"One. You are going to fall asleep now."

The gently curved, ketchup-streaked forefinger delicately brushed the tip of Little Eddie's nose, and stayed there while Eddie sagged against the back of the chair.

Harry's heart beat so loudly that he feared the sound would bring Eddie out of his trance. Eddie remained motionless. Harry breathed quietly by himself for a moment. "Now you can lower your hand to your lap, Eddie. You are going deeper and deeper into sleep. Deeper and deeper and deeper."

Eddie's hand sank gracefully downward.

The attic seemed hot as the inside of a furnace to Harry. His fingers left blotches on the open pages of the book. He wiped his face on his sleeve and looked at his little brother. Little Eddie had slumped so far down in the chair that his head was no longer visible in the tilting mirror. Perfectly still and quiet, the attic stretched out on all sides of them, waiting (or so it seemed to Harry) for what would happen next. Maryrose's trunks sat in rows under the eaves far behind the mirror, her old dresses hung silently within the dusty wardrobe. Harry rubbed his hands on his jeans to dry them, and flicked a page over with the neatness of an old scholar who had spent half his life in libraries.

"You're going to sit up straight in your chair," he said.

Eddie pulled himself upright.

"Now I want to show you that you're really hypnotized, Little Eddie. It's like a test. I want you to hold your right arm straight out before you. Make it as rigid as you can. This is going to show you how strong you can be."

Eddie's pale arm rose and straightened to the wrist, leaving his fingers dangling.

Harry stood up and said, "That's pretty good." He walked the two steps to Eddie's side and grasped his brother's arm and ran his fingers down the length of it, gently straightening Eddie's hand. "Now I want you to imagine that your arm is getting harder and harder. It's getting as hard and rigid as an iron bar. Your whole arm is an iron bar, and nobody on earth could bend it. Eddie, it's stronger than Superman's arm." He removed his hands and stepped back.

"Now. This arm is so strong and rigid that you can't bend it no matter how hard you try. It's an iron bar, and nobody on earth could bend it. Try. Try to bend it."

Eddie's face tightened up, and his arm rose perhaps two degrees. Eddie grunted with invisible effort, unable to bend his arm.

"Okay, Eddie, you did real good. Now your arm is loosening up, and when I count backwards from ten, it's going to get looser and looser. When I get to *one,* your arm'll be normal again." He began counting, and Eddie's fingers loosened and drooped, and finally the arm came to rest again on his leg.

Harry went back to his chair, sat down, and looked at Eddie with great satisfaction. Now he was certain that he would be able to do the next demonstration, which Dr. Mentaine called "The Chair Exercise."

"Now you know that this stuff really works, Eddie, so

we're going to do something a little harder. I want you to stand up in front of your chair."

Eddie obeyed. Harry stood up too, and moved his chair forward and to the side so that its cane seat faced Eddie, about four feet away.

"I want you to stretch out between these chairs, with your head on your chair and your feet on mine. And I want you to keep your hands at your sides."

Eddie hunkered down uncomplainingly and settled his head back on the seat of his chair. Supporting himself with his arms, he raised one leg and placed his foot on Harry's chair. Then he lifted the other foot. Difficulty immediately appeared in his face. He raised his arms and clamped them in so that he looked trussed.

"Now your whole body is slowly becoming as hard as iron, Eddie. Your entire body is one of the strongest things on earth. Nothing can make it bend. You could hold yourself there forever and never feel the slightest pain or discomfort. It's like you're lying on a mattress, you're so strong."

The expression of strain left Eddie's face. Slowly his arms extended and relaxed. He lay propped string-straight between the two chairs, so at ease that he did not even appear to be breathing.

"While I talk to you, you're getting stronger and stronger. You could hold up anything. You could hold up an elephant. I'm going to sit down on your stomach to prove it."

Cautiously, Harry seated himself down on his brother's midriff. He raised his legs. Nothing happened. After he had counted slowly to fifteen, Harry lowered his legs and stood. "I'm going to take my shoes off now, Eddie, and stand on you."

He hurried over to a piano stool embroidered with fulsome roses and carried it back; then he slipped off his moccasins and stepped on top of the stool. As Harry

stepped on top of Eddie's exposed thin belly, the chair supporting his brother's head wobbled. Harry stood stock-still for a moment, but the chair held. He lifted the other foot from the stool. No movement from the chair. He set the other foot on his brother. Little Eddie effortlessly held him up.

Harry lifted himself experimentally up on his toes and came back down on his heels. Eddie seemed entirely unaffected. Then Harry jumped perhaps half an inch into the air, and since Eddie did not even grunt when he landed, he kept jumping, five, six, seven, eight times, until he was breathing hard. "You're amazing, Little Eddie," he said, and stepped off onto the stool. "Now you can begin to relax. You can put your feet on the floor. Then I want you to sit back up in your chair. Your body doesn't feel stiff anymore."

Little Eddie had been rather tentatively lowering one foot, but as soon as Harry finished speaking he buckled in the middle and thumped his bottom on the floor. Harry's chair (Maryrose's chair) sickeningly tipped over, but landed soundlessly on a neat woolen stack of layered winter coats.

Moving like a robot, Little Eddie slowly sat upright on the floor. His eyes were open but unfocused.

"You can stand up now and get back in your chair," Harry said. He did not remember leaving the stool, but he had left it. Sweat ran into his eyes. He pressed his face into his shirt sleeve. For a second, panic had brightly beckoned. Little Eddie was sleepwalking back to his chair. When he sat down, Harry said, "Close your eyes. You're going deeper and deeper into sleep. Deeper and deeper, Little Eddie."

Eddie settled into the chair as if nothing had happened, and Harry reverently set his own chair upright again. Then he picked up the book and opened it. The print swam before his eyes. Harry shook his head and

looked again, but still the lines of print snaked across the page. (When Harry was a sophomore at Adelphi College he was asked to read several poems by Guillaume Apollonaire, and the appearance of the wavering lines on the page brought back this moment with a terrible precision.) Harry pressed the palms of his hands against his eyes, and red patterns exploded across his vision.

He removed his hands from his eyes, blinked, and found that although the lines of print were now behaving themselves, he no longer wanted to go on. The attic was too hot, he was too tired, and the toppling of the chair had been too close a brush with actual disaster. But for a time he leafed purposefully through the book while Eddie tranced on, and then found the subheading "Post-Hypnotic Suggestion."

"Little Eddie, we're just going to do one more thing. If we ever do this again, it'll help us go faster." Harry shut the book. He knew exactly how this went; he would even use the same phrase Dr. Mentaine used with his patients. *Blue rose*—Harry did not quite know why, but he liked the sound of that.

"I'm going to tell you a phrase, Eddie, and from now on whenever you hear me say this phrase, you will instantly go back to sleep and be hypnotized again. The phrase is 'blue rose.' 'Blue rose.' When you hear me say 'blue rose,' you will go right to sleep, just the way you are now, and we can make you stronger again. 'Blue rose' is our secret, Eddie, because nobody else knows it. What is it?"

"Blue rose," Eddie said in a muffled voice.

"Okay. I'm going to count backward from ten, and when I get to 'one' you will be wide awake again. You will not remember anything we did, but you will feel happy and strong. Ten."

As Harry counted backwards, Little Eddie twitched

and stirred, let his arms fall to his sides, thumped one foot carelessly on the floor, and at "one" opened his eyes.

"Did it work? What'd I do? Am I strong?"

"You're a bull," Harry said. "It's getting late, Eddie —time to go downstairs."

Harry's timing was accurate enough to be uncomfortable. As soon as the two boys closed the attic door behind them they heard the front door slide open in a cacophony of harsh coughs and subdued mutterings followed by the sound of unsteady footsteps proceeding to the bathroom. Edgar Beevers was home.

VI

Late that night the three homebound Beevers sons lay in their separate beds in the good-sized second-floor room next to the attic stairs. Directly above Maryrose's bedroom, its dimensions were nearly identical to it except that the boys' room, the "dorm," had no window seat and the attic stairs shaved a couple of feet from Harry's end. When the other two boys had lived at home, Harry and Little Eddie had slept together, Albert had slept in a bed with Sonny, and only George, who at the time of his induction into the Army had been six feet tall and weighed two hundred and one pounds, had slept alone. In those days, Sonny had often managed to make Albert cry out in the middle of the night. The very idea of George could still make Harry's stomach freeze.

Though it was now very late, enough light from the street came in through the thin white net curtains to give complex shadows to the bunched muscles of Albert's upper arms as he lay stretched out atop his sheets. The voices of Maryrose and Edgar Beevers, one approximately sober and the other unmistakably

drunk, came clearly up the stairs and through the open door.

"Who says I waste my time? I don't say that. I don't waste my time."

"I suppose you think you've done a good day's work when you spell a bartender for a couple of hours—and then drink up your wages! That's the story of your life, Edgar Beevers, and it's a sad, sad story of w-a-s-t-e. If my father could have seen what would become of you . . ."

"I ain't so damn bad."

"You ain't so damn good, either."

"Albert," Eddie said softly from his bed between his two brothers.

As if galvanized by Little Eddie's voice, Albert suddenly sat up in bed, leaned forward, and reached out to try to smack Eddie with his fist.

"I didn't do nothin'!" Harry said, and moved to the edge of his mattress. The blow had been for him, he knew, not Eddie, except that Albert was too lazy to get up.

"I hate your lousy guts," Albert said. "If I wasn't too tired to get out of this-here bed, I'd pound your face in."

"Harry stole my birthday car, Albert," Eddie said. "Makum gimme it back."

"One day," Maryrose said from downstairs, "at the end of the summer when I was seventeen, late in the afternoon, my father said to my mother, 'Honey, I believe I'm going to take out our pretty little Maryrose and get her something special,' and he called up to me from the drawing room to make myself pretty and get set to go, and because my father was a gentleman and a Man of His Word, I got ready in two shakes. My father was wearing a very handsome brown suit and a red bow tie and his boater. I remember just like I can see it now. He stood at the bottom of the staircase, waiting for me,

and when I came down he took my arm and we just went out that front door like a courting couple. Down the stone walk, which my father put in all by himself even though he was a white-collar worker, down Majeski Street, arm in arm down to South Palmyra Avenue. In those days all the best people, all the people who counted, did their shopping on South Palmyra Avenue."

"I'd like to knock your teeth down your throat," Albert said to Harry.

"Albert, he took my birthday car, he really did, and I want it back. I'm ascared he busted it. I want it back so much I'm gonna die."

Albert propped himself up on an elbow and for the first time really looked at Little Eddie. Eddie whimpered. "You're such a twerp," Albert said. "I wish you *would* die, Eddie, I wish you'd just drop dead so we could stick you in the ground and forget about you. I wouldn't even cry at your funeral. Prob'ly I wouldn't even be able to remember your name. I'd just say, 'Oh yeah, he was that little creepy kid used to hang around cryin' all the time, glad he's dead, whatever his name was.'"

Eddie had turned his back on Albert and was weeping softly, his unwashed face distorted by the shadows into an uncanny image of the mask of tragedy.

"You know, I really wouldn't mind if you dropped dead," Albert mused. "You neither, shitbird."

". . . realized he was taking me to Alouette's. I'm sure you used to look in their windows when you were a little boy. You remember Alouette's, don't you? There's never been anything so beautiful as that store. When I was a little girl and lived in the big house, all the best people used to go there. My father marched me right inside, with his arm around me, and took me up in the elevator and we went straight to the lady who managed the dress department. 'Give my little girl the best,' he

said. Price was no object. Quality was all he cared about. 'Give my little girl the best.' *Are you listening to me, Edgar?"*

Albert snored face-down into his pillow; Little Eddie twitched and snuffled. Harry lay awake for so long he thought he would never get to sleep. Before him he kept seeing Little Eddie's face all slack and dopey under hypnosis—Little Eddie's face made him feel hot and uncomfortable. Now that Harry was lying down in bed, it seemed to him that everything he had done since returning from Big John's seemed really to have been done by someone else, or to have been done in a dream. Then he realized that he had to use the bathroom.

Harry slid out of bed, quietly crossed the room, went out onto the dark landing, and felt his way downstairs to the bathroom.

When he emerged, the bathroom light showed him the squat black shape of the telephone atop the Palmyra directory. Harry moved to the low telephone table beside the stairs. He lifted the phone from the directory and opened the book, the width of a Big 5 tablet, with his other hand. As he had done on many other nights when his bladder forced him downstairs, Harry leaned over the page and selected a number. He kept the number in his head as he closed the directory and replaced the telephone. He dialed. The number rang so often Harry lost count. At last a hoarse voice answered. Harry said, "I'm watching you, and you're a dead man." He softly replaced the receiver in the cradle.

VII

Harry caught up with his father the next afternoon just as Edgar Beevers had begun to move up South Sixth Street toward the corner of Livermore. His father wore

his usual costume of baggy gray trousers cinched far above his waist by a belt with a double buckle, a red-and-white plaid shirt, and a brown felt hat stationed low over his eyes. His long fleshy nose swam before him, cut in half by the shadow of the hat brim.

"Dad!"

His father glanced incuriously at him, then put his hands back in his pockets. He turned sideways and kept walking down the street, though perhaps a shade more slowly. "What's up, kid? No school?"

"It's summer, there isn't any school. I just thought I'd come with you for a little."

"Well, I ain't doing much. Your ma asked me to pick up some hamburg on Livermore, and I thought I'd slip into the Idle Hour for a quick belt. You won't turn me in, will you?"

"No."

"You ain't a bad kid, Harry. Your ma's just got a lot of worries. I worry about Little Eddie too, sometimes."

"Sure."

"What's with the books? You read when you walk?"

"I was just sort of looking at them," Harry said.

His father insinuated his hand beneath Harry's left elbow and extracted two luridly jacketed paperback books. They were titled *Murder, Incorporated* and *Hitler's Death Camps*. Harry already loved both of these books. His father grunted and handed *Murder, Incorporated* back to him. He raised the other book nearly to the tip of his nose and peered at the cover, which depicted a naked woman pressing herself against a wall of barbed wire while a uniformed Nazi aimed a rifle at her back.

Looking up at his father, Harry saw that beneath the harsh line of shadow cast by the hat brim his father's whiskers grew in different colors and patterns. Black and brown, red and orange, the glistening spikes swirled across his father's cheek.

"I bought this book, but it didn't look nothing like that," his father said, and returned the book.

"What didn't?"

"That place. Dachau. That death camp."

"How do you know?"

"I was there, wasn't I? You wasn't even born then. It didn't look anything like that picture on that book. It just looked like a piece a shit to me, like most of the places I saw when I was in the Army."

This was the first time Harry had heard that his father had been in the service.

"You mean, you were in World War II?"

"Yeah, I was in the Big One. They made me a corporal over there. Had me a nickname too. 'Beans.' 'Beans' Beevers. And I got a Purple Heart from the time I got a infection."

"You saw Dachau with your own eyes?"

"Damn straight, I did." He bent down suddenly. "Hey—don't let your ma catch you readin' that book."

Secretly pleased, Harry shook his head. Now the book and the death camp were a bond between himself and his father.

"Did you ever kill anybody?"

His father wiped his mouth and both cheeks with one long hand. Harry saw a considering eye far back in the shadow of the brim.

"I killed a guy once."

A long pause.

"I shot him in the back."

His father wiped his mouth again, and then motioned forward with his head. He had to get to the bar, the butcher, and back again in a very carefully defined period of time. "You really want to hear this?"

Harry nodded. He swallowed.

"I guess you do, at that. Okay—we was sent into this camp, Dachau, at the end of the war to process the prisoners and arrest the guards and the commandant.

Everything was all arranged. A bunch of brass hats from Division were going to come on an inspection, so we had to wait there a couple days. We had these guards lined up, see, and these skinny old wrecks would come up and give 'em hell. We wasn't supposed to let 'em get too near."

They were passing Mr. Petrosian's little tar-paper house, and Harry felt a spasm of relief that Mr. Petrosian was not out on his tiny porch working on his case of beer. The Idle Hour was only a few paces ahead.

"Anyhow, one of these guards, one of the worst ones, suddenly decided he's going to run for it. He takes off, runnin' like crazy toward the woods. What do I do? I ask. Nobody knows what the hell to do. Shoot him, somebody says. So I shot him in the back. That was all she wrote."

Now they had reached the screen door which led into the Idle Hour, and the smells of malt and hops filled the air. "See you back at the house," his father said, and disappeared through the screen door like a magician.

VIII

After Harry had read a hundred pages of *Murder, Incorporated*, his favorite murderers were Louis "Lepke" Buchalter and Abe "Kid Twist" Reles. They were dependable professionals. A kind of black light surrounded them and made them glitter. Lepke Buchalter and Abe Reles looked out at the world from the shadows of their hat brims. They lived in shadowy rooms and peered out through the curtains. They appeared on a dark corner before their terrified victim, did their work, and walked away, turning up their coat collars.

Suppose you had some kind of job that took you around the country, like a salesman's job, Harry

thought as he read away the afternoon in the porch swing; suppose you had a job that took you from one town to another. Suppose you killed someone in each one of those towns, carefully and quietly, and hid the bodies so it would take people a long time to find them. Your work would never be done.

IX

"Blue rose," Harry said.

Little Eddie sagged openmouthed against the cane of his chair, his hands loose in his lap.

It had worked. Harry looked around as if he expected applause, and did feel that all the things in the attic looked back at him with warm approval. It was nine-thirty at night; he and Eddie, alone in the house, occupied the attic in perfect safety. Harry wanted to see if he could put other people under and make them do things, but for now, for tonight, he was content to experiment with Eddie.

"You're going deeper and deeper asleep, Eddie, deeper and deeper, and you're listening to every word I say. You're just sinking down and down, hearing my voice come to you, going deeper and deeper with every word, and now you are real deep asleep and ready to begin."

Little Eddie sat sprawled over Maryrose's cane-backed chair, his chin touching his chest and his little pink mouth drooping open. He looked like a slightly undersized seven-year-old, like a second-grader instead of the fourth-grader he would be when he joined Mrs. Franken's class in the fall. Suddenly he reminded Harry of the Ultraglide Roadster, scratched and dented and stripped of its tires.

"Tonight you're going to see how strong you really are. Sit up, Eddie."

Eddie pulled himself upright and closed his mouth, almost comically obedient.

Harry thought it would be fun to make Little Eddie believe he was a dog and trot around the attic on all fours, barking and lifting his leg. Then he saw Little Eddie staggering across the attic, his tongue bulging out of his mouth, his own hands squeezing and squeezing his throat. Maybe he would try that too, after he had done several other exercises he had discovered in Dr. Mentaine's book. He checked the underside of his collar for maybe the fifth time that evening, and felt the long thin shaft of the pearl-headed hatpin he had stopped reading *Murder, Incorporated* long enough to smuggle out of Maryrose's bedroom after she had left for work.

"Eddie," he said, "now you are very deeply asleep, and you will be able to do everything I say. I want you to hold your right arm straight out in front of you."

Eddie stuck his arm out like a poker.

"That's good, Eddie. Now I want you to notice that all the feeling is leaving that arm. It's getting number and number. It doesn't even feel like flesh and blood anymore. It feels like it's made out of steel or something. It's so numb that you can't feel anything there anymore. You can't even feel pain in it."

Harry stood up, went toward Eddie, and brushed his fingers along his arm. "You didn't feel anything, did you?"

"No," Eddie said in a slow gravel-filled voice.

"Do you feel anything now?" Harry pinched the underside of Eddie's forearm.

"No."

"Now?" Harry used his nails to pinch the side of Eddie's biceps, hard, and left purple dents in the skin.

"No," Eddie repeated.

"How about this?" He slapped his hand against

Eddie's forearm as hard as he could. There was a sharp loud smacking sound, and his fingers tingled. If Little Eddie had not been hypnotized, he would have tried to screech down the walls.

"No," Eddie said.

Harry pulled the hatpin out of his collar and inspected his brother's arm. "You're doing great, Little Eddie. You're stronger than anybody in your whole class—you're probably stronger than the whole rest of the school." He turned Eddie's arm so that the palm was up and the white forearm, lightly traced by small blue veins, faced him.

Harry delicately ran the point of the hatpin down Eddie's pale, veined forearm. The pinpoint left a narrow chalk-white scratch in its wake. For a moment Harry felt the floor of the attic sway beneath his feet; then he closed his eyes and jabbed the hatpin into Little Eddie's skin as hard as he could.

He opened his eyes. The floor was still swaying beneath him. From Little Eddie's lower arm protruded six inches of the eight-inch hatpin, the mother-of-pearl head glistening softly in the light from the overhead bulb. A drop of blood the size of a watermelon seed stood on Eddie's skin. Harry moved back to his chair and sat down heavily. "Do you feel anything?"

"No," Eddie said again in that surprisingly deep voice.

Harry stared at the hatpin embedded in Eddie's arm. The oval drop of blood lengthened itself out against the white skin and began slowly to ooze toward Eddie's wrist. Harry watched it advance across the pale underside of Eddie's forearm. Finally he stood up and returned to Eddie's side. The elongated drop of blood had ceased moving. Harry bent over and twanged the hatpin. Eddie could feel nothing. Harry put his thumb and forefinger on the glistening head of the pin. His

face was so hot he might have been standing before an open fire. He pushed the pin a further half inch into Eddie's arm, and another small quantity of blood welled up from the base. The pin seemed to be moving in Harry's grasp, pulsing back and forth as if it were breathing.

"Okay," Harry said. "Okay."

He tightened his hold on the pin and pulled. It slipped easily from the wound. Harry held the hatpin before his face just as a doctor holds up a thermometer to read a temperature. He had imagined that the entire bottom section of the shaft would be painted with red, but saw that only a single winding glutinous streak of blood adhered to the pin. For a dizzy second he thought of slipping the end of the pin in his mouth and sucking it clean.

He thought: Maybe in another life I was Lepke Buchalter.

He pulled his handkerchief, a filthy square of red paisley, from his front pocket and wiped the streak of blood from the shaft of the pin. Then he leaned over and gently wiped the red smear from Little Eddie's underarm. Harry refolded the handkerchief so the blood would not show, wiped sweat from his face, and shoved the grubby cloth back into his pocket.

"That was good, Eddie. Now we're going to do something a little bit different."

He knelt down beside his brother and lifted Eddie's nearly weightless, delicately veined arm. "You still can't feel a thing in this arm, Eddie, it's completely numb. It's sound asleep and it won't wake up until I tell it to." Harry repositioned himself in order to hold himself steady while he knelt, and put the point of the hatpin nearly flat against Eddie's arm. He pushed it forward far enough to raise a wrinkle of flesh. The point of the hatpin dug into Eddie's skin but did not break it.

Harry pushed harder, and the hatpin raised the little bulge of skin by a small but appreciable amount.

Skin was a lot tougher to break through than anyone imagined.

The pin was beginning to hurt his fingers, so Harry opened his hand and positioned the head against the base of his middle finger. Grimacing, he pushed his hand against the pin. The point of the pin popped through the raised wrinkle.

"Eddie, you're made out of beer cans," Harry said, and tugged the head of the pin backwards. The wrinkle flattened out. Now Harry could shove the pin forward again, sliding the shaft deeper and deeper under the surface of Little Eddie's skin. He could see the raised line of the hatpin marching down his brother's arm, looking as prominent as the damage done to a cartoon lawn by a cartoon rabbit. When the mother-of-pearl head was perhaps three inches from the entry hole, Harry pushed it down into Little Eddie's flesh, thus raising the point of the pin. He gave the head a sharp jab, and the point appeared at the end of the ridge in Eddie's skin, poking through a tiny smear of blood. Harry shoved the pin in further. Now it showed about an inch and a half of gray metal at either end.

"Feel anything?"

"Nothing."

Harry jiggled the head of the pin, and a bubble of blood walked out of the entry wound and began to slide down Eddie's arm. Harry sat down on the attic floor beside Eddie and regarded his work. His mind seemed pleasantly empty of thought, filled only with a variety of sensations. He *felt* but could not hear a buzzing in his head, and a blurry film seemed to cover his eyes. He breathed through his mouth. The long pin stuck through Little Eddie's arm looked monstrous seen one way; seen another, it was sheerly beautiful. Skin, blood,

and metal. Harry had never seen anything like it before. He reached out and twisted the pin, causing another little blood-snail to crawl from the exit wound. Harry saw all this as if through smudgy glasses, but he did not mind. He knew the blurriness was only mental. He touched the head of the pin again and moved it from side to side. A little more blood leaked from both punctures. Then Harry shoved the pin in, partially withdrew it so that the point nearly disappeared back into Eddie's arm, moved it forward again; and went on like this, back and forth, back and forth as if he were sewing his brother up, for some time.

Finally he withdrew the pin from Eddie's arm. Two long streaks of blood had nearly reached his brother's wrist. Harry ground the heels of his hands into his eyes, blinked, and discovered that his vision had cleared.

He wondered how long he and Eddie had been in the attic. It could have been hours. He could not quite remember what had happened before he had slid the hatpin into Eddie's skin. Now his blurriness really was mental, not visual. A loud uncomfortable pulse beat in his temples. Again he wiped the blood from Eddie's arm. Then he stood on wobbling knees and returned to his chair.

"How's your arm feel, Eddie?"

"Numb," Eddie said in his gravelly sleepy voice.

"The numbness is going away now. Very, very slowly. You are beginning to feel your arm again, and it feels very good. There is no pain. It feels like the sun was shining on it all afternoon. It's strong and healthy. Feeling is coming back into your arm, and you can move your fingers and everything."

When he had finished speaking Harry leaned back against the chair and closed his eyes. He rubbed his forehead with his hand and wiped the moisture off on his shirt.

"How does your arm feel?" he said without opening his eyes.

"Good."

"That's great, Little Eddie." Harry flattened his palms against his flushed face, wiped his cheeks, and opened his eyes.

I can do this every night, he thought. I can bring Little Eddie up here every single night, at least until school starts.

"Eddie, you're getting stronger and stronger every day. This is really helping you. And the more we do it, the stronger you'll get. Do you understand me?"

"I understand you," Eddie said.

"We're almost done for tonight. There's just one more thing I want to try. But you have to be really deep asleep for this to work. So I want you to go deeper and deeper, as deep as you can go. Relax, and now you are really deep asleep, deep deep, and relaxed and ready and feeling good."

Little Eddie sat sprawled in his chair with his head tilted back and his eyes closed. Two tiny dark spots of blood stood out like mosquito bites on his lower right forearm.

"When I talk to you, Eddie, you're slowly getting younger and younger, you're going backward in time, so now you're not nine years old anymore, you're eight, it's last year and you're in the third grade, and now you're seven, and now you're six years old . . . and now you're five, Eddie, and it's the day of your fifth birthday. You're five years old today, Little Eddie. How old are you?"

"I'm five." To Harry's surprised pleasure, Little Eddie's voice actually seemed younger, as did his hunched posture in the chair.

"How do you feel?"

"Not good. I hate my present. It's terrible. Dad got it,

and Mom says it should never be allowed in the house
because it's just junk. I wish I wouldn't ever have to
have birthdays, they're so terrible. I'm gonna cry."

His face contracted. Harry tried to remember what
Eddie had gotten for his fifth birthday, but could
not—he caught only a dim memory of shame and
disappointment. "What's your present, Eddie?"

In a teary voice, Eddie said, "A radio. But it's busted
and Mom says it looks like it came from the junkyard. I
don't want it anymore. I don't even wanna *see* it."

Yes, Harry thought, yes, yes, yes. He could remember. On Little Eddie's fifth birthday, Edgar Beevers had
produced a yellow plastic radio which even Harry had
seen was astoundingly ugly. The dial was cracked, and
it was marked here and there with brown circular
scablike marks where someone had mashed out ciga-
rettes on it.

The radio had long since been buried in the junk
room, where it now lay beneath several geological layers
of trash.

"Okay, Eddie, you can forget the radio now, because
you're going backwards again, you're getting younger,
you're going backwards through being four years old,
and now you're three."

He looked with interest at Little Eddie, whose entire
demeanor had changed. From being tearfully unhappy,
Eddie now demonstrated a self-sufficient good cheer
Harry could not ever remember seeing in him. His
arms were folded over his chest. He was smiling, and
his eyes were bright and clear and childish.

"What do you see?" Harry asked.

"Mommy-ommy-om."

"What's she doing?"

"Mommy's at her desk. She's smoking and looking
through her papers." Eddie giggled. "Mommy looks
funny. It looks like smoke is coming out of the top of
her head." Eddie ducked his chin and hid his smile

behind a hand. "Mommy doesn't see me. I can see her, but she doesn't see me. Oh! Mommy works hard! She works hard at her desk!"

Eddie's smile abruptly left his face. His face froze for a second in a comic rubbery absence of expression; then his eyes widened in terror and his mouth went loose and wobbly.

"What happened?" Harry's mouth had gone dry.

"No, Mommy!" Eddie wailed. "Don't, Mommy! I wasn't spying, I wasn't, I promise—" His words broke off into a screech. "NO, MOMMY! DON'T! DON'T, MOMMY!" Eddie jumped upward, sending his chair flying back, and ran blindly toward the rear of the attic. Harry's head rang with Eddie's screeches. He heard a sharp *crack!* of wood breaking, but only as a small part of all the noise Eddie was making as he charged around the attic. Eddie had run into a tangle of hanging dresses, spun around, enmeshing himself deeper in the dresses, and was now tearing himself away from the web of dresses, pulling some of them off the rack. A long-sleeved purple dress with an enormous lace collar had draped itself around Eddie like a ghostly dance partner, and another dress, this of dull red velvet, snaked around his right leg. Eddie screamed again and yanked himself away from the tangle. The entire rack of clothes wobbled and then went over in a mad jangle of sound.

"NO!" he screeched. "HELP!" Eddie ran straight into a big wooden beam marking off one of the eaves, bounced off, and came windmilling toward Harry. Harry knew his brother could not see him.

"Eddie, stop," he said, but Eddie was past hearing him. Harry tried to make Eddie stop by wrapping his arms around him, but Eddie slammed right into him, hitting Harry's chest with a shoulder and knocking his head painfully against Harry's chin; Harry's arms closed on nothing and his eyes lost focus, and Eddie

went crashing into the tilting mirror. The mirror
yawned over sideways. Harry saw it tilt with dreamlike
slowness toward the floor, then in an eye blink drop and
crash. Broken glass sprayed across the attic floor.

"STOP!" Harry yelled. "STAND STILL, EDDIE!"

Eddie came to rest. The ripped and dirty dress of dull
red velvet still clung to his right leg. Blood oozed down
his temple from an ugly cut above his eye. He was
breathing hard, releasing air in little whimpering exha-
lations.

"Holy shit," Harry said, looking around at the attic.
In only a few seconds Eddie had managed to create
what looked at first like absolute devastation.
Maryrose's ancient dresses lay tangled in a heap of
dusty fabrics from which wire hangers skeletally protruded; gray Eddie-sized footprints lay like a pattern
over the muted explosion of colors the dresses now
created. When the rack had gone over, it had knocked a
section the size of a dinner plate out of a round wooden
coffee table Maryrose had particularly prized for its
being made from a single section of teak—"a single
piece of *teak*, the rarest wood in all the world, all the
way from Ceylon!" The much-prized mirror lay in
hundreds of glittering pieces across the attic floor. With
growing horror, Harry saw that the wooden frame had
cracked like a bone, showing a bone-pale, shockingly
white fracture in the expanse of dark stain.

Harry's blood tipped within his body, nearly tipping
him with it, like the mirror. "Oh God oh God oh God."

He turned slowly around. Eddie stood blinking two
feet to his side, wiping ineffectually at the blood
running from his forehead and now covering most of
his left cheek. He looked like an Indian in war paint—a
defeated, lost Indian, for his eyes were dim and his
head turned aimlessly from side to side.

A few feet from Eddie lay the chair in which he had
been sitting. One of its thin curved wooden arms lay

beside it, crudely severed. It looked like an insect's leg, Harry thought, like a toy gun.

For a moment Harry thought that his face too was red with blood. He wiped his hand over his forehead and looked at his glistening palm. It was only sweat. His heart beat like a bell. Beside him Eddie said, "Aaah . . . what . . . ?" The injury to his head had brought him out of the trance.

The dresses were ruined, stepped on, tangled, torn. The mirror was broken. The table had been mutilated. Maryrose's chair lay on its side like a murder victim, its severed arm ending in a bristle of snapped ligaments.

"My head *hurts*," Eddie said in a weak, trembling voice. "What happened? Ah! I'm all blood! I'm all blood, Harry!"

"You're all blood, you're all blood?" Harry shouted at him. "Everything's *all blood,* you dummy! Look around!" He did not recognize his own voice, which sounded high and tinny and seemed to be coming from somewhere else. Little Eddie took an aimless step away from him, and Harry wanted to fly at him, to pound his bloody head into a pancake, to destroy him, smash him . . .

Eddie held up his bloodstained palm and stared at it. He wiped it vaguely across the front of his T-shirt and took another wandering step. "I'm ascared, Harry," his tiny voice uttered.

"Look what you did!" Harry screamed. "You wrecked everything! Damn it! What do you think is going to happen to us?"

"What's Mom going to do?" Eddie asked in a voice only slightly above a whisper.

"You don't know?" Harry yelled. "You're dead!"

Eddie started to weep.

Harry bunched his hands into fists and clamped his eyes shut. They were both dead, that was the real truth. Harry opened his eyes, which felt hot and oddly heavy,

and stared at his sobbing, red-smeared, useless little brother. "Blue rose," he said.

X

Little Eddie's hands fell to his sides. His chin dropped, and his mouth fell open. Blood ran in a smooth wide band down the left side of his face, dipped under the line of his jaw, and continued on down his neck and into his T-shirt. Pooled blood in his left eyebrow dripped steadily onto the floor, as if from a faucet.

"You are going deep *asleep*," Harry said. Where was the hatpin? He looked back to the single standing chair and saw the mother-of-pearl head glistening on the floor near it. "Your whole body is *numb*." He moved over to the pin, bent down, and picked it up. The metal shaft felt warm in his fingers. "You can feel no *pain*." He went back to Little Eddie. "Nothing can *hurt* you." Harry's breath seemed to be breathing itself, forcing itself into his throat in hot harsh shallow pants, then expelling itself out.

"Did you *hear* me, Little Eddie?"

In his gravelly, slow-moving hypnotized voice, Little Eddie said, "I heard you."

"And you can feel no *pain*?"

"I can feel no pain."

Harry drew his arm back, the point of the hatpin extending forward from his fist, and then jerked his hand forward as hard as he could and stuck the pin into Eddie's abdomen right through the blood-soaked T-shirt. He exhaled sharply, and tasted a sour misery on his breath.

"You don't feel a thing."

"I don't feel a thing."

Harry opened his right hand and drove his palm against the head of the pin, hammering it in another

few inches. Little Eddie looked like a voodoo doll. A kind of sparkling light surrounded him. Harry gripped the head of the pin with his thumb and forefinger and yanked it out. He held it up and inspected it. Glittering light surrounded the pin too. The long shaft was painted with blood. Harry slipped the point into his mouth and closed his lips around the warm metal.

He saw himself, a man in another life, standing in a row with men like himself in a bleak gray landscape defined by barbed wire. Emaciated people in rags shuffled up toward them and spat on their clothes. The smells of dead flesh and of burning flesh hung in the air. Then the vision was gone, and Little Eddie stood before him again, surrounded by layers of glittering light.

Harry grimaced or grinned, he could not have told the difference, and drove his long spike deep into Eddie's stomach.

Eddie uttered a small *oof.*

"You don't feel anything, Eddie," Harry whispered. "You feel good all over. You never felt better in your life."

"Never felt better in my life."

Harry slowly pulled out the pin and cleaned it with his fingers.

He was able to remember every single thing anyone had ever told him about Tommy Golz.

"Now you're going to play a funny, funny game," he said. "This is called the Tommy Golz game because it's going to keep you safe from Mrs. Franken. Are you ready?" Harry carefully slid the pin into the fabric of his shirt collar, all the while watching Eddie's slack blood-streaked person. Vibrating bands of light beat rhythmically and steadily about Eddie's face.

"Ready," Eddie said.

"I'm going to give you your instructions now, Little Eddie. Pay attention to everything I say and it's all going to be okay. Everything's going to be okay—as

long as you play the game exactly the way I tell you. You understand, don't you?"

"I understand."

"Tell me what I just said."

"Everything's gonna be okay as long as I play the game exactly the way you tell me." A dollop of blood slid off Eddie's eyebrow and splashed onto his already soaked T-shirt.

"Good, Eddie. Now the first thing you do is fall down—not now, when I tell you. I'm going to give you all the instructions, and then I'm going to count backwards from ten, and when I get to *one,* you'll start playing the game. Okay?"

"Okay."

"So first you fall down, Little Eddie. You fall down real hard. Then comes the fun part of the game. You bang your head on the floor. You start to go crazy. You twitch, and you bang your hands and feet on the floor. You do that for a long time. I guess you do that until you count to about a hundred. You foam at the mouth, you twist all over the place. You get real stiff, and then you get real loose, and then you get real stiff, and then real loose again, and all this time you're banging your head and your hands and feet on the floor, and you're twisting all over the place. Then when you finish counting to a hundred in your head, you do the last thing. You swallow your tongue. And that's the game. When you swallow your tongue you're the winner. And then nothing bad can happen to you, and Mrs. Franken won't be able to hurt you ever ever ever."

Harry stopped talking. His hands were shaking. After a second he realized that his insides were shaking too. He raised his trembling fingers to his shirt collar and felt the hatpin.

"Tell me how you win the game, Little Eddie. What's the last thing you do?"

"I swallow my tongue."

"Right. And then Mrs. Franken and Mom will never be able to hurt you, because you won the game."

"Good," said Little Eddie. The glittering light shimmered about him.

"Okay, we'll start playing right now," Harry said. "Ten." He went toward the attic steps. "Nine." He reached the steps. "Eight."

He went down one step. "Seven." Harry descended another two steps. "Six." When he went down another two steps, he called up in a slightly louder voice, "Five."

Now his head was beneath the level of the attic floor, and he could not see Little Eddie anymore. All he could hear was the soft, occasional plop of liquid hitting the floor.

"Four."

"Three."

"Two." He was now at the door to the attic steps. Harry opened the door, stepped through it, breathed hard, and shouted "One!" up the stairs.

He heard a thud, and then quickly closed the door behind him.

Harry went across the hall and into the dormitory bedroom. There seemed to be a strange absence of light in the hallway. For a second he saw—was sure he saw—a line of dark trees across a wall of barbed wire. Harry closed this door behind him too, and went to his narrow bed and sat down. He could feel blood beating in his face; his eyes seemed oddly warm, as if they were heated by filaments. Harry slowly, almost reverently extracted the hatpin from his collar and set it on his pillow. "A hundred," he said. "Ninety-nine, ninety-eight, ninety-seven, ninety-six, ninety-five, ninety-four . . ."

When he had counted down to "one," he stood up and left the bedroom. He went quickly downstairs without looking at the door behind which lay the attic

steps. On the ground floor he slipped into Maryrose's bedroom, crossed over to her desk, and slid open the bottom right-hand drawer. From the drawer he took a velvet-covered box. This he opened, and jabbed the hatpin in the ball of material, studded with pins of all sizes and descriptions, from which he had taken it. He replaced the box in the drawer, pushed the drawer into the desk, and quickly left the room and went upstairs.

Back in his own bedroom, Harry took off his clothes and climbed into his bed. His face still burned.

He must have fallen asleep very quickly, because the next thing he knew Albert was slamming his way into the bedroom and tossing his clothes and boots all over the place. "You asleep?" Albert asked. "You left the attic light on, you fuckin' dummies, but if you think I'm gonna save your fuckin' asses and go up and turn it off, you're even stupider than you look."

Harry was careful not to move a finger, not to move even a hair.

He held his breath while Albert threw himself onto his bed, and when Albert's breathing relaxed and slowed, Harry followed his big brother into sleep. He did not awaken again until he heard his father half screeching, half sobbing up in the attic, and that was very late at night.

XI

Sonny came from Fort Sill, George all the way from Germany. Between them, they held up a sodden Edgar Beevers at the gravesite while a minister Harry had never seen before read from a Bible as cracked and rubbed as an old brown shoe. Between his two older sons, Harry's father looked bent and ancient, a skinny old man only steps from the grave himself. Sonny and

George despised their father, Harry saw—they held him up on sufferance, in part because they had chipped in thirty dollars apiece to buy him a suit and did not want to see it collapse with its owner inside into the lumpy clay of the graveyard. His whiskers glistened in the sun, and moisture shone beneath his eyes and at the corners of his mouth. He had been shaking too severely for either Sonny or George to shave him, and had been capable of moving in a straight line only after George let him take a couple of long swallows from a leather-covered flask he took out of his duffel bag.

The minister uttered a few sage words on the subject of epilepsy.

Sonny and George looked as solid as brick walls in their uniforms, like prison guards or actual prisons themselves. Next to them, Albert looked shrunken and unfinished. Albert wore the green plaid sport jacket in which he had graduated from the eighth grade, and his wrists hung prominent and red four inches below the bottoms of the sleeves. His motorcycle boots were visible beneath his light gray trousers, but they, like the green jacket, had lost their flash. Like Albert, too. Ever since the discovery of Eddie's body, Albert had gone around the house looking as if he'd just bitten off the end of his tongue and was trying to decide whether or not to spit it out. He never looked anybody in the eye, and he rarely spoke. Albert acted as though a gigantic padlock had been fixed to the middle of his chest and *he* was damned if he'd ever take it off. He had not asked Sonny or George a single question about the Army. Every now and then he would utter a remark about the gas station so toneless that it suffocated any reply.

Harry looked at Albert standing beside their mother, kneading his hands together and keeping his eyes fixed as if by decree on the square foot of ground before him. Albert glanced over at Harry, knew he was being looked at, and did what to Harry was an extraordinary thing.

Albert *froze*. All expression drained out of his face, and his hands locked immovably together. He looked as little able to see or hear as a statue. *He's that way because he told Little Eddie that he wished he would die,* Harry thought for the tenth or eleventh time since he had realized this, and with undiminished awe. Then was he lying? Harry wondered. And if he really did wish that Little Eddie would drop dead, why isn't he happy now? Didn't he get what he wanted? Albert would never spit out that piece of his tongue, Harry thought, watching his brother blink slowly and sightlessly toward the ground.

Harry shifted his gaze uneasily to his father, still propped up between George and Sonny, heard that the minister was finally reaching the end of his speech, and took a fast look at his mother. Maryrose was standing very straight in a black dress and black sunglasses, holding the straps of her bag in front of her with both hands. Except for the color of her clothes, she could have been a spectator at a tennis match. Harry knew by the way she was holding her face that she was wishing she could smoke. Dying for a cigarette, he thought, ha-ha, the Monster Mash, it's a graveyard smash.

The minister finished speaking, and made a rhetorical gesture with his hands. The coffin sank on ropes into the rough earth. Harry's father began to weep loudly. First George, then Sonny, picked up large damp shovel-marked pieces of the clay and dropped them on the coffin. Edgar Beevers nearly fell in after his own tiny clod, but George contemptuously swung him back. Maryrose marched forward, bent and picked up a random piece of clay with thumb and forefinger as if using tweezers, dropped it, and turned away before it struck. Albert fixed his eyes on Harry—his own clod had split apart in his hand and crumbled away between his fingers. Harry shook his head *no*. He did not want to drop dirt on Eddie's coffin and make that noise. He did

not want to look at Eddie's coffin again. There was enough dirt around to do the job without him hitting that metal box like he was trying to ring Eddie's doorbell. He stepped back.

"Mom says we have to get back to the house," Albert said.

Maryrose lit up as soon as they got into the single black car they had rented through the funeral parlor, and breathed out acrid smoke over everybody crowded into the backseat. The car backed into a narrow grave-yard lane, and turned down the main road toward the front gates.

In the front seat, next to the driver, Edgar Beevers drooped sideways and leaned his head against the window, leaving a blurred streak on the glass.

"How in the name of hell could Little Eddie have epilepsy without anybody knowing about it?" George asked.

Albert stiffened and stared out the window.

"Well, that's epilepsy," Maryrose said. "Eddie could have gone on for years without having an attack." That she worked in a hospital always gave her remarks of this sort a unique gravity, almost as if she were a doctor.

"Must have been some fit," Sonny said, squeezed into place between Harry and Albert.

"Grand mal," Maryrose said, and took another hungry drag on her cigarette.

"Poor little bastard," George said. "Sorry, Mom."

"I know you're in the armed forces, and armed forces people speak very freely, but I wish you would not use that kind of language."

Harry, jammed into Sonny's rock-hard side, felt his brother's body twitch with a hidden laugh, though Sonny's face did not alter.

"I said I was sorry, Mom," George said.

"Yes. Driver! Driver!" Maryrose was leaning forward, reaching out one claw to tap the chauffeur's

shoulder. "Livermore is the next right. Do you know South Sixth Street?"

"I'll get you there," the driver said.

This is not my family, Harry thought. I came from somewhere else and my rules are different from theirs.

His father mumbled something inaudible as soon as they got in the door and disappeared into his curtained-off cubicle. Maryrose put her sunglasses in her purse and marched into the kitchen to warm the coffee cake and the macaroni casserole, both made that morning, in the oven. Sonny and George wandered into the living room and sat down on opposite ends of the couch. They did not look at each other—George picked up a *Reader's Digest* from the table and began leafing through it backward, and Sonny folded his hands in his lap and stared at his thumbs. Albert's footsteps plodded up the stairs, crossed the landing, and went into the dormitory bedroom.

"What's she in the kitchen for?" Sonny asked, speaking to his hands. "Nobody's going to come. Nobody ever comes here, because she never wanted them to."

"Albert's taking this kind of hard, Harry," George said. He propped the magazine against the stiff folds of his uniform and looked across the room at his little brother. Harry had seated himself beside the door, as out of the way as possible. George's attentions rather frightened him, though George had behaved with consistent kindness ever since his arrival two days after Eddie's death. His crew cut still bristled and he could still break rocks with his chin, but some violent demon seemed to have left him. "You think he'll be okay?"

"Him? Sure." Harry tilted his head, grimaced.

"He didn't see Little Eddie first, did he?"

"No, Dad did," Harry said. "He saw the light on in the attic when he came home, I guess. Albert went up there, though. I guess there was so much blood Dad

thought somebody broke in and killed Eddie. But he just bumped his head, and that's where the blood came from."

"Head wounds bleed like bastards," Sonny said. "A guy hit me with a bottle once in Tokyo. I thought I was gonna bleed to death right there."

"And Mom's stuff got all messed up?" George asked quietly.

This time Sonny looked up.

"Pretty much, I guess. The dress rack got knocked down. Dad cleaned up what he could, the next day. One of the cane-back chairs got broke, and a hunk got knocked out of the teak table. And the mirror got broken into a million pieces."

Sonny shook his head and made a soft whistling sound through his pursed lips.

"She's a tough old gal," George said. "I hear her coming, though, so we have to stop, Harry. But we can talk tonight."

Harry nodded.

XII

After dinner that night, when Maryrose had gone to bed—the hospital had given her two nights off—Harry sat across the kitchen table from a George who clearly had something to say. Sonny had polished off a six-pack by himself in front of the television and gone up to the dormitory bedroom by himself. Albert had disappeared shortly after dinner, and their father had never emerged from his cubicle beside the junk room.

"I'm glad Pete Petrosian came over," George said. "He's a good old boy. Ate two helpings too."

Harry was startled by George's use of their neighbor's first name—he was not even sure that he had ever heard it before.

Mr. Petrosian had been their only caller that afternoon. Harry had seen that his mother was grateful that someone had come, and despite her preparations wanted no more company after Mr. Petrosian had left.

"Think I'll get a beer, that is if Sonny didn't drink it all," George said, and stood up and opened the fridge. His uniform looked as if it had been painted on his body, and his muscles bulged and moved like a horse's. "Two left," he said. "Good thing you're underage." George popped the caps off both bottles and came back to the table. He winked at Harry, then tilted the first bottle to his lips and took a good swallow. "So what the devil was Little Eddie doing up there anyhow? Trying on dresses?"

"I don't know," Harry said. "I was asleep."

"Hell, I know I kind of lost touch with Little Eddie, but I got the impression he was scared of his shadow. I'm surprised he had the nerve to go up there and mess around with Mom's precious stuff."

"Yeah," Harry said. "Me too."

"You didn't happen to go with him, did you?" George tilted the bottle to his mouth and winked at Harry again.

Harry just looked back. He could feel his face getting hot.

"I just was thinking maybe you saw it happen to Little Eddie, and got too scared to tell anybody. Nobody would be mad at you, Harry. Nobody would blame you for anything. You couldn't know how to help someone who's having an epileptic fit. Little Eddie swallowed his tongue. Even if you'd been standing next to him when he did it and had the presence of mind to call an ambulance, he would have died before it got there. Unless you knew what was wrong and how to correct it. Which nobody would expect you to know, not in a million years. Nobody'd blame you for anything, Harry, not even Mom."

"I was asleep," Harry said.

"Okay, okay. I just wanted you to know."

They sat in silence for a time, then both spoke at once.

"Did you know—"

"We had this—"

"Sorry," George said. "Go on."

"Did you know that Dad used to be in the Army? In World War II?"

"Yeah, I knew that. Of course I knew that."

"Did you know that he committed the perfect murder once?"

"What?"

"Dad committed the perfect murder. When he was at Dachau, that death camp."

"Oh Christ, is that what you're talking about? You got a funny way of seeing things, Harry. He shot an enemy who was trying to escape. That's not murder, it's war. There's one hell of a big difference."

"I'd like to see war someday," Harry said. "I'd like to be in the Army, like you and Dad."

"Hold your horses, hold your horses," George said, smiling now. "That's sort of one of the things I wanted to talk to you about." He set down his beer bottle, cradled his hands around it, and tilted his head to look at Harry. This was obviously going to be serious. "You know, I used to be crazy and stupid, that's the only way to put it. I used to look for fights. I had a chip on my shoulder the size of a house, and pounding some dipshit into a coma was my idea of a great time. The Army did me a lot of good. It made me grow up. But I don't think you need that, Harry. You're too smart for that—if you have to go, you go, but out of all of us, you're the one who could really amount to something in this world. You could be a doctor. Or a lawyer. You ought to get the best education you can, Harry. What you have to do is stay out of trouble and get to college."

"Oh, college," Harry said.

"Listen to me, Harry. I make pretty good money, and I got nothing to spend it on. I'm not going to get married and have kids, that's for sure. So I want to make you a proposition. If you keep your nose clean and make it through high school, I'll help you out with college. Maybe you can get a scholarship—I think you're smart enough, Harry, and a scholarship would be great. But either way, I'll see you make it through." George emptied the first bottle, set it down, and gave Harry a quizzical look. "Let's get one person in this family off on the right track. What do you say?"

"I guess I better keep reading," Harry said.

"I hope you'll read your ass off, little buddy," George said, and picked up the second bottle of beer.

XIII

The day after Sonny left, George put all of Eddie's toys and clothes into a box and squeezed the box into the junk room; two days later, George took a bus to New York so he could get his flight to Munich from Idlewild. An hour before he caught his bus, George walked Harry up to Big John's and stuffed him full of hamburgers and french fries and said, "You'll probably miss Eddie a lot, won't you?" "I guess," Harry said, but the truth was that Eddie was now only a vacancy, a blank space. Sometimes a door would close and Harry would know that Little Eddie had just come in; but when he turned to look, he saw only emptiness. George's question, asked a week ago, was the last time Harry had heard anyone pronounce his brother's name.

In the seven days since the charmed afternoon at Big John's and the departure on a southbound bus of George Beevers, everything seemed to have gone back

to the way it was before, but Harry knew that really everything had changed. They had been a loose, divided family of five, two parents and three sons. Now they seemed to be a family of three, and Harry thought that the actual truth was that the family had shrunk down to two, himself and his mother.

Edgar Beevers had left home—he too was an absence. After two visits from policemen who parked their cars right outside the house, after listening to his mother's muttered expressions of disgust, after the spectacle of his pale, bleary, but sober and clean-shaven father trying over and over to knot a necktie in front of the bathroom mirror, Harry finally accepted that his father had been caught shoplifting. His father had to go to court, and he was scared. His hands shook so uncontrollably that he could not shave himself, and in the end Maryrose had to knot his tie—doing it in one, two, three quick movements as brutal as the descent of a knife, never removing the cigarette from her mouth.

Grief-stricken Area Man Forgiven of Shoplifting Charge, read the headline over the little story in the evening newspaper which at last explained his father's crime. Edgar Beevers had been stopped on the sidewalk outside the Livermore Avenue National Tea, T-bone steaks hidden inside his shirt and a bottle of Rheingold beer in each of his front pockets. He had stolen two steaks! He had put beer bottles in his pockets! This made Harry feel like he was sweating inside. The judge had sent him home, but home was not where he went. For a short time, Harry thought, his father had hung out on Oldtown Road, Palmyra's Skid Row, and slept in vacant lots with winos and bums. (Then a woman was supposed to have taken him in.)

Albert was another mystery. It was as though a creature from outer space had taken him over and was using his body, like *Invasion of the Body Snatchers.*

Albert looked like he thought somebody was always standing behind him, watching every move he made. He was still carrying around that piece of his tongue, and pretty soon, Harry thought, he'd get so used to it that he would forget he had it.

Three days after George left Palmyra, Albert had actually tagged along after Harry on the way to Big John's. Harry had turned around on the sidewalk and seen Albert in his black jeans and grease-blackened T-shirt halfway down the block, shoving his hands in his pockets and looking hard at the ground. That was Albert's way of pretending to be invisible. The next time he turned around, Albert growled, "Keep walking."

Harry went to work on the pinball machine as soon as he got inside Big John's. Albert slunk in a few minutes later and went straight to the counter. He took one of the stained paper menus from a stack squeezed in beside a napkin dispenser and inspected it as if he had never seen it before.

"Hey, let me introduce you guys," said Big John, leaning against the far side of the counter. Like Albert, he wore black jeans and motorcycle boots, but his dark hair, daringly for the nineteen-fifties, fell over his ears. Beneath his stained white apron he wore a long-sleeved black shirt with a pattern of tiny azure palm trees. "You two are the Beevers boys, Harry and Bucky. Say hello to each other, fellows."

Bucky Beaver was a toothy rodent in an Ipana television commercial. Albert blushed, still grimly staring at his menu sheet.

"Call me Beans," Harry said, and felt Albert's gaze shift wonderingly to him.

"Beans and Bucky, the Beevers boys," Big John said. "Well, Buck, what'll you have?"

"Hamburger, fries, shake," Albert said.

Big John half turned and yelled the order through the hatch to Mama Mary's kitchen. For a time the three of them stood in uneasy silence. Then Big John said, "Heard your old man found a new place to hang his hat. His new girlfriend is a real pistol, I heard. Spent some time in County Hospital. On account of she picked up little messages from outer space on the good old Philco. You hear that?"

"He's gonna come home real soon," Harry said. "He doesn't have any new girlfriend. He's staying with an old friend. She's a rich lady and she wants to help him out because she knows he had a lot of trouble and she's going to get him a real good job, and then he'll come home, and we'll be able to move to a better house and everything."

He never even saw Albert move, but Albert had materialized beside him. Fury, rage, and misery distorted his face. Harry had time to cry out only once, and then Albert slammed a fist into his chest and knocked him backwards into the pinball machine.

"I bet that felt real good," Harry said, unable to keep down his own rage. "I bet you'd like to kill me, huh? Huh, Albert? How about that?"

Albert moved backward two paces and lowered his hands, already looking impassive, locked into himself.

For a second in which his breath failed and dazzling light filled his eyes, Harry saw Little Eddie's slack, trusting face before him. Then Big John came up from nowhere with a big hamburger and a mound of french fries on a plate and said, "Down, boys. Time for Rocky here to tackle his dinner."

That night Albert said nothing at all to Harry as they lay in their beds. Neither did he fall asleep. Harry knew that for most of the night Albert just closed his eyes and faked it, like a possum in trouble. Harry tried to stay awake long enough to see when Albert's fake sleep

melted into the real thing, but he sank into dreams long before that.

He was rushing down the stony corridor of a castle past suits of armor and torches guttering in sconces. His bladder was bursting, he had to let go, he could not hold it more than another few seconds . . . at last he came to the open bathroom door and ran into that splendid gleaming place. He began to tug at his zipper, and looked around for the butler and the row of marble urinals. Then he froze. Little Eddie was standing before him, not the uniformed butler. Blood ran in a gaudy streak from a gash high on his forehead over his cheek and right down his neck, neat as paint. Little Eddie was waving frantically at Harry, his eyes bright and hysterical, his mouth working soundlessly because he had swallowed his tongue.

Harry sat up straight in bed, about to scream, then realized that the bedroom was all around him and Little Eddie was gone. He hurried downstairs to the bathroom.

XIV

At two o'clock the next afternoon Harry Beevers had to pee again, and just as badly, but this time he was a long way from the bathroom across from the junk room and his father's old cubicle. Harry was standing in the humid sunlight across the street from 45 Oldtown Way. This short street connected the bums, transient hotels, bars, and seedy movie theaters of Oldtown Road with the more respectable hotels, department stores, and restaurants of Palmyra Avenue—the real downtown. 45 Oldtown Way was a four-story brick tenement with an exoskeleton of fire escapes. Black iron bars covered the ground-floor windows. On one side of 45 Oldtown

Way were the large soap-smeared windows of a bank-rupted shoe store, on the other a vacant lot where loose bricks and broken bottles nestled amongst dandelions and tall Queen Anne's lace. Harry's father lived in that building now. Everybody else knew it, and since Big John had told him, now Harry knew it too.

He jigged from leg to leg, waiting for a woman to come out through the front door. It was as chipped and peeling as his own, and a broken fanlight sat drunkenly atop it. Harry had checked the row of dented mailboxes on the brick wall just outside the door for his father's name, but none bore any names at all. Big John hadn't known the name of the woman who had taken Harry's father, but he said that she was large, black-haired, and crazy, and that she had two children in foster care. About half an hour ago a dark-haired woman had come through the door, but Harry had not followed her because she had not looked especially large to him. Now he was beginning to have doubts. What did Big John mean by "large" anyhow? As big as he was? And how could you tell if someone was crazy? Did it show? Maybe he should have followed that woman. This thought made him even more anxious, and he squeezed his legs together.

His father was in that building now, he thought. Harry thought of his father lying on an unmade bed, his brown winter coat around him, his hat pulled low on his forehead like Lepke Buchalter's, drawing on a cigarette, looking moodily out the window.

Then he had to pee so urgently that he could not have held it in for more than a few seconds, and trotted across the street and into the vacant lot. Near the back fence the tall weeds gave him some shelter from the street. He frantically unzipped and let the braided yellow stream splash into a nest of broken bricks. Harry looked up at the side of the building beside him. It

looked very tall, and seemed to be tilting slightly toward him. The four windows on each floor looked back down at him, blank and fatherless. Just as he was tugging at his zipper, he heard the front door of the building slam shut.

His heart slammed too. Harry hunkered down behind the tall white weeds. Anxiety that she might walk the other way, toward downtown, made him twine his fingers together and bend his fingers back. If he waited about five seconds, he figured, he'd know she was going toward Palmyra Avenue and would be able to get across the lot in time to see which way she turned. His knuckles cracked. He felt like a soldier hiding in a forest, like a murder weapon.

He raised up on his toes and got ready to dash back across the street, because an empty grocery cart closely followed by a moving belly with a tiny head and basketball shoes, a cigar tilted in its mouth like a flag, appeared past the front of the building. He could go back and wait across the street. Harry settled down and watched the stomach go down the sidewalk past him. Then a shadow separated itself from the street side of the fat man, and the shadow became a black-haired woman in a long loose dress now striding past the grocery cart. She shook back her head, and Harry saw that she was tall as a queen and that her skin was darker than olive. Deep lines cut through her cheeks. It had to be the woman who had taken his father. Her long rapid strides had taken her well past the fat man's grocery cart. Harry ran across the rubble of the lot and began to follow her up the sidewalk.

His father's woman walked in a hard, determined way. She stepped down into the street to get around groups too slow for her. At the Oldtown Road corner she wove her way through a group of saggy-bottomed men passing around a bottle in a paper bag and cut in front of two black children dribbling a basketball up the

street. She was on the move, and Harry had to hurry along to keep her in sight.

"I bet you don't believe me," he said to himself, practicing, and skirted the group of winos on the corner. He picked up his speed until he was nearly trotting. The two black kids with the basketball ignored him as he kept pace with them, then went on ahead. Far up the block, the tall woman with bouncing black hair marched right past a flashing neon sign in a bar window. Her bottom moved back and forth in the loose dress, surprisingly big whenever it bulged out the fabric of the dress; her back seemed as long as a lion's. "What would you say if I told you . . ." Harry said to himself.

A block and a half ahead, the woman turned on her heel and went through the door of the A&P store. Harry sprinted the rest of the way, pushed the yellow wooden door marked ENTER, and walked into the dense, humid air of the grocery store. Other A&P stores may have been air-conditioned, but not the little shop on Oldtown Road.

What was foster care anyway? Did you get money if you gave away your children?

A good person's children would never be in foster care, Harry thought. He saw the woman turning into the third aisle past the cash register. He saw with a small shock that she was taller than his father. If I told you, you might not believe me. He went slowly around the corner of the aisle. She was standing on the pale wooden floor about fifteen feet in front of him, carrying a wire basket in one hand. He stepped forward. What I have to say might seem . . . For good luck, he touched the hatpin inserted into the bottom of his collar. She was staring at a row of brightly colored bags of potato chips. Harry cleared his throat. The woman reached down and picked up a big bag and put it in the basket.

"Excuse me," Harry said.

She turned her head to look at him. Her face was as

wide as it was long, and in the mellow light from the store's low-wattage bulbs her skin seemed a very light shade of brown. Harry knew he was meeting an equal. She looked like she could do magic, as if she could shoot fire and sparks out of her fierce black eyes.

"I bet you don't believe me," he said, "but a kid can hypnotize people just as good as an adult."

"What's that?"

His rehearsed words now sounded crazy to him, but he stuck to his script.

"A kid can hypnotize people. I can hypnotize people. Do you believe that?"

"I don't think I even care," she said, and wheeled away toward the rear of the aisle.

"I bet you don't think I could hypnotize you," Harry said.

"Kid, get lost."

Harry suddenly knew that if he kept talking about hypnotism the woman would turn down the next aisle and ignore him no matter what he said, or else begin to speak in a very loud voice about seeing the manager. "My name is Harry Beevers," he said to her back. "Edgar Beevers is my dad."

She stopped and turned around and looked expressionlessly into his face.

Harry dizzyingly saw a wall of barbed wire before him, a dark green wall of trees at the other end of a barren field.

"I wonder if you maybe call him Beans," Harry said.

"Oh, great," she said. "That's just great. So you're one of his boys. Terrific. *Beans* wants potato chips, what do you want?"

"I want you to fall down and bang your head and swallow your tongue and *die* and get buried and have people drop dirt on you," Harry said. The woman's mouth fell open. "Then I want you to puff up with *gas*. I

want you to *rot*. I want you to turn green and *black*. I want your *skin* to slide off your bones."

"You're crazy!" the woman shouted at him. "Your whole family's crazy! Do you think your mother wants him anymore?"

"My father shot us in the back," Harry said, and turned and bolted down the aisle for the door.

When he got outside he began to trot down seedy Oldtown Road. When he came to Oldtown Way he turned left. When he ran past number 45, he looked at every blank window. His face, his hands, his whole body felt hot and wet. Soon he had a stitch in his side. Harry blinked, and saw a dark line of trees, a wall of barbed wire before him. At the top of Oldtown Way he turned into Palmyra Avenue. From there he could continue running past Alouette's boarded-up windows, past all the stores old and new, to the corner of Livermore, and from there, he only now realized, to the little house that belonged to Mr. Petrosian.

XV

On a sweltering midafternoon eleven years later at a camp in the Central Highlands of Vietnam, Lieutenant Harry Beevers closed the flap of his tent against the mosquitoes and sat on the edge of his temporary bunk to write a long-delayed letter back to Pat Caldwell, the young woman he wanted to marry—and to whom he would be married for a time, after his return from the war to New York State.

This is what he wrote, after frequent crossings-out and hesitations. Harry later destroyed this letter.

> *Dear Pat:*
> *First of all I want you to know how much I miss*

*you, my darling, and that if I ever get out of this
beautiful and terrible country, which I am going to
do, that I am going to chase you mercilessly and
unrelentingly until you say that you'll marry me.
Maybe in the euphoria of relief (YES!!!), I have the
future all worked out, Pat, and you're a big part of
it. I have eighty-six days until DEROS, when they
pat me on the head and put me on that big bird out
of here. Now that my record is clear again, I have
no doubts that Columbia Law School will take me
in. As you know, my law board scores were pretty
respectable (modest me!) when I took them at
Adelphi. I'm pretty sure I could even get into
Harvard Law, but I settled on Columbia because
then we could both be in New York.*

*My brother George has already told me that he
will help out with whatever money I—you and
I—will need. George put me through Adelphi. I
don't think you knew this. In fact, nobody knew
this. When I look back, in college I was such a jerk.
I wanted everybody to think my family was well-to-
do, or at least middle-class. The truth is, we were
damn poor, which I think makes my accomplishments all the more noteworthy, all the more
loveworthy!*

*You see, this experience, even with all the ugly
and self-doubting and humiliating moments, has
done me a lot of good. I was right to come here,
even though I had no idea what it was really like. I
think I needed the experience of war to complete
me, and I tell you this even though I know that you
will detest any such idea. In fact, I have to tell you
that a big part of me loves being here, and that in
some way, even with all this trouble, this year will
always be one of the high points of my life. Pat, as
you see, I'm determined to be honest—to be an*

honest man. If I'm going to be a lawyer, I ought to be honest, don't you think? (Or maybe the reverse is the reality!) One thing that has meant a lot to me here has been what I can only call the close comradeship of my friends and my men—I actually like the grunts more than the usual officer types, which of course means that I get more loyalty and better performance from my men than the usual lieutenant. Some day I'd like you to meet Mike Poole and Tim Underhill and Pumo the Puma and the most amazing of all, M. O. Dengler, who of course was involved with me in the Ia Thuc cave incident. These guys stuck by me. I even have a nickname, "Beans." They call me "Beans" Beevers, and I like it.

There was no way my court-martial could have really put me in any trouble, because all the facts, and my own men, were on my side. Besides, could you see me actually killing children? This is Vietnam and you kill people, that's what we're doing here—we kill Charlies. But we don't kill babies and children. Not even in the heat of wartime— and Ia Thuc was pretty hot!

Well, this is my way of letting you know that at the court-martial of course I received a complete and utter vindication. Dengler did too. There were even unofficial mutterings about giving us medals for all the BS we put up with for the past six weeks—including that amazing story in Time *magazine. Before people start yelling about atrocities, they ought to have all the facts straight. Fortunately, last week's magazines go out with the rest of the trash.*

Besides, I already knew too much about what death does to people.

I never told you that I once had a little brother

named Edward. When I was ten, my little brother wandered up into the top floor of our house one night and suffered a fatal epileptic fit. This event virtually destroyed my family. It led directly to my father's leaving home. (He had been a hero in WWII, something else I never told you.) It deeply changed, I would say even damaged, my older brother Albert. Albert tried to enlist in 1964, but they wouldn't take him because they said he was psychologically unfit. My mom too almost came apart for a while. She used to go up in the attic and cry and wouldn't come down. So you could say that my family was pretty well destroyed, or ruined, or whatever you want to call it, by a sudden death. I took it, and my dad's desertion, pretty hard myself. You don't get over these things easily.

The court-martial lasted exactly four hours. Big deal, hey?—as we used to say back in Palmyra. We used to have a neighbor named Pete Petrosian who said things like that, and against what must have been million-to-one odds, who died exactly the same way my brother did, about two weeks after— lightning really did strike twice. I guess it's dumb to think about him now, but maybe one thing war does is to make you conversant with death. How it happens, what it does to people, what it means, how all the dead in your life are somehow united, joined, part of your eternal family. This is a profound feeling, Pat, and no damn whipped-up failed court-martial can touch it. If there were any innocent children in that cave, then they are in my family forever, like little Edward and Pete Petrosian, and the rest of my life is a poem to them. But the Army says there weren't, and so do I.

I love you and love you and love you. You can stop worrying now and start thinking about being married to a Columbia Law student with one hell

of a good future. I won't tell you any more war stories than you want to hear. And that's a promise, whether the stories are about Nam or Palmyra.

Always yours,
Harry
(aka "Beans!")

Arthur Machen (1863–1947)

THE GREAT GOD PAN

Arthur Machen is one of the greatest writers of supernatural horror in the English language. The *Penguin Encyclopedia of Horror and the Supernatural* calls him "one of supernatural fantasy's greatest stylists; with the eye of a visionary and a language that is, at times, truly incantatory, he reveals the wonder—and terror—lying hidden behind everyday scenes." He never wrote a ghost story. Philip Van Doren Stern said, "Machen dealt with the elemental forces of evil, with spells that outlast time, and with the malign powers of folklore and fairy tale." His most important books are *The Great God Pan and The Inmost Light* (1894), *The Three Imposters* (1895), *The House of Souls* (1906), and his selected *Tales of Horror and the Supernatural* (1949). His "The White People" (1899) was a seminal influence on H. P. Lovecraft, and Helen Vaughan of "The Great God Pan" inspired the femme fatale in Peter Straub's *Ghost Story* (1979). Machen's influence is widespread, though his stories are infrequently reprinted today. "The Great God Pan" was a cause célèbre when it appeared—it certainly horrified the critics—and was one of the works of fiction that gave the 1890s a reputation for decadence. A tale of science gone awry, it descends from Mary Shelley and Robert Louis Stevenson, but introduces Machen's unique vision and lush, lurid style. It is Machen's most famous story and shows him at the start of his career already a master of horror.

I   The Experiment

"I am glad you came, Clarke; very glad indeed. I was not sure you could spare the time."

"I was able to make arrangements for a few days; things are not very lively just now. But have you no misgivings, Raymond? Is it absolutely safe?"

The two men were slowly pacing the terrace in front of Dr. Raymond's house. The sun still hung above the western mountain line, but it shone with a dull red glow that cast no shadows, and all the air was quiet; a sweet breath came from the great wood on the hillside above, and with it, at intervals, the soft murmuring call of the wild doves. Below, in the long lovely valley, the river wound in and out between the lonely hills, and, as the sun hovered and vanished into the west, a faint mist, pure white, began to rise from the banks. Dr. Raymond turned sharply to his friend.

"Safe? Of course it is. In itself the operation is a perfectly simple one; any surgeon could do it."

"And there is no danger at any other stage?"

"None; absolutely no physical danger whatever, I give you my word. You are always timid, Clarke, always; but you know my history. I have devoted myself to transcendental medicine for the last twenty years. I have heard myself called quack and charlatan and impostor, but all the while I knew I was on the right path. Five years ago I reached the goal, and since then every day has been a preparation for what we shall do tonight."

"I should like to believe it is all true." Clarke knit his brows, and looked doubtfully at Dr. Raymond. "Are you perfectly sure, Raymond, that your theory is not a phantasmagoria—a splendid vision, certainly, but a mere vision after all?"

Dr. Raymond stopped in his walk and turned sharp-

ly. He was a middle-aged man, gaunt and thin, of a pale yellow complexion, but as he answered Clarke and faced him, there was a flush on his cheek.

"Look about you, Clarke. You see the mountain, and hill following after hill, as wave on wave, you see the woods and orchards, the fields of ripe corn, and the meadows reaching to the reed beds by the river. You see me standing here beside you, and hear my voice; but I tell you that all these things—yes, from that star that has just shone out in the sky to the solid ground beneath our feet—I say that all these are but dreams and shadows: the shadows that hide the real world from our eyes. There *is* a real world, but it is beyond this glamour and this vision, beyond these 'chases in Arras, dreams in a career,' beyond them all as beyond a veil. I do not know whether any human being has ever lifted that veil; but I do know, Clarke, that you and I shall see it lifted this very night from before another's eyes. You may think all this strange nonsense; it may be strange, but it is true, and the ancients knew what lifting the veil means. They called it seeing the god Pan."

Clarke shivered; the white mist gathering over the river was chilly.

"It is wonderful indeed," he said. "We are standing on the brink of a strange world, Raymond, if what you say is true. I suppose the knife is absolutely necessary?"

"Yes; a slight lesion in the grey matter, that is all; a trifling rearrangement of certain cells, a microscopical alteration that would escape the attention of ninety-nine brain specialists out of a hundred. I don't want to bother you with 'shop,' Clarke; I might give you a mass of technical detail which would sound very imposing, and would leave you as enlightened as you are now. But I suppose you have read, casually, in out-of-the-way corners of your paper, that immense strides have been made recently in the physiology of the brain. I saw a paragraph the other day about Digby's theory, and

Browne Faber's discoveries. Theories and discoveries! Where they are standing now, I stood fifteen years ago, and I need not tell you that I have not been standing still for the last fifteen years. It will be enough if I say that five years ago I made the discovery to which I alluded when I said that then I reached the goal. After years of labour, after years of toiling and groping in the dark, after days and nights of disappointment and sometimes of despair, in which I used now and then to tremble and grow cold with the thought that perhaps there were others seeking for what I sought, at last, after so long, a pang of sudden joy thrilled my soul, and I knew the long journey was at an end. By what seemed then and still seems a chance, the suggestion of a moment's idle thought followed up upon familiar lines and paths that I had tracked a hundred times already, the great truth burst upon me, and I saw, mapped out in lines of light, a whole world, a sphere unknown; continents and islands, and great oceans in which no ship has sailed (to my belief) since Man first lifted up his eyes and beheld the sun, and the stars of heaven, and the quiet earth beneath. You will think all this high-flown language, Clarke, but it is hard to be literal. And yet; I do not know whether what I am hinting at cannot be set forth in plain and homely terms. For instance, this world of ours is pretty well girded now with the telegraph wires and cables; thought, with something less than the speed of thought, flashes from sunrise to sunset, from north to south, across the floods and the desert places. Suppose that an electrician of today were suddenly to perceive that he and his friends have merely been playing with pebbles and mistaking them for the foundations of the world; suppose that such a man saw uttermost space lie open before the current, and words of men flash forth to the sun and beyond the sun into the systems beyond, and the voices of articulate-speaking men echo in the waste void that

bounds our thought. As analogies go, that is a pretty good analogy of what I have done; you can understand now a little of what I felt as I stood here one evening; it was a summer evening, and the valley looked much as it does now; I stood here, and saw before me the unutterable, the unthinkable gulf that yawns profound between two worlds, the world of matter and the world of spirit; I saw the great empty deep stretch dim before me, and in that instant a bridge of light leapt from the earth to the unknown shore, and the abyss was spanned. You may look in Browne Faber's book, if you like, and you will find that to the present day men of science are unable to account for the presence, or to specify the functions of a certain group of nerve-cells in the brain. That group is, as it were, land to let, a mere waste place for fanciful theories. I am not in the position of Browne Faber and the specialists, I am perfectly instructed as to the possible functions of those nerve-centres in the scheme of things. With a touch I can bring them into play, with a touch, I say, I can set free the current, with a touch I can complete the communication between this world of sense and—we shall be able to finish the sentence later on. Yes, the knife is necessary; but think what that knife will effect. It will level utterly the solid wall of sense, and probably, for the first time since man was made, a spirit will gaze on a spirit world. Clarke, Mary will see the god Pan!"

"But you remember what you wrote to me? I thought it would be requisite that she—"

He whispered the rest into the doctor's ear.

"Not at all, not at all. That is nonsense, I assure you. Indeed, it is better as it is; I am quite certain of that."

"Consider the matter well, Raymond. It's a great responsibility. Something might go wrong; you would be a miserable man for the rest of your days."

"No, I think not, even if the worst happened. As you

know, I rescued Mary from the gutter, and from almost certain starvation, when she was a child; I think her life is mine, to use as I see fit. Come, it is getting late; we had better go in."

Dr. Raymond led the way into the house, through the hall, and down a long dark passage. He took a key from his pocket and opened a heavy door, and motioned Clarke into his laboratory. It had once been a billiard-room, and was lighted by a glass dome in the centre of the ceiling, whence there still shone a sad grey light on the figure of the doctor as he lit a lamp with a heavy shade and placed it on a table in the middle of the room.

Clarke looked about him. Scarcely a foot of wall remained bare; there were shelves all around laden with bottles and phials of all shapes and colours, and at one end stood a little Chippendale bookcase. Raymond pointed to this.

"You see that Parchment Oswald Crollius? He was one of the first to show me the way, though I don't think he ever found it himself. That is a strange saying of his: 'In every grain of wheat there lies hidden the soul of a star.'"

There was not much furniture in the laboratory. The table in the centre, a stone slab with a drain in one corner, the two arm-chairs on which Raymond and Clarke were sitting; that was all, except an odd-looking chair at the furthest end of the room. Clarke looked at it, and raised his eyebrows.

"Yes, that is the chair," said Raymond. "We may as well place it in position." He got up and wheeled the chair to the light, and began raising and lowering it, letting down the seat, setting the back at various angles, and adjusting the foot-rest. It looked comfortable enough, and Clarke passed his hand over the soft green velvet, as the doctor manipulated the levers.

"Now, Clarke, make yourself quite comfortable. I have a couple of hours' work before me; I was obliged to leave certain matters to the last."

Raymond went to the stone slab, and Clarke watched him drearily as he bent over a row of phials and lit the flame under the crucible. The doctor had a small hand-lamp, shaded as the larger one, on a ledge above his apparatus, and Clarke, who sat in the shadows, looked down the great dreary room, wondering at the bizarre effects of brilliant light and undefined darkness contrasting with one another. Soon he became conscious of an odd odour, at first the merest suggestion of odour, in the room; and as it grew more decided he felt surprised that he was not reminded of the chemist's shop or the surgery. Clarke found himself idly endeavouring to analyse the sensation, and, half conscious, he began to think of a day, fifteen years ago, that he had spent in roaming through the woods and meadows near his old home. It was a burning day at the beginning of August, the heat had dimmed the outlines of all things and all distances were a faint mist, and people who observed the thermometer spoke of an abnormal register, of a temperature that was almost tropical. Strangely that wonderful hot day of the 'fifties rose up in Clarke's imagination; the sense of dazzling all-pervading sunlight seemed to blot out the shadows and the lights of the laboratory, and he felt again the heated air beating in gusts about his face, saw the shimmer rising from the turf, and heard the myriad murmur of the summer.

"I hope the smell doesn't annoy you, Clarke; there's nothing unwholesome about it. It may make you a bit sleepy, that's all."

Clarke heard the words quite distinctly, and knew that Raymond was speaking to him, but for the life of him he could not rouse himself from his lethargy. He could only think of the lonely walk he had taken fifteen

years ago; it was his last look at the fields and woods he had known since he was a child, and now it all stood out in brilliant light, as a picture, before him. Above all there came to his nostrils the scent of summer, the smell of flowers mingled, and the odour of the woods, of cool shaded places, deep in the green depths, drawn forth by the sun's heat; and the scent of the good earth, lying as it were with arms stretched forth, and smiling lips, overpowered all. His fancies made him wander, as he had wandered long ago, from the fields into the wood, tracking a little path between the shining undergrowth of beech-trees; and the trickle of water dropping from the limestone rock sounded as a clear melody in the dream. Thoughts began to go astray and to mingle with other recollections; the beech alley was transformed to a path beneath ilex trees, and here and there a vine climbed from bough to bough, and sent up waving tendrils and drooped with purple grapes, and the sparse grey-green leaves of a wild olive tree stood out against the dark shadows of the ilex. Clarke, in the deep folds of dream, was conscious that the path from his father's house had led him into an undiscovered country, and he was wondering at the strangeness of it all, when suddenly, in place of the hum and murmur of the summer, an infinite silence seemed to fall on all things, and the wood was hushed, and for a moment of time he stood face to face there with a presence, that with neither man nor beast, neither the living nor the dead, but all things mingled, the form of all things but devoid of all form. And in that moment, the sacrament of body and soul was dissolved, and a voice seemed to cry "Let us go hence," and then the darkness of darkness beyond the stars, the darkness of everlasting.

When Clarke woke up with a start he saw Raymond pouring a few drops of some oily fluid into a green phial, which he stoppered tightly.

"You have been dozing," he said: "the journey must have tired you out. It is done now. I am going to fetch Mary; I shall be back in ten minutes."

Clarke lay back in his chair and wondered. It seemed as if he had but passed from one dream into another. He half expected to see the walls of the laboratory melt and disappear, and to awake in London, shuddering at his own sleeping fancies. But at last the door opened, and the doctor returned, and behind him came a girl of about seventeen, dressed all in white. She was so beautiful that Clarke did not wonder at what the doctor had written to him. She was blushing now over face and neck and arms, but Raymond seemed unmoved.

"Mary," he said, "the time has come. You are quite free. Are you willing to trust yourself to me entirely?"

"Yes, dear."

"You hear that Clarke? You are my witness. Here is the chair, Mary. It is quite easy. Just sit in it and lean back. Are you ready?"

"Yes, dear, quite ready. Give me a kiss before you begin."

The doctor stooped and kissed her mouth, kindly enough. "Now shut your eyes," he said. The girl closed her eyelids, as if she were tired, and longed for sleep, and Raymond held the green phial to her nostrils. Her face grew white, whiter than her dress: she struggled faintly, and then with the feeling of submission strong within her, crossed her arms upon her breast as a little child about to say her prayers. The bright light of the lamp beat full upon her, and Clarke watched changes fleeting over that face as the changes of the hills when the summer clouds float across the sun. And then she lay all white and still, and the doctor turned up one of her eyelids. She was quite unconscious. Raymond pressed hard on one of the levers and the chair instantly sank back. Clarke saw him cutting away a circle, like a tonsure, from her hair, and the lamp was moved nearer.

Raymond took a small glittering instrument from a little case, and Clarke turned away shuddering. When he looked again the doctor was binding up the wound he had made.

"She will awake in five minutes." Raymond was still perfectly cool. "There is nothing more to be done; we can only wait."

The minutes passed slowly; they could hear a slow, heavy ticking. There was an old clock in the passage. Clarke felt sick and faint; his knees shook beneath him, he could hardly stand.

Suddenly, as they watched, they heard a long-drawn sigh, and suddenly did the colour that had vanished return to the girl's cheeks, and suddenly her eyes opened. Clarke quailed before them. They shone with an awful light, looking far away, and a great wonder fell upon her face, and her hands stretched out as if to touch what was invisible; but in an instant the wonder faded, and gave place to the most awful terror. The muscles of her face were hideously convulsed, she shook from head to foot; the soul seemed struggling and shuddering within the house of flesh. It was a horrible sight, and Clarke rushed forward, as she fell shrieking to the floor.

Three days later Raymond took Clarke to Mary's bedside. She was lying wide-awake, rolling her head from side to side, and grinning vacantly.

"Yes," said the doctor, still quite cool, "it is a great pity; she is a hopeless idiot. However, it could not be helped; and, after all, she has seen the Great God Pan."

II   Mr. Clarke's Memoirs

Mr. Clarke, the gentleman chosen by Dr. Raymond to witness the strange experiment of the god Pan, was a person in whose character caution and curiosity were

oddly mingled; in his sober moments he thought of the unusual and the eccentric with undisguised aversion, and yet, deep in his heart, there was a wide-eyed inquisitiveness with respect to all the more recondite and esoteric elements in the nature of men. The latter tendency had prevailed when he accepted Raymond's invitation, for though his considered judgment had always repudiated the doctor's theories as the wildest nonsense, yet he secretly hugged a belief in fantasy, and would have rejoiced to see that belief confirmed. The horrors that he witnessed in the dreary laboratory were to a certain extent salutary; he was conscious of being involved in an affair not altogether reputable, and for many years afterwards he clung bravely to the commonplace, and rejected all occasions of occult investigation. Indeed, on some homoeopathic principle, he for some time attended the séances of distinguished mediums, hoping that the clumsy tricks of these gentlemen would make him altogether disgusted with mysticism of every kind, but the remedy, though caustic, was not efficacious. Clarke knew that he still pined for the unseen, and little by little, the old passion began to reassert itself, as the face of Mary, shuddering and convulsed with an unknowable terror, faded slowly from his memory. Occupied all day in pursuits both serious and lucrative, the temptation to relax in the evening was too great, especially in the winter months, when the fire cast a warm glow over his snug bachelor apartment, and a bottle of some choice claret stood ready by his elbow. His dinner digested, he would make a brief pretence of reading the evening paper, but the mere catalogue of news soon palled upon him, and Clarke would find himself casting glances of warm desire in the direction of an old Japanese bureau, which stood at a pleasant distance from the hearth. Like a boy before a jam-closet, for a few minutes he would hover indecisive, but lust always prevailed, and Clarke ended by

drawing up his chair, lighting a candle, and sitting down before the bureau. Its pigeon-holes and drawers teemed with documents on the most morbid subjects, and in the well reposed a large manuscript volume, in which he had painfully entered the gems of his collection. Clarke had a fine contempt for published literature; the most ghostly story ceased to interest him if it happened to be printed; his sole pleasure was in the reading, compiling, and rearranging what he called his "Memoirs to Prove the Existence of the Devil," and engaged in this pursuit the evening seemed to fly and the night appeared too short.

On one particular evening, an ugly December night, black with fog, and raw with frost, Clarke hurried over his dinner, and scarcely deigned to observe his customary ritual of taking up the paper and laying it down again. He paced two or three times up and down the room, and opened the bureau, stood still a moment, and sat down. He leant back, absorbed in one of those dreams to which he was subject, and at length drew out his book, and opened it at the last entry. There were three or four pages densely covered with Clarke's round, set penmanship, and at the beginning he had written in a somewhat larger hand:

Singular Narrative told me by my Friend, Dr. Phillips. He assures me that all the facts related therein are strictly and wholly True, but refuses to give either the Surnames of the Persons concerned, or the Place where these Extraordinary Events occurred.

Mr. Clarke began to read over the account for the tenth time, glancing now and then at the pencil notes he had made when it was told him by his friend. It was one of his humours to pride himself on a certain literary ability; he thought well of his style, and took pains in

arranging the circumstances in dramatic order. He read the following story:—

The persons concerned in this statement are Helen V., who, if she is still alive, must now be a woman of twenty-three, Rachel M., since deceased, who was a year younger than the above, and Trevor W., an imbecile, aged thirteen. These persons were at the period of the story inhabitants of a village on the border of Wales, a place of some importance in the time of the Roman occupation, but now a scattered hamlet, of not more than five hundred souls. It is situated on rising ground, about six miles from the sea, and is sheltered by a large and picturesque forest.

Some eleven years ago, Helen V. came to the village under rather peculiar circumstances. It is understood that she, being an orphan, was adopted in her infancy by a distant relative, who brought her up in his own house till she was twelve years old. Thinking, however, that it would be better for the child to have playmates of her own age, he advertised in several local papers for a good home in a comfortable farmhouse for a girl of twelve, and this advertisement was answered by Mr. R., a well-to-do farmer in the above-mentioned village. His references proving satisfactory, the gentleman sent his adopted daughter to Mr. R., with a letter, in which he stipulated that the girl should have a room to herself, and stated that her guardians need be at no trouble in the matter of education, as she was already sufficiently educated for the position in life which she would occupy. In fact, Mr. R. was given to understand that the girl was to be allowed to find her own occupations, and to spend her time almost as she liked. Mr. R. duly met her at the nearest station, a town some seven miles away from his house, and seems to have remarked nothing extraordinary about the child, except that she

was reticent as to her former life and her adopted father. She was, however, of a very different type from the inhabitants of the village; her skin was a pale, clear olive, and her features were strongly marked, and of a somewhat foreign character. She appears to have settled down easily enough into farmhouse life, and became a favourite with the children, who sometimes went with her on her rambles in the forest, for this was her amusement. Mr. R. states that he has known her to go out by herself directly after their early breakfast, and not return till after dusk, and that, feeling uneasy at a young girl being out alone for so many hours, he communicated with her adopted father, who replied in a brief note that Helen must do as she chose. In the winter, when the forest paths are impassable, she spent most of her time in her bedroom, where she slept alone, according to the instructions of her relative. It was on one of these expeditions to the forest that the first of the singular incidents with which this girl is connected occurred, the date being about a year after her arrival at the village. The preceding winter had been remarkably severe, the snow drifting to a great depth, and the frost continuing for an unexampled period, and the summer following was as noteworthy for its extreme heat. On one of the very hottest days in this summer, Helen V. left the farmhouse for one of her long rambles in the forest, taking with her, as usual, some bread and meat for lunch. She was seen by some men in the fields making for the old Roman Road, a green causeway which traverses the highest part of the wood, and they were astonished to observe that the girl had taken off her hat, though the heat of the sun was almost tropical. As it happened, a labourer, Joseph W. by name, was working in the forest near the Roman Road, and at twelve o'clock his little son, Trevor, brought the man his dinner of bread and cheese. After the meal, the boy,

who was about seven years old at the time, left his father at work, and, as he said, went to look for flowers in the wood, and the man, who could hear him shouting with delight over his discoveries, felt no uneasiness. Suddenly, however, he was horrified at hearing the most dreadful screams, evidently the result of great terror, proceeding from the direction in which his son had gone, and he hastily threw down his tools and ran to see what had happened. Tracing his path by the sound, he met the little boy, who was running headlong, and was evidently terribly frightened, and on questioning him the man at last elicited that after picking a posy of flowers he felt tired, and lay down on the grass and fell asleep. He was suddenly awakened, as he stated, by a peculiar noise, a sort of singing he called it, and on peeping through the branches he saw Helen V. playing on the grass with a "strange naked man," whom he seemed unable to describe more fully. He said he felt dreadfully frightened, and ran away crying for his father. Joseph W. proceeded in the direction indicated by his son, and found Helen V. sitting on the grass in the middle of a glade or open space left by charcoal burners. He angrily charged her with frightening his little boy, but she entirely denied the accusation and laughed at the child's story of a "strange man," to which he himself did not attach much credence. Joseph W. came to the conclusion that the boy had woke up with a sudden fright, as children sometimes do, but Trevor persisted in his story, and continued in such evident distress that at last his father took him home, hoping that his mother would be able to soothe him. For many weeks, however, the boy gave his parents much anxiety; he became nervous and strange in his manner, refusing to leave the cottage by himself, and constantly alarming the household by waking in the night with cries of "The man in the wood! Father! Father!"

In course of time, however, the impression seemed to have worn off, and about three months later he accompanied his father to the house of a gentleman in the neighbourhood, for whom Joseph W. occasionally did work. The man was shown into the study, and the little boy was left sitting in the hall, and a few minutes later, while the gentleman was giving W. his instructions, they were both horrified by a piercing shriek and the sound of a fall, and rushing out they found the child lying senseless on the floor, his face contorted with terror. The doctor was immediately summoned, and after some examination he pronounced the child to be suffering from a fit, apparently produced by a sudden shock. The boy was taken to one of the bedrooms, and after some time recovered consciousness, but only to pass into a condition described by the medical man as one of violent hysteria. The doctor exhibited a strong sedative, and in the course of two hours pronounced him fit to walk home, but in passing through the hall the paroxysms of fright returned and with additional violence. The father perceived that the child was pointing at some object and heard the old cry. "The man in the wood," and looking in the direction indicated saw a stone head of grotesque appearance, which had been built into the wall above one of the doors. It seems that the owner of the house had recently made alterations in his premises, and on digging the foundation for some offices, the men had found a curious head, evidently of the Roman period, which had been placed in the hall in the manner described. The head is pronounced by the most experienced archaeologists of the district to be that of a faun or satyr.[1]

From whatever cause arising, this second shock

[1] Dr. Phillips tells me that he has seen the head in question, and assures me that he has never received such a vivid presentment of intense evil.

seemed too severe for the boy Trevor, and at the present date he suffers from a weakness of intellect, which gives but little promise of amending. The matter caused a good deal of sensation at the time, and the girl Helen was closely questioned by Mr. R., but to no purpose, she steadfastly denying that she had frightened or in any way molested Trevor.

The second event with which the girl's name is connected took place about six years ago, and is of a still more extraordinary character.

At the beginning of the summer of 1882 Helen contracted a friendship of a peculiarly intimate character with Rachel M., the daughter of a prosperous farmer in the neighbourhood. This girl, who was a year younger than Helen, was considered by most people to be the prettier of the two, though Helen's features had to a great extent softened as she became older. The two girls, who were together on every available opportunity, presented a singular contrast, the one with her clear, olive skin and almost Italian appearance, and the other of the proverbial red and white of our rural districts. It must be stated that the payments made to Mr. R. for the maintenance of Helen were known in the village for their excessive liberality, and the impression was general that she would one day inherit a large sum of money from her relative. The parents of Rachel were therefore not averse from their daughter's friendship with the girl, and even encouraged the intimacy, though they now bitterly regret having done so. Helen still retained her extraordinary fondness for the forest, and on several occasions Rachel accompanied her, the two friends setting out early in the morning, and remaining in the wood till dusk. Once or twice after these excursions Mrs. M. thought her daughter's manner rather peculiar; she seemed languid and dreamy, and as it has been expressed, "different from herself," but these

peculiarities seem to have been thought too trifling for remark. One evening, however, after Rachel had come home, her mother heard a noise which sounded like suppressed weeping in the girl's room, and on going in found her lying, half undressed, upon the bed, evidently in the greatest distress. As soon as she saw her mother, she exclaimed, "Ah, Mother, Mother, why did you let me go to the forest with Helen?" Mrs. M. was astonished at so strange a question, and proceeded to make inquiries. Rachel told her a wild story. She said—

Clarke closed the book with a snap, and turned his chair towards the fire. When his friend sat one evening in that very chair, and told his story, Clarke had interrupted him at a point a little subsequent to this, had cut short his words in a paroxysm of horror. "My God!" he had exclaimed, "think, think what you are saying. It is too incredible, too monstrous; such things can never be in this quiet world, where men and women live and die, and struggle, and conquer, or maybe fail, and fall down under sorrow, and grieve and suffer strange fortunes for many a year; but not this, Phillips, not such things as this. There must be some explanation, some way out of the terror. Why, man, if such a case were possible, our earth would be a nightmare."

But Phillips had told his story to the end, concluding: "Her flight remains a mystery to this day; she vanished in broad sunlight: they saw her walking in a meadow, and a few moments later she was not there."

Clarke tried to conceive the thing again, as he sat by the fire, and again his mind shuddered and shrank back, appalled before the sight of such awful, unspeakable elements enthroned as it were, and triumphant in human flesh. Before him stretched the long dim vista of the green causeway in the forest, as his friend had

described it; he saw the swaying leaves and the quivering shadows on the grass, he saw the sunlight and the flowers, and far away, far in the long distance, the two figures moved toward him. One was Rachel, but the other?

Clarke had tried his best to disbelieve it all, but at the end of the account, as he had written it in his book, he had placed the inscription:

ET DIABOLUS INCARNATUS EST.
ET HOMO FACTUS EST.

III   The City of Resurrections

"Herbert! Good God! Is it possible?"

"Yes, my name's Herbert. I think I know your face too, but I don't remember your name. My memory is very queer."

"Don't you recollect Villiers of Wadham?"

"So it is, so it is. I beg your pardon, Villiers, I didn't think I was begging of an old college friend. Goodnight."

"My dear fellow, this haste is unnecessary. My rooms are close by, but we won't go there just yet. Suppose we walk up Shaftsbury Avenue a little way? But how in heaven's name have you come to this pass, Herbert?"

"It's a long story, Villiers, and a strange one too, but you can hear it if you like."

"Come on, then. Take my arm, you don't seem very strong."

The ill-assorted pair moved slowly up Rupert Street; the one in dirty, evil-looking rags, and the other attired in the regulation uniform of a man about town, trim, glossy, and eminently well-to-do. Villiers had emerged from his restaurant after an excellent dinner of many

courses, assisted by an ingratiating little flask of Chianti, and, in that frame of mind which was with him almost chronic, had delayed a moment by the door, peering round in the dimly lighted street in search of those mysterious incidents and persons with which the streets of London teem in every quarter and at every hour. Villiers prided himself as a practised explorer of such obscure mazes and byways of London life, and in this unprofitable pursuit he displayed an assiduity which was worthy of more serious employment. Thus he stood beside the lamp-post surveying the passers-by with undisguised curiosity, and with that gravity only known to the systematic diner, had just enunciated in his mind the formula: "London has been called the city of encounters; it is more than that, it is the city of resurrections," when these reflections were suddenly interrupted by a piteous whine at his elbow, and a deplorable appeal for alms. He looked around in some irritation, and with a sudden shock found himself confronted with the embodied proof of his somewhat stilted fancies. There, close beside him, his face altered and disfigured by poverty and disgrace, his body barely covered by greasy ill-fitting rags, stood his old friend Charles Herbert, who had matriculated on the same day as himself, with whom he had been merry and wise for twelve revolving terms. Different occupations and varying interests had interrupted the friendship, and it was six years since Villiers had seen Herbert; and now he looked upon this wreck of a man with grief and dismay, mingled with a certain inquisitiveness as to what dreary chain of circumstance had dragged him down to such a doleful pass. Villiers felt together with compassion all the relish of the amateur in mysteries, and congratulated himself on his leisurely speculations outside the restaurant.

They walked on in silence for some time, and more

than one passer-by stared in astonishment at the unaccustomed spectacle of a well-dressed man with an unmistakable beggar hanging on to his arm, and, observing this, Villiers led the way to an obscure street in Soho. Here he repeated his question.

"How on earth has it happened, Herbert? I always understood you would succeed to an excellent position in Dorsetshire. Did your father disinherit you? Surely not?"

"No, Villiers; I came into all the property at my poor father's death; he died a year after I left Oxford. He was a very good father to me, and I mourned his death sincerely enough. But you know what young men are; a few months later I came up to town and went a good deal into society. Of course I had excellent introductions, and I managed to enjoy myself very much in a harmless sort of way. I played a little, certainly, but never for heavy stakes, and the few bets I made on races brought me in money—only a few pounds, you know, but enough to pay for cigars and such petty pleasures. It was in my second season that the tide turned. Of course you have heard of my marriage?"

"No, I never heard anything about it."

"Yes, I married, Villiers. I met a girl, a girl of the most wonderful and strange beauty, at the house of some people whom I knew. I cannot tell you her age; I never knew it, but, so far as I can guess, I should think she must have been about nineteen when I made her acquaintance. My friends had come to know her at Florence; she told them she was an orphan, the child of an English father and an Italian mother, and she charmed them as she charmed me. The first time I saw her was at an evening party. I was standing by the door talking to a friend, when suddenly above the hum and babble of conversation I heard a voice which seemed to thrill to my heart. She was singing an Italian song. I was

introduced to her that evening, and in three months I married Helen. Villiers, that woman, if I can call her 'woman,' corrupted my soul. The night of the wedding I found myself sitting in her bedroom in the hotel, listening to her talk. She was sitting up in bed, and I listened to her as she spoke in her beautiful voice, spoke of things which even now I would not dare whisper in blackest night, though I stood in the midst of a wilderness. You, Villiers, you may think you know life, and London, and what goes on day and night in this dreadful city; for all I can say you may have heard the talk of the vilest, but I tell you you can have no conception of what I know, not in your most fantastic, hideous dreams can you have imagined forth the faintest shadow of what I have heard—and seen. Yes, seen. I have seen the incredible, such horrors that even I myself sometime stop in the middle of the street, and ask whether it is possible for a man to hold such things and live. In a year, Villiers, I was a ruined man, in body and soul—in body and soul."

"But your property, Herbert? You had land in Dorset."

"I sold it all; the field and woods, the dear old house—everything."

"And the money?"

"She took it all from me."

"And then left you?"

"Yes; she disappeared one night. I don't know where she went, but I am sure if I saw her again it would kill me. You may think, Villiers, that I have exaggerated and talked for effect; but I have not told you half. I could tell you certain things which would convince you, but you would never know a happy day again. You would pass the rest of your life, as I pass mine, a haunted man, a man who has seen hell."

Villiers took the unfortunate man to his rooms, and

gave him a meal. Herbert could eat little, and scarcely touched the glass of wine set before him. He sat moody and silent by the fire, and seemed relieved when Villiers sent him away with a small present of money.

"By the way, Herbert," said Villiers, as they parted at the door, "what was your wife's name? You said Helen, I think? Helen what?"

"The name she passed under when I met her was Helen Vaughan, but what her real name was I can't say. I don't think she had a name. No, no, not in that sense. Only human beings have names, Villiers; I can't say anymore. Good-bye; yes, I will not fail to call if I see any way in which you can help me. Good-night."

The man went out into the bitter night, and Villiers returned to his fireside. There was something about Herbert which shocked him inexpressibly; not his poor rags nor the marks which poverty had set upon his face, but rather an indefinite terror which hung about him like a mist. He had acknowledged that he himself was not devoid of blame; the woman, he had avowed, had corrupted him body and soul, and Villiers felt that this man, once his friend, had been an actor in scenes evil beyond the power of words. His story needed no confirmation: he himself was the embodied proof of it. Villiers mused curiously over the story he had heard, and wondered whether he had heard both the first and the last of it. "No," he thought, "certainly not the last, probably only the beginning. A case like this is like a nest of Chinese boxes; you open one after another and find a quainter workmanship in every box. Most likely poor Herbert is merely one of the outside boxes; there are stranger ones to follow."

Villiers could not take his mind away from Herbert and his story, which seemed to grow wilder as the night wore on. The fire began to burn low, and the chilly air of the morning crept into the room; Villiers got up with

a glance over his shoulder, and shivering slightly, went to bed.

A few days later he saw at his club a gentleman of his acquaintance, named Austin, who was famous for his intimate knowledge of London life, both in its tenebrous and luminous phases. Villiers, still full of his encounter in Soho and its consequences, thought Austin might possibly be able to shed some light on Herbert's history, and so after some casual talk he suddenly put the question:

"Do you happen to know anything of a man named Herbert—Charles Herbert?"

Austin turned round sharply and stared at Villiers with some astonishment.

"Charles Herbert? Weren't you in town three years ago? No; then you have not heard of the Paul Street case? It caused a good deal of sensation at the time."

"What was the case?"

"Well, a gentleman, a man of very good position, was found dead, stark dead, in the area of a certain house in Paul Street, off Tottenham Court Road. Of course the police did not make the discovery; if you happen to be sitting up all night and have a light in your window, the constable will ring the bell, but if you happen to be lying dead in somebody's area, you will be left alone. In this instance as in many others the alarm was raised by some kind of vagabond; I don't mean a common tramp, or a public-house loafer, but a gentleman, whose business or pleasure, or both, made him a spectator of the London streets at five o'clock in the morning. This individual was, as he said, "going home," it did not appear whence or whither, and had occasion to pass through Paul Street between four and five AM. Something or other caught his eye at Number 20; he said, absurdly enough, that the house had the most unpleasant physiognomy he had ever observed, but, at any rate,

he glanced down the area, and was a good deal astonished to see a man lying on the stones, his limbs all huddled together, and his face turned up. Our gentleman thought his face looked peculiarly ghastly, and so set off at a run in search of the nearest policeman. The constable was at first inclined to treat the matter lightly, suspecting common drunkenness; however, he came, and after looking at the man's face, changed his tone, quickly enough. The early bird, who had picked up this fine worm, was sent off for a doctor, and the policeman rang and knocked at the door till a slatternly servant girl came down looking more than half asleep. The constable pointed out the contents of the area to the maid, who screamed loudly enough to wake up the street, but she knew nothing of the man; had never seen him at the house, and so forth. Meanwhile the original discoverer had come back with a medical man, and the next thing was to get into the area. The gate was open, so the whole quartet stumped down the steps. The doctor hardly needed a moment's examination; he said the poor fellow had been dead for several hours, and it was then the case began to get interesting. The dead man had not been robbed, and in one of his pockets were papers identifying him as—well, as a man of good family and means, a favourite in society, and nobody's enemy, so far as could be known. I don't give his name, Villiers, because it has nothing to do with the story, and because it's no good raking up these affairs about the dead when there are no relations living. The next curious point was that the medical men couldn't agree as to how he met his death. There were some slight bruises on his shoulders, but they were so slight that it looked as if he had been pushed roughly out of the kitchen door, and not thrown over the railings from the street or even dragged down the steps. But there were positively no other marks of violence about him, cer-

tainly none that would account for his death; and when they came to the autopsy there wasn't a trace of poison of any kind. Of course the police wanted to know all about the people at Number 20, and here again, so I have heard from private sources, one or two other very curious points came out. It appears that the occupants of the house were a Mr. and Mrs. Charles Herbert; he was said to be a landed proprietor, though it struck most people that Paul Street was not exactly the place to look for country gentry. As for Mrs. Herbert, nobody seemed to know who or what she was, and, between ourselves, I fancy the divers after her history found themselves in rather strange waters. Of course they both denied knowing anything about the deceased, and in default of any evidence against them they were discharged. But some very odd things came out about them. Though it was between five and six in the morning when the dead man was removed, a large crowd had collected, and several of the neighbours ran to see what was going on. They were pretty free with their comments, by all accounts, and from these it appeared that Number 20 was in very bad odour in Paul Street. The detectives tried to trace down these rumours to some solid foundation of fact, but could not get hold of anything. People shook their heads and raised their eyebrows and thought the Herberts rather 'queer,' 'would rather not be seen going into their house,' and so on, but there was nothing tangible. The authorities were morally certain that the man met his death in some way or another in the house and was thrown out by the kitchen door, but they couldn't prove it, and the absence of any indications of violence or poisoning left them helpless. An odd case, wasn't it? But curiously enough, there's something more that I haven't told you. I happened to know one of the doctors who was consulted as to the cause of death, and some

time after the inquest I met him, and asked him about it. 'Do you really mean to tell me,' I said, 'that you were baffled by the case, that you actually don't know what the man died of?' 'Pardon me,' he replied. 'I know perfectly well what caused death. Blank died of fright, of sheer, awful terror; I never saw features so hideously contorted in the entire course of my practice, and I have seen the faces of a whole host of dead.' The doctor was usually a cool customer enough, and a certain vehemence in his manner struck me, but I couldn't get anything more out of him. I suppose the Treasury didn't see their way to prosecuting the Herberts for frightening a man to death; at any rate, nothing was done, and the case dropped out of men's minds. Do you happen to know anything of Herbert?"

"Well," replied Villiers, "he was an old college friend of mine."

"You don't say so? Have you ever seen his wife?"

"No, I haven't. I have lost sight of Herbert for many years."

"It's queer, isn't it, parting with a man at the college gate or at Paddington, seeing nothing of him for years, and then finding him pop up his head in such an odd place. But I should like to have seen Mrs. Herbert; people said extraordinary things about her."

"What sort of things?"

"Well, I hardly know how to tell you. Everyone who saw her at the police court said she was at once the most beautiful woman and the most repulsive they had ever set eyes on. I have spoken to a man who saw her, and I assure you he positively shuddered as he tried to describe the woman, but he couldn't tell why. She seems to have been a sort of enigma; and I expect if that one dead man could have told tales, he would have told some uncommonly queer ones. And there you are again in another puzzle; what could a respectable country gentleman like Mr. Blank (we'll call him that if you

ber Mary. She was the mother of Helen Vaughan, who was born nine months after that night.

Mary never recovered her reason. She lay, as you saw her, all the while upon her bed, and a few days after the child was born she died. I fancy that just at the last she knew me; I was standing by the bed, and the old look came into her eyes for a second, and then she shuddered and groaned and died. It was an ill work I did that night when you were present; I broke open the door of the house of life, without knowing or caring what might pass forth or enter in. I recollect your telling me at the time, sharply enough, and rightly enough too, in one sense, that I had ruined the reason of a human being by a foolish experiment, based on an absurd theory. You did well to blame me, but my theory was not all absurdity. What I said Mary would see, she saw, but I forgot that no human eyes could look on such a vision with impunity. And I forgot, as I have just said, that when the house of life is thus thrown open, there may enter in that for which we have no name, and human flesh may become the veil of a horror one dare not express. I played with energies which I did not understand, and you have seen the ending of it. Helen Vaughan did well to bind the cord about her neck and die, though the death was horrible. The blackened face, the hideous form upon the bed, changing and melting before your eyes from woman to man, from man to beast, and from beast to worse than beast, all the strange horror that you witnessed, surprises me but little. What you say the doctor whom you sent for saw and shuddered at I noticed long ago; I knew what I had done the moment the child was born, and when it was scarcely five years old I surprised it, not once or twice but several times with a playmate, you may guess of what kind. It was for me a constant, an incarnate horror, and after a few years I felt I could bear it no

longer, and I sent Helen Vaughan away. You know now what frightened the boy in the wood. The rest of the strange story, and all else that you tell me, as discovered by your friend, I have contrived to learn from time to time, almost to the last chapter. And now Helen is with her companions. . . .